SWEET
&
BITTER
MAGIC

BY
ADRIENNE TOOLEY

MARGARET K. McELDERRY BOOKS
New York London Toronto Sydney New Delhi

ĄET K. McELDERRY BOOKS

print of Simon & Schuster Children's Publishing Division

Avenue of the Americas, New York, New York 10020

Text © 2021 by Adrienne Tooley

Jacket illustration © 2021 by Tara Phillips

Front case image by the8monkey/Essentials Collection/iStock

Jacket design by Laura Eckes © 2021 by Simon & Schuster, Inc.

Map illustration © 2021 by Virginia Allyn

MARGARET K. McELDERRY BOOKS is a trademark of Simon & Schuster, Inc.

For information about special discounts for bulk purchases, please contact Simon & Schuster Special Sales at 1-866-506-1949 or business@simonandschuster.com.

The Simon & Schuster Speakers Bureau can bring authors to your live event. For more information or to book an event contact the Simon & Schuster Speakers Bureau at 1-866-248-3049 or visit our website at www.simonspeakers.com.

Interior design by Tom Daly

The text of this book was set in ScotchFBText.

Manufactured in the United States of America

10 9 8 7 6 5 4 3 2

Library of Congress Cataloging-in-Publication Data

Names: Tooley, Adrienne, author.

Title: Sweet & bitter magic / by Adrienne Tooley.

Other titles: Sweet and bitter magic

Description: New York : Margaret K. McElderry Books, [2021] * Summary: When seventeen-year-old Tamsin, a cursed witch who must steal love from others, meets Wren, a girl hiding her own dangerous magic, they strike a love bargain with life-or-death consequences.

Identifiers: LCCN 2020008924 (print) * LCCN 2020008925 (ebook) * ISBN 9781534453852 (hardcover) * ISBN 9781534453876 (ebook)

Subjects: CYAC: Witches—Fiction. * Magic—Fiction. * Fantasy.

Classification: LCC PZ7.1.T6264 Swe 2021 (print) * LCC PZ7.1.T6264 (ebook) * DDC [Fic]—dc23

LC record available at https://lccn.loc.gov/2020008924

LC ebook record available at https://lccn.loc.gov/2020008925

FOR YOU, IF YOU NEED IT.
NEVER DOUBT THAT YOU ARE WORTHY OF LOVE.

ONE

TAMSIN

The salt was dull on Tamsin's tongue. The mild spice had meant something to her once, had made a difference when sprinkled with a deft hand on her boiled eggs or her smoked fish. Now it tasted like everything else, in that it tasted like despair, like the whisper of a faraway fire. Like the rest of her stale, wasted life.

The woman was staring at Tamsin expectantly. Tamsin shook her head. "The salt from your tears is useless to me." She forced the small brown pouch back into the trembling woman's hand.

"But my nursemaid said . . . this is the same price she paid the witch in Wells." The woman's eyes looked ready to spill more salt.

Tamsin blinked, her face blank as a slate. "Go to the witch in Wells, then."

She knew the woman wouldn't. Tamsin was twelve times more powerful than the witch in Wells, and everyone, including the simpering woman standing before her, knew it.

The woman's eyes grew wide. "But my child."

She held out the unmoving bundle in her arms. Tamsin ignored it, turning toward the fireplace, which had been stoked to a blazing roar despite the midsummer heat. The flames danced merrily. Mockingly. The fire did nothing to shake the chill in Tamsin's bones. She pulled her shawl tighter, swept her long hair around her, but it made not a single bit of difference. She was freezing.

The fire crackled. The woman wept. Tamsin waited.

"Please." The woman's voice caught at the end of the word, her plea transformed into a cough, a desperate whimper. "Please save my son."

But Tamsin did not turn. The woman was so close—*so close* to uttering the three words Tamsin needed to hear.

"I'll do anything."

Tamsin's lips curled. She turned, gesturing for the woman to hand over the bundle of blankets. The woman hesitated, eyes darting nervously over the objects assembled on Tamsin's cluttered wooden table: hazy, sharp-edged crystals; bundles of sage and lavender tied with white string; thick, leather-bound books with creamy, black-inked pages.

Tamsin needed none of those things, of course. Witches themselves were the vessels, intermediaries siphoning natural magic from the world around them and nudging it in the right direction.

Still, in her nearly five years serving the townspeople of Ladaugh, Tamsin had found that most of them felt more at ease in her cottage when they had something concrete to focus on. Something that wasn't her.

The baby didn't stir when he was transferred from his mother's arms to Tamsin's. Tamsin used a finger to push aside the blanket obscuring his tiny face. He was a sickly yellow gray, the color stark against Tamsin's pale skin. His little body was so feverish she could almost feel its heat. His temperature was much too high for his tiny heart to handle.

Tamsin murmured a few soft nonsense words to the child. Then she glanced up at his mother, almost as if she had forgotten.

"Oh. My payment." Tamsin tried to situate her face in such a way to appear casual. Apologetic. "I'll simply need you to part with some of your love."

She considered the two children before her. Although the woman had braved Tamsin's cottage out of devotion to her son, the emotional bond between mother and daughter had existed for two additional years. That level of unconditional love would last Tamsin much longer than a bond to a child barely three months old.

"The love for your daughter would be best." Tamsin gestured to the little girl, who was examining the crystals with wide, thoughtful eyes.

The woman blanched, her face turning nearly as gray as her son's. "You cannot be serious."

Tamsin shrugged, rocking the baby gently. "I'm afraid those

are my terms. Surely you've heard whispers at the market."

She did her best not to waver. It was just as unconscionable a request as the woman's face reflected. Other witches worked for the price of a baby's laugh, for fresh bread, for a new pewter cauldron. Yet love was Tamsin's price.

It was the only way to defy the curse that had been placed upon her nearly five years prior.

Tamsin could no longer love, and therefore was doomed never to feel any of the joys life had to offer. She could only get a glimpse of what she had lost by taking love from another. If she held tight—and the person's love was pure—it was enough to give her a few moments of feeling. To experience the warmth of the world despite the cold uselessness of her heart.

The woman's eyes had gone blank, and when she spoke, it was softly, as if to herself. "They warned me, but I couldn't believe a young woman could be so cruel. So cold."

"That sounds like a personal problem." Tamsin shifted the baby to her other arm. She knew the townspeople talked about her, hurriedly exchanging whispers and angry words as they waited at the butcher's stall for their paper-wrapped packages. Still, Tamsin knew the woman would pay. In the end, people always paid.

"I'd rather seek out a sprite." The woman's voice was ragged through her tears. "The river is only two days' walk."

Tamsin snorted. That was the trouble with ordinary folk. They loved magic, but they were frightfully flippant about the consequences. They'd trade a cow for a handful of magic seeds. They would offer up their voice to a mermaid in exchange for a smaller nose. They would seek out the trolls that lurked beneath bridges in the swampy Southlands, hoping to be granted a wish. But there was always a price for their impulsivity—the seeds bloomed flowers that sang incessantly, the new nose was always running, and trolls, who were notoriously indifferent to nuance, tended to misinterpret intention.

The only way to ensure that a magical request was balanced, legal, and properly interpreted was to barter with a witch. Since the Year of Darkness—a time still spoken of in hushed whispers despite the nearly thirty years that had passed—relations between witches and ordinary folk had been closely regulated by both the Coven and the queen to ensure the safety of the ordinary folk and the responsibility of the witch.

Tamsin, despite having been expelled from the academy and banished from the witches' land, Within, was not exempt from that responsibility. If anything, her isolation and her curse were added reminders that magic had consequences. It was a blessing that Tamsin was allowed to practice village magic. It was a mercy that she was even *alive*.

Of course, it rarely felt like a mercy. But that was probably because the Coven had made it so she could not *feel* at all.

"If you want to take your chances with a sprite, by all means, let one give your baby gills," Tamsin said with a shrug, offering the woman the bundle in her arms. "But you and I both know your child won't make it through the night."

The woman deflated. She shook her head, then grabbed for the girl, who had toddled forward toward Tamsin's table of knickknacks. The girl squirmed in protest. Tamsin cooed emptily at the unmoving baby.

The mother held her daughter firmly by the shoulders, staring tenderly at the little girl's pinched, reddening face. Then the woman's head snapped up. "Take my love for my husband." Her eyes were wild, focused on something far away. "Please."

Tamsin sighed, long and loud. People always tried to exchange romantic love for unconditional love, as though the two were interchangeable. But there was a significant difference. Conditional love was fickle. Often it fizzled and stalled, burning out so quickly that Tamsin hardly got more than a handful of uses from it. A mother's love for her child, however, could last her several months if she rationed it carefully.

A child for a child. Tamsin thought it fair. But the woman felt otherwise. Her eyes were as fiery as the flames roaring in Tamsin's hearth.

"Take it," she said, advancing toward the witch, who was still cradling the child. "I give it to you willingly. Please"—her eyes blazed—"I beg of you. Take it. You must."

Tamsin took an inadvertent step backward, nearly tripping over an empty basket. She recovered quickly, both her balance and her impassive expression.

"How long have you been married?"

The woman furrowed her brow in confusion. "Three winters."

Tamsin considered it. Longer relationships often bore more fruitful love, but there was always a chance that the love between the couple had begun to sour or turn stale. Shorter relationships were riskier: They carried less romantic weight but could provide a similar bounty if the couple in question radiated passion.

The woman had been married for three years. She had two children and, if Tamsin wasn't mistaken, another on the way. Clearly, it wasn't for lack of trying.

Sensing a lapse in her mother's attention, the little girl squirmed out of her grip and wrapped a tiny, plump hand around the quartz sitting on the table's edge. Her eyes were wide with wonder as she cradled it in her palm.

The woman lunged forward, flinging the quartz from her daughter's hand without touching it herself. It clattered to the floor near the stone hearth. The little girl let out a loud wail and scampered toward the crystal. But the mother was quicker, scooping her daughter into her arms. The girl continued to struggle, pounding at her mother with her tiny fists.

Tamsin felt a rush of appreciation for the little girl's resolve. She reminded Tamsin of Marlena. Headstrong. Curious. Impossible to wrangle. The memory made her blood run even colder. Carved a desperate, aching hole in her useless heart.

"Fine," she snapped, cursing herself inwardly the moment the word slipped through her lips. It appeared that her most recent store of love—a crush on the smith's apprentice given in exchange for a spool of unbreakable thread—hadn't run out the way she'd thought. She'd had one small ounce of compassion left in her. And, thanks to her ever-present guilt, she'd wasted it on a squalling two-year-old.

Whatever Tamsin had felt, it was gone as quickly as it had appeared. She watched impassively as the woman fell to her knees, sobbing no longer with anguish but with relief.

"Get up," Tamsin said, her voice sharp.

The woman did.

Tamsin gestured for the woman to come closer. The mother took several hesitant steps, eyes wide like a startled deer. Tamsin covered the remaining distance quickly and placed her hand over the woman's heart. The mother squirmed beneath her touch.

"Think of him," Tamsin commanded.

The woman closed her eyes. Tamsin kept her gaze steady on the woman's face. The palm of her hand grew warm. The woman's love ran up Tamsin's arm and into her bloodstream. The room began to brighten—the greens of her freshly gathered herbs were bright and waxy; their sharp scents wafted through the afternoon air, tickling the inside of her nose. Tamsin's spirits rose as she reveled in the warmth spreading through her body, into her bones.

She had already started to waste it.

Her hand still on the woman, Tamsin focused on the love running through her, sending it to her center. She ushered it carefully to her chest, where her heart sat empty, good for nothing but keeping a steady beat.

Tamsin tucked the love into the left-hand corner of her rib cage, trying to corral it as best she could—although, of course, love could never truly be controlled. It was like trying to trap flies in a birdcage. All Tamsin could do was try to keep her wits about her and stay as levelheaded as possible so that the love would only be used when she chose to access it. She could not afford another slip of compassion. Not when customers were already so few and far between.

When she was quite certain everything was properly secured,

Tamsin removed her hand. The room darkened, the scent faded, and the chill returned, settling into her body familiarly, like a cat in a favorite chair. The woman had gone ashen and expressionless.

"Now, then." Tamsin returned her attention to the child in her arms. Seven times she swept a finger from his tiny forehead down the bridge of his nose, over his lips, and past his chin. Magic flowed from her finger, spreading slowly through the tiny life she cradled. The cottage was silent, save for Tamsin's whispers and the crackling of the flames.

Then the bundle twitched.

Tamsin removed her finger, breaking the stream of magic. The baby's skin was no longer gray but the soft brown of his mother's. Two tiny pink spots spread across his cheeks. He opened his mouth, letting loose a screech so loud Tamsin's head began to scream in response.

The woman let go of her struggling daughter and rushed forward, all but ripping her son from Tamsin's arms. She cradled her screaming baby close, tears falling from her face.

Tamsin had quite preferred the child when he was quiet, but the mother seemed pleased. She thanked Tamsin in a babbling, wet whirlwind before taking her daughter by the hand and rushing from the hut.

Tamsin slumped into a hard-backed wooden chair and eased off her leather boots. She rolled out her ankles, wincing as they cracked. Her head was pounding, and her littlest toe ached.

It was, Tamsin knew, a truly mild price to pay for the magic she had just performed. Most witches her age would have been bedridden for days after untangling and extracting such a severe sickness from another person's body. Of course, most witches her age were still at the academy, where they weren't allowed to perform such a spell at all.

No other young witch was as powerful as Tamsin, but then, no other witch had been cursed and banished from the world Within, either. No other witch had spent her seventeenth birthday cooing emptily over a baby, trying not to shrink beneath the hateful eyes of his mother.

For it *was* her birthday, the first day of what was supposed to be the most important year of her life. Seventeen was the age witches graduated from the academy. It marked the year they could decide their destiny—to stay Within and serve the Coven, or to go beyond the Wood and live among the ordinary folk.

Tamsin had always dreaded her seventeenth birthday, because while she had only ever wanted to stay Within, her sister, Marlena, had only ever wanted to leave.

In the end, good-bye had come much sooner than she'd expected.

Once Tamsin had been relegated to Ladaugh, a provincial farming town in the ordinary world beyond the Wood, seventeen became nothing more than a number. Now it was merely a reminder that she had been on her own for nearly five years and a disgrace for even longer.

Tamsin smacked her palm against the smooth wooden table. She hated herself for her power. No good had ever come from it. If she weren't so desperate to take a break from the swirling gloom in her head and the emptiness of her heart, she might have hung up her cloak altogether. But in order to feel, Tamsin needed love. And casting spells for ordinary folk was the only way to get it.

The pain in her temple pounding a steady rhythm against her brain, Tamsin pushed herself begrudgingly to her feet, ladled water from her drinking bucket into her iron kettle, and set the kettle over the fire to heat. She pried the wooden shutters away from her lone window and peered outside. The sun was sinking in the sky. Several people on the path to the square pointed upward in awe. Tamsin slammed the shutters closed. She had loved sunsets once. Now, no matter the hour, the sky was a singularly unremarkable gray. The colors she'd once delighted in were dilapidated and dull.

The kettle howled, as piercing as the baby's cry. As her long fingers plucked dried leaves of feverfew and buds of chamomile from the bundles hung above her sink, Tamsin thought idly of the reunion the woman would have with her husband that night. At first he'd be confused by her disinterest. Then hurt. Then resigned. Tomorrow he'd spread stories about the witch, threaten to storm her cottage—to kill her, even.

Tamsin wasn't concerned. People were always shooting dark looks and whispers her way each time she ventured into town. There were slighted lovers who lingered outside her front gate a moment too long, but who fled the moment she opened her front door.

Tamsin was still but a girl. That alone was nearly enough to scare them away. Her reputation did the rest.

Using a pestle to grind the leaves, Tamsin diminished the herbs and petals to dust. She shook the pieces carefully into a scrap of cheesecloth, which she tossed into her mug and submerged in boiling water. She didn't want to give the dregs a chance to settle in the bottom of the cup. She didn't want to give herself the chance to read them.

She sank into the chair next to the fire, the soles of her feet dangerously close to the dancing flame. Tamsin shifted slightly. Even if she placed her feet directly into the embers, she would get none of its welcome warmth. She would garner nothing but blistering pain.

Steam billowed from the mug in her hands, the tea's phantom heat teasing her frozen bones as it caressed her cheek. She felt nothing. She took a sip of the tea. It tasted of nothing, with a lingering hint of bog water.

She didn't know why she bothered.

Tamsin dumped the tea onto the fire, and the flames sputtered for a second before returning to their dance. She rolled her eyes. The motion forced her attention back toward the thundering in her head, which was worsened by an incessant pounding on her front door.

Tamsin scrutinized the door suspiciously. Sunset marked the end of her business hours, and since most people in Ladaugh either resented her or feared her, she wasn't often the subject of social calls.

She strode forward and unhitched the small window at the top of the door to peer out at the intruder. A small boy, no older than seven or eight, shifted his weight nervously from one bare foot to the other. Probably a pawn in another of the farmer's son's pranks. The farmer's son was a stupid boy, always trying to one-up the witch for bragging rights. He never succeeded.

She swung the door open, glowering expectantly at the child. "What?"

The poor boy looked as though he wished the earth would swallow him whole. While Tamsin could have arranged that, instead she waited for him to speak.

"Pardon, ma'am," the boy squeaked.

"*Miss*," Tamsin snapped, putting a hand to her still-pounding head. The boy looked at her questioningly. "I am not your mother. You will address me as *miss*."

The boy's eyes widened, and he bobbed his head quickly. "Miss?"

Tamsin drew herself up to her full height and nodded her assent.

"Two of Her Majesty's riders are in the town square." The boy spoke quickly, his words crashing into one another. "They've called a meeting. Everyone is to come immediately." He finished with a hiccup, stumbling to catch his breath. He bounced on his toes, clearly anxious to move on.

"And they told you to summon the witch?" Tamsin raised a dark eyebrow.

The boy's eyes were so wide they nearly fell out of his head. "No, ma'am." He gasped at his error. "Miss. They just said get everyone, and quick."

Tamsin laughed humorlessly. "Very well. Message received." She waved her hand. "Go on, then." The boy's face slumped in relief. He was out of the garden before Tamsin had shut the door.

A town meeting. How quaint. There was nothing the queen

had to say that interested her. Whatever the news, it would work its way through town four times over before the moon had settled in the sky. She would surely hear of it tomorrow from no less than six separate individuals when she went to the market for her eggs.

Perhaps there was yet another royal ball—the southern duke's son was close to marrying age by now and had rejected every lord and lady the Queendom of Carrow had to offer. That, or the ogres had finally found their way around the strongholds erected between the Wastelands and the East.

Whatever the news, it was of no consequence to Tamsin. Despite the fact that Queen Mathilde's relationship with the Coven's current High Councillor had held strong for nearly twenty years, Tamsin could not find it in her to care about the politics of the world Beyond.

She scratched her left forearm, where the Coven's sigil was supposed to be. The skin, mottled and burned where the mark had been stripped from her, was a reminder of what she had done.

A reminder of whom she had lost.

Tamsin gave a strangled cry, sweeping her arm across her cluttered tabletop, relishing the chaos and clatter of her belongings tumbling to the stone floor. A crystal splintered. Her mug shattered, scattering chunks of hardened clay across the room. Loose papers floated into the fire, the flames devouring the dark ink until the words no longer existed.

She hated her cottage. It was a small, suffocating disaster. It wasn't home. Nothing about Ladaugh was home.

Tamsin's hand moved instinctively to her heart.

It was her birthday, after all. It couldn't hurt to use a little bit of love. Just for a moment of peace. Tamsin's curse left her with nothing but guilt and regret. Her existence was lifeless—a banished witch relegated to lowering fevers in babies and aiding this year's corn crop. She'd had so much potential. Could have been so much more if she hadn't been so impulsive. So careless. So desperate.

Now Tamsin was nothing but bitter and dark and cold— always so impossibly cold.

Pressing her hand harder against her chest, Tamsin closed her eyes and unraveled the knot inside her. She siphoned out the smallest pinch of the woman's love for her husband. Immediately she was flooded with warmth. She shrugged off her shawl and moved lazily through the house, her long homespun skirt tickling her toes, her fingers trailing across the cloudlike quilt, her palms pressing against the smooth edges of her crystals. She rummaged through several unmarked jars for a cinnamon stick, then brought it to her nose and inhaled the sharp spice's subtle nuttiness.

She rushed to the window and pried away the shutters again, her heart catching in her throat as she glimpsed the tail end of the sunset—the sharp reds fading into golds streaked with pinks that turned blue black. She was using too much, was wasting her supply on little frivolities, but she needed to do one last thing before she cut herself off. Before she squirreled the love away for when she needed it most.

Tamsin shuttered the window and turned to the table. She took a pinch of seasoning from a small leather sack and sprinkled several tiny grains on the tip of her tongue.

The salt tasted tangy and bright.

TWO

WREN

The candle's tiny flame flickered, then failed. Wren swore, her voice barely a whisper, more of a suggestion than a sound. If her father woke, he would beg her not to go, and it would be another hour before she could lull him back to sleep. By the time she made it to market, everyone would have gotten their eggs from Lensla, the miserable woman who lived near the bog, and Wren would be without coins. Again.

She'd heard a rumor that girls in the North had offered a stiltzkin their names for the ability to turn straw into gold. What she would have given to make such a trade. Wren didn't need a name. Not if it meant she'd have gold to spare, a full belly, and proper medicine for her father. She had been named for a bird, after all. It wouldn't be a terrible loss.

Tiptoeing carefully across the small room, Wren cringed as she stumbled over her father's boots at the foot of the bed. She paused, keeping her breath trapped in her lungs. There was no sound from her father. Exhaling gently, Wren stayed rooted to the floor until her eyes grew accustomed to the darkness. Only then did she bend down to grab the boots, the leather soft and worn from their many years guarding her father's feet. She settled them carefully in the corner so she would not trip again.

She fumbled with the door, opening it just wide enough to slip through before shutting it quickly to shield her father's sickbed from the sunlight spilling through the cottage's front windows.

Wren sighed again, at full volume this time. It had been a particularly unpleasant night, her father complaining of a headache so searing he was unable to keep down even the smallest spoonful of water. She had finally lulled him to sleep with a warm mustard-seed compress and the hint of a song, her voice low and husky from her own lack of sleep.

"I'd be dead without you, little bird," her father had murmured, minutes before falling into a fitful slumber. Wren wished she could chalk the sentiment up to feverish exaggeration, but it was the truth. *You must promise never to leave me, Wren,* her father had said, the day after her mother died, *for without you, I do not think I would survive.* In the five years since, he'd never let her forget it.

Wren ran a hand through her hair, her fingers catching in the tangled plait, the same fiery-red shade as her mother's.

Most days she wanted to chop it all off, but that would break her father's heart. And so she kept her hair, the weight of it always on her shoulders. A memory she always had to carry.

She quickly washed her face and hands, the cold water shocking her senses awake. She retied her hair into a neat braid and pulled on her boots, lacing them with quick efficiency. She rolled out the crick in her neck and stretched her hands to the ceiling. Her pale fingertips brushed the bottom of the roof's wooden beam.

Wren was beginning to outgrow her life.

Each day she struggled to fold herself up into the small, perfect pieces the world demanded. The freckle-faced village girl who peddled eggs at market to support her family. The dutiful daughter who spent every waking moment nursing her perpetually ill father back to health. The quiet girl who was trying not to drown in an ocean of her own secrets.

For sleep was not the only thing Wren had sacrificed for her father.

Wren gathered two large baskets and lined their insides with soft, brightly colored cloth. A basket on each arm, she headed outside, around the corner of their small, thatched cottage toward the chicken coop. The air smelled of freshly clipped lavender, the scent wafting across the morning in a purple haze. Of course, it wasn't actually lavender Wren was smelling—it was magic.

Ignore it, ignore it, ignore it.

She couldn't. The magic swirled around her even as she turned her back, caressing her cheek, light as a feather, while she shooed her hens away from their nests. She gathered their small, warm bounty determinedly, wiping the eggs clean and tucking them carefully between the worn tea towels. The magic draped itself around her like a scarf. Wren swatted at the air, trying to dispel it. It wasn't like she could do anything with the purple haze of magic. She wasn't a witch.

She was a source.

For years Wren had believed that everyone saw the world the way she did. That other people could see magic's shining colors twisting through the sky like ribbons, could recognize its pungent scent. Wren couldn't imagine life without magic's soft, soothing whisper, without being able to touch its pillowy lightness or taste its hint of sweetness, like a ripe berry ready to burst. It wasn't until she was met with the blank stares of her playmates that Wren realized that there was something different about her. That no one else could see the swirling, colorful cloud of magic that always hung above her head.

She should have gone straight to the Witchlands. The Coven required any ordinary folk who believed they possessed power to enter the Witchwood, the border of enchanted trees surrounding their country. Were they to make it through the Wood to the Witchlands, they would train with the Coven and carve out a place for themselves in the world of magic. Should they refuse to come of their own accord, they would be tracked down and taken by force, never allowed to return to the world beyond the Wood.

Wren was supposed to be there. Sources were highly valued: They housed pure magic, magic witches could draw from in order to supplement their own power. The Coven would have taken her in without a moment's hesitation and kept her well compensated for the rest of her life.

But magic had torn her family apart once before. During the Year of Darkness, when her parents were young and newly married, they'd had a child, a boy who was only days old when he caught the sickness cast by the dark witch Evangeline. Wren came along nearly twelve years later. By then her parents were old and haunted, grief-stricken and set in their fear and hatred of all things magic. When her mother died, her father became even more delicate.

And so Wren kept her true self hidden. She would run a hand through her braid, tugging loose the plait so her father wouldn't notice that when the wind blew, not a single hair fell out of place. She forced herself to shiver in the winter, despite the fact that she was never cold, not even when she walked barefoot through the snow. The world bent toward her, like recognizing like. Magic recognizing magic.

Her father could never know. So Wren tried to ignore the way magic pulled at her. She chose not to go to the Witchlands to train, the way the Coven's edict required. She kept her distance from any and all magic lest she be found out and punished for her defection.

Wren did her best to pretend she hadn't wanted that life anyway.

After slipping the final egg into her basket and tucking the cloth protectively around her precious wares, Wren closed the latch on the coop and moved swiftly through her front gate, which slammed behind her. She winced despite herself, thinking of her father and his already-unsteady slumber.

A deeper, darker part of her hoped it had woken him up.

Before her feet met the path, soft black fur brushed against her ankle—the scruffy stray cat that often hung around her house. Wren knelt, balancing her baskets as she scratched him behind the ears. She'd always had a way with animals—birds settling on her shoulder as she walked to town, dogs following dutifully at her heels, even horses occasionally coming to nuzzle her neck despite her empty pockets.

"I know, I know." Wren rummaged in her basket for a crumb but came up with nothing. "You're hungry. I'm sorry." The cat's yellow eyes stared accusingly up at her. "So am I, you know. Not that you care." The cat let out a soft mewl.

Wren ran her hand across the creature's matted back, extracting a burr that had stuck near the base of his tail. The cat nipped affectionately at her finger. "That's all I can do," Wren murmured apologetically. "Unless I have a *very* good day at market." Though of course that wasn't likely. The cat nuzzled her knee, leaving black fur clinging to the green wool of her trousers. "Okay, greedy. I'll do my best." Wren gave the cat a final scratch behind the ears, then hauled herself up, careful not to jostle her eggs.

The cat shot Wren an affronted look.

Wren glanced back up at the purple haze of magic. It pointed down the path to the left, toward the town of Wells. She glanced to the right, toward Ladaugh. It was a similar walk to each town's main square, but the sky in that direction was a clear, normal blue.

It wasn't even a choice, really.

Magic made Wren a bit . . . odd. She was forever shooing it

away, constantly smoothing down the hair that stood up on the back of her neck in its presence, always trying to explain why she'd stopped a conversation midsentence, listening to a shriek no one else could hear. Sometimes she gave in to it, closed her eyes and tried to will it in her direction, to parse its dazzling ribbons and unravel its secrets. But there she was less successful. Mostly she just waved her hands about and felt ridiculous.

Still, the purple ribbon felt like a sign. If she followed, it might lead her to a field of wildflowers or to a tiny creek running with the freshest water she had ever tasted. It might take her to a den of baby foxes that would chase their tails and nuzzle her arm with their wet, black noses. . . .

Wren's baskets weighed heavily on her arms as she let her daydream die. She needed to head to market to trade for food and herbs for her father. She could not afford the distraction. And so Wren turned right, leaving the magic—and her desperate glimmer of wanting—behind.

Her footsteps crunched on the road to Ladaugh, kicking up dust that danced around her ankles. Her baskets swung jauntily as the path wound its way through Farmer Haddon's field, where his four sons chased one another with sticks. The wheat was tall, nearly to Wren's waist. It had been a wet spring, but summer had driven away the clouds, leaving the days crisp and bright and warm. The sun was hot against her cheek. Soon her face would bloom with freckles, and the bridge of her nose would turn a perpetual pink.

Wren walked past towering hay bales and endless fields of corn, stopping once to offer her hand to a field mouse, which settled on her shoulder, its tiny claws tangling in her hair. She waved at Amelia, the butcher's wife, who was loaded down with three baskets and nearly as many crying children. She crossed a great stone bridge, passing others carrying their market wares in baskets or strapped upon their backs. Despite their friendly greetings, their faces were set.

Something had shifted since she'd crossed the river. It hung sourly in the air, was present in the townspeople's grim expressions. Even the field mouse had scampered down her back and into the tall summer grass. When she came upon a family—a father, mother, and little boy, doubtfully older than three—pulling a wooden cart loaded with everything they owned, her curiosity got the best of her.

"Hello, friends." She raised a hand in greeting. "Where are you headed this morning?"

"South, of course." The woman looked at Wren with wide eyes, her face frantic. "Haven't you heard? There's a plague sweeping its way through the queendom." She shivered, pulling her child close.

"Were you not at the meeting?" the father asked, noting Wren's confusion. "Queen Mathilde has fled from Farn and headed to the Winter Palace. The capital has been completely ravaged by the sickness. Once the plague makes its way over the mountains, we will be next."

"What are the symptoms?" Wren tugged sharply on the end of her braid. Her father could not afford another sickness. He was already feverish and bedridden, his illness unresponsive to her remedies. "The usual sorts?"

The woman shook her head sharply. "It isn't a physical sickness."

That was a relief. Her father's symptoms were very much physical. Whatever he had wasn't this plague.

"They said . . ." The woman paused, putting her hands over her child's tiny ears. The boy squirmed beneath her touch, burying his face in her linen trousers. "They said it creeps inside your mind, siphons out your memories and your joys. Leaves the afflicted bodies empty, like"—the woman glanced side to side, her voice dropping to barely a whisper—"walking ghosts."

Wren's body went cold. What sort of sickness was strong enough to rob a person of their soul?

The father looked over his shoulder, down the road to Ladaugh, eager to move on. He put an arm around his wife. "Excuse us," he said, smiling emptily at Wren. He ushered his family forward, their backs bent with the weight of their cart, their heads bowed in fear. Wren raised a hand in parting, but the family did not look back.

Ladaugh's bustling town square assailed Wren's senses with the shrill scrape of knives being sharpened and the savory scent of meat roasting over an open flame. Vendors called across the market, chiding their competitors; children played tag in front of the bookseller's cart. Wren, distracted by their game, tripped, her toe catching on a loose cobblestone.

"Whoa there, girlie." A strong hand gripped her elbow as she struggled to steady herself.

"Tor." Wren smiled easily. The tailor was a kind man and,

perhaps more important, a consistent customer. She squinted at his vest. The fabric was shimmering with magic, as though it existed behind a curtain of smoke. The pattern was beginning to make her a bit dizzy.

"Wren?" The old man waved a hand before her eyes to reclaim her attention. She tried to look apologetic. Tor smiled stiffly. "How's your da?"

Wren's own smile slipped several notches. "Not well."

Tor's grip on her arm grew tighter. "The plague?" The bags beneath his eyes were nearly black. It appeared that Wren was not the only one who had gone without sleep.

She shook her head. "The symptoms aren't the same."

Tor loosened his grip. "Be careful, will you? My cousin in Farn sent a raven last night, said the sickness has ravaged the capital like I wouldn't believe. The afflicted are empty-eyed, and even the earth is affected. He said the ground shook until it opened up and swallowed a hundred people whole."

A chill ran up the back of Wren's arm. She shifted her baskets nervously.

Tor's eyes were dark and hard. "You weren't alive for the Year of Darkness, but this is how the sickness started then, too. There's a new dark witch. I know it." He ran a hand through his thinning hair. "The Coven claimed they would protect us, but why would witches care about ordinary folk?" He laughed darkly. "Anyway, even Queen Mathilde has denounced the Coven. If our queen is willing to turn her back on witches, well . . ." He trailed off, pursing his lips. "It must be bad. Watch yourself, will you? And that da of yours." His eyes lingered on

Wren, his pity nearly tangible. "I'll take five eggs, if you have them."

He offered her three needles, six mismatched buttons, and a spool of black thread. Wren accepted his barter gratefully, passing over her eggs one by one as Tor nestled them carefully into his sack. She bid him farewell and continued on, grateful for the silent, solid ground beneath her feet.

Wren continued to circle the market, trading her speckled eggs for a purple-leafed head of cabbage, the bones of a turkey, and a loaf of dense brown bread. She exchanged pleasantries with the other vendors, but despite the usual niceties of market day, the air in the square was stilted and strange.

Wren stopped to browse a small cart of polished pink apples, her fingers lingering longingly on their waxy skin. It had been close to a year since she'd tasted the crisp, sweet fruit. A woman in the South had tasked a wood nymph with poisoning a single golden apple to kill her stepdaughter. But the spell had gone rogue. The southern orchards had withered away, and an entire year's harvest had burned. The ghastly green flames had been seen all the way in the West.

That woman had been a fool. Even Wren, who was the first to find any excuse to avoid an encounter with a witch, who nursed her father back to health with herbs and broths made from the jelly marrow of bones rather than seek out spells and enchantments, knew better than to trust a nymph with poison.

"She didn't even come to the meeting," a woman whispered, pulling Wren's attention from the apple's smooth skin. "I bet she already knew."

"I bet she caused the entire thing," a second woman replied, her face pinched.

Wren shifted her baskets and made a show of polishing the apple on her skirt, listening closely.

"I wouldn't put it past her. I always thought there was something wrong there. I mean, her *prices*," the first woman said. "It's not natural."

"Nothing about that witch is natural," said the other. "She's so young. Too young, if you ask me."

A shiver of magic crept down Wren's neck. It felt like the insistent eyes of a stranger, but stronger. Magic danced around her body, wrapping her in an embrace. She tried to shake it, but in her haste, the apple tumbled from her hand and rolled all the way across the market, landing at the feet of a tinker displaying a lush purple cloak with seemingly endless pockets. The apple's once-bright skin was left broken and bruised.

The women stopped talking and stared at Wren, scandalized. The merchant started yelling, his voice low and gruff, his long brown beard trembling as he glowered down at her.

Wren tried to slow her hammering heart. The price of apples was twice what it had been before the poisoning. The fruit was a delicacy she could not afford.

Wren tried to stammer out an apology, but the words caught in her throat. The slithering feeling of eyes on the back of her neck returned, but this time it wasn't magic. People had started to stare. Wren's face was on fire, the merchant's loud voice ringing in her ears. She offered him the buttons and thread from Tor as well as her loaf of bread. The man scowled but accepted her payment.

Wren tried not to cry as she picked up the bruised, brown apple, repositioned her much lighter baskets, and turned away.

Only two eggs remained, their speckled brown shells delicate and smooth. Two was hardly enough to barter for dry crusts of bread. Still, she had to try. Wren swallowed the lump in her throat and called out to the crowd.

"Did you say eggs?" The voice behind her was lush as velvet, dark as midnight.

Wren wheeled around, her eyes widening as she took in the face of the girl who had spoken.

Tamsin, the witch of Ladaugh, stood before her, buried beneath a sweeping cloak of forest green. Wren took a step back. She'd been so desperate to trade that she'd forgotten to look for the source of the magic that had sent the apple tumbling to the cobblestones. She had failed to watch for the streaks of earthy red magic, ruddy like wet clay, that radiated from Tamsin. Had forgotten to turn and run, unsold eggs be damned. Had broken the one and only rule upon which her life depended: Never come face-to-face with a witch.

"Well, do you have eggs or not?" Tamsin snapped. She brushed back her hair, dark as a raven's wing, a thick eyebrow arching up with scorn.

Wren was having difficulty finding her voice. She rummaged quickly through her basket, nearly shattering the shells as she scooped the eggs into her hand and held them out to the witch.

Tamsin took them, eyes narrowed. "How much?"

Wren shrugged, waving her other hand in the air in an uncertain gesture, all the while fighting the urge to bolt. She was acting a fool, but she had never been so close to a witch in her life, and certainly not one as powerful as Tamsin. She squirmed beneath the witch's stare. The green flecks in Tamsin's brown eyes were the same color as her cloak.

Tamsin clucked her tongue impatiently and dropped a handful of coins into Wren's basket before turning on her heel, her cloak flaring out behind her like a cape. Wren gaped after her, catching a hint of fresh sage on the morning breeze.

She scrambled to collect the coins, nearly ten times what the eggs were worth, the heat of them sparking excitement in her chest. Perhaps she had been wrong to steer clear of witches. Wren had always assumed they were just as awful as her father said. But it was clear to her now that Tamsin's sour expression did not accurately reflect the fullness of her heart.

Wren breezed through the market, handing over a copper coin for a loaf of coarse, dark bread five times finer than the one she had parted with. She purchased fresh herbs and a cut of venison, little luxuries she normally wouldn't dare dream of. And still, despite the weight of her replenished baskets, one solid silver coin remained.

Wren made quick time of the walk back home. She sauntered through the front gate, a smile playing about her lips. It slipped as she heard a noise from the back room. Wren settled her baskets on the table and scooped a ladleful of water, which she carried carefully to her father.

She inched the door open slowly, drops of water falling on her boots. "Papa?"

He made a soft sound, his lips curling into a weak smile.

Wren helped him sit up, tipped the ladle gently toward his parched lips. Several drops dribbled down his chin.

"There's my little bird," he said, his voice a thick whisper. His skin was slick with sweat, his hair grayer even than it had been that morning, fading into shocks of white near his temples. He looked a fright. But he recognized her. His mind was still his own. Wren exhaled a soft sigh of relief.

Her father put a hand on her cheek, his skin flaky and paper-thin. "You know I'd be lost without you. Dead, even." He tried to grin, but it was more like a grimace.

"Don't say that," she whispered, her tongue stale. "You always say that. You're going to be fine." She removed his hand and settled it back at his side under the heavy pile of rough wool blankets. "I'll make you a broth."

"Damn the broth," he said, his grimace widening. Wren faked a laugh, though they both knew he could stomach little else.

"Sleep," she commanded, and it was testament to her father's frailty that he didn't even try to fight her.

She slipped back into the main room and put water, turkey bones, and herbs in a pot to boil. She hung the empty baskets on their hooks near the door, then folded the tea towels and tucked them safely back into their cupboard.

Once everything was in its place, Wren pulled a chair in front of the fireplace, using it to reach the brown jug on the top of the mantel. The jug was innocuous and plain, like Wren herself. The most unlikely place to hide something valuable.

Wren glanced warily at the door to her father's room. He

knew nothing about the meager savings she had scraped together, the meals she'd skipped in order to hear the satisfying clink of coins. The hens were old. They couldn't lay eggs forever. Wren needed a backup plan.

She uncorked the jug and let the coins spill out onto the worn wooden table. She sorted them into piles—several copper, two brass, and one precious gold, already reserved for the tax collectors come autumn.

Still, there was so much she could do with this money. She could pocket it and run off to a new life. There was enough to serve her until she got on her feet, found a job and a room with a proper bed. Perhaps she could even go to the Witchlands and finally learn everything about magic. About who she was.

Wren turned Tamsin's coin over in her hand, soothed by the warmth of it. She had sacrificed everything for her father—her heart, her future, her magic. Surely she was owed something too.

There was a splutter and a hiss from the hearth. Guiltily, she swept the coins and her daydreams back into their respective hiding places. Her father was all she had left. She couldn't turn away from him now. Wren sighed as she replaced the jug on the mantel and peeked into the pot. She was back to the bleak reality of her life. The water had begun to boil.

THREE

TAMSIN

No one had called on Tamsin in four days.

Her mornings bled into afternoons that melted into evenings like fire turned to embers turned to dust. Her fingers itched to work. Panic flared in her chest, rising higher each day her door went without a knock. Her store of love continued to wane.

Thanks to the rapid spread of the plague, she feared it might never be refilled.

Tamsin tried to distract herself. She stared at the walls, searching for shapes in the discolored stones: a cloud above the hearth, an ear of corn by the crack near the window, and a tiny dog next to the door that was visible only when she turned her head and squinted so hard she could feel it in her brain.

Tamsin took a needle to several hole-ridden pairs of thick woolen socks. She told herself that she wore through socks so quickly it wasn't worth using magic to mend them. She didn't need to battle hiccups every time her big toe forced its way through the worn wool.

But of course that wasn't the whole truth.

After her banishment, Tamsin's relationship with her power had changed. Gone were the days of fulfilling every whim with the flick of her wrist. No longer did she flaunt her prowess or push her abilities to their limits. This Tamsin no longer trusted her instincts. This Tamsin no longer deserved the convenience her talent provided. Not when she was living and Marlena was dead.

The needle plunged itself into the thin skin beneath her fingernail as though in confirmation.

Putting her darning aside, Tamsin used a long iron poker to stoke the fading flames in the fireplace. She was nearly out of firewood, running low on supplies and sustenance. She glanced at the basket she had taken to market five days earlier. There was nothing left inside save a head of pale green cabbage and a single brown-speckled egg.

It was hardly enough to feed a child, yet Tamsin could not be bothered to venture back to the town's square to fill her pantry. Not when the townspeople's opinion of witches had shifted so dramatically. She had gone from being tentatively trusted to fully vilified. Hated, even.

Their whispers had trailed Tamsin home from the market,

pushing against her throat like a cloak tied too tight. In the days that followed, their accusations began to root themselves into the walls of her cottage, carving out spaces between the loose stones, swirling beneath the boiling kettle, nestling themselves atop her worn gray rug until Tamsin felt she had always lived with their words.

Her fault, this dark magic. She's dangerous. Evil. Steer clear of the witch.

Tamsin had heard similar sentiments before. Only then she had actually deserved them.

Now she was alone, trapped within the confines of her hut. Each day that she went without a visitor, the walls seemed a little bit closer, the roof a little bit lower. Her house was closing in around her, inch by inch. Soon she would no longer be able to move. Soon she might actually be as useless as she felt.

A light rain began to fall, tapping a steady beat against the roof of the hut, pattering softly against the wooden shutters barring the window. Tamsin sat, stoic and silent. Once, the sound of rain had been comforting, had given her a clear mind and a sense of peace. But now it was just water, falling from the sky, hitting her house. A sound and nothing more.

Tamsin reached for the shawl draped across the back of her chair and wrapped it tightly around her shoulders. She cleared her throat, the sound sticking. She wished she had someone to talk to.

She'd had someone, once. Leya, with her big eyes, was a source: a girl made of pure magic. But Tamsin could not remember her best friend's laugh or the heat of her hand in Tamsin's as they snuck out of the dorms to lie in the long grass and stare up at the stars. She could, however, recall the way her heart had broken as Leya shouted at her retreating back: "You're going to regret this."

As usual, Leya had been right.

Her throat grew tight with the memory. Tamsin reached for her jug of water, hoping to rinse the sour taste from her mouth. Instead her fingers grazed something soft. Her hand closed around a black leather-bound book.

One that had *definitely* not been there moments before.

Tamsin flung it across the room as though it were on fire. The book skittered and stopped, landing open to a creamy white page covered with loopy handwriting. Heart hammering, she grabbed the iron poker from the hearth and approached the book like it was a feral creature she was trying to tame. She kept her eyes carefully averted from the words scrawled across the pages.

Tamsin nudged the book with the sharp end of the poker. It did not jump to life, did not leap forward to attack. For all intents and purposes, it appeared to be nothing more than a book.

But it *was* more.

This diary had lived buried at the bottom of Tamsin's cupboard for nearly five years. It had taken the journey from Within to Ladaugh tucked into the waistband of Tamsin's travel skirt, the only relic from her old life. Never once had she peered at its pages. Never once had she taken it from its hiding place.

Yet here it was before her, laid out like a curse.

Tamsin backed away from the diary slowly, reaching for a tea towel. Once she had it in hand, she sucked in a shaking breath, then lunged for the book, using the cloth to fling it into the cupboard. She slammed the doors shut and leaned back against the wood, trying to catch her breath.

The sour taste of grief had been replaced by a dry-tongued sense of discomfort. Tamsin's cottage had an order; everything had a place. Then again, she *had* gone four days without human contact. She was starting to feel suffocated. Maybe she had taken out the diary and merely . . . forgotten.

Tamsin rubbed the back of her neck nervously. That couldn't be the case—she hadn't touched the diary in years. Whatever was happening, Tamsin was not the one instigating it.

It was raining harder now, the water falling with a hiss, then a crackle. Tamsin glanced idly at her fireplace, expecting a shower of sparks as a flame devoured the log. But the fire had faded to embers. The hearth sat dark and empty.

That was when she noticed the glow. The sky had gone a sickly brownish green, and a thick, sharp scent pooled in Tamsin's nostrils, all putrid ash and burning spice.

She was tempted to close the shutters, brew herself a sleeping draught, and go to bed. She was fairly certain she was having delusions. Perhaps she hadn't had enough to eat.

Then she saw the smoke coming from her herb garden. Flames devoured her carefully cultivated plants—tiny leaves of basil, frail fronds of rosemary, thin tendrils of dill. Tamsin rubbed her eyes quickly, but the scene didn't change. She stared, bewildered, wondering if this misunderstanding was part of her delusion too.

It was raining. Nothing was supposed to be on fire.

Tamsin, who had been gripping the sill so tightly that the tips of her fingers had gone a ghostly white, pried herself away from the window and ran to the door. Fury flooded her, filling the empty cavern in her chest.

She had invested so much time in her garden, had nursed the tiny seedlings into full-fledged plants, had watched them take root and explode across the once-barren soil. While she couldn't enjoy their scents or notice the subtle flavor they imparted in her food, she had made them, had tended to the little plants the way she wasn't allowed to tend to her own heart, to her memories, to the people she had once loved and then lost.

They were only plants, but the garden was all she had.

Tamsin's fingers fumbled unsteadily with the lock, the metal bar sticking unhelpfully, before she finally managed to pry it open with a grimace-inducing scrape.

Giant droplets of rain plummeted to the ground, turning the long summer grass a singed brown that reeked of death. The sky was darker now, inky and ominous.

There was a creak, then a terrible groan as Tamsin's fence shattered. One of the wooden fence posts toppled onto her patch of chamomile. She rushed out into her garden only for the rain to turn its violence on her—burning holes into the hem of her skirt, sizzling the ends of her hair, and leaving droplet-size blisters on her skin. She tried to cover her face with her arm, but the pain soon grew too much to bear. Reluctantly, she retreated to the safety of her cottage and its slate-shingled roof, while the heavy rain continued to eat away at the earth.

She settled herself shakily on her too-firm bedroll, rubbing camphor on the angry red welts. She had scoffed when she over-heard the tailor tell the butcher how the ground in Farn had opened up, swallowing its citizens whole. But now it was unde-niably clear: The plague had been cast using dark magic.

Tamsin's gut clenched at the thought.

Dark magic, while appealing in its all-encompassing power, drained the earth rather than the witch who cast the spell. As the world tried to overcompensate for the loss of its natural resources, the magic that filled its empty wells became twisted and impure. The side effects of a spell borne from dark magic were endless and horrifying.

Magic was, after all, about *balance*. That was the first les-son Tamsin had ever learned. The Coven's High Councillor had warned the young witch that no matter how strong she believed herself to be, magic itself was always much more powerful. And when magic was pulled directly from the earth, the earth had a tendency to rebel.

Tamsin's empty heart twisted in her chest. When she thought about balance, she thought of her twin sister, of their palms pressed together, of staring into each other's eyes like a mirror without the glass. Together, they had been their own kind of magic.

Tamsin wished that when she thought of Marlena, she could remember what it had felt like to love her. She wished she could remember more than her sister's cold, clammy skin and the eerie blue of her lips against the crisp white sheets of the infirmary.

Tamsin could only remember clawing at the cold, wet earth, the dirt caked so thick beneath her fingernails that it took a whole week's scrubbing to get clean. She could only recall how the ancient words, faded and smudged on the aged scrap of parchment, had stuck in her throat as she spoke them aloud, summoning the magic from the earth below to bind her power to her twin sister's life.

But though the spell had been successful in saving Marlena, the dark magic hadn't stopped there. It had slipped through Tamsin's grasp, taking on a life of its own.

Taking lives.

Tamsin spent most of her mornings wondering why her classmate Amma had still been asleep in the dormitory when the rest of the students had evacuated to higher ground. She agonized over the way Amma must have struggled to breathe as the water poured in—flooding the room in a matter of seconds. Every night, Tamsin replayed the moment when the High Councillor had broken the bond between the sisters and the life had drained from Marlena, too.

She had done that. Tamsin had caused that. Two people were dead thanks to her misguided, desperate attempt to keep her sister alive.

Under the Coven's rule, the punishment for using dark magic was death. Tamsin had been desperate enough to reach for it anyway. She knew what she had been willing to sacrifice, twelve years old and reckless. But her dark magic hadn't been strong enough to make it past the Wood, the border of trees that separated the world Within from the world Beyond. Her spell had stayed contained, and only those Within knew the enormity of what she had done. This new plague, however, was affecting ordinary folk at a dizzying rate, which meant the spell had to have been cast by a witch older and more powerful than Tamsin had been.

The High Councillor was surely fuming. She was the one who had taken down the dark witch thirty years prior, when Evangeline had used dark magic to cause her own plague. The High Councillor was the one who had founded the Coven, had made it her life's work to create and enforce a system that would educate the young witches in her care and prevent the use of dark magic. Before the Coven's takeover, the world of magic had been rogue and chaotic. Now there was an order. There were laws and due process and consequences.

Five years ago, Tamsin had betrayed the High Councillor's trust. Now another witch had done the same.

Tamsin's cupboard doors flew open with a sharp bang. The diary shot toward her, slamming into her gut with a shocking amount of force. Tamsin stumbled backward, gasping for air, her eyes never leaving the black book.

The first time, she had been able to write off the diary's appearance as odd. The second time, she could find no reasonable explanation. She took a swift, shaking breath. Had *she* summoned it as she recalled her own use of dark magic? Or maybe it was the dark magic *itself*, messing with her balance. Trying to rekindle her grief. Poking at the yellow bruise of loss she tried so desperately to ignore.

Whatever was happening, Tamsin could not bear to face it. She flung the book back into the crowded cupboard, burying it beneath a moth-eaten quilt. Then she turned to the hearth, where the embers of her earlier fire had all but faded to nothing. Shivering, she took one of the few remaining pieces of firewood from her meager pile and nestled it into the ashes.

She fiddled with the flint, her shaking hands missing a strike once, twice, three times before she saw a spark. Tamsin spoke to the fire, her voice cracking with fear as she coaxed it to life. Once the hearth was filled with a flickering flame, Tamsin turned toward the table.

The diary was lying open to a page filled with loopy black handwriting.

Tamsin swore, her vision swimming as panic crawled its way up her throat. She scooped the book up, ready to fling it into the fire, when her eyes caught on the loop of a letter *T*.

Her name scribbled in her sister's handwriting.

Marlena had always been writing. During lessons, meals, free spell periods, she was always scribbling, sometimes so quickly that the ink smeared on her page and splattered her left hand. She was messy, imprecise, and seemingly never out of secrets. Secrets she refused to share.

Tamsin had often tried to read over her sister's shoulder, sometimes catching the hint of a word before Marlena slammed the cover closed or swatted her roughly away. It had been a part of her sister, that book, the words on the page an extension of Marlena's soul.

It was one of the reasons Tamsin had never allowed herself to open it. She couldn't bear to look at her sister's handwriting and feel nothing but idle curiosity about someone she had once been willing to die for.

Tamsin's curse had been placed by the Coven as a way to make sure Tamsin's love for another would never again cloud her judgment. Now the sight of her dead sister's handwriting brought her nothing but a creeping sense of disquiet.

Even as she settled into a kitchen chair, Tamsin tried to talk herself out of it. But her eyes had already begun to catch on full sentences. The last time a witch had used dark magic, two girls had died. Marlena had been one of them. And now that another spell had been cast, her diary was haunting Tamsin. Hounding her.

It couldn't be a coincidence. Things either were, or they were not, Councillor Mari used to say. Clearly, the diary wanted something from her. So, Tamsin began to read.

Tamsin is testing me again. I know I shouldn't blame her—I know it's just my own jealousy rearing its ugly head—but you'd think she was a princess (one of those relentlessly privileged people that the ordinary folk are forced to worship), walking the halls, laughing with Leya like she doesn't have a care in the world.

I suppose she doesn't. It must be so easy to be her. But to be honest (and if you can't be honest to a book with paper that can't talk back, where can you be?), I wonder if she isn't just the slightest bit tired. It must be exhausting, trying to maintain that level of perfection.

I've seen the way the councillors look at her when it's her turn to cast. There's so much weight there. Such expectation. Me, I can try until my face turns red and my blood runs blue and my vision goes black, and they'll just sigh that little sigh (you know that sigh, the one I've gotten my entire life since my magic "appeared") and pat me on the back and tell me "nice try," and then I want to run away and die (but of course I only end up bedridden for days, my brain foggy and my limbs so heavy they might as well be rocks).

I don't know what I'd do without Amma. I really don't. Yes, her sight is becoming more advanced, but so are the headaches. What's a gift if you don't also have a curse? I'm sure I don't know. But my sister might.

Sometimes I wish (and yes, I know wishing is futile—my mother is my mother, after all) that I knew what it was like to be her. Really and truly knew. I understand that's a strange thing to feel about a girl who has the same face as I do (although I do maintain that I'm the prettier one; I've got to have something), but that's where the similarities stop.

Do you know that we used to switch places all the time, laughing behind our little fists as we tricked some of the savviest witches

in the world into calling us by the wrong names?
(Of course you didn't know that; you're a diary.)
We played that game for ages, and it always
worked, until the day sparks first shot from
her fingers and mine stayed perfectly normal.
Until there was no fooling anyone because her
magic was a river and mine was a raindrop. I
still remember the day I couldn't be Tamsin
anymore and realized that all there was left
to be was me.

It was the worst day of my life.

FOUR

WREN

The baker had no bread.

It was just after daybreak. The market in Wells had been open no more than a matter of minutes, but already the loaves had been picked over, nothing left but a handful of crumbs and a light dusting of white powder. Wren tried not to let her face twist into a grimace as she surveyed the scraps.

"The ones I sold were near two days old," the baker said, wringing her hands nervously. "Last night I found my flour turned to ash, right in the barrel." Her voice was hushed, almost as though she didn't believe it herself.

Next to the baker stood her wife, weeping steadily into a

yellowing handkerchief. Both women had dark circles beneath their eyes. Both glanced darkly around the meager market.

Most of the merchants hadn't even bothered to come. The ones who had were armed with wares that lacked their usual liveliness. Potatoes were withered, their peels nearly black, their eyes blooming strange, gnarled roots larger than the starch itself. Milk, once white as fresh snow, now shone a sickly silver blue in bottles only half-full. The only vendor with a fully stocked stand was a tinker, selling bottles of bright purple potion—PLAGUE PREVENTERS, his sign said—for the criminal price of pure silver. Wren wasn't certain if the reason his stand was empty of customers was the asking price or the potion's impossible promise.

Even her own basket was lighter than usual. The henhouse had been filled with the stink of sulfur, and though she had searched high and low, she'd found nothing but nest after empty nest. The chickens had been eerily still, nothing like the usual squawking and ruffled feathers that came when dragon hatchlings snuck inside and swallowed the still-warm eggs whole. It wasn't a creature that had stolen her eggs. It was the plague.

Wren waved away the baker's string of apologies. She didn't blame the woman for her misfortune. Everything was harder these days. Tensions between witches and ordinary folk were at an all-time high. The Coven's High Councillor had issued a statement proclaiming the emergence of another dark witch, who had used dark magic to create the memory-stealing plague. The minds were the first to go, but—as everyone who had survived the Year of Darkness knew—it was only a matter of time before the bodies followed.

Crops were withering. Giant waves of water flowed through the streets, soaking everyone's ankles and ruining their shoes. The wolves had left the forests and had begun feasting on farm animals. Farmer Haddon's youngest son insisted they'd start eating little girls next.

Stepping out of the house had begun to feel like darting, unarmed, through a battle zone. Wren hadn't wanted to go outside, not after the raindrops that had left behind the smell of sizzling skin, but her cupboard was down to its last onion, and if her father was going to get better, he needed something solid to eat.

His system couldn't handle the disappointment of hunger.

Hers couldn't handle the disappointment of disappointing him.

"It's so quiet." Wren's voice was no more than a whisper. The baker's eyes went as dark as the heavy gray clouds hanging low in the sky.

"Most took off west, toward the sea. As though sickness can't reach the water." She frowned, her eyes flashing with annoyance. "Some are caring for the fallen. The rest, well . . ."

She didn't need to finish.

Around them, the air crackled with caustic energy, the scuffling of scattered footsteps, the swish of cloaks as the wearers drew them more tightly around their noses and mouths despite the heat of the summer sun. The first case had struck the town of Wells three days prior. For two days the plague limited itself to the ill and elderly, but then yesterday a ten-year-old had come running to the town square, shouting that his sister had dropped to the ground before springing up and running, screaming, into the fields.

The townspeople had sent out a search party, but no one had found her. Now neighbors looked upon neighbors suspiciously, scouring for symptoms. No one knew how to prevent the plague. They only knew it was spreading through their town faster than the wind, which had taken to blustering at speeds capable of toppling an ox. The world was falling apart, and not a single person knew how to save it. They hardly knew how to save themselves.

Wren bid the baker and her wife a somber farewell. Each step she took left her uneasy. The magic from the stones beneath her feet made her feel as though someone were churning butter inside her stomach.

She made her way quickly through the rest of the market, picking up a limp head of cabbage and a cut of meat so small it wouldn't fill a child. Wren cringed as she parted with two copper coins. Her savings were already dwindling.

At the market's edge, a foul taste overtook her, as though her tongue had been coated with ash. Her attention caught on something moving swiftly across the square. At first she thought it a snake, but upon closer inspection, she realized it was magic—thick, dark, and slimy—oozing across the cobblestones.

Wren had never seen magic so gruesome. The longer she watched it, the more it became clear that the slithering shadow was dark magic. Panicked, Wren tried to stop it, tried to will it back with her mind, but of course her effort made no difference. The magic continued on undisrupted, creeping determinedly behind a couple walking arm in arm in the middle of the square.

Wren wanted to call out to them, to stop the magic coursing swiftly toward its prey, but of course there was nothing she could do. Even if she did reveal herself as a source and tell the couple what she saw, it would be useless trying to convince them of a danger they could not see for themselves. They might think her a *witch*.

And so she stayed still and looked on in horror as the dark magic wrapped itself around the man's ankle and pulled him roughly to the ground. He hit the cobblestones with a dull thud, his head bouncing limply once before coming to rest. The woman fell to her knees beside him, shaking his shoulder insistently.

"Henry," the woman cried. "Someone help my husband."

A ring of wary onlookers gathered but kept their distance. Wren shivered, her arms covered with goose bumps as she watched the dark magic creep across the length of the man's body like a horde of spiders. When the magic reached his mouth, it hesitated. Then the darkness disappeared up his nose. The man's entire being shuddered, and then he gasped, his eyes shooting open. Even from where Wren stood, she could see the wildness within.

"Henry." The man's wife flung herself on him, tears still falling from her face. But instead of returning her embrace, the man pawed at his wife, pushing her off and away until he could scramble backward.

"What are you doing?" The man's teeth chattered wildly. "What do you want?"

The woman stopped mid-sob. "Henry, please, it's me." She flung herself forward, grabbing her husband by the arm. He shook her off roughly, his fear palpable.

"Don't touch me," the man said. "Please, leave me alone."

The crowd of onlookers began to disperse. Signs of the plague were evident in the man's actions. No one wanted to risk contamination. Wren, however, could not seem to pull her eyes away as the man got shakily to his feet. The woman flung herself at his ankle. "Your name is Henry. I am your wife. We have three sons."

The man's expression was haunting. The woman's words meant nothing to him, were so impossible he could not even fathom their meaning. He bent down, trying to extract the woman from his limb.

"Please, Henry." The woman had returned to sobbing. "You know me. You *love* me." Her voice broke, her desperation tangible. It sent a shiver up Wren's spine.

All the while, the man remained unchanged, methodically trying to remove the woman from his person. The wife held on tight, but in the end the man triumphed.

"I know not who you are or what you want," the man said, his voice booming in the empty square, "but, woman, leave me be." With that he turned and fled, leaving his wife crying and crumpled on the cobblestones.

As he ran, a black curtain of magic trailed behind him like a shroud.

Wren's heart ached for the woman. Her instinct was to offer comfort, but in the end, fear won, as it often did. She hoisted her nearly empty basket over her shoulder and made her way quickly down the path toward her cottage. Now that she knew what to look for, she began to notice dark magic clinging to the homes of the afflicted like a shadow. Now, with just a glance at the smoke emanating from the chimneys of her neighbors, she could identify who the plague's next victim would be.

It was too much. Her stomach churned with unease as she inhaled the sulfurous stink of the dark magic. The sickness was spreading. It was only a matter of time before it came for her father. She was surprised it hadn't already struck.

Wren shivered as she maneuvered her way around a patch of weeds with razor-sharp thorns. She stumbled, sinking into a puddle of bubbling mud and walking straight into a tree branch stuck sideways from its fallen trunk. It tore into her shoulder, catching her sleeve and slicing open her skin.

Wren swore, struggling to extract herself from the clutches of the sharp stick. She was so used to branches bending away from her that she had forgotten to pay attention to her surroundings. Three tiny drops of blood soaked through the thin, flax-colored linen of her shirt. Wren rolled her eyes to the sky, cursing her clumsiness, when her attention caught on a newly unfurled ribbon of black. Her jaw clenched with dread before her eyes had even finished tracing the streak of magic to the worn, thatched roof of her own cottage.

She ran home so quickly she had trouble coming to a stop. Her shaking hands struggled with the latch on the front gate long enough that she finally decided to vault over it. She moved awkwardly, ungracefully. Too much momentum barreled her forward into the door. She didn't have time to consider her actions, didn't think what was next; she just fell into the front room of the cottage, her father's name on her lips.

"Papa." Wren's voice fell flat. The door to her father's room was ajar, sunlight spilling into the usually darkened space. There was no sound, not the shifting of sheets nor any murmurs of pain. Only silence.

"Papa." Wren spoke more forcefully this time, one hand on the door to his room, the other pulling on the end of her braid so hard it made her head ache. She needed to check on him, and yet she couldn't bear to.

There was a metallic tang on her tongue. A low, rumbling moan came from the back room. A draft blew through the room, despite the fact that the front door was closed and the windows were sealed. Wren swallowed the lump in her throat. She had to know.

She pushed her way into the room. Her whole body relaxed at the sight of her father sitting up in bed. He was smiling.

"Well, hello." Her father's voice was steady and strong.

Wren couldn't remember the last time she had seen him looking so well. Her knees, which had gone weak from her rush of panic, gave out with relief. She sank onto the edge of the bed, careful to avoid his feet.

"What's wrong?" Her father examined her face sympathetically.

"I thought . . ." Wren struggled to catch her breath.

The coppery taste still sat on her tongue, but seeing her father so alert and alive made it difficult for her to take the flavor of the magic seriously. It was only because she had watched the scene in the marketplace that she had panicked so. She suddenly felt ridiculous.

"You worry too much." Her father gave Wren a pointed look.

She didn't have the energy to protest. He was right. Worrying had taken the place of any hobbies, of any hopes or dreams for the future. "In fact, I'm beginning to think my lungs could use some fresh air. What say we take a walk?"

Wren's smile wavered. The outside world had turned so volatile and vicious, her father would hardly recognize it. "I'm not so sure about that." She motioned for her father to lean forward, plumping the pillows that had gone flat beneath his back.

"Stop that," her father laughed, waving away her effort. "Really, Eve, I'm fine."

Wren froze. "What?"

"You fuss too much, Evie. I'm all right."

Nothing about her father calling Wren by her mother's name was all right. Wren turned to face him. "Papa."

But the word held no weight. His face twisted in confusion. His glassy eyes looked past Wren. Looked right through her.

"*No*," she said. Her father flinched at her harsh tone, but for once Wren didn't care. She could only see what was to come next: He would lose his resilient spirit and forget his family completely. All those years of nursing him back to health would have been for nothing.

"Let me find you something to eat." Wren's voice shook, but she did her best to keep a smile on her face as she guided her father back onto the pillows and inched slowly out of the room, pulling the door shut behind her. She had no intention of cooking; she merely needed a rational reason to flee her father's hollow gaze.

Wren paced the floor of the main room, tugging at her braid.

The dark magic now hung so low in the sky that she could see it out of every window. It draped itself across the cottage like a cloak. She murmured nonsense words under her breath as she drew all the shutters. She sank into a chair, rested her elbows on the table, and held her head in her hands.

She had tried so hard. Had been so careful. She had burned sage to purify their small space. She had put elderberries in his tea and broth. She had covered her mouth each time she left the cottage, and upon her return she had scrubbed her hands until they were raw and red. Yet her father had been struck anyway. It felt personal, as though Wren herself had done something to cause it. As though she hadn't protected her father the way she should have.

But Wren had done everything for him, given up *everything* for him. Her entire life had been one endless sacrifice—ignoring hunger's rumble as she offered up her portion of broth to her father, peddling eggs when she should have been attending school with the village children, staying far from the Witchlands so that her father would never know what she truly was.

Or perhaps it *was* her fault, but not for the reasons she thought. Perhaps her constant wanting, the ache in her chest every time she turned away from magic, the awe she felt having stood before Tamsin the witch—perhaps those things were the reason he had fallen ill.

Maybe Wren had compromised her father not with her actions but with her thoughts.

And he *was* compromised, her existence already scrubbed from his memory. If her father did not remember his daughter, all of Wren's sacrifices had been for naught. Her life would leave absolutely no mark on the world. She could have passed through the Witchwood and entered the Witchlands. She could have studied under the Coven, learned how to harness all the magic swirling within her. She could have been different. She could have been *more*.

If her father succumbed to the plague, Wren would have nothing a thousand times over.

Her sacrifice needed to matter. Her decision to put her father first needed to matter.

Wren laid her hands flat on the bare table, stared at her long, crooked fingers, her dirty nails, her bloody cuticles. Wren had the hands of a worker. The hands of someone who didn't give up.

So she wouldn't.

The sky had turned a glowing green. The air held a hint of bile. Wren held a sleeve to her nose, but the scent seeped through her skin, settling in the back of her mouth atop the already bitter taste of desperation. She hurried down the path toward Wells, darting past the same dangers she had encountered only hours before. Her body moved quickly, but her heart was heavy, her anxiety weighing her down.

She shoved her hand in her pocket, touching the silver for reassurance. It was the last of Tamsin's coins. Perhaps it was silly to spend the coin from a witch on a remedy sold by a tinker, but it was the only option she could see through the fog of panic that had settled atop her brain.

The town square was even more deserted than before. The

baker and her wife had packed up. The butcher, too, had closed his stall. Only the tinker and a woman offering wilting bouquets of herbs remained.

"Is this enough?" Wren stood before the wizened man, the silver coin clutched in her shaking fingers.

"What's that, now?" The tinker did not look up from where he was fussing with his display of tiny glass vials. The bright purple liquid inside sloshed merrily.

"I have silver," Wren said sharply. "Will that be enough?"

The tinker finally looked up. "That'll do, lass. Although your manners could use a touch of work." The old man cracked a smile missing several teeth.

Wren pursed her lips, trying to tamp down a sigh. She forced a smile. Far be it from her to test the limits of a tinker.

"That's better," he said, offering his palm for her coin.

Wren tried not to cringe as she handed it over. She knew she was being reckless, spending impulsively, but her father was afflicted. She didn't have time to waste worrying. Wren always worried. Wren always wasted.

This time, she would *do*.

But the moment the coin hit the tinker's skin, his face darkened. "Ah, lass. Someone's been fooled."

Wren glanced warily around the deserted square. "What do you mean?"

The tinker wrinkled his nose. "This is a witch's coin."

"A what?"

The tinker smiled sadly at her. "A fake. I once traded a witch my right big toe for the ability to spot a counterfeit coin. Comes in handy in my line of business, let me tell you. Anyway, if I had to guess, I'd say this one was once a button. Either way . . ." He shrugged apologetically and handed it back to Wren.

"This coin isn't real?"

The tinker let out a tiny sigh of exasperation. "That's what I told you. Any chance you've got another?"

But Wren hardly heard him, so loud was the fury running through her blood. Not only had Tamsin made her look a fool, but she had given Wren many coins—coins Wren had spent on goods and wares, which made Wren a thief too.

Such carelessness, such cruelty, when ordinary folk were already suffering, was unfathomable. The witch needed to answer for her actions. At the very least, Tamsin needed to supply Wren with enough true coins to repay her debt and secure a vial of the tinker's potion for her father. If he had fallen ill because of Wren's dark thoughts, it was up to her to cure him too.

And so Wren bid the tinker a grim farewell and prepared herself to extort a witch.

FIVE

TAMSIN

The shrieking was louder than usual.

Tamsin reached for a pillow to muffle the sharp caws of the black-winged birds that had perched on her ruined fence. The birds were especially restless in the early afternoon, when Tamsin had taken to napping. But instead of closing around fabric, her fingers caught on something unfamiliar that fell to pieces against her palm.

Tamsin cracked an eyelid.

There were flowers everywhere. Long-stemmed, white-petaled things that covered every inch of her patchwork quilt, draping across her body from her neck to her toes. Tamsin scrambled from the bed, knocking the contents of her bedside table to the floor. A black leather-bound book landed at her feet. Its inexplicable appearance was even more ominous than the flowers'.

The diary's first entry had unsettled her. Tamsin had never known her sister to be jealous. Marlena was not a skilled witch, but she hadn't needed magic. She'd been the type of strong-willed, confident person everyone adored, the kind of girl everyone wanted as their best friend. She had been elusive, secretive, and special.

She had also wanted nothing to do with Tamsin. As soon as they'd moved into the academy dormitories, Tamsin had found herself in constant competition for her sister's attention, and, worse than that, on the losing side of it.

Tamsin had always been applauded for her power, given special attention from the High Councillor, admiration from her teachers. But at the academy she'd found that getting attention was not the same thing as being liked.

She'd been so jealous of the easy way Marlena made friends. The way people cared for her despite her lack of talent. Tamsin had never imagined that Marlena might be jealous of *her*.

It didn't make any sense. It couldn't possibly be the truth. And so Tamsin had buried the book beneath the dirt of her ruined garden, promising herself that she would not let the diary's words pollute her memory.

Clearly, it had other plans.

Tamsin pointedly ignored the small leather book as she used an arm to sweep the flowers off the blanket. They tumbled to the floor, white petals floating down like snow—or ash. Both were likely these days, despite the fact that it was the middle of summer.

Everything in the entire world was wrong.

Tamsin surveyed the chaos of her tiny cottage, arms crossed tightly against her chest. She just needed to breathe, that was all. She closed her eyes and inhaled sharply.

When she opened them, the diary was sitting on her bed.

"This isn't funny." Tamsin's voice cracked from disuse. But no one replied. Instead a gust of wind blew through the room, ruffling the pages of the journal. Tamsin glanced around warily. The window was closed.

Fear gripped her, like a hand wrapped around her throat. This wasn't her imagination. She wasn't being paranoid. Something was happening, something beyond her reach. Tamsin was very much used to being in control. She was not enjoying the alternative.

Running a hand through her hair, Tamsin sank tentatively onto the edge of the bed. Every single part of her was shaking, although from the cold or from fear, Tamsin couldn't tell. Dark magic was ravaging the world, and her dead sister's diary was taunting her. It was punishment she was due, but the timing made no sense. She'd had the diary for years. Five silent, solitary years. Why now?

"What do you want, Marlena?" Tamsin whispered softly, running a finger idly across a stray petal on her quilt. She tried to turn the diary's page using only the nail of her pinky finger, but the paper didn't budge. She tried harder, to no avail. Tamsin even tried to shut the book, but the cover was like steel. There was only one entry the diary wanted her to read. So Tamsin did.

I woke up in the infirmary. Again. Honestly, I might as well just move in here. Who needs a dormitory when you can have scratchy, starched sheets and the dulcet tones of Healer Elthe's voice instructing me to wake up?

I was out for nearly twelve hours this time. It's taking me longer to recover. I used to just lose consciousness for a few minutes, which was annoying but manageable. But now I'm starting to lose hours. Pieces of my days disappear. I'm missing out on my own life. At this rate, I'll spend more of my existence sleeping than living.

I hate that I can't depend on my body. That my mind needs to take breaks. I have no control. I'm at the mercy of myself. And I'm so envious of those people who can just do whatever they want to do. Go wherever they want to go. Be whatever they want to be without considering the consequences.

People like Tamsin.

She came to visit, of course, loaded down with a giant bouquet of lilies. They don't even bloom this time of year, but I can appreciate the effort, even though their petals are the same color as the sparse, sanitized interior of the infirmary. We had a nice enough conversation, but then, as she was leaving, she pulled my blanket up to my chin and stroked my cheek like I was a baby bird who had fallen from the nest. Sometimes I wonder if she loves this, all the fussing over me, the mothering (because we all know our mother doesn't have time for such things), the helping. She's always trying to help.

But I just can't seem to let her. And I know sometimes I can be cruel, but I couldn't help feeling resentful that here I was, sprawled out in the bed the infirmary should probably just name after me, and she didn't even appear to have so much as a hangnail after performing the exact same spell. So much for "magic has consequences." Tamsin has no idea how I feel, and worse yet, she never will.

Tamsin tried to turn the page, but the diary wouldn't budge. It was just like Marlena to pique her interest and then deny her further information. She threw the book back onto the bed. She hadn't meant for her actions to come off as patronizing. She'd truly wanted to help.

There had always been an imbalance between them. No matter how hard Marlena worked, magic only ever seemed to hurt her, to turn itself against her. Magic left Marlena dizzy and numb. It sometimes took her days to return to her usual self.

Tamsin, on the other hand, hardly needed to blink, and magic poured through her, always at her beck and call. The lesson that had landed Marlena in the infirmary that time had garnered Tamsin nothing more than a faint pressure in her ear, which had popped the moment she yawned. She emerged from spells unscathed while her sister slipped slowly into sleep.

But her magic *did* have consequences. Tamsin now suffered them every single day of her bleak, bitter existence. And she suffered those consequences *because* of her sister. Because of the spell Tamsin had used to save her.

It hadn't mattered, in the end.

She'd still laid flowers on her sister's grave.

Tamsin glanced at the petal she continued to clutch, at the stems strewn across the floor. They were lilies, Marlena's favorite flower. The ones Tamsin always brought to her bedside. The ones she had left on the packed earth during her final good-bye. Was someone threatening her? Were these flowers the same ones that would lie on *her* grave too?

She was having trouble breathing. She gasped great hiccupping gulps of air, choking and spluttering as the room pitched and darkened around her. Before, she had been unnerved. But now she was really and truly afraid.

She needed to calm down, but as she dug her nails into the flesh of her palm, she knew she couldn't do it alone. She reached within for a thread to grip and coaxed the love out from its hiding place. Instantly she was flooded with a steadying warmth. She took three giant, calming breaths. The room stopped spinning. Her vision stopped receding.

Then she was flooded again with the icy grip of fear.

Desperate, Tamsin tried to pull more love but found there was nothing left inside her to hold. The last of the young mother's love was gone, and she had absolutely no idea if or when she would ever replenish her stash. After she had explained to several teary-eyed parents that she could not reverse the effects of dark magic, the people of Ladaugh had given her a wide berth. At market they made their opinions about Tamsin inarguably clear: She was a stain on the world, entirely at fault.

Those were the same words whispered by her fellow witches just before the Coven had voted to banish her from Within.

A banging started up on her front door, so hard it threatened to rattle the door off its hinges. Outside, the birds squawked and screeched. The doorknob jiggled. Tamsin's blood ran cold. She tried to imagine what kind of person could possibly be on the other side. She glanced at the flowers on the floor. At the book on her bed.

She wasn't ready to face her past.

There was one second of blissful silence. Even the birds outside stopped their squawking. Then the person started shouting. The strong, high voice didn't sound especially threatening, but Tamsin wasn't taking any chances. She made her way toward the door, pausing at the table to pick up a knife still slick from buttering a slice of bread. Tamsin held it carefully in front of her as she slid aside the bolt and swung the door open.

The girl stopped shouting. For it was a village girl, her long hair pulled back in a messy braid, her trousers full of deftly repaired holes, her boots all but falling off her feet. Her forehead was pinched in frustration, her mouth still puckered, ready to shout again. Her wide gray eyes caught on Tamsin's knife.

"I thought you were a witch."

The girl's voice was melodic yet grating, like a song sung in the wrong key. There was something about the stranger that was familiar, although Tamsin was having trouble placing her. She glowered at the girl in an attempt to overcompensate for her uncertainty.

The stranger seemed impervious to Tamsin's scrutiny. She simply sidestepped the knife and brushed brusquely past Tamsin into the cottage without looking back.

"Yes, please, do come in," Tamsin muttered darkly under her breath, closing the door behind the girl. She left the bolt unlocked.

The girl slumped into one of Tamsin's kitchen chairs, red-faced and panting. Sweat dripped down her temple. "I suppose you know why I'm here, then."

"I suppose I don't," Tamsin snapped, her guard on high as she glanced warily at the flowers littering the floor. She didn't know who this girl was, why she looked familiar, or what she was doing in her house. Tamsin didn't like not knowing things.

"My father has been afflicted by the plague."

"I'm sorry for your loss." Tamsin was not very sorry at all. In fact, she was rather relieved. This girl hadn't come to finish her off. She was just another ordinary person desperate for a cure.

The stranger's expression crumpled. She tugged at the end of her long braid so sharply that Tamsin's scalp began to ache in sympathy.

"It isn't a loss," she insisted. "The tinker sells a plague pre-venter. Says it's a cure. Which is why I'm here, actually—"

"Tinker teas will do nothing more than give you indigestion," Tamsin cut her off. "If there were a cure to the plague, do you think anyone in this town would have fallen victim to it?"

The girl blinked blankly at her. "What does that mean?"

Tamsin drew herself up to her full height. Her reputation was supposed to precede her, yet somehow this girl did not seem very impressed. "That I'm very good at my job."

"Very good at stealing eggs, more like," the stranger muttered under her breath.

Recognition clicked into place. The last time Tamsin had seen this girl she'd been babbling pathetically in the marketplace, unable to put a price on her eggs. The relief was overwhelming. When the knocking had begun, Tamsin had feared a face-off with an angry witch. Instead she was holding court with a girl who peddled eggs. She let out a humorless cackle. The girl's eyes darkened.

"Don't know what's so funny about stealing from a girl with a sick father," she said, tugging again on the tail of her braid. "It's criminal is what it is."

Tamsin shrugged. "I gave you coins."

"*Fake* coins," the girl said sharply. "You owe me."

Tamsin snorted with surprise. "I do not."

A self-righteous expression spread across the girl's face. "You stole from me. I demand payment. I'll . . . report you."

Tamsin raised an eyebrow. "To whom?"

The girl looked around the cottage, clearly grasping for an answer. "I'll take it up with the Coven."

Tamsin was growing annoyed. Yes, she had given the girl some buttons charmed to look like coins, but she had been doing the same to Ladaugh's merchants for years. None of them had thrown a fit. None of them had had the audacity to show up to her cottage and demand payment. The townspeople might be giving her a wide berth at present, but at least that showed they still respected her. At least they knew—and feared—what she could do.

This girl had no such respect. Her small nose was wrinkled, as though she smelled something unexpected she didn't know how to place. Her eyes roved about the room, sticking for several seconds on the ceiling before she forced her gaze back onto Tamsin, who was still staring at her with suspicion. She was terribly odd.

"The Coven would never listen to the likes of you. Just cut your losses and go."

The girl's gray eyes blazed with fury. "Would they listen to me if I was a source?"

Tamsin looked the girl up and down. The sheer audacity of her claim was almost impressive. "Well, you're not, so that's rather a moot hypothetical, don't you think?"

"How do you know I'm not?" The girl jutted her chin out defiantly.

Tamsin stared at her uncomprehendingly. "Because you look to be my age. I knew every single person who studied at the academy, and I don't even know your name."

The girl scowled. "I'm—"

"No, no," Tamsin said, holding her hands to her ears. "I don't know, but more important"—she leaned closer and whispered conspiratorially—"I don't care. Now stop wasting my time and get out of my house."

The girl gaped at her. Tamsin idly untangled a knot in her hair. The verbal sparring had been entertaining if nothing else. A welcome distraction from flowers and leather-bound books. It had even given her a momentary glimmer of feeling—not joy, of course, but *something*. Now, however, she wanted the girl gone.

"Go on, then." She gave the girl a small wave of dismissal.

"My name is Wren."

Tamsin raised both eyebrows. "Good for you?"

The girl, Wren, pushed her chair away from the table with a terrible scrape. "Are all witches so awful?" It sounded as though she didn't really want an answer.

Tamsin pursed her lips but didn't say anything. Let the girl believe what she wanted. She wouldn't be the first.

"Anyway, here." Wren got to her feet and produced a letter from the back pocket of her trousers. "It was nailed to your front door. Don't get out much, do you?" Her eyes lingered on Tamsin's for a moment before sweeping across the dusty cottage.

Tamsin snatched the parchment from the girl's grasp, her irritation fading as she caught sight of the sigil stamped into the sealing wax.

"Where did you get this?" Her voice was sharp.

Wren looked confused. "The front door. I already said . . ." She trailed off as Tamsin turned her attention to the words spelled out in black ink.

> *Due to the rapidly deteriorating relations between*
> *witches and ordinary folk, the Coven cordially*
> *invites you to join the hunt for the dark witch.*

*Return Within to register. The one who locates
the witch responsible for the dark magic will be
rewarded a boon without limitations. Anything
your magical heart desires.
Happy hunting.*

It was signed with the High Councillor's name.

Tamsin had gone a bit light-headed. *Return Within,* the letter read, but she couldn't, could she? Not after what she'd done. She was banished, after all. Yet the note had arrived on her doorstep. Someone wanted her to return. It made sense, really. Tamsin was the only witch alive who had dabbled in dark magic.

The rest had been put to death.

She alone knew what it felt like to hold that raw, electric power in her hands. She alone knew how desperate a person had to be to use it. She alone knew what it was like to suffer the consequences.

Perhaps that gave her valuable insight. She understood. She could connect. And if Tamsin found the dark witch, all of Within would be indebted to her. She could stop the spell before anyone lost their life. She could redeem herself in the Coven's eyes.

If the Coven forgave her, maybe one day Tamsin could forgive herself, too.

"Are you going?"

Tamsin shrieked, dropping the letter as she leaped away from the voice in her ear. She had completely forgotten about Wren.

"Why were you reading over my shoulder?" Tamsin brushed away a stray hair from her face, trying to regain her composure.

"Your face got all pinched." Wren tried to mimic the witch's expression. "I was curious." She shrugged lightly, like she wasn't nosy in the slightest. "So, are you?"

"No." Tamsin pressed her lips together into a thin line. All the possibility of the moment had vanished. She didn't deserve to be forgiven. She had been banished for a reason. Whoever had sent the call simply hadn't been paying attention. It was a blanket spell, nothing more.

"But it's dark magic." Wren had picked the letter up from the floor and was jabbing it violently with her finger. "It says right there."

"I know what dark magic is," Tamsin snapped. She had to get this girl out of her house.

"Well, then, why don't you want to stop it?" The girl leveled her gaze at Tamsin, almost as though she were staring into the heart of her.

"I do." The words escaped Tamsin's lips before she could stop them.

"Brilliant." Wren's eyes were bright. "We'll go together, then."

"What are you talking about?"

"I already told you," she said, her brow furrowed with confusion. She took a long, deep breath. "I'm a source."

Tamsin was starting to worry about the girl's sanity. "No," she said, taking a careful step backward, "you're not."

Wren crossed the room with surprising speed. She reached for Tamsin's hand and interlaced their fingers. Tamsin began to struggle, tried to get the strange girl off her, but even as she flailed, something unfamiliar and warm spread through her, moving up her arm, nestling in her chest, fluttering in her stomach. For a moment, it felt like feeling.

At first Tamsin thought it was the sheer unfamiliarity of touching another person, that the sensation came from holding the hand of a girl who was probably pretty. Before the curse, pretty girls had always given Tamsin fluttering feelings. But then understanding clicked into place. It was the way she'd felt with Leya when they'd worked together in lessons as witch and source. Tamsin was like a bucket lowered into a well. The source was the water, spilling over Tamsin's every surface, filling her to the very brim with magic.

Wren had been telling the truth.

She was not only a source, but a strong one, albeit chaotically untrained. She housed the kind of magic that would allow Tamsin to walk through walls by simply nodding at solid stone. Tamsin might one day be able to manipulate the hearts and minds of ordinary folk with the barest flick of her wrist. With Wren's aid, someday Tamsin might be strong enough to cross from one corner of the world to another with a single step.

Currently, that sort of magic was merely aspirational due to the havoc it would wreak upon a witch's body, not to mention the danger it posed to an untrained source. Sources were made of magic, and releasing too much of it too quickly had the potential to throw their beings into chaos. They could overcompensate and overheat their organs. They might accidentally drain all their body heat and freeze to death. But with the right training and cooperation between witch and source, the possibilities became endless.

Icy shame flooded her like a bucket of water. Tamsin had no right to imagine the possibility of further power. In fact, she deserved to have much less.

She dropped Wren's hand, and the sensation stopped. Tamsin studied the girl's face, the symmetrical nature of it. A pink flush had spread across her freckled cheeks. Tamsin tried to imagine marching into the academy to ask for a hunting license with this strange, unknown girl in tow. The Coven would throw a fit.

In the early days of her rise to power, the dark witch Evangeline had targeted the sources first. Back then, sources did not live Within; they were not raised nor educated alongside witches. In fact, most witches *feared* sources, for they knew the whispers of the ancients—that sources held the potential to reach the heart of a witch's power and cut off her access to magic altogether.

But there were pages missing from the ancients' writings. Pages whose absence implied a secret that sources did not want witches to discover. Evangeline, who had never been afraid of anyone, set out to uncover what that secret might be.

She devoted years to scouring the world for the truth, seeking out those who were made of the magic she so desperately craved. Evangeline used her charms to gain a source's trust, muffling her power until the source believed she was one of the ordinary folk, until the witch had flattered the source enough to learn that spells cast from a source's magic left not a single consequence to a witch's being. A source could provide a witch near-unlimited power.

Power Evangeline had had no trouble taking.

But of course, sources were still people. They needed rest,

care, tenderness. Evangeline offered them none of those things. When their human limitations became too inconvenient, she disposed of them and turned to the earth, siphoning out its magic and sending the world into chaos. Thus began the Year of Darkness.

After Evangeline's downfall, the Coven became militant about rounding up magical children. Sources, they now knew, were natural gateways to the use of dark magic. Where before, Within had been only for witches, now the Coven searched all four corners of the world for witches and sources alike. They housed them together at the academy, where they could keep an eye on them. Train them. Protect them. Study them.

Tamsin didn't know how Wren had managed to slip through the cracks.

If they were to go Within, it would be quite the strange homecoming for both of them.

Tamsin shook her head wildly. She could not believe she was even entertaining the idea. "I'm not going." She couldn't. Her eyes fell on the diary, still open on her bed. She couldn't set foot Within. Not after what she had done to Marlena. Not after what had happened to Amma.

"Please." Wren was in front of her again, her gray eyes wide with emotion. Tamsin felt no sympathy for her. She couldn't. "I have to end the plague." The girl bit her lip, clearly grappling with something. "And I need your help to do it."

Tamsin kicked at a stray flower petal. If nothing else, the foreboding she'd felt when Wren first entered her cottage had all but disappeared. The girl wasn't threatening. But she *was* irritating. "Why is this so important to you?"

Wren wrapped her arms around herself like a cloak. "My father."

A buzzing started in the back of Tamsin's brain.

"You care for your father, do you?"

Wren looked at Tamsin with confusion. "Of course I do. I love my father more than anything in this world. He's all I have."

The buzzing grew louder. "And that's why you want to stop the plague?"

"I have to save him." Wren stepped forward, closing the space between them. "Please." Tamsin took a step back. Wren took another forward. "I'll do anything."

The buzzing in Tamsin's head stopped, leaving a perfect plane of quiet. There were suddenly two options, each of them appealing. Either she agreed to help the girl and was paid in love so good and pure it would last her years, *or* Wren would blanch at the asking price and leave Tamsin alone once and for all.

Either outcome would suffice.

"All right," Tamsin finally said. "I'll help you hunt the dark witch."

Wren exhaled a sob so sharp that she collapsed to the floor, a bundle of elbows and knees. Tamsin nudged the ball of girl gingerly with her toe. "But I will require payment. And I have to warn you, I do not come cheap."

Wren looked up at Tamsin with dewy eyes. "I don't have much money."

"I don't take coins." A sneer spread across Tamsin's lips. She had the upper hand once again. It felt familiar. It felt *right*. "I deal in love."

SIX

WREN

"But I don't want to love you."

The incredulous words burst forth before Wren had time to truly appreciate what she was saying. "I just think that's a bit . . . odd, isn't it?" she backtracked quickly, trying to abate the judgment radiating from the witch. "To force someone to fall in love with you?" Wren's cheeks blazed with embarrassment. She was certain her face was as fiery red as her hair.

Tamsin sighed wearily, rolling her eyes so far back in her head that Wren could see only the whites. "I don't want you to love *me*."

"Oh." That was a relief. Wren had heard stories of love potions, how they made a person highly suggestible, always at another's beck and call. The idea of being controlled, especially by the likes of Tamsin, was nothing less than horrifying.

"I want your love for your father."

The totality of Tamsin's demand hit Wren like a load of bricks. She had hinged her entire life on being her father's dutiful daughter. What would happen if she no longer was? Who would she be?

I'd be dead without you, little bird. Her father's voice echoed in her ear. Her entire life, Wren had known that to be the truth.

But what if it isn't? Another voice drowned out the memory, this one darker, sharper. *Wouldn't this be the way to find out?*

"Absolutely not." Wren shook away the wicked thought. The cost was simply too high.

"You didn't even consider it." Tamsin's voice had taken on a particular whine.

"Do you understand what you're asking me to part with?"

Wren was incredulous. If she no longer loved her father, she would hardly care if he died from the plague or not. Their entire quest would be moot. Even if they did manage to somehow end the plague, wouldn't her father then die from starvation once Wren felt no bond, no duty to continue to care for him? Her father's life hung in the balance either way.

"Love is not something to be taken lightly."

Tamsin laughed humorlessly, her expression wry. "I wouldn't know."

Wren frowned, even as understanding dawned upon her. The witch's eerily icy detachment. The dullness behind her brown eyes. "You can't love."

"Well, you don't have to sound so smug about it," Tamsin snapped.

"You know, that actually makes quite a bit of sense," Wren said, laughing through the panic that had settled in her chest. "I was having trouble understanding how a person could ask for something so cruel, but now I understand. You're heartless."

Wren reveled in the pained look that flashed across Tamsin's face. Perhaps it was the proximity of the empty-hearted girl, or the fact that she was acting so flippant about taking the most valuable thing Wren had to offer, but she wanted the witch to hurt as much as she did. "What would you do with it, anyway?"

"That's none of your concern," Tamsin said sharply.

"Of course it is."

But the witch had turned away from Wren. Tamsin grabbed a broom and began to sweep the white-petaled flowers from the floor into the hearth.

"If I don't love him, no one will." Wren's voice was weak with the truth of it.

"If we fail, I hardly think that will matter much." The broom bristled against the stone hearth. "The dead can't love you back."

Wren recoiled as though she'd been slapped. Tamsin spoke of death so casually. Wren had been taught to fear it, but it sounded as though Tamsin and death were old friends. It sent a shiver down Wren's spine.

"You're a monster," she breathed. The witch's shoulders tensed. But when she turned, she did not speak, just stared at Wren with her endless dark eyes.

Wren needed a moment away from the cottage, its consequences, and its dizzying array of magic. She wanted to exhale
without her breath disrupting the swirling earth-red ribbons
that hung about Tamsin. There were puddles of power all
around the cottage that felt like sinking into quicksand. Her
head was heavy with the impossibility of the witch's asking
price. It was all too much.

Tamsin clucked her tongue against the roof of her mouth but
said nothing.

Wren moved to the door, desperate for a lungful of air that
didn't taste like Tamsin's particular brand of magic—the bright,
bitter bite of fresh herbs. She needed to go back to the safety of her
home, to the comfort of knowing that her feelings were her own.
Wren had been wrong to come to the witch. To try anything other
than what she had always known.

"Good-bye, then," she said, manners winning out despite
herself.

Wren thought she saw something like relief flash across
Tamsin's face as she closed the door behind her.

The cat was back, mewling for milk. "Sorry, friend." Wren moved
to pet his silky head. "I've nothing to give." The cat hissed, and
the fur on his back stood up straight. His yellow eyes stared at her
suspiciously.

"It's okay," Wren said softly, holding her hand in front of
her. "It's only me. It's all right." She reached slowly for the stray,
but his paw met her hand in midair, slicing sharp red scratches
on her palm. He hissed again before backing slowly, guard-

edly, away. Wren watched in horror as dark magic clung to his retreating figure like a shadow.

Another victim of the plague. Another of her sacrifices forgotten.

Wren glanced up at the cloud of magic that clung to the cottage's roof, the color as dark as tar, the scent nearly as terrible. It was worse than it had been earlier, which meant her father must be worse too. Wren opened the front door, her heart braced for a terrible sight.

Her father stood at the table, slicing an onion with his pocketknife. He was engrossed in his work, his brow furrowed familiarly with concentration. Wren hadn't seen him focused in quite some time. She hadn't seen him standing in even longer.

The door swung shut with a slam. Her father looked up, a mildly perplexed expression sweeping across his face.

"Oh, hello." He offered his daughter a hesitant smile.

Wren nearly collapsed with relief. Her father looked better than he had in years. He had color in his cheeks. His movements were steady and sure.

And to think there had been a moment when she had almost said yes to Tamsin. Wren bit back a laugh. She had been overreacting. Again. She didn't need the witch. Didn't need her sour expression or her impossible demands. Wren had a handle on the situation. Her father was going to be fine.

She slumped against the door frame and began to unlace her boots. She had walked the distance of two towns and back. Her feet were killing her.

"Can I help you?"

Wren stopped, hand still tangled in her laces. Her father's smile had slipped into a wary grimace. "It's me." She spoke softly, fighting the muscles in her face, forcing a smile that made her cheeks burn with effort.

Her father's eyes narrowed. "I'm sorry, but I don't know who you are."

Wren's heart skipped a beat. Her whole body silenced for one moment of searing white-hot pain. She had been prepared for her father to call her by her mother's name. She hadn't been ready for him to forget them both.

"I . . ." But it didn't matter what she said, so Wren closed her mouth. She stood on the threshold of their small cottage, looking at the little life they had maintained. At the father who had convinced her that family was the ultimate end.

Without you, I do not think I would survive.

But now that he no longer carried the memory of his dead wife and his lost son, suddenly he was not bedridden by his grief. Without the memory of Wren, the daughter who attended to his every need, he was finally able to stand on his own two feet.

Still, Wren knew, he would not be well for long. Dark magic swirled about the small room. It had claimed his memory. It was only a matter of time before her father fell victim to the plague's physical consequences as well.

Wren bit back a scream. She tugged sharply at the end of her braid, pulling until her head ached. She needed to think. She had to find a way around this.

Her eyes landed on her patchwork bedroll in the corner. She could tell her father she was the cleaning girl. She could secure herself a place in her home, could tend to the daily tasks of cleaning and cooking and caretaking without raising his suspicion.

Wren could continue to carry the weight of the household, of her father's emotional well-being. She could continue to sacrifice, all while playing the role of a serving girl. Perhaps as time went on, her father would warm to her. Maybe one day even come to think of her like a daughter.

The thought caught in Wren's throat. Her father did not know her, which meant he could not love her. He could not lean on his love for a person who did not exist.

Oh.

That was it, then, wasn't it? What the witch had been trying to tell her. It didn't matter how much she loved her father if the plague claimed his life the way it had already claimed his memory. Wren could hold as tightly as she wanted to her love for him, could claim it was all that she was, but that identity would no longer exist if her father did not survive.

There was no other way. For her sacrifices to matter, Wren had to give up the one thing she held dearest. Love had driven her every step of her seventeen years, so love would guide her again, until it no longer could.

Wren sighed, steeling herself. The answer was so clear as to be inevitable. It was hardly a choice at all. If her father no longer knew her, there was no place for her here.

Which meant she was free to go.

Free.

What a strange concept, after dreaming of the word for so

many years. It almost meant nothing, so great were the possibilities it encompassed.

But then her eyes met the furrowed brow of her father, and she feared she might be sick. It was easy to speculate. It was another thing to *do*.

"Forgive me." Wren cleared her throat, pitching her voice down, in hopes she would sound more certain than she felt. "Let me introduce myself." She took a careful step back to give her father space.

Her eyes darted around the room. If she was going to travel with Tamsin to the Witchlands, she needed a way to get her things from the cottage without her father thinking her a thief.

"I am here to collect your taxes." Her voice came out in a rush, the words crashing into one another. She took a shaky, steadying breath. "Our records show you have been ill. While we were generous enough to let you defer, we are no longer able to extend that courtesy. Your payment is now drastically overdue."

Her father's face paled. He still knew what taxes were, at least, though that knowledge did not make Wren feel better in the slightest.

"I . . ." His eyes glanced helplessly around the room. He knew nothing about the stash of savings Wren had scraped together. "I have nothing to offer you. No food in my cupboard save this onion." His hands were shaking. Wren's heart was breaking. She wasn't going to be able to do this if she felt, so Wren conjured up the image of the most unfeeling person she knew and tried to emulate Tamsin.

She sniffed, drawing herself up to her full height. "In that case,

I will take some of your belongings, items valued high enough to ease your debt. I trust you will not fight me on this. Queen Mathilde does not look kindly upon those who shirk their duties."

Her father ran a hand across the back of his neck. "I, uh, suppose that will be fine."

Wren nodded and moved deliberately around the room, trying to look at objects that featured in her earliest memories as though they were brand-new. She hemmed over a chair her father had built and hawed over the rug her mother had made, keeping her father's worried face always in her line of sight. Once she was certain she knew what she needed, Wren asked him to point her to a burlap sack.

Wren filled the bag quickly. She had very few things: an extra pair of trousers, two clean shirts, a needle, thread, thick socks, a length of rope, undergarments, rags for her monthlies, and an embroidered tea towel. She saved the jug for last, her eyes scanning the mantel as though arbitrarily. After a moment of staged contemplation, Wren managed to shrug and sigh loftily.

"I suppose this will do," she said, plucking it from its place and feigning surprise as its contents jangled. She moved swiftly to the table, where she shook out the coins, letting them clatter heavily onto the table. She began to separate the coins into two piles.

Her father's eyes were as wide as saucers. He gaped down at the table as though he had never before seen so much money in one place.

In that moment, Wren understood that her father had never truly known the lengths she had gone to for him—the sleepless nights, her empty belly, the magic flowing uselessly through her veins. She didn't know if the lurch in her stomach was from pride or sadness.

"These"—she pushed the first, larger pile toward the end of the table—"are to be reserved for our next collection." The true tax collectors were due in less than a season. It pained Wren to realize that she did not know if she would be back by then. When she no longer loved her father, would she feel any duty to return?

"And these," Wren said, hurriedly pocketing the smaller pile of coins, "ease the rest of your debt." She kept her head down as she tied the sack up with a tight knot and hauled it over her shoulder.

As she moved toward the door, her eyes fell on her father's boots. They were exactly where she'd left them those few mornings ago, when her greatest fear had been nothing more than a fever. Wren glanced down at her own ragged boots, then over to her father. The cloud above him was growing larger. Soon he would hardly remember how to tie his laces. He wouldn't need the boots. She did.

"One last thing." Wren smiled broadly, apologetically, as she gathered up the boots. "There we are." Her eyes lingered on her father's face.

"Good-bye," she whispered.

Her father raised a hand in a halfhearted wave.

"I love you."

Wren knew her words would confuse him, knew they would run right through him, but she needed to say them, needed to speak them one last time while they were still true.

For one brief moment, their eyes met. The emptiness of her father's expression broke Wren's heart into a million pieces.

She was out the door before he could respond, stopping only at the gate to pull off her sorry excuse for boots and step into her father's worn yet sturdy pair. Wren laced them as tightly as they would go. They were several sizes too big, but with a bit of padding they would surely suffice.

She left her own dilapidated pair hanging from the gate, their broken soles the only remaining proof that she had ever been there at all.

She set off back toward Ladaugh, her load much heavier than before. She moved the sack to the other shoulder, the jangle of coins in her pocket reminding her she still had unfinished business.

Wren might have been leaving her father behind, but that didn't mean she was leaving him alone.

She pushed open the door to the tailor's shop, grateful to find it empty, save for Tor, who was poring over numbers at a desk in the back. He looked surprised to see her. Wren couldn't blame him. She had been repairing her own clothes for so long she could hardly remember the last time she'd purchased anything new.

"I have a favor to ask," Wren said, in lieu of a greeting.

The old man peered at her curiously. "Go on, then."

Wren dropped her sack with a soft thump. "My father has become afflicted. I have to leave town, but I need to be sure he's taken care of. Fed, hydrated, kept inside so he doesn't hurt himself."

Anger flashed in Tor's eyes. "You're a sweet girl, but surely you can't be asking me to put myself in that kind of danger."

Wren looked desperately at him. "You don't have to go inside. Just leave some food on the step, knock on the door, and run."

She pulled her hand from her pocket and dropped a mess of

coins onto his desk. They clattered wildly. A copper farthing rolled to the floor. Wren stopped it with her foot.

"Please, Tor." She pressed the rogue coin onto the desk with a sharp clink.

Tor did not look away.

"*Please.*"

"And where are you going, then?" When the tailor finally spoke, Wren knew it was as close to an agreement as she was likely to get.

"You wouldn't believe me," Wren said quietly. "Please"— she bent down to retie her bag—"take care of him. He needs someone."

The tailor let out a long, low sigh. "Fine," he said. "I'll do all I can until I'm unable."

Wren had half a mind to throw her arms around the man, but she refrained. "Thank you," she said instead, and hoped it was enough.

Tor slipped the coins into his pocket and bade her farewell. Wren's load wasn't lighter, necessarily, but it felt more manageable.

Wren didn't bother to knock. She simply barged into the witch's hut and dumped her sack by the door, startling Tamsin so intensely that she fell from a kitchen chair to the floor with a loud thump.

"Okay."

The witch's face flashed with surprise. "Okay what?"

"Okay, I'll do it. I'll pay you in love."

"I thought I was a monster." Tamsin was back on her feet, one hand on her hip, her eyebrow cocked in challenge.

Wren's cheeks burned. She had spoken rashly, let her anger get the better of her. What if the witch had been so insulted that she refused to accept?

"I'm sorry," she said, trying to choose her words carefully. "I shouldn't have . . . I wasn't . . ." Tamsin watched her struggle, eyebrow raised. Wren finally let herself lapse into silence. The room was quiet, save for the crackle of the fire.

"Fine." There was a flicker of something frantic behind the witch's eyes. Excitement and fear fought a battle to claim her expression. It made Wren anxious. Apprehensive. Still, the word offered a welcome relief from the suffocating silence between them.

"Give me your hand." Tamsin extended her own, displaying a long palm and thin fingers.

Wren stepped back, cradling her hands near her heart. "Why?"

"I don't work until my payment is received. You pay me with love; I accompany you on your hunt. Get it?" She gave Wren a withering look, as though she thought perhaps she didn't understand.

Wren shook her head sharply. "If I give you my love now, I'll no longer have motivation to end the plague. That doesn't make any sense."

Tamsin scowled. "I don't see how that's my problem."

"If you want my love for my father, it is your problem." Wren was bluffing. She needed Tamsin much more than the witch needed her.

"I don't like problems," Tamsin said. "No deal." She turned away, her spine rigid. "I am paid in advance, or not at all."

Wren's heart sank to her toes. Only moments ago, the girl's eyes had gleamed hungrily. Now she was refusing. Still, there was something desperate lingering in the crack of her voice.

"What if I gave you a taste?" Wren took an inadvertent step forward. The witch spun on her heel to face her again. "Just a *little* bit," she clarified quickly. "So you know I'm good for it. Would that work?"

Wren had already resigned herself to this fate. So what if it came a bit sooner than she had expected?

The witch closed the distance between them in one swift stride. Tamsin wrapped her clawlike fingers around Wren's wrist tightly. "Think of him," she demanded.

Wren did. She conjured the image of her father, his smile, his eyes crinkled in the corners, his swoop of tawny hair patched with gray. And as Wren thought, she felt a tug right behind her heart. Just as when the two had first touched, Wren felt something inside her flowing toward the witch, like Wren was a river that opened up to Tamsin's sea.

"What are you doing?" Wren tried to pull away, but Tamsin only held on harder. Wren caught a whiff of fresh herbs, felt the tickle of a summer breeze upon the back of her neck, despite the fact that the cottage was quite sealed to the outside world.

The witch's features changed. A smile floated gently across her face—a very nice face, Wren had to admit begrudgingly, when it wasn't tensed in a scowl. Tamsin looked younger. Friendlier. Freer.

"Focus," the witch nudged gently, and Wren returned to the image of her father. His smile, his hair mottled with gray. His eyes.

What color were his eyes?

"Stop!" she shrieked, wrenching her arm out of the witch's

grasp. If the witch held on any longer, Wren feared she would lose the ability to picture her father's face entirely.

The moment she broke contact, Tamsin's expression changed, her smile slipping into a sneer. The soft, gentle person was gone, as if she had been a ghost. A mirage of a girl. It was as though that version of Tamsin had never existed at all.

"What now?" The witch's voice was impatient, the rosy glow fading quickly from her cheeks.

"I couldn't . . . I can't remember what color his eyes are."

Tamsin clucked her tongue. "That's normal." She waved off Wren's frantic expression, turning away. "It's not like you know what color my eyes are."

"They're brown," Wren answered automatically. The witch turned back to face her, eyebrows raised, her brown eyes wide.

"So, what?" Wren demanded, trying to calm the panic buzzing in her brain. "You take my love, and I get . . . what?"

"My company." Tamsin lifted her lips in the pretense of a smile. "I accompany you with the intention of seeking the dark witch and securing the Coven's boon. Once the hunt is complete, either by our hand or another's, you will give me the love you hold for your father. After that, we won't ever have to see each other again."

Wren swallowed thickly, her mouth dry. "Okay," she said finally. "Where do I sign?"

Tamsin frowned. "Sign? You don't *sign* anything."

"What, so we're just supposed to trust each other?" It was Wren's turn to raise her eyebrows.

"Of course not." Tamsin looked disgusted. "All pacts dealing in the future trade of love must be sealed with a kiss. The kiss serves as your promise."

It was, perhaps, the last thing Wren had expected. She squirmed beneath the witch's stare, a hundred emotions rushing through her head. She had shared one awkward, teeth-knocking kiss with Farmer Haddon's eldest son, but she had never kissed a girl. She certainly hadn't imagined it happening for the first time like this.

"Trust me," Tamsin said, misinterpreting her hesitation. "I get no pleasure from this either." She let out a little laugh, light and musical, like a flute. "Get it? Because of my curse?" She trailed off, frowning, as though surprised by herself. She gave Wren a searching look. "Your love was stronger than I thought." Then Tamsin's face darkened again, the corners of her lips slipping back into a small frown. "Don't look so frightened; it's just a quick peck. Surely you *have* kissed someone before?"

Wren's curiosity at the witch's changing moods quickly soured into resentment. She heaved a giant sigh, her expression dour. "Go on, then, let's get this over wi—" But before she could finish her sentence, the witch stepped forward and silenced her with a kiss.

SEVEN

TAMSIN

Technically, Wren was a very good kisser. It was a shame that it sparked absolutely nothing in Tamsin—no butterflies, no warm glow, no fire burning deep and dark within.

She knew what she was supposed to feel, had felt those things before with Leya, their lips pressed together behind the stacks in the dustiest corner of the library next to the books with magic so ancient they practically snored.

There was a second—one single second where the tiny glimmer of love tried to slip out of her grasp—when Tamsin thought she felt a flutter in her stomach. But just as quickly as it struck, the feeling was gone. She pulled her lips away from Wren's and sent a black ribbon winding around the girl's pale throat.

Wren clawed at the magic, her voice high and breathy. "What's happening?" the source shrieked. "What did you do?"

Tamsin merely stood still, letting the magic wrap a ribbon around her own neck and tie itself neatly into a bow. "It's just a ribbon," she said, blinking blankly at Wren's outsize panic. "If you stop pawing at it, you'll find that it hasn't actually harmed you." She swept her hair away to show Wren her own throat. "See? I have one too." She tugged sharply on the end of the ribbon, but the knot didn't budge. "It's not going anywhere, so don't waste your time trying."

Wren shakily sucked in a small breath. "But . . . why?"

"Just in case." Tamsin swept around the table, lifting a basket from the floor and hanging it on a peg by the door. "Should you choose to deny me my due, the ribbon will strangle you." Her shoulders quirked up slightly, almost like a hiccup. It was a simple enough explanation. She thought she ought to take it slow with Wren. Despite being a source, she didn't seem to be particularly versed in magic.

Wren did not take the news very well. She was breathing too quickly, air escaping her mouth in little gasps. A tiny bead of sweat dripped down her temple. "You've got one too," she finally managed. There was accusation in her voice.

"Yes, well, it's a pact," Tamsin said flatly. She really thought it should be self-explanatory. "It took two of us to make it, which means it's possible for either of us to break it." She waved her hand unconcernedly. "Think of it as security. Don't forget: I'm bound to you, too."

"Oh, good," Wren said darkly.

Tamsin closed her eyes as she exhaled her frustration. Wren was being quite dramatic. After all, the decision to hunt had been *her* idea. Tamsin hadn't asked for any of this. This was not a game, not something to be taken lightly. Dark magic was out there, and if they could not find the witch responsible, it was impossible to tell what might happen, both to the world and to them.

The banging of a cupboard pulled Tamsin from her thoughts. Her muscles tensed, her body flooding with panic as she waited for the weight of her sister's diary to come barreling forward. She couldn't handle another entry. Not here in front of this ridiculous girl. Not now, knowing what they had to do. Where they had to go.

But it was only Wren, rummaging through her cupboard and pulling out an armload of objects.

"What are you doing?" Tamsin asked, bewildered, as Wren dumped feathers, crystals, a bundle of dried sage, and a tarot deck onto her kitchen table.

"Packing for you, since you seem incapable of doing it your-self." Wren pointed to the spot where Tamsin still stood frozen. "Do you have a bag?"

"Incredible." Tamsin shook her head in amazement.

Wren scowled. "What's incredible?"

"How someone filled with so much magic can know so little about it." Tamsin gathered up the objects and shoved them hap-hazardly back into the cupboard. "Those are trinkets to trick the simple minds of ordinary folk." She let her eyes rove over Wren, who was appearing more and more ordinary with each passing moment. The girl squirmed beneath her stare.

When Tamsin finally grew bored with making Wren uncomfortable, she fluttered her fingers, and a small rucksack packed itself with a change of clothing and several bundles of herbs. For a moment she considered summoning the diary, but the panic she'd felt had not fully ebbed. She'd read the entries it had asked of her. She knew how her sister had felt, could taste the bitterness dripping from each page.

Marlena had resented her, and Tamsin had never known. But she did now, with her sister's loopy handwriting seared into her memory, frustration and pain preserved in the pages Tamsin had read. She didn't *want* to know the side of Marlena that the diary showed.

And so she sent it burrowing beneath her mattress, throwing a sticking spell on the book for good measure. As a consequence, Tamsin coughed until her throat went raw. Wren watched it all, openmouthed, her eyes sweeping across Tamsin's body, not like she was looking at her but like she was looking through her.

"What?" Tamsin slung the bag over her shoulder, suddenly self-conscious.

"Sorry." Wren shut her mouth. "It's just that I've never actually seen magic coming from a witch before."

Tamsin took a step back. "You can *see* my magic?" It felt vaguely intrusive, as though Wren knew more about Tamsin than Tamsin knew about herself.

"I can see all magic." Wren offered up the ghost of a grin. "I told you, remember? I can help with the hunt. I'm not the burden you're making me out to be."

Tamsin highly doubted that. Still, if they were going to find the dark witch, the ability to track magic was likely to come in handy at some point, although she had no intention of telling Wren that. Tamsin wiggled her fingers again. The fire doused itself; the shutters sealed themselves. The house went quiet and still. Quiet, save for Wren, who sniffed loudly, her nose wrinkled with effort. Tamsin stared at her suspiciously.

"Are you smelling me?"

"No," Wren snapped, turning away quickly.

"You are," Tamsin said, barking out a laugh. "You're smelling my magic." Leya had been distractible too, more attuned to the world around her than Tamsin, but even she hadn't been as obvious about it as Wren was.

"I wasn't. . . ." Wren trailed off, her shoulders hunched, her body stiff.

"Sure you weren't." Tamsin sighed deeply, the ribbon around her neck tightening ever so slightly, as though mocking her impulsivity, mocking her decision to accept this impossible quest with this ridiculous person. "Let's go," she snapped, pulling her cloak from its peg and striding out the front door into the gray afternoon air, Wren at her heels.

As they walked from her cottage to the town square, Tamsin had to glance over her shoulder every few moments to make sure Wren was still there. The girl's eyes clung to the sky, squinting up at the roof of every cottage they passed. She stopped more than once, biting her lip so hard she drew blood.

Tamsin hated the idea that there was something Wren could see that she couldn't, that the world kept secrets only Wren could reveal. She knew she was more powerful than Wren, who couldn't actually do anything with her magic besides house it. Still, after so many years of being the best, Tamsin did not enjoy the feeling of inadequacy that came from knowing the source could do something she could not.

"Wren," Tamsin finally snapped, shifting her bag to the other shoulder. The world Within was already nearly five days' trek from Ladaugh. At Wren's current pace, it would take them closer to ten. "Can we at the very least get outside the village before the sun goes down?"

Wren jumped, startled. "Sorry, what?"

Tamsin sighed exasperatedly. "Walk. Faster."

Wren hoisted her bag higher on her shoulder and hurried to catch up. She glanced backward. "It's getting worse," she said, her voice hushed. "The plague, I mean." She pointed at something Tamsin could not see. "What kind of person casts a spell that steals memories?" She stared at Tamsin intently, as though she expected an answer.

"Someone with something they want to forget," Tamsin said darkly.

"It's evil," Wren said, and chewed on her bottom lip. "To strip away everything that makes a person human. And *then* to steal their life? What's it all for?"

Tamsin didn't know. It did seem mercilessly cruel. To prolong death by first taking the things that made life worth living. There was a difference between existing and living. That was something Tamsin knew well.

"I can't imagine what kind of monster chooses to use dark

magic." Wren shivered. "Surely even witches have morals?"

Tamsin went cold. Despite the fact that Wren couldn't possibly know about her past, it still felt personal.

"You really do walk extraordinarily slowly," she snapped. "If we're going to end the plague, we need to first actually leave Ladaugh."

She looked pointedly at her companion, who shut her mouth and turned her eyes to the dirt below her feet.

When they reached the square, Tamsin stopped walking abruptly, causing Wren—who was still watching the ground—to barrel right into her, sending a spark of heat across Tamsin's shoulder.

The town square was surprisingly bustling for a gloomy afternoon. A small group of villagers watched as fifty-some strangers moved about it, drinking from the fountain, bartering with one another for bread and nuts. Wooden carts were loaded with armchairs, barrels of water, and even beds. Women corralled children, shouting instructions to the newcomers, their sharp consonants catching on the wind. Their clothes were covered in dust and dirt, their faces sunbaked, their eyes weary.

Tamsin examined their goods, richly colored and gilded, things fine enough to have come from Farn, the queen's city. It would account for the group's weariness. Farn was the final city in the Queendom of Carrow before the Wood that led Within. The caravan had come from the place where Tamsin and Wren were set to go. The Queen's Road would bring them to the city of Farn, but first they had to journey through the mazelike caverns below the mountains that divided the country. Some travelers hated the dark dampness of the caves, but Tamsin much preferred the ease of an existing path over the idea of actually *climbing* a mountain.

They watched the procession in silence, gloom settling in Tamsin's gut as she took in the tired faces of the endless parade of people. She caught snippets of their conversations as they passed. The word "witch" was always accompanied by a scowl.

"What happened to their horses?" Wren's eyes were stuck on the carts, which, though harnessed for the giant animals, were each drawn by several men instead.

"Spiders," said a voice to their left. Wren jumped, and Tamsin adjusted her cloak so as not to give away her own surprise. It was a wizened old woman, hunched over nearly double, draped in a worn brown cloak.

"What's that, Mother?" Wren's tone was unflinchingly polite, despite the fact that the woman was more of a crone than a kindly grandmother.

"Spiders," the woman repeated. Her voice was brittle, but a sparkle behind her eyes betrayed the joy of spreading gossip. "Came from the great caverns beneath the mountain two days past. Took the horses in the night."

Tamsin tensed with understanding, but Wren frowned. "That doesn't seem right," she said, eyeing the woman suspiciously. "It would take millions of spiders to carry away a horse. There's no such way. They were likely just frightened off."

"Oh, they were mighty scared." The woman gave Wren a pitying grin. "But no, dear. It only takes one spider if that spider is big enough."

Wren let out a laugh that tipped toward the hysterical. "You can't mean . . ." She waved her hands around, gesturing wildly. "That's not . . ." She looked to Tamsin, her eyes widening with horror. "They couldn't be . . ."

But of course they could. That was the trouble with dark magic. People always assumed that the stories were exaggerated, that the truth was not nearly so terrible, when in fact the opposite was true.

Even five years prior, twelve years old and filled to the brim with anxious dreams and an impossible imagination, Tamsin had not been able to fathom the consequences of the spell she had cast in hopes of saving her sister's life. It had swept the world Within with a vengeance unimaginable in even her most paralyzing nightmares. The earth, drained of its magic, rocked like a ship at sea. Trees crashed to the ground like hammers to anvils. Lightning lit up the sky, turning it an eerie, deathly purple. Water flooded the streets, slipped through the cracks in windows, and filled the dormitories to the brim. Most girls got out.

One girl didn't.

Now another witch had unleashed dark magic. The longer it remained at work, the more aggressively the world would rebel, which meant that spiders large enough to eat horses would be the least of Wren's worries.

Tamsin, though, was worried enough for both of them.

Wren shot her a wary look. "Are we . . ." Tamsin shook her head sharply, trying to get the stupid girl to be quiet, but Wren didn't seem to notice. "Will we pass through those caverns on our way?"

The old woman peered at Tamsin suspiciously. "What are two nice girls like you doing headed north? Nothing there but destruction." Her eyes narrowed. "Unless, of course, one of you's a witch."

Tamsin tried to laugh lightheartedly, but it came out sounding more like a bark. "Of course not. We are going nowhere." She shot Wren a sharp look before turning back to the woman. "Truth be told, I fear my cousin has started to show symptoms of the plague. Best be off, old woman, lest you catch the sickness too."

The woman's eyes widened warily, and she hurried away to rejoin the caravan, her cloak held tightly against her nose and mouth.

"Oh, now, that was awful," Wren said mournfully. "She was so frightened."

Tamsin elbowed the girl sharply. "You can't go around hollering about heading north when people are moving south in droves. The only ones going north will be witches. Calling that sort of attention to us will only make the journey more difficult." Tamsin rubbed her left forearm absentmindedly.

She was taking a gigantic risk, the sort of risk that Wren could not possibly appreciate. But Tamsin was on edge, alone in a sea of judgment, a flurry of uncertainty and fear. She did not know if the place where she was born would welcome her back. She did not know if she still had a home at all.

Wren's mouth was set. "You seem to quite like attention," she said sourly, sounding for all the world like she was reading from Marlena's diary.

Tamsin bristled. For the past five years she had done her best to serve the people of Ladaugh and keep her head down. To stay out of the limelight. To be nothing more than a common witch.

"Let's go." She tugged on Wren's wrist, pulling her off balance as they moved away from the square. The road was still filled with people following the caravan. Tamsin wanted to walk in peace, so she led them to the cornfields. It took a bit of thrashing to move through the giant green stalks, but the lack of people made the effort worthwhile.

"Okay," Wren muttered behind her, "this is ridiculous."

Tamsin ignored her. Stumbling through cornfields would be the least of their worries as they followed the Queen's Road to the north, beyond the spindly mountains that rose like spikes in the distance. Atop the tallest peak was the palace where Queen Mathilde held court. Below it lay the ruined capital of Farn. Beyond the city proper was the Wood.

The common folk told their non-magic children nighttime tales of the forest's dangers—bandits, giants, and wolves alike, each deadlier than the last, depending on who did the telling—but in reality it was only a swath of charms and enchantments that made it impossible for ordinary folk to pass through the seemingly endless expanse of trees. The Wood kept them from traveling to the world Within. Within was for witches.

Witches who weren't Tamsin.

In fact, she did not know if she would be allowed to pass through the trees at all. Perhaps the ancient spells would sense the mottled scar on her arm and refuse to part the serpentine branches. It was possible the High Councillor had placed a ward around the Wood to prevent Tamsin from ever returning. Every uncertain step she took might be in vain.

The not knowing was the worst part, clawing at her insides like the sharp nails of Councillor Mari's cat, which had never liked her but had adored Marlena.

The weight of her sister's memory bent Tamsin's head over, sent a shooting pain down her back. It was a complicated weight, awkward and lopsided. For so long, Tamsin had mourned the sister she remembered—although, of course, her curse had blurred some of Marlena's edges. But now, thanks to the diary, Tamsin was starting to fear that the sister she thought she had known had never truly existed at all. That the Marlena she missed was a figment of her imagination. Her warped memories. Her desperation.

Tamsin scratched at her left arm, nails digging into her scar. Already she was exhausted, and they had yet to leave Ladaugh.

At least the diary wasn't with her. Its smooth leather cover could not dig into her side. Its words could not swim before her eyes. Tamsin was grateful for small mercies. Small mercies like silence.

Too much silence.

Tamsin whirled around, coming face-to-face with endless ears of corn. Wren was nowhere to be seen. Tamsin, having been wrapped up in her own fragmented memories, had no idea how long she had been missing.

"Wren?" She hadn't wanted to phrase it as a question. Statements were controlled. Questions were dependent. And if there was one thing Tamsin did not want to be, it was dependent on Wren.

There was no reply. Against her better judgment, Tamsin shouted Wren's name again, louder this time.

A rustling—several stalks bristled, swaying lightly in the afternoon breeze. Tamsin held her breath. The sound was chaotic, a tangle of feet that made it difficult to determine if the limbs belonged to a human or an animal. She tried to brush away the fear creeping up her spine. Giant spiders were just the beginning. Perhaps there were poisonous beetles, or the farmer's scarecrow had come to life. Maybe it had taken Wren, tying *her* to the post to keep watch over the crops.

Tamsin fingered the ribbon around her neck, a glimmer of hope swirling in her chest. If Wren were dead, the ribbon would unfurl. Tamsin would be free to return home and forget this altogether-terrible idea. But the necklace stayed firmly tied at her throat. Tamsin sighed with annoyance. Wren wasn't dead, then.

"Wren." This time it wasn't a question.

"What?" Wren came crashing through the field, bobbing and ducking between the stalks. Her eyes were as wide as a baby deer's, the spring in her step more joyful than the season's first warm day. "I caught sight of these blooming along the road." She shoved a fistful of wildflowers at Tamsin. The flowers' thin roots were perfectly intact. It appeared that Wren had not picked the flowers so much as gently coaxed the spindly roots to remove *themselves* from the ground.

Tamsin stared at the bouquet blankly. "What am I supposed to do with those?"

"Look at them?" Wren scrunched her brow with confusion. "Smell them?"

"That seems like an extraordinary waste of time."

Wren's jaw dropped as she examined Tamsin's pinched expression. "You can't even love a *flower*?"

Tamsin clenched her jaw in fury. "What of it?"

"That's so sad." Wren's eyes were wide but not mocking. She frowned. "So, when you look at these flowers, what do you see?" She shoved the bundle into Tamsin's unwilling hands.

"The petals are . . . white?" Tamsin held a stem up to her nose and inhaled. It smelled of nothing, of course. "This is ridiculous." She threw the flowers on the ground, then stomped on them with her heel for good measure.

Wren flinched. "You hurt them."

"They're flowers."

"They have magic," Wren insisted. "They can feel."

Tamsin rolled her eyes. "What did they say when I stomped on them?" Her voice was jangling, mocking. Wren looked pained.

"They didn't *say* so much as scream." She tugged on her braid. "Anyway, the petals aren't white; they're pink, like the sky just before the sun sets. Their scent is sweet, like the grass after a summer rain." She crouched down and ran a finger over a petal. "And they're soft, like a baby chick."

Tamsin tsked in annoyance. "They are not."

"They are," Wren insisted. The earnestness of her expression only served to fuel Tamsin's fury. Not only could this girl feel, but she described things just poorly enough for Tamsin to remember exactly how much of the world she was missing. Just well enough that she hungered for more.

"We don't have to talk."

"Oh." Tamsin could hear the hurt in Wren's voice, but the sudden quiet was so blissful she had trouble finding it within herself to care.

The sun was low in the sky when the cornfields opened up into a vast, grassy expanse. Tamsin and Wren were far from the road now, though if Tamsin squinted, she could make out the shapes of people heading for the town she and Wren had finally left. The grass beneath their feet was marshy and wet despite the fact that it hadn't rained in weeks.

"Stop." Tamsin held out a hand. Wren barreled into her. "I'm hungry."

Wren regained her balance. "Oh, good, you brought food."

Tamsin frowned. "You didn't bring any?"

Wren's eyes narrowed. "You didn't bring any either?"

Tamsin shrugged. "Well, I thought you'd bring some."

Wren gaped at her. "I'm supposed to be reading your mind now?"

"That would save us both quite a bit of trouble, yes."

"You're impossible," Wren huffed, flinging herself onto a low stone wall that snaked up and down the valley.

Tamsin ignored her. They were on farmland, after all. It wouldn't be terribly difficult to summon something proper to sup on. She reached for Wren.

The girl swatted her hand away. "What are you doing?"

"I want some of your magic. I need to keep myself in one piece. We've got quite the journey ahead of us." She grabbed Wren's arm and pulled the source's magic toward her. She whispered a summoning spell, and in moments there was a certifiable feast: a loaf of bread still steaming from the oven, four links of sausage, and a basket of pears. Tamsin could hardly believe how simple it had been. She felt nothing, no consequences, not even a moment of light-headedness from the effort.

To some, it might have been a thrilling moment, but Tamsin refused to revel in power without consequence. She did not want to invite any further similarities between herself and the dark witch Evangeline than she already had.

Wren gaped at her. "You can't just take my magic without asking." But her eyes betrayed both her awe and her hunger, and she got to eating, shoving handful after handful into her mouth. She was really rather feral.

Wren stopped chewing mid-bite. "Wait." She set her handful of bread back on the tea towel it had appeared with. "Where did this come from?"

Tamsin shrugged. "I summoned it from a nearby farmhouse."

Wren stared indignantly at her. "But that's awful. Now someone doesn't have bread for the night. What if these pears were for a tart?"

Tamsin shook her head uncomprehendingly. "Then they won't make a tart?" She pulled off a piece of bread and chewed it slowly.

Wren looked pained. "Have you ever wanted for *anything*?"

"I've wanted plenty," Tamsin snapped, though her tone was softened by the bread in her mouth. She did not appreciate this girl acting as though she knew her after they'd traveled together for less than a day.

"Unbelievable," Wren muttered to her hands.

"Fine." Tamsin swallowed thickly. "Keep your morals. Starve for all I care."

Wren sat, arms crossed, staring determinedly anywhere but the food. Tamsin carried on eating. The food was tasteless, but she still managed to put on quite a show of enjoyment, moaning and groaning as she took several exaggerated bites.

Finally, Wren dropped her piteous act and scrambled for the final sausage.

"Thought so." Tamsin took a triumphant bite out of the largest pear.

Wren scowled and turned her attention toward a bird that had landed on the wall beside her, murmuring to the creature quietly. Tamsin smiled through a mouthful of fruit, though the bite was devoid of any pleasure. That was all she had sometimes: her spite. It didn't make her any friends, but it gave her something to focus on. Something to feel. She imagined it as a fire within her, even as her limbs froze, as people frowned and turned away, as her empty cottage echoed with loneliness.

Who was Wren to say she'd never wanted? She had lost. She had yearned. She had settled into a life she wasn't meant for. Tamsin was never supposed to have been alone. She was a twin, one part of a whole set of sisters. It was always supposed to have been TamsinandMarlena, spoken in one breath so that their names crashed together the way their lives had once collided.

Again Tamsin thought of the diary, barreling into her every chance it had. Her past was creeping back to haunt her from all sides—dark magic hanging in the air, her sister's words swimming before her eyes. But Tamsin had the sort of past that should stay buried. If she held too tightly to it, she would only be dragged down into its dark depths.

Twins were supposed to be equals, two sides of the same coin, only she and her sister weren't and never had been. Tamsin had been greedy, had stolen all the strength in their mother's womb. Had left nothing for her sister, so that magic had been her undoing. So that, in the end, Marlena had died of the exact thing that made Tamsin so strong.

Wren was wrong.

Tamsin had wanted.

Tamsin *wanted* to turn and run back toward Ladaugh, *wanted* to stay far from the home where she was no longer welcome. She *wanted* her sister to be more than a memory.

As it was now, the nothing Tamsin felt when she thought of her sister—the way Marlena always took the high harmony when they sang songs that echoed off the vaulted ceilings of the academy's Grand Hall, the way she tied her hair into knots when she was anxious, the way she never quite gave anyone her full attention—made Tamsin want to scream. But *wanting*, Tamsin knew, begot nothing, and so her scream echoed inside herself. Left nothing but silence ringing in her head.

EIGHT

WREN

Wren had never spent the night beneath a bridge before. "You're acting like a child," Tamsin snapped from the shadows as she shoved her rucksack beneath her head and draped her cloak across her like a blanket.

"But trolls live under bridges." Wren hung back, tugging on her braid anxiously. She was having trouble shaking the stories she had been told as a child, the warnings she had been given by a father who was afraid of everything magical and a mother who knew nothing of the wider world.

"I take it back. A child has more sense than you." Wren couldn't see Tamsin's face, but she was certain the witch had rolled her eyes. "Trolls are only native to the South. They thrive in warm, marshy climates." Tamsin turned over, her back to Wren, her voice muffled. "Now get out of sight and go to sleep."

Wren hesitated, staring up at the starry sky, but eventually she gave in, settling herself as far from Tamsin as possible.

The witch snored, but sleep evaded Wren.

They had planned to stop at an inn. Tamsin had hoped for a bath. Wren had hoped for other people, for anyone who wasn't Tamsin with her bitter chuckle and her constant whining about her feet. The girl was likely no older than Wren's own seventeen years, and yet she complained more than any old woman—even Saroya, the woman from Wells who had spent years playing the harp for Oöna, the queen of the giants. Saroya's hands were gnarled and ruined, yet she always had a spare smile for Wren on market day.

If Wren hadn't seen Tamsin filled with a momentary flash of love, she wouldn't have believed the witch's lips could do anything other than sneer. And kiss.

But that was beside the point.

Sure enough, even as Tamsin slept, her face was screwed up with displeasure. Wren thought Tamsin's muscles must be exhausted from such strain. Wren herself was exhausted simply from staring at Tamsin's sour expression for an entire day.

Even the nearness of the witch was draining. Wren seemed to be drawn to Tamsin the same way magic was drawn to Wren. While she had no desire to be any nearer to Tamsin than she absolutely had to be, she couldn't seem to help it. Tamsin, too, had kept her close. The witch seemed to believe she had free rein over Wren's power. Thrice that day the witch had poked her shoulder with a long finger, sending ice through Wren's body as her magic moved toward Tamsin.

As if the journey hadn't been difficult enough. Wren rolled out her neck. Her legs felt weak and gooey as she stretched out on the dirt. She walked often, but not nearly so *far*. And not with such chaos, the ribbons of natural and dark magic twisting around one another like serpents, the sweet, sour smell of them clouding her nostrils.

They had come to a town as the sun set, the scent of sulfur overwhelming Wren the moment they'd set foot on the cobblestones. The light from the small lantern Tamsin carried had been strong enough to illuminate windows and doorways boarded up from the outside. The wood, nailed to the front doors of nearly half the cottages, was warped and cracked as though an animal had attempted to escape captivity. Tamsin had dismissed the houses as abandoned, but Wren could see the black ribbons of dark magic hanging above the huts. There were plague-riddled people trapped inside.

The realization had turned her stomach. Wren knew that no matter how desperate she was for a bed, she could not stay in a town with people who would treat others in such a way. And so they had walked on, and settled in the dried-up creek beneath a stone bridge instead.

The witch gave a gigantic snore, thick and phlegmy. It was unfair that sleep came to Tamsin so easily. Wren could not recall a night that she hadn't spent tossing and turning, her mind replaying her actions and her words, analyzing what she could have done to appear more normal, things she could have said to have been more polite. Worrying over how she could have better served her father. Wren could hardly remember the last time she'd woken feeling refreshed.

She didn't know why she'd assumed things would be any different now. Yet everything else was. Wren *herself* was different, lying under a bridge in a small town, far from home and everything she'd ever known.

Wren, who had never been farther than the marketplace in Ladaugh, had often dreamed about the wider world, and yet she had never understood exactly how vast it would be when she got there. The sky stretched on forever; the rocks beneath her feet were endless. With each step, she stretched a bit of herself. The small girl with the small life in the small town was starting to grow. There was so much to see.

She might never be finished looking.

Wren had sacrificed so much, not knowing exactly what that meant. But now, surrounded by flowers with colors she had never learned to name, watching people pass with clothes cut from fabrics she'd never touched, hearing voices with accents she could not place—a reminder of so many cities she still did not know—Wren again felt something dark rear its ugly head. That evil, suffocating thought that she had made her father sick because she had yearned for more.

Her father's face swam before her. Pieces of her memory were hazy—his eyes still evaded her—but it was there. He was there, still, in both her head and her heart.

But not for long, she reminded herself, fighting back a wave of nausea. For Wren had given away the one thing upon which she could always depend: her father. She'd left him behind, fading, like embers dying in the hearth. Had *chosen* to do so.

And when he was well and truly gone, scrubbed from every inch of her heart, Wren didn't know who she would be or if the trade would feel justified. Would it be worth it in the end, when she was finally allowed to embrace all the pieces of herself she had spent so much time trying to deny?

Magic had killed her brother, and Wren felt that weight fully each time the wind shifted and she caught a taste of sunshine. Each time a star shot across the sky and her own heart glowed. Wren was more than her life had ever allowed her to be. When she no longer loved her father, would she love her freedom more than she had ever loved him?

Her throat tightened, making it difficult to breathe. Wren inhaled slowly, trying to focus on the flow of air through her lungs rather than the ragged sound of her breath catching. She had gone a bit light-headed.

And then a voice, so faint she almost missed it. One tiny, terrified word: "Help."

Wren sat up so quickly that the world around her began to spin.

Tamsin didn't stir.

For a moment there was nothing but the night. Then, the voice again. Louder this time. Desperate. Haunted.

"Help."

Wren turned toward Tamsin, who was still scowling in her sleep. She moved to shake her but stopped before her fingers could close around the witch's shoulder. Tamsin was already the crankiest person Wren had ever met, and that was in her waking hours. She shivered at the thought of the ire she would invoke if she pulled the witch from sleep.

Carefully, so as not to disturb a single pebble, Wren got to her feet. She stumbled through patches of sharp summer grass on shaking legs. When she was far enough away that she would not wake the witch, she too called out. "Hello?"

"Hello?" The voice again, excited and eager. "I'm here."

The night was still, the starlight illuminating nothing but the rocks at her feet. "Where?"

"Here," the voice insisted. Wren wheeled all the way around, but there was no one there. "No," the voice said, sighing heavily. "Not there. Down *here*." Something sticky skimmed her ankle. Wren shrieked, jumping back. "Careful," the voice snapped, affronted. Wren peered down into the shadowy grass.

It was a frog.

Wren didn't know whether to laugh or run away. "I don't understand." She was probably delirious.

The frog peered up at her with buggy eyes, its long tongue lapping out to catch a passing fly. "I'm a lord," it said simply. "Cursed by an evil witch."

"I know one of those," she muttered despite herself.

The frog looked relieved, insomuch as a frog could. "Then you'll help me?"

Wren bent down to kneel in the grass, pebbles pressing uncomfortably into her knees. "Help you how?"

"My father will be most grateful," the frog continued, as though he had not heard her. "He's a duke, you know. Of course you'll be rewarded quite handsomely." The creature was speaking very fast.

"Help you how?" Wren asked again, curiosity getting the best of her.

"Oh!" The frog bounced up and down on his spongy toes. "It's really very simple. All you have to do is give me a kiss."

"A kiss?" Wren frowned.

"That's it, just one peck and it's over. It's nothing, really. Just pick me up, give me a quick smack, and I'll be forever in your debt."

Wren shifted her weight onto her heels. It seemed too simple. The answer made her suspicious, although she didn't understand exactly why.

"Why were you cursed?" she asked, trying to buy herself time.

The frog blinked up at her. "It was a simple misunderstanding," he said. "She had a horrible temper. Wouldn't even let me explain."

That certainly sounded like someone Wren knew. She felt a pang of sympathy for the frog. The lord?

"All right." It was just a kiss, after all. Something she could easily give. An action she could take to help someone, the way she couldn't yet help her father. The way she couldn't help herself. And it was such a simple ask. Lips pressed to lips. Nothing more. Hadn't she just kissed Tamsin? It certainly wasn't as though *that* had meant anything.

Wren offered her hand to the frog, who hopped into it. His skin was clammy and slick against her palm. It wasn't the most comforting sensation, but, she supposed, it would only take a second. One second to free a person from a terrible spell.

Surely that was worth a single moment of absurdity.

Wren brought her hand toward her face. The frog blinked at her. His long pink tongue flapped out of his mouth onto her palm. She shuddered, her own tongue flooding with a sharp, metallic tang. Perhaps if she just closed her eyes . . .

"Wren." Her eyes flew open. "What are you doing?" The witch stalked toward her, hair mussed, one cheek pink and imprinted with the stitching from her rucksack.

Wren glanced desperately from the witch to the frog, which was waiting patiently in her hand. "He needs help," she said quickly, raising the frog up so Tamsin could see him. "He's a lord who was turned into a frog."

Tamsin took a step forward, squinting at the creature in Wren's palm. Her face was unreadable in the starlight. "First of all," she said sharply, "that's a toad."

Wren squinted down. "But . . . he was cursed by a witch."

Tamsin shot her a withering look. "Oh, really?"

"Yes," she said, confidence waning as she stared at the nervously flopping creature. "So . . . you're not a lord?" She felt quite foolish, addressing a toad.

Tamsin snickered. "No, he's a nasty little swamp sprite who should be squashed," she said, swatting the toad out of Wren's hand. Wren gasped as the creature fell. Tamsin rolled her eyes. "Don't know how long it must have taken that one to hop up here from the South, but you're lucky I woke up. If you'd kissed him, you would have turned into a toad as well."

Wren's eyes widened in horror. She tried to wipe all traces of the toad off her hand and onto the grass. She had only been trying to help. All Wren *ever* wanted to do was help, and yet, time and time again, she was the one who got hurt.

"Rule of thumb," Tamsin said, staring down at her. "Never trust something that talks when it shouldn't."

Wren stopped scraping at the skin of her palm. "But what if it *had* been a lord?"

"You still should have walked away." The witch shrugged lightly. "You can't save everyone. Especially not if you're a toad." She looked as though she was biting back a grin.

"It isn't funny," Wren said sharply, getting to her feet and turning back toward the bridge.

"It's sort of funny," Tamsin said, following behind her. "If only I could laugh."

Wren didn't reply.

She was a source, a girl made of magic, and still she had nearly been played by a toad. It was another thing she hadn't known. Another brand-new failing. Normally, Wren wouldn't have minded the lesson. But Tamsin had been a witness.

It wasn't that Wren cared what Tamsin thought of her. It was that she knew Tamsin was judging her for not knowing anything about magic. For agreeing to a journey she was nowhere near capable of completing. For caring about her father so much that she was willing to sacrifice everything for him, even when he hadn't asked her to.

It was that she knew Tamsin could see everything Wren hated about herself. That Tamsin wasn't wrong for thinking Wren was unworthy of her power. That, maybe, Wren truly was.

* * *

Wren woke with a start to the blinding white of the morning sky. She was shivering, as though her being had been drenched in icy water. Her tongue, thick with sleep, held the faint taste of cherries. She inhaled shakily. Honey hung in the air.

Magic.

As she scrambled to sit upright, her foot nudged something solid. She wiped the sleep from her eyes as she reached for the small leather-bound book.

Wren frowned. It was a nice book, the black leather smooth and worn in a well-loved way. But she hadn't noticed it among Tamsin's things before and didn't think the witch would simply leave something lying around for prying eyes.

Her mood darkened as she remembered that the witch had seen her nearly press her lips to a toad's. It couldn't hurt for Wren to gain a little leverage. Yet when she tried to pry open the book's cover, it would not budge. She grunted and pulled and pushed and, yes, even kicked, but still the book would not open.

Its lack of cooperation only served to make her more curious. What sort of secrets did Tamsin possess that she'd lock into such a well-protected book? Perhaps it held special spells for being a grump, or maybe a list of people she wanted to hex. Wren giggled, forgetting herself.

Tamsin's eyes snapped open. At first she looked vulnerable, caught between sleep and wakefulness. But then her eyes caught on the book in Wren's hands, and she sat up, her face as white as a sheet. Wren could have sworn she saw fear flash behind the witch's eyes.

"Where did you get that?" Tamsin demanded, face flushing from a furious red to a sickly green.

"I didn't—" Wren gaped at the witch's outsize reaction. It was only a book. "I just found it. There." She pointed to the patch of dirt where it had been. Tamsin's eyes barely left the book. Wren offered it to her gently.

The second the book was in her hand, the witch relaxed. But her relief did not last long. "Get up." Tamsin snapped her fingers, and her pack was in her hand. "We have to go."

"Why?" Wren clumsily gathered her things, her limbs still heavy with exhaustion. "What's wrong?"

"Nothing." Tamsin tucked the book carefully into the waistband of her long skirt and stomped out from beneath the bridge.

The morning air was crisp and bright as they climbed up the bank of the river and emerged onto the road. The sky was streaked with pink. Birds rustled their wings, waking up their voices with tinny shrieks.

"What is that?" Wren rushed to catch up with the witch, nodding pointedly at the book, which was resting at Tamsin's left hip.

Tamsin pressed a hand idly to the soft leather cover. "Nothing."

"It's clearly not nothing," Wren said. "You practically fainted when you saw me holding it."

Tamsin shot her a withering look.

"It wouldn't open for me, if that makes you feel any better," Wren added darkly, almost as an afterthought. The witch did look a bit relieved. "Which makes me wonder," she continued, reaching for the witch, her fingers grazing Tamsin's wrist, "what it is that you don't want me to see. Do you write poetry? Are you the first romantic poet without a heart?"

Wren was positively tickled by the thought.

"*Stop*," Tamsin snapped, her voice harsh and broken.

Wren stopped, hand outstretched. They stared at each other in silence.

"It's private," Tamsin finally said, her tone soft but pained.

"All right," Wren said, just as quietly. "I'm sorry. It's private."

She did not appreciate being chastised. She had only been curious, wanting a bit of insight into the girl Tamsin was. Wren had shared so much already: her father, her love, her naivety. But Tamsin was a closed book. Literally.

She trudged after the witch, her feet kicking up more dust than perhaps was necessary as they walked past a wide field littered with hay bales the size of horses. The moment she began to wish she had someone kind to talk to, a bird flitted past her. Almost without thinking, Wren offered up her finger. The little creature landed on it, and she nearly squealed with surprise. Its tiny body was squat and round, its feathers dappled brown and white. It was a wren, the little bird from which she'd gotten her name. It felt like a sign.

"Hello, friend," she cooed softly to the creature, and its orange beak trembled furiously as it let out a string of high-pitched whistles in response.

"Oh, you have got to be kidding me." Tamsin had stopped, her eyes lingering on the hand that held the baby bird. Wren stared back defiantly, but her cheeks burned with embarrassment. "Don't try to kiss it," Tamsin warned, rolling her eyes as she turned back to the road.

Wren stuck her tongue out at the witch's back.

"She's just angry," she told the bird. "She doesn't like it when I talk, but you don't mind, do you?" She used a finger to carefully pet the wren's soft feathers. It let out an appreciative whistle. "That's right," Wren said quietly. "You like me just fine. The problem isn't me, after all. It's her." The tiny bird gave her finger a soft nip before flittering away to the trees, still warbling a flurry of whistles.

Wren's eyes bored into the back of Tamsin. She was such an impossible presence, always saying what she wanted, taking what she needed, never worrying about anyone else or what they might think of her. Wren felt a twinge of envy as she watched the witch walk, head held high, shoulders back, as though she didn't care whose eyes looked upon her face. As though she wanted to be seen.

Wren had spent so much of her life trying to be smaller, trying to take up less space. She feared the eyes of others, worried someone would see the power she had worked so hard to suppress. Wren kept herself small and unassuming in hopes that if no one ever told her what she wanted to hear, she could tell herself that what she wanted didn't matter. Even now she walked hunched over, her shoulders sagging, her back bent. Her boots shuffled against the dirt, as though she was too afraid to even lift her feet fully from the ground.

The more she noticed their differences, the harder it became for Wren to pull her eyes from the witch. She straightened her shoulders, shook out her limbs. She wanted some of the witch's certainty. She wanted to give the witch some of her self-restraint. So focused was Wren on comparing their personality traits that she didn't notice the witch stop walking. She barreled directly into Tamsin. A jolt of cold, sharp as ice, ran down the back of her neck.

A barn was on fire. The smell was terrible, like the moment after a slaughter, cloyingly rank and tinged with fear. The flames darted and leaped, bright blue and blazing. This was no ordinary fire. Smoke rose from the barn, thick and toxic, mingling with the dark magic that hovered above the roof like a cloud.

Tiny sparks exploded in the morning sky, so bright they burned Wren's eyes. Embers rained down from the roof, catching on the dry summer grass below. The field began to smoke. Wren looked on in panic as she gauged the length of the farmland, the giant bales of hay they'd passed. Everything would take to the fire in an instant. The whole countryside would burn until it reached the houses with the boarded-up windows and doors. The village would burn. The people inside would burn with it.

Panic rose in Wren's throat. She reached for Tamsin, who was watching the raging flames with wide eyes.

"We have to do something."

The road was empty, the field abandoned—the farmer and his family perhaps still sleeping soundly in their beds. There was no one around to help, no one to stop the fire but them.

But Tamsin shook her head. "We can't just douse it with water. It's dark magic. It would take nearly a day to quell flames like that, even if I used your power, too."

"But we *can* stop it," Wren said, tugging at the witch's wrist. She couldn't believe she had to fight Tamsin about this. She knew the girl was cold, but this was negligence bordering on pure evil. "We can't just let the country burn."

"What part of 'it would take nearly a day' do you not understand?" Tamsin didn't snap, but her harsh tone still stung. "If someone sees us here, they'll think we're involved. If they find out I'm a witch, they won't hesitate to throw me into the flames too. If you want to leave this land alive, we have to go. Now."

The sour, stale taste of dread settled on Wren's tongue. "You're saying we do nothing?"

"We can't save everyone, Wren." Wren could have sworn Tamsin's eyes flashed with sorrow. "It's the fire or your father. Take your pick."

Horror pooled in Wren's stomach as she watched the barn blaze, watched the flames race across the summer grass. Her body was slick with sweat. And yet, even as she tried to consider, there was only one answer she was able to give.

"My father," she whispered hoarsely. Tamsin nodded sharply and carried on walking. The beam of the barn sizzled and snapped. It fell to the ground with a great, thundering crack. To Wren, it sounded like a heart breaking.

Living with the feeling that the world was on fire, Wren now knew, was nothing compared to watching it burn.

NINE

TAMSIN

There was no way around it. They were going to have to climb a mountain.

"You're sure this is the only way?" Tamsin asked the scrawny man before her, his hair matted with filth, his stench so rank her eyes began to water. She was hungry, and she was exhausted. The mountain loomed above them, casting a shadow so dark that the morning looked like twilight.

"Sorry, lass," he said, his voice surprisingly soft for a man so grimy, "but the tunnel's collapsed. If you want to make it to Farn, the only way is up and over. We're taking the scenic route."

"I can't believe this," Wren moaned as she stared at the entrance to the cavern, which was completely caved in. "That caravan came through here just days ago."

"Didn't think you'd be so sorry to miss the giant spiders." But Tamsin's taunt fell flat. It really was a horrible mess. Boulders had tumbled down to create an endless wall of stone and sand, decorated with broken branches, withered moss, and decaying greenery. It was a wonder the entire mountain hadn't cracked right down the middle.

Still there was a flurry of activity. Several men as dirty as the one before her were hauling boulders away from the cavern's mouth. They called and shouted to one another, their gravelly voices filling the late-morning air. Several cleaner people lingered near the cavern's mouth as well, uncertain amid the chaos. One of the women looked familiar enough that Tamsin drew up the hood of her cloak to hide her face. She did not need to be recognized here, of all places.

"Any of youse who's coming with, gather round," the scrawny, dirty man called. "My name's Boor, and I'll be taking you upward. For a price, of course." The man smiled to reveal a mouth of missing teeth.

"What might that price be?" A thin, reedy man in traveler's clothes stared at Boor suspiciously. "And what sort of name is *Boor*?"

"The kind of name that suits me," Boor said. "It's six silvers per person. Ten for you, though," he said to the man, who gaped at him wordlessly.

"Six silvers?" Wren turned to Tamsin with horror. She pulled a handful of coins from her pocket. "I don't have enough for the both of us."

"Put those away," Tamsin snapped. "These men are bandits. They probably blew the caverns up themselves so they could make some extra money." She rummaged around in her cloak until she came up with two small black buttons. She whispered a quiet word and the buttons gleamed gold. "That should satisfy them," she said, shaking out her left hand, which had gone numb.

"But . . ." Wren trailed off, looking uncertain.

"Bandits," Tamsin said again. The girl was really too kind for her own good. Sometimes terrible people deserved the terrible things that were coming to them. Tamsin dropped the coins into Boor's hand. "Keep the change," she said, her voice low. "I don't ask questions if you offer me the same courtesy." Boor's eyes gleamed in agreement.

Only three others stepped forward to offer the men their coins. The rest turned back the way they had come, their faces dark.

Tamsin studied the remaining group and their desperate, determined expressions. Ordinary folk were moving south in droves. Anyone intentionally going north—toward the plague— must be heading toward something they valued more than their lives. More than their memories. Perhaps, like Wren, they were hoping to save someone they loved. Perhaps, like Tamsin, they were on their way home.

"All right, then," a second man called, waving the pack of people over with a large, grubby hand. "Come on. I hope you're ready to climb."

He led them around the ruined mouth of the cavern to a set of steep stone stairs built into the side of the mountain.

"Absolutely not." Wren skittered to a halt beside Tamsin, shaking her head vehemently. "I'm not climbing those." She dropped her voice to a whisper. "You're a witch. Can't you just"—she waved her hand vaguely in the air—"magic us over?"

Tamsin elbowed her sharply. "Can you not?" She glanced pointedly at their fellow travelers. For all she knew, they'd try to stone her atop the mountain. "And no, I can't just 'magic us over.'" Her whisper did nothing to hide her disgusted tone. "What do you think a witch actually *does*?"

Wren frowned. "I don't know. Whatever they want?"

Tamsin pursed her lips together in annoyance. She would hardly have believed that someone with such a strong reserve of magic could know so little about it, except that she had been on the road with Wren for several days, and so, of course, she could.

"It isn't that easy," Tamsin sighed, keeping her voice low. "Am I powerful? Absolutely. Can I whisk us up and over a mountain without losing a leg?" She frowned theatrically. "Unlikely."

"But I'm a source. Surely that would help."

"Great, so I'll only lose *half* the leg." Tamsin rolled her eyes, but Wren still looked confused. Tamsin sighed. She was going to have to explain as though teaching a child. "Think of it like a scale." Tamsin held out both her hands, palms up. "The amount of magic it would require to move us up and over *stone* is immense. If I take that much now"—she dropped her left hand and raised her right—"I'm going to have to pay it back." She glanced at her right hand, which rested near her ear. "Where is that energy going to come from? I got no sleep, so I don't have any to spare." She shot Wren a dark look. "And I am responsible not only for myself, but for you, too. That's now double the magic I need." She sank her left hand even deeper, so that it hung near her hip.

Wren opened her mouth to protest, but Tamsin cut her off with a glare.

"Fine, say I pull magic from you." She moved her left hand back up so it hit near her waist and let the right one droop down near her shoulder. "But you haven't been trained properly, so it's likely you'd overcompensate and offer too much too quickly, which would deplete your resources, not to mention probably make you ill, leaving me with most of the grunt work. That's still a lot of energy that *I* have to make up for. So either the magic chooses for me and I lose a limb"—she balanced her hands out—"or I sleep for the next half century in an attempt to repay my debt to the earth. While I would be a lovely sleeping corpse, I'm sure"—she smiled sardonically at Wren—"it might be easier if you just got over yourself and started climbing the stairs."

Wren stared at her, openmouthed.

"There's a railing. You'll be fine." Tamsin swatted the girl's shoulder. "Go on." Surprisingly, Wren obeyed, falling into step behind two middle-aged women.

Tamsin watched her climb the first few steps before sighing and starting her own ascent. She did not bother with the railing. The steps were clearly the work of witches. She knew she would not fall. Instead Tamsin fiddled with the journal tucked into the waistband of her skirt.

She had been so certain she had escaped the diary's clutches. But that had been foolish—*she* had been foolish, to forget that when dark magic took hold of something, it pushed and pushed until it destroyed.

Her legs burned as she continued to climb. The stairs were

short and steep, just wide enough to fit two climbers side by side. A tapestry of thick moss clung to the side of the peak, giving the air a heavy, humid quality. The higher they climbed, the harder it became to breathe. Yet Wren still insisted on talking.

"That explanation seemed a bit simplistic." She glanced over her shoulder at Tamsin, then stopped, clutching the rail with white knuckles. "I shouldn't have looked down."

"Novice mistake." Tamsin clucked her tongue. "And I explained it simplistically because that seems to be the only way to make you understand."

Wren's face soured. "It isn't my fault I don't know things. You don't have to be so patronizing."

"Actually," Tamsin said, keeping her own eyes on the back of Wren's head so they would not stray to the ground far below, "it *is* your fault. You're supposed to report to the Coven upon recognition of your talent so they can train you. Technically, you broke the highest law of the world Within."

"Where?" Wren paused, frowning.

Tamsin, too, stopped climbing. "Within," she repeated. Wren's face remained blank. "The Coven's land. Beyond the Wood."

Wren's face lit with understanding. "Oh. I didn't know it had a proper name. Most people just call it the Witchlands."

"The *Witchlands*?" Tamsin would not have been surprised to learn her eyebrows had become permanently attached to her hairline. "Is everything a story to the ordinary folk?"

Wren looked a bit embarrassed. "Mostly. Yes."

Tamsin sighed as they continued to climb.

"You know, it is rather beautiful up here," Wren said after several more steps. "It smells like salt, and that breeze . . ." She sighed contentedly as the wind whipped at them, blowing Tamsin's hair in her face.

"So?" She tried to sound cross, but as she was extracting hair from her mouth, it sounded more like a mumble.

"And the sky. It's so blue it's practically clear. It's almost as if we're high enough above the world that the plague doesn't exist. That the dark magic cannot reach us." There was a hint of hope in Wren's voice, as though speaking it could make it so.

Tamsin glanced around, a pang of longing in her chest. She often forgot exactly how much of the world her curse kept her from enjoying. Even colors were impossible to remember. In Tamsin's eyes, they were merely climbing up the side of a gigantic rock. She gleaned no pleasure from the act, no enjoyment from the height, just a turning of her stomach when her foot missed a step. There was nothing beautiful here but Wren's ability to be nauseatingly optimistic. Still, she kept silent. Wren's words were something, even if they were simple and fleeting. They weren't a feeling, but they were a reminder of one.

A person could feel. A person could hurt. Tamsin wished there were more nuance to her personal emotional spectrum. It was exhausting, being angry. Feeling bitter. Biting back. She pulled the diary from her hip and turned it over in her hands.

"Okay, seriously, what is that?"

Tamsin hadn't noticed Wren stop walking. "Nothing," she said quickly. But Wren didn't budge.

"Your face looks strange." She stared suspiciously down at Tamsin from her step.

"My face is fine," Tamsin snapped. "Keep walking."

"I'm not an idiot." Wren's words were a challenge. "I know you think I'm stupid, but I'm not. You're hiding something from me."

Tamsin sighed. For a moment she considered telling the source everything. Her entire history, everything about her sister, about her banishment, all of it. But if she did that, Wren's feelings toward her would change. She would stop being in awe and start being afraid. With the world in chaos and the dark magic getting stronger, the only way Tamsin would survive this trip Within was to go with someone who did not know all the deep, dark parts of her. For their bargain to work, Tamsin could show no weakness.

"I mean it." Wren watched Tamsin with cloudy eyes. "You can trust me."

"Trust you?" Tamsin laughed, hard and harsh, but she felt no relief. "You don't even trust yourself. You know nothing about your magic, nothing about my world. So don't pretend you know anything about me."

Wren dropped her hands and stared at Tamsin incredulously. "That's only because you're too self-absorbed to share a single thing with me. I've asked you so many questions, and all you've ever given me are half answers, brushed away because you think I'm a fool. Well, so are you." Wren shook her head.

"Fine," Tamsin said. "I'll tell you." If Wren wanted to call her a fool, she would act like one. "They're love notes. From a secret admirer." That got a laugh from Wren. Tamsin set her shoulders and brushed carefully past Wren. The group was nearly a hundred steps ahead of them. "Just because you haven't fallen victim to my charm doesn't mean other people don't find me delightful."

Wren hurried to catch up with her. "You're lying."

"That's my prerogative," Tamsin said over her shoulder. "I'm not one of the fair folk."

Wren gaped at her. "You're impossible," she hissed. "I wish I'd never met you. I'd be better off with my father. At least he appreciates me."

"Are you sure about that?" From what she could gather, Wren's father was a selfish, simpering man. The kind of person who took but never gave. To hear Wren tell it, though, her father might as well have been a saint.

Wren narrowed her eyes. "What are you talking about?"

Tamsin shrugged. "Don't be so quick to think your sacrifices are appreciated."

Wren's face had gone red. "What does that mean?"

"You didn't join the Coven." It wasn't that Tamsin was sorry she and Wren hadn't been classmates—the girl was infuriating at best—but she couldn't ignore the flash of interest that sparked behind Wren's eyes every time Tamsin talked about magic. It wasn't innocent curiosity. It was a raw, powerful hunger.

"I couldn't." Wren's eyes were wide. "By the time I understood what I was, my mother had died. I was all that my father had left. I couldn't just leave him."

Tamsin arched an eyebrow. "Why not?"

"It was my duty."

"Why?"

"What do you mean, 'why?'" Wren snapped.

Tamsin shrugged. "Why did you give up your life for your father's?"

"That's not what happened," Wren said fiercely. "He would have died without me."

Tamsin looked her over coolly. "I'm sure he liked to tell you that."

Wren looked ready to cry. "I love my father."

"Convenient, considering that's my payment." Tamsin sighed, brushing her long hair around her shoulders. "But just because you love him doesn't mean he loves you back."

Wren let out an incredulous laugh. "You know, I felt sorry for you, not being able to love. But now I wonder if maybe you'd have been this way anyway. You don't care about anything or anyone. So you can pick and pick and pick at me and my father and my decisions, but at least I know I love someone. At least I have someone I would do anything for. Someone I would give up my life to protect. Can you say the same?" Wren's voice hit a register so high she might as well have been shrieking. But her words sliced Tamsin at the center of her useless, dark heart.

"You have no idea what you're talking about," she said, voice shaking. Her hands were clenched into fists, the world wobbling at the edges.

Tamsin was so used to viewing grief and sadness as an extension of love that she had nearly forgotten she had the capacity for it at all. But now, here, she wasn't hurt because she cared about someone. She was hurt because she didn't. Because she *couldn't*. Because the useless, driveling girl standing before her had abilities that Tamsin did not. To see magic. To love her family. To shame Tamsin for choices Wren knew nothing of.

"Who hurt you?" Wren squinted at the witch, her voice barely a whisper, nearly lost in the wind that had begun to roar.

Tamsin said nothing.

Wren looked at her a moment, disappointment etched across her face, before pushing past her, taking the stairs two at a time to catch up with the rest of the group.

Tamsin let her go, and the diary fell open in her hands. She looked down at Marlena's loopy scribbles. The answer to Wren's question was complicated. There were a great many people Tamsin blamed for her pain. But the fact was that, in the end, the person she blamed the most was herself.

My sister is keeping secrets. Not that it's anything new for her. Did you know that she found her power nearly three years before I did? And she refused to tell anyone so we could enter the academy at the same time. She wanted so badly for us to do everything together that she didn't even tell me for over a year. It's lucky Vera wasn't the kind of person to dress us in matching outfits, but I know Tamsin ached for it. Every time I changed my hair, she'd change hers, too. If I started wearing green, she'd enchant all her clothes the same shade. She was so desperate for us to be the same that she never stopped to consider how fundamentally different we were.

But that's beside the point. Right now, something's going on, something weird, even for her. She keeps looking at me all teary and shifty-eyed, and her lips are chapped and cracked. It's a telltale giveaway that she has a secret. Tamsin's such a goody-goody she always wants to be honest and pure, and the only way she can keep herself quiet is to bite her mouth shut. And she just hovers over me. No matter the hour, she's always popping her head in to check on me, like she's making sure I haven't died.

Not that she's the only one. Healer Elthe is looking at me like I've come back to life. You should have seen it: The moment I opened my eyes, she gasped and clutched her heart like she'd seen a ghost. Apparently, I was unconscious for close to a week, my pulse so faint it was nearly nonexistent. Everyone fully expected me to die. Instead they're getting ready to discharge me. That's right: I get to leave this terrible, sterile place!

So yes, here I am, back among the living. Fundamentally not dying, which, I know, is unusual for me. Yet my sister continues to bite her tongue. She's keeping a secret, something *bigger than she's ever held, and it's eating her alive. Amma told me she's been fighting with Leya. And they never fight. Honestly, it's disgusting how in tune they are. Apparently, Tamsin's been sitting alone, always tapping her foot on the floor or her quill against the table, so agitated that she doesn't even participate in lessons anymore. Within's golden child has suddenly come undone. But by what???*

She hasn't even bothered to scrub her fingernails. They're caked with dirt. I mean, honestly . . . you'd think she'd care a bit more about appearances. But maybe that's just me.

Tamsin and Marlena had been twelve years old when it happened. In a particularly tense lesson, the students had been tasked with battling the blue flames of an enchanted fire. Marlena's attempt sent her crumpling to the floor. When Tamsin abandoned her own flame to aid her sister, the fire grew tenfold, injuring several students and incinerating the instructor's desk.

"You are superior," the High Councillor told her as Tamsin sat, chastised, in the woman's stone chambers. "Even in the womb, you sensed your mother's power, and so you took it for yourself." The High Councillor's eyes danced with something frightfully close to pride. "But," she warned, "if you continue to trouble yourself with Marlena, you will never live up to your full potential. You made a decision then. You must honor it now."

Nearly a week passed, but still Marlena did not wake. Healer

Elthe was growing more concerned by the day, her lips pressing into the thinnest of lines each time Tamsin showed up to inquire about her sister. Although the healer wouldn't say it aloud, Tamsin knew the truth: Her sister was going to die.

Marlena had always been weak, compromised by even the faintest use of magic. But Tamsin's twin was not the kind to sit idly by. She always forged ahead. Pushed harder than she should. Ended up in the infirmary just as often as she slept in her own dormitory, all while Tamsin continued to grow stronger, her stamina longer, her power tangible. Magic was about balance, but the sisters were as imbalanced as it was possible to be.

Tamsin had appealed to the High Councillor, begged her to tend to Marlena, to use a source, use any means necessary to wake her sister up. But the High Councillor had refused. "One must not dabble in death," she told Tamsin, her lips quirking downward. "There is a rule of returns. It is a rule we witches cannot afford to break. For death is not kind. It does not understand. It only feeds." The woman had smiled at Tamsin sadly. "Someday you will understand."

But Tamsin hadn't.

If she held enough power for two people, she should be able to share it with another. Or so she had reasoned as she spent hours poring through the library stacks, looking for a spell that would allow her to share her strength. When she found none, Tamsin turned her attention elsewhere. She slipped out of her dormitory after dark, seeking out elderly witches in shadowy taverns who whispered stories about Evangeline and dark magic. When she learned that Evangeline and the High Councillor had been best friends, Tamsin snuck into the High Councillor's study, a place where she was trusted and welcome, and stole pages from her private notes. When she had everything she needed, Tamsin begged Leya to help her plan, to accompany her on the night she attempted the spell, but the source refused. Leya understood the consequences Tamsin had chosen to ignore.

So Tamsin fumbled through the ancient ritual alone. She summoned forbidden dark magic from the cool clay of the soil, dug her fingers into the earth, and spoke the fearful, caustic words that bound her sister's life to Tamsin's power.

It had worked, for a time.

And then the rains came.

TEN

WREN

Wren took the stairs two at a time. Even as she stomped upward, she kept an eye on Tamsin nearly ten feet below. Clearly, the witch couldn't be bothered with her. Tamsin wasn't even looking where she stepped. Instead her face was buried in that book. Surrounded by her own secrets.

Well.

Wren had only been trying to help. But lately she had started to worry that being willing to offer help—a trait she'd always considered a strength—might actually be a weakness.

When she had agreed to trade away her love for her father, she'd thought she was choosing to do something noble. Something good. But if her help always hurt, well, then what was she really doing?

Her foot caught on the stone stair. She was climbing, that was what, up a mountain in the company of bandits. *Bandits.* Honestly. And the worst part, Wren knew, was that as far up as they climbed, they had just as far to go back down. In her misery, she barreled into the squat woman before her, who was not nearly as out of breath as she.

"Why are we stopping?"

The woman shrugged. "Ask him. What's his name? Boomer?"

"Boor," the man said, wheezing slightly. "And we're stopping because we're here."

Wren looked around blankly. "Where?"

Boor clucked his tongue loudly as though he was disappointed by her. "The palace, lass. We've made it to the palace."

Wren blanched. "The queen's palace?"

"No, the pig's palace," he snapped. "Of course the queen's palace."

"But . . ." Wren could hardly believe she was the only one protesting. "I thought you were taking us to Farn."

"Well, naturally you can get to the queen's city from the queen's palace." Boor sighed loudly. "Saints, lass, you're awfully picky for a girl heading north." His eyes lingered on hers knowingly, almost as if he could see the magic moving within her.

Wren shifted beneath his gaze. "But . . . we're halfway up a mountain."

Boor rolled his eyes, his pinched expression reminiscent of Tamsin's. "Exactly. Didn't your mother ever tell you the stories of the palace on the mountain? How the queen rules above her subjects?"

"My mother's dead," Wren said without thinking.

Boor looked uncomfortable. He kicked idly at a cracked stair. "Well, the palace isn't actually *on* a mountain, is it? It's *in* a mountain. Everyone knows that. But what they *don't* all know is how to get in through the back entrance. Lucky for you, you've got one of the finest tour guides in the West."

He fumbled around in the greenery until his hand caught on something solid. He gave a hearty yank, and a door the color of moss swung forward, revealing a dark chamber. Wren glanced over her shoulder, but Tamsin was still far behind.

"What is this place?" Wren hesitated at the chamber's entrance.

"Escape route. In case of a revolt. Or a memory-stealing plague." Boor's laugh came out more like a cough. "In you go, lass. Where's your friend?"

"She's not my friend," Wren snapped.

"All right, all right, no harm meant." Boor shook his head, hands extended out protectively.

Wren rolled her eyes and stepped into the stone corridor. Their footsteps echoed against the low ceiling. The passageway was long and squat, the light behind them dimming with each step. The taller travelers had to walk hunched over.

Something skittered across the floor, and in her terror Wren stumbled, her foot catching on a gap in the stone. A hand as cold as ice closed around her arm. Wren shrieked.

"Calm down, will you? I'm trying to help you."

"Tamsin?" Wren barely managed to stop herself from shrieking again.

"Who else would it be?"

"Oh, I don't know, a *bandit*." Wren's tone was scathing.

"Hey," came Boor's indignant wheeze.

"I'm sure these men are very nice," Tamsin said loudly. "Will you please shut up," she snapped, lowering her voice to a whisper. "They don't ask me questions; I don't ask them any."

Wren scoffed. "Don't you think we maybe should? How do we know this is even a palace? How did *they* know about this entrance?" She could not believe she had allowed dangerous men to lead her through dark passageways. She had been on the road only a few days and already she had all but abandoned her usual sense.

Wren felt the witch shift beside her. "Look, *you're* the one who followed them in here. You knew just as well as I did that we needed a way onward. They had a way. Now stop asking questions. It's very irritating."

They joined the rest of the group, who were huddled around a great steel door. Boor shoved his way forward, a match burning between his fingers.

"I can't believe we get to see the inside of the palace," one of the women whispered loudly to her companion.

"Hate to disappoint you lot, but there's not much left to see," Boor said, swinging open the steel door and gesturing for the group to step inside. The woman who had whispered hurried forward, but Wren hung back.

"Doesn't the palace have guards? Do you think there's a battalion of armed knights on the other side of this door ready to hack us to pieces?" She glanced desperately at Tamsin, who did not seem to share her concern.

"Not a chance. The queen fled to her winter palace before the news of the plague had even reached our town," Tamsin said, shaking her head lightly. "This palace is abandoned. Anyway, I'd bet you a true coin that these bandits have already gone through the entire place and taken every single thing of value for themselves."

When Wren had first learned about the plague from that family on the road outside Ladaugh, they had mentioned something similar about the queen and her winter palace. Still, she stayed at the end of the line, ready to flee back down the long, dark corridor at the first hint of danger. But all she heard was Boor's maniacal cackle.

Tamsin swept forward, squinting into the light of the queen's chambers. Wren followed begrudgingly after her, glass crunching beneath her boot.

"Told you," Tamsin said as Wren took in the decimated room with its ripped curtains and torn pillows, its slashed portraits and its ransacked drawers.

"All right, then," Boor said, nudging the empty spine of a book with the toe of his boot. "I'm off. Keep your health, or whatever lie people are offering these days." He spat loudly on the dirty carpet.

"This is it?" Tamsin's voice was flat. "This is as far as you take us?" She sighed darkly, crossing her arms over her chest. Boor nodded his affirmative, then slipped back through the shadows of the passageway, off to take the coins from another group of unsuspecting travelers.

Wren was beginning to feel a bit dizzy. The acrid taste of ash caught in the back of her throat. She coughed, eyes watering with the terrible flavor. As she blinked, trying to regain her focus, her attention caught on a shadow of magic, thick and black, coiled like a rope. It slinked across the marble floor, tugging at Wren's attention until she could ignore it no longer, her feet moving before her brain had caught up.

"What are you . . . ?" Behind her, Wren heard Tamsin sigh, heard the reluctant swish of her cloak as she strode after her, leaving the bandits and their fellow travelers behind. Wren followed the magic down a maze of hallways hung with gold-framed portraits and littered with piles of tarnished armor. Even the people in the paintings frowned down at the chaos—the puddles of water (or worse) in the corners of the corridors; the stench of rotten cabbage and spoiled eggs that clung to the velvet curtains, which hung in tatters; the torn tapestries; the bent swords. The giant glass windows were shattered. Tangles of deep green vines twisted their way inside, snaking up the marble pillars. Black mold sank into the carpets.

She lost sight of it then, amid the wreckage. Everything was shrouded in shadow. Everything was black and bleak. After standing helpless in the middle of the spongy carpet, she begrudgingly let Tamsin nudge her toward and down a spiral staircase, their feet silent against the stone as they descended.

Wren was having trouble keeping herself quiet. "Oh," she gasped again and again as they entered room after ruined room.

The ghosts of finery were everywhere in the dining hall, from the gnarled candlesticks to the puddles of melted pewter chalices to the long wooden tables now reduced to firewood. In what had likely once been the library, they came across several pyres, now only ashes. The stink of sweat and fear stained the lush carpets, and not a single book could be found on the endless expanse of shelves.

People were huddled in corners, their faces gaunt, their bodies wrapped in the black ribbons of dark magic.

Wren and Tamsin found the first true sign of life in the kitchens. Wren assumed the scuffling was an animal—even when the form emerged from the pantry, she still thought it a stray dog. It wasn't until the thing righted itself that she realized it was a child.

"Don't," she said, grabbing Tamsin's wrist before she could cast a spell. Wren took a step forward and knelt. The child stared warily at her, his eyes wide, his clothing blackened with soot. He carefully clutched a rotten apple core.

"It smells awful," the witch said, her voice muffled from behind her sleeve. Wren flashed her a fierce look.

"Hello, there." She gave the child a careful smile. "Are you hungry?" The child's eyes flickered over her face with disdain. The answer was so obvious as to be rude. "Here." Wren dropped her sack and rummaged around for a piece of the now slightly stale bread Tamsin had stolen for supper the night before. Wren held the offering out carefully. The child said nothing. Then he lunged, snatching up the bread with one hand while holding tightly to the apple's core with the other. "Are you alone?" she asked.

The child shook his head, crumbs flying as he shoved the bread in his mouth with a grubby little fist. "My ma's here." His words were garbled through his giant bite. "She's hurt."

"Will you show me?" Wren kept her voice soft. Careful. The child eyed her, crumbs spilling from his lips. Then he nodded.

"What are you doing?" Tamsin whispered roughly.

"His mother's hurt. We have to help her."

Behind her, the witch grumbled. "We really don't. For all you know he'll lead us to a group of looters who will use our bodies for firewood."

Wren turned, anger boiling in her veins. "Have you no compassion? No sympathy for anyone but yourself?"

Tamsin stared at her blankly. "No," she finally said. "I'm cursed. That was sort of the point."

"Fine." Wren let of a groan of frustration. She should not have expected better from Tamsin, but of course she had. She always looked for the best in people, even when they gave her reason not to. "Go away, then. But I'm going to see if I can help." She turned to follow the child, who had scampered away, past the giant ovens and the overturned produce baskets. The kitchen floor was littered with rotting onion skins, broken chicken bones, and giant piles of dust so thick and gray they might have been the corpses of mice.

Wren hurried after the child, who had taken a hard right. Something loosened in her chest when she heard Tamsin's footsteps behind her. The witch was still grumbling, but she was there. Wren turned in time to watch the child disappear through a trapdoor in the floor. Tamsin grabbed her wrist.

"You can't be serious." Tamsin gave her a sharp look. "This is stupid, even for you. You don't know who or what might be lurking down there. It's too dangerous."

Wren didn't care. All she could think of was the emptiness in the child's eyes, the way hunger had stripped him down and made him weak. Wanting. She had been that way too. Wren knew what it was to feel hunger—not just the growling of the stomach but the pang of guilt, the fear that she deserved the sick, impossible feeling. The light-headedness. The *hopelessness*.

She could not turn her back now. Not when she knew so intimately what that child was up against. Wren pulled her wrist from Tamsin's grasp and followed the child through the trapdoor.

The stink was much worse below, pungent and hot and stale. Wren tensed at every scuffle, every sniffle, every sob. The dark was so deep that she could see nothing, not even in her mind's eye. When a tiny blue flame flickered to life, she momentarily lost her bearings.

Tamsin hopped down the final rung of the ladder, the light she held illuminating the distaste upon her face. "Hey." The witch's voice was hard. "Stop that."

Wren looked down. The child had pressed a kitchen knife against her hip, the point poking her skin through the thin fabric.

"He wouldn't . . ." But Wren trailed off at the determination on the child's face.

"What do you want?" The voice that came from the shadows was hoarse and thin, like the croaking of a toad. Tamsin lifted her light higher. Wren braced herself, but it illuminated only the face of a woman, defeat written across it in the purple bags beneath her eyes, in the greasy strands of hair, in the dirt that clung to her clothes.

"I'm Wren." She smiled cautiously. The woman didn't look fearsome, nor had the child moved to break her skin with the knife. "I just wanted to see if I could help."

The woman shifted, at great personal cost. She let out a moan, deep and guttural, like a sow ready to birth. It was then that Wren saw the comparison continued. The woman's belly was swollen, apparent even through her many layers of grimy garments.

"Can't help me," the woman groaned, a hand resting against her stomach. "Nothing t'be helped now. Leo, come." Her accent was sharp, like the women in the caravan they'd passed in Ladaugh, her vowels quick and hardly apparent.

Wren felt the child shift, the pressure disappearing as he retreated. She took a hesitant step closer. "Are you in pain?"

The woman grunted. Or laughed? Perhaps neither. Maybe both. "I don't know. All I know's this babe was due three weeks past. She's still in there, kicking. Won't come out. Not now, perhaps not ever, thanks t'this plague." She glanced darkly at her stomach. "Can't say I blame her." She looked up at Wren. "No, lass, just leave me be. Nothing t'be done. Any rate, she's safer in there than out."

The woman's resignation was so absolute that Wren didn't know what to do. "Here." She fumbled in her bag for a few coins. "Take these, at least." Wren's body shuddered as she held them out, her brain rebelling against her heart's offering. But the woman smiled sadly up at her.

"Ah, lass, you're not from here, then. Coins get you nothing. There's nothing t'be got. The queen is gone, left us to die." Her face darkened. "Never mind that I gave up all my years to cook her food. Scrubbed her potatoes, I did, baked her pies with little birds on the crust, and all I've got to show for it is this miserable life. Don't trust a queen, girl. Not even when her face gleams like the sun at the taste of one of your roasts. Never learn to love someone untouchable. They'll only disappoint you in the end."

Wren's throat tightened, and she felt her heart clench at the woman's words, although she could not determine what about them, exactly, affected her so. "No," she said finally, her voice cracking despite her best efforts. "You will not die." She turned to Tamsin, who was wringing her hands helplessly. "Stop that," Wren commanded her, trying to get ahold of herself. "Get this woman some food. Leave her with endless fire and blankets to keep warm."

Tamsin widened her eyes in protest, trying to communicate without speech. Wren sighed.

"Mother, I cannot help you deliver your child, but I can make sure you are well taken care of with food, and blankets, and fire. Do you protest if these items come from a witch's hands?" She stared down at the woman, who blinked blankly at her.

"Lass, I cannot move. I care not where the help comes from— only that it does."

"Well, then." Wren turned to Tamsin. "That settles it. Here." She offered her hand to the witch.

"What's that for?" Tamsin studied her suspiciously.

"To help," Wren snapped. "You keep forgetting that I can help."

Tamsin reached for Wren, and her frozen fingers closed around Wren's palm. Wren shivered, both from the shock and from how quickly the witch had resigned herself to help. She watched as her magic flowed toward Tamsin, turning the color of clay. There was a crackle, the sound of a flame. Tamsin spoke a few words. Magic swirled around the witch and Wren, and for a moment the two of them were surrounded by a tornado of light. It was oddly intimate—ruined, of course, by Tamsin's scowl.

Items burst forth from their magic, settling themselves around the woman and her child: heaping piles of blankets, candles and flint, loaves of dense brown bread still steaming, links of plump sausages, baskets of crisp red apples.

The woman's eyes were so wide they threatened to fall from her face. Leo, the little boy, had already pounced, an entire sausage hanging from his mouth. Tears spilled down the woman's cheeks. "Thank you," she said, her voice breaking. "I cannot thank you enough."

"Then don't," Wren said quietly. "Just take care." She wanted to promise the woman a cure, wanted to reassure her the way she could not reassure herself. But she could offer the woman nothing more than what she had already given. Still, the woman managed a small smile before collapsing back into tears.

Wren turned to usher Tamsin back up the ladder, but the woman stopped her. "That way," she said, pointing into the darkness. "It's how they smuggled wine in from the East. They say the queen is pure of heart"—the woman made a sour face—"but she does still love her drink. There's another trapdoor that'll lead you down the mountain and land you in the center of Farn. Take care. There are men with sharper knives than my Leo here."

She ruffled the boy's hair, but the child was so immersed in his sausage that he did not look up. Wren bid them farewell, her heart heavy. She had done something, but it was not nearly enough.

"Well, that was quite the production," Tamsin said, flicking her wrist at the trapdoor. A rope of magic swirled about the iron ring and pulled it open effortlessly. Daylight flooded the dark room.

"That," Wren said, smiling serenely at the witch, "was called kindness. I thought you could use an education." Her tone was chastising, but not cruel. For Tamsin had aided her, and more willingly than Wren had expected. It had reminded her of that flash she'd seen of Tamsin filled with love, open and thoughtful and full of hope.

Wren glanced down through the hole in the floor. Ladder rungs clung to the side of the mountain. She wondered at the dedication of men carrying crates of wine up to such a precarious entry point. The things people did out of duty. She slipped carefully onto the rungs, her feet finding solid purchase, her fingers wrapping around the iron as tightly as they could. There was still a long way to go.

Halfway down the side of the mountain, Wren glanced up at Tamsin, who was several rungs above. She could see nothing but the worn soles of the witch's boots and the dusty, burr-covered hem of her skirt. Wren carried a similar level of filth. She had taken to breathing mostly through her mouth in order to avoid the sweet, sour smell of herself. Her hopes rose each time they came across a riverbank or stream, and yet every time she got close enough to the sound of running water, she was put off by the sludgy, bubbling mud that filled the banks. Without Tamsin's ability to conjure, Wren would not have had a single drop to drink in days.

Tamsin's heel came down on Wren's fingers. She yelped, letting go for one precarious second to shake out the pain radiating through her hand. Tamsin craned her neck down to see what she was doing.

"What happened?"

"I got distracted." Wren's fingers had turned purple.

"Something new and different for you," Tamsin muttered.

Wren shot her a sharp look but continued her descent. It was quiet save for the fluttering of the breeze and the ever-present grumbling of stone. Lately even the sound of magic had turned dour. Where once stone had sung, now it groaned. Trees that had whispered now shrieked. Even water, which used to jangle merrily, like bells or copper coins, now rang out stiffly, like iron against an anvil.

After a few minutes, Tamsin stopped moving and peered down at her. "I didn't steal any of that stuff."

Wren blinked, not following. "Sorry, what?"

"The food and blankets we gave to the woman," Tamsin said. "I conjured it. Brand-new, just for her. I never thought about where things came from before you. But this time I did. No one was left wanting because we helped her."

Wren stared up at her, frowning slightly. "Okay?"

"I just thought, if you're distracted because you're trying to come up with another way to lecture me, you should know I didn't steal it." The corners of Tamsin's mouth turned downward slightly before she shook her head. "It was more work—a *lot* more—but I did it. So I really, really don't need another lecture, okay?"

"Hmm." Wren made a soft, noncommittal noise. She couldn't help but feel like Tamsin was trying to be kind. It wasn't really working, but it did seem like she was trying. That was something. "Let's maybe finish this conversation when we're both on solid ground?"

"No conversation to have," Tamsin said quickly. "Just thought you ought to know. Don't look down."

Of course that was exactly what Wren did. They had gone a long way, but the height was still dizzying. "Yep," she said shakily, "I'm just going to focus on these rungs now."

But it wasn't so simple. She started to consider Tamsin, the way the witch lacked her usual bite. The way she had been almost kind. Wren knew Tamsin was keeping secrets from her—the leather-bound book, for one, and the way her eyes went cloudy sometimes, like she was looking far, far away, her sarcastic tone a clear defense mechanism for some sort of grief—but now she wondered if Tamsin had other secrets too. Secrets about herself, about the person she would be without her curse. The person she would be if she could love.

Wren shook her head. She was being ridiculous. She put the witch out of her mind, focused on keeping herself steady and balanced. Her arms were shaking. Her stomach growled. Still they descended. When finally her foot found solid ground, Wren was exhausted, from both steeling her mind and manipulating her body. Tamsin hopped down from the final rung, her boots smacking the cobblestones with a thud.

They had come out in an alley. The buildings around them were strange, a jumble of dark wood and light stone, pressed together and stacked upon one another like teetering piles of coins. Wren had never seen anything like them. The people of Farn practically lived on top of one another, whereas her closest neighbor was an entire cornfield away.

Tamsin, sidestepping puddles and discarded trash, led them under several low-hanging archways and down tiny steps built into the sloping hill. Wren followed, watching her feet. It was eerily silent. Despite the number of buildings, there seemed to be very few people in them. The people they did encounter were empty-eyed, huddled in corners, dressed in dirty rags, covered in their own sick. The black mark of the plague hung about the afflicted like blankets. Still, they shivered despite the late-afternoon heat. Their patches of lank, greasy hair, their brittle bones, their blank expressions, haunted her even after she passed.

Was that what her father looked like now?

Her stomach still squirming uncomfortably, Wren hurried after Tamsin, who had stopped a good thirty paces ahead, where the twisting alleyway opened up to the center of the city. Wren came to a halt beside her.

This must have been a marketplace once, a giant square filled with vendors and goods and wares. But now a great rift had run through the cobblestones to create a vast canyon. Wren took a careful step forward, still far from the edge but at a better vantage point. Far below lay the splintered remains of stalls and wooden carts, the carcasses of horses, and the bones of many, many people.

Giant black birds, their feathers gleaming blue in the late-afternoon light, circled overhead. Several perched on a horse's giant rib cage, surveying their domain. One had a strip of flesh hanging from its beak. The stench was overwhelming, the sun so strong against the pavement that the heat shimmered before their eyes.

Bile rose in the back of Wren's throat. She was suddenly and violently sick across the cobblestones. "Get me out of here," she said sharply, her breath catching, her vision going spotty as she struggled to fill her lungs with air. "Please, I can't look anymore. I can't."

Tamsin rolled her eyes. "Very well. Should've guessed you'd have a weak stomach." But she ushered Wren away, offering up a corner of her cloak. "To mask the smell." Wren took it. While the cloak had a musty scent to it from so many days on the road, there was still a hint of Tamsin's magic, the bite of fresh herbs.

Wren focused on those herbs, listing as many as she could in order to distract herself from the horrors she had seen. Rosemary. Dill. Thyme. Sage. Tarragon. The birds' black feathers glinted blue in the sun. Wren gasped and shivered, stumbling after Tamsin, not knowing where they were headed, not caring in the least so long as they got far, far away from the hole in the ground and the rank, rotten smell of the dead.

ELEVEN

TAMSIN

Had Tamsin not been so focused on corralling a simpering, spluttering Wren, she would have noticed the men. There were two of them in the alley ahead, each nearly twice the girls' size in both height and mass, their skin so pale it was almost translucent. One was bent over a corpse, rummaging through the poor man's pockets. The other was picking dirt from beneath his fingernails with a knife.

Tamsin stopped. Wren, her face still buried in Tamsin's cloak, rammed into her, causing Tamsin to stumble and swear. The men looked up with interest. The one in front was tall, with long hair so fair it might have been white. It was braided into thick ropes that were tied beneath his chin like a second beard.

The man behind him had brown hair down to his waist, his beard just as long.

"Why are we stop—oh." Wren's eyes narrowed as she took in the scene before her.

Tamsin grabbed Wren's wrist sharply in warning, sparks of magic pooling in her palm. Wren had the propensity to act rashly in the name of morality. These men were stealing from the dead. Wren could hardly be trusted to keep her mouth shut. And indeed, as she realized what was happening, Wren's expression shifted from confusion to contempt. "What are you—ow!" The shout was directed at Tamsin, who had dug her fingernails deep into the girl's flesh.

"Oh, come now," the fair-haired man said, his accent clipped, his tone mocking, "I don't bite." He flashed them a glittering smile, made more unnerving by the exceptional whiteness of his teeth. Teeth that blinding were out of place against the man's rough, rugged appearance. His clothing was smudged and fraying, his boots caked with dirt, and he wore a series of increasingly vicious-looking knives tucked into his black belt. The dark-haired man wore a grubby, matted fur and carried a giant bow slung over his shoulder.

Tamsin swallowed thickly. The blond man handled his knives too tenderly to have stolen them, which meant he was from Orathe, the wintry village in the North. Orathen hunters were well known for both their violence and their superstitions. Not the sort of men a witch wanted to meet in a darkening alley—for the sun was now setting, drifting behind the stone buildings of the city and bathing the streets in shadow.

"You shouldn't be out on the streets alone," the dark-haired man said. "You need someone to protect you. Lucky for you, we take all kinds of payment." He smiled wolfishly, revealing similarly garish teeth.

"No, thank you." Tamsin kept her voice clipped and detached. "We're fine." She took a step backward, pulling Wren along with her. The man's beady eyes narrowed, and he crossed the cobblestones quickly. So quickly that Tamsin knew it would be useless to try to outrun them.

"What," he said, his breath hot and putrid even from a distance, "too good?" He eyed Tamsin with disdain.

The blond man sauntered toward them. "Maybe your friend here feels differently." He held out a grubby hand, his nails caked with dirt, his skin stained with blood. Wren visibly recoiled. The man's face twisted with fury, and he moved to grab her.

Tamsin flicked her wrist. The man's long blond braids fell into a heap on the cobblestones. Braids that would have taken him years to grow, countless kills to earn. The man stumbled backward, his eyes wide—first from panic as he realized his hair had been shorn, then from anger as he realized it was Tamsin who had done it.

"Witch!" he roared, reaching for the largest knife in his belt. Beside him, the dark-haired man had removed the bow from his shoulder. Tamsin blinked quickly, trying to clear away the floating spots of light that had appeared in her vision as a consequence of the spell.

Wren tugged urgently on her hand, but it was useless. They couldn't outrun the men who were glowering down at them with their weapons drawn. It wasn't until Tamsin felt a rush of magic flowing up her arm that she realized Wren wasn't trying to pull her away. She was trying to help. Tamsin's vision cleared. The fair-haired man, who had located his preferred knife, stopped cold, his eyes on Tamsin's and Wren's intertwined hands.

"What's this?" His snarl turned into a sneer as he examined Wren with disdain. "You'll let a witch touch you"—he practically spat in Tamsin's direction—"yet you recoil from me?" He took one deliberate step forward. Careful. Contained. The moment before the kill.

"My people are dying because of you and yours," he said, his full range of fury now directed at Tamsin. He held his knife casually, in a way that belied his skill. "Your death won't change that," he said as Tamsin and Wren took a collective step back, "but it will certainly make me feel better." He flashed them another blinding grin, and then he lunged forward, the tip of his knife aimed at the base of Tamsin's throat.

Tamsin hardly had time to think. With one hand tightly wrapped around Wren's, she spoke a long string of words, the harsh consonants sharp as they rolled off her tongue, and the magic flowed through her as surely as blood through her veins.

The ground beneath the blond man's feet shuddered and cracked. Both men were jerked downward, their hulking figures falling through the cobblestones and hitting the bottom of Tamsin's makeshift pit with thuds so heavy the ground trembled a second time. The men were trapped in a smaller version of the gaping fissure in the square, just large enough for their two hulking bodies and just deep enough that, even if one climbed upon the other's shoulders, they would be unable to get out. Wren hurried to the edge and peered down into the darkness, but Tamsin hung back.

Without the warmth of Wren's magic, cold came sweeping back into her bones. The adrenaline had already begun to wear off, leaving her with the slimy, sticky feeling of wrongness. Once again she had behaved rashly, choosing action over consideration. Once again she had used her power to hurt.

The men below were silent. Tamsin choked down the bile rising in her throat. Soon Wren would turn around and look at her with unmasked horror. She would realize the enormity of Tamsin's power and the fact that she did not deserve to use it, not when it continued to destroy the lives of so many.

Tamsin squeezed her eyes shut. She couldn't bear to see that particularly pained grimace splash itself across Wren's round face. Before, she had been just another witch to Wren. But that was about to change, and for some strange reason, she didn't *want* Wren to see her for the monster she truly was.

"I helped, right?"

Tamsin's eyes flew open. Wren was staring at her eagerly, her expression wide and hopeful.

Tamsin's stomach clenched. "I used your magic, if that's what you mean." She braced herself for the look of horror sure to come when Wren realized that she had aided in the takedown of the two men.

Instead Wren beamed, the smile lighting up her entire face. "That was incredible. I mean, I'm tired, but also I feel . . . exhilarated. Oh, you have a bit of blood." Wren reached for the corner of Tamsin's cloak and used it to dab away the streak of red from the nick on Tamsin's neck. "I was always taught not to hurt anyone, but surely they deserved it. Is it wrong that I'm feeling this way? What *is* this that I'm feeling? Why am I talking so much?" Her face was flushed, her shoulders rising and falling with each quick intake of air.

Tamsin eyed the girl warily. Something was different about her. She looked taller somehow, her face vivid and visibly striking in a way Tamsin had never before noticed. She looked settled. Present. Alive.

It was entirely the opposite of what Tamsin had expected. But the joy was there, written on Wren's face plain as day. A feeling so far from Tamsin that all she could do was marvel at it.

"What?" Wren's smile slipped slightly. "What's the matter?"

"Nothing," Tamsin said, more confidently than she felt. If Wren wasn't deterred by her action, if she felt something *good*, then maybe that meant Tamsin wasn't as terrible as she currently felt. Maybe that meant that her actions had been justified.

"Agency looks good on you," she told the girl honestly. "You look taller."

"What?" Wren spluttered, pressing a hand to her cheek.

Tamsin narrowed her eyes uncomprehendingly. "Why are you flailing?"

"I—" Wren gaped at her. "You just gave me a compliment." Her tone was accusatory.

Tamsin took a step back. "I did not." She hadn't meant to, at any rate. She'd simply been making an observation. Wren *did* look better when she wasn't hunched over, when she wasn't tugging on her hair or picking at her cuticles. Wren was always worrying. Of course Tamsin would notice when she wasn't.

It seemed simple enough. She didn't know why Wren had to start blushing everywhere. Tamsin straightened her cloak. "Come on, then."

"Wait." Wren cast a glance over her shoulder, biting her lip as she stared at the pit. Tamsin's heart sank. The longer the girl looked, the more certain Tamsin was that Wren had changed her mind about the situation. "Do you think they're going to die here?" Wren turned toward Tamsin, eyes worried.

"I don't know." Tamsin's voice was so soft she hardly heard it herself. She didn't want Wren to turn her back on her now. Not when they were so close to the Wood. Tamsin didn't have the strength to go Within alone. It would be too easy to walk away.

Wren was silent for what seemed like an eternity, eyes fixed on the gaping hole in the earth. Then she seemed to make some sort of decision, nodding once, sharp and short. "I want his knife. The one he cut you with."

Tamsin blinked at her uncomprehendingly. "Why?"

Wren took a moment to answer. "So he can't ever use it again."

"Do you even know how to use a knife?" She could only imagine the sort of inadvertent damage Wren could do with that sort of weapon. Yet there was something else, something in her that wanted to see what Wren would look like holding one.

And so Tamsin did not wait for an answer. She simply called for it, and the vicious, beautiful thing flew through the air toward her like an arrow. She admired it for a moment, the etching so delicate it could only have been done with a needle, before handing it over to Wren, who tucked the blade into her belt as though it had always belonged there.

They turned away, a surprisingly amicable silence between them. Neither Tamsin nor Wren looked back.

They were close to the Wood. Tamsin could hear it, the soft swishing of wind through the leaves, the names of the runes carved into the twisted trunks by the hands of her ancestors. It was an ancient magic, heavy and powerful.

A magic Tamsin had never expected to witness again.

She ran a hand over the mottled skin on her left arm. She wondered if the Wood would recognize her, or if it would send out a call alerting the Coven of her imminent return. She hoped it was not so specific. She hoped that it would sense only her power and offer her safe passage.

She hated that she did not know for sure.

"What's wrong?" Wren was nearly ten paces ahead of her. Tamsin had not realized she had stopped walking.

"Nothing." But her tone was not as sharp as she hoped. It seemed to only offer proof that the opposite was true.

Wren frowned but did not push. She merely waited for Tamsin to catch up before continuing on.

The trees were getting louder, their creaks and moans reminding Tamsin of the last time she had made her way through the tangled Wood, away from the life and the world she had always known. Away from the lifeless body of her sister. Cursed to be forever alone. She still remembered the way the trees had shrieked as she hurried past.

When the dark witch Evangeline had been caught using dark magic, the High Councillor had killed her. Everyone, including Tamsin herself, had expected that she'd meet the same fate.

But the High Councillor had banished Tamsin instead. Cursed her, yes, but let her go alive. She had been twelve years old. A child. Still, the rest of the Coven had wanted her dead. She was certain they still did.

If they tried to kill her upon her return, she wondered if she would mind. Tamsin had a tenuous relationship with life. It still seemed strange that she should live while her sister was dead. It seemed as though the lives of twins should be similar to the balance required of magic and the earth. One was not right without the other. One should not die without the other. That was why she had worked so hard to save Marlena's life.

Tamsin stumbled, weighed down by more than just her memories. A pocket of her cloak tore, as though it were stuffed with stones rather than a thin black book. She sighed, the message clear as day. She pulled out the diary, and, sure enough, the pages fell open to a new entry.

After darting a quick glance ahead at Wren, who was humming softly to herself as she walked with her face raised toward the sky, Tamsin looked down at her sister's words. The handwriting spilled across the page. The ink bled with tears.

Tamsin's heart sank. She should have known this entry was coming. She had been tracking the timeline, the entries the diary chose to show her. Everything led to this one terrible moment when the world began to fall apart.

She wanted to shut the book, but the cover wouldn't budge. Instead she stared at Marlena's words, reminding herself it was all her fault.

I don't want to write it down. I can't write it down. Because if I write it down, that means it's true, and Amma can't be dead. See? It looks ridiculous, written down. Girls don't die Within. Witches don't die (unless they're me, but even I didn't actually die despite the number of times I was told my chances looked grim). I hate myself for making this about me. For trying to be funny the way you can't when something has ripped your heart out and left you numb. Empty. Cold.

It's been raining for thirty-one days, and my best friend is dead. Drowned in her own bed. It's cruel the way magic works. Amma had sight, so no one thought they had to warn her. Everyone thought she'd be the first one out. But she had a headache that day. She'd come to my room, asked to sleep in my bed, but I'd only just come from the infirmary and didn't want to lie still in a dark room. And so I sent her away. Away to a room where the water seeped through the windowsill until it filled her lungs.

She's dead. And the world is wrong. It has taken on a tilt, just the slightest angle,

everything sharp, even with all the water.
Everything off.

Tamsin's stopped talking. I swear, you'd
think it was her best friend who died, the way
she carries on, eyes ringed red. She didn't
even like Amma. Always resented her, I think,
because Amma "stole" me away. Not that it's
stealing if you go willingly. But Tamsin never
understood that, did she? No, it was only ever
about what she wanted. Who she thought I was.
Who she wanted me to be. It was always about
Tamsin. It was never about me.

She hasn't even come to see me. Not that
I'd let her, mind you—I'd turn everyone away,
even the High Councillor, although of course she
hasn't got the time. She's getting nervous, you
can tell. No one knows what's going on, not even
the Coven. Her grip is slipping. And she can't
afford to let go.

Me, on the other hand, well, I've got nothing
left to lose.

"Seriously, what is the matter with you?" Wren's hands were
on her hips, her expression impossible to decipher.

"Nothing." Tamsin's tone was particularly vicious, a grating octave that usually stopped Wren from pressing the way she
always pressed. Marlena's entries were changing; her resentment
was now tinged with hatred. Her bitterness was now disgust.

Tamsin had always thought she'd done a good job disguising her anxiety over their dark-magic bond. She thought she'd muffled her guilt and grief over Amma's death. But Marlena had seen right through her.

And hadn't said a word.

"Tamsin." That was all Wren said, just her name, in a voice so patient it made her want to scream. She was staring at the book still open in Tamsin's shaking hands.

Tamsin deserved this uncertainty—the sour taste of fear on her tongue—and Wren deserved the truth. But if Tamsin made it through the Wood, if she was able to set foot Within, she needed someone on her side. Someone who didn't look at her with trepidation. With fear.

Wren couldn't know that Tamsin was a murderer, however inadvertent. She would turn away, would cut and run, and any chance of finding the witch responsible for the dark magic would vanish. Tamsin wasn't brave enough to step into the Wood on her own. She needed Wren. Which meant she could only offer her a glimpse of her past.

"The last time a witch used dark magic, a girl in my class died. Two girls, actually." The hollow rasp of her voice was not an act. She fumbled with the diary, shoving it in a pocket so that it disappeared from view. "Seeing the world like this now, it . . . it brings it all back. Every awful thing. I want to stop this, but . . . I'm afraid."

She couldn't believe she'd said it out loud.

Neither, apparently, could Wren. "Why didn't you tell me?" She stared at Tamsin with wide eyes, sympathy sticking to every syllable she spoke. The softness of her tone made Tamsin feel guilty. Still, she had to admit it was nice to have someone who didn't know the truth. A girl who didn't look at her like she was a monster.

"It hurts too much," Tamsin finally admitted, reveling for just a moment in the truth. "The remembering. Being here. I . . ." She trailed off helplessly, the forest looming ahead, greater and more terrible than her memories. Towering higher than her fear. What if the trees did not offer her entry?

Oh, but what if they did?

Tamsin had been born Within, had never moved through the Wood on her way *toward* the world of magic. She did not know what to expect. Could not gauge what would happen next.

"We'll go together." Wren's voice was no more than a whisper, her face guarded but hopeful. "Into the Wood." She offered a hand to Tamsin, who stared at it blankly. "You're not alone," Wren tried again. "You don't have to be afraid."

But the words were so foreign as to be nonsense. Tamsin was alone, and she always would be. That was the nature of her curse. The nature of *her*.

When she did not reach for Wren's hand, Wren reached for hers instead, and Tamsin let herself be led toward the tangle of trees.

"Are you ready?" Wren gave Tamsin a significant look.

They both knew the answer was no. They both knew the answer didn't matter in the end.

Stomach squirming, Tamsin pressed a hand against a knotted trunk. With a creak and a groan, the branches began to recoil, twisting away from her touch like a hand from fire. Instead of finding relief in the fact that the trees were prepared to offer her entry, Tamsin's entire being was charged with a great, deep fear.

"I don't know what we'll find in there," she whispered, the truth bitter on her tongue. She had asked Leya what it had been like to walk through the trees. Leya had shuddered, never giving her a complete answer. All she'd ever offered was that it felt like the Wood was asking her two questions: *Are you one of us?* and *Can you survive?*

"That's okay." Wren's eyes were wide, filled with a wonder Tamsin could not fathom. Perhaps it was the source's certainty of her own power, a concept unimaginable to Tamsin, who could think only of her own failings. But then Wren smiled, and the longing within her was so earnest it made Tamsin want to pinch her. "I've been waiting my whole life to find out."

"Lucky you," Tamsin said, her sarcasm erased by the warble of fear in her voice.

"Lucky us," Wren said, squeezing Tamsin's hand.

The witch took a deep breath, Wren set her shoulders, and together they stepped into the shadow of the Wood.

TWELVE

WREN

It was dark beneath the canopy of trees, the moon peeking through the thick leaves in slivers just wide enough to give the illusion of light. The silence of the grove had given way to whispers in a language Wren couldn't understand—unrelenting whispers that grew more urgent with every step she took.

She was all alone now. Just a girl in a grove—her hand empty, her skin cold with the ghost of Tamsin's grip. The moment she had set foot inside the trees, they had been yanked apart. And though Wren had called for her, there was no sign of the witch's brown eyes, no cascade of soft, dark hair. There was only Wren.

Wren and slippery, silky magic.

She had disturbed something when she stepped into the

Wood. It moved around her as though she were a stone casting ripples in a pond. The magic within her was drawn to the magic of this place. The power inside her was begging to belong to the trees.

She thought she ought to panic. She thought she ought to be afraid. Instead something within her swelled. She was in the *Witchwood*. It was a moment she had spent her life dreaming of—the sort of dream that existed only in the darkest part of the night. It had never occurred to her that such a dream could come true. Yet here she was, between the trees. Each step forward took her closer to the world Within. To the Witchlands.

To the place where she belonged.

For the longer Wren had spent on the road with Tamsin, and the more she learned about the world that she had always denied herself, the more certain she was that she needed to see it. She had to *know*. No more running. It was time to start embracing her true self.

And her true self was brought out by Tamsin. There was a tentative kindness forming there. Taking down the men together had been exhilarating, had made Wren feel invincible. It had made her feel like the connection between them wasn't a coincidence—that they had been meant to find each other.

And then, before they'd stepped into the Wood, all her hard work had paid off. Tamsin had shared a secret of her own accord. She had finally stopped fighting Wren, stopped hiding, and had offered a momentary view of true vulnerability. They were making progress. Progress toward what, Wren didn't know. But it felt like something vast and wild and important.

Almost as important as the way the hair stood up straight on her arms, the way a chill trickled down her spine. The way the sharp, warm spice of the solstice settled on her tongue. Her body was at odds with her mind. The magic draped lazily across her. Yet she could not quite give in. In the back of her mind, her father's voice lingered.

Warning her of the way magic crept in to corrupt a soul.

Wren paused before a ring of trees, their trunks covered in symbols—crude, unintelligible carvings that looked as impossible as the whispers sounded. Between the trunks hung a gossamer layer of magic, thin and delicate as a spider's web. Wren brushed her fingers against it, testing for a hint of pain or sharp heat. Instead the magic whispered against her hand like a feather across soft skin.

She moved through as though she were moving through water, the steady trickle of magic washing over her. Past the shimmering waterfall of power, colors became so sharp Wren could taste them. Lush lilac-purple lavenders, blushing powdered-sugar pinks, and creamy sky blues all settled themselves on her tongue.

The trees around her creaked and moaned, their branches lifting up toward the sky. The wildflowers at her feet opened their mouths to take great, gasping breaths. Wren's presence had stirred something. Had caused the Witchwood to wake.

Each time she lifted a foot, tiny toadstools burst up in her track, their reds bright against the damp, mossy brown of the forest floor. She was altering the Witchwood, leaving a mark. It was exactly where she was supposed to be. The forest needed her.

For the first time, Wren felt powerful.

And then the whispers changed. Their words became decipherable, the accents familiar. The consonants slapped against the back of teeth. The same way her father rounded his Os. Her heart caught in her throat. The strength she had felt only moments ago dissipated.

"No!" her father's voice shouted, and Wren knew exactly whom he was facing. The memory swirled around her, vivid yet unstable.

She was a child again, barely eight, crouching in the chicken coop, surrounded by the squawking of the hens. Their feathers ruffled as she invaded their space, but she ignored them, pressing her eye against a hole in the warped wooden slats.

A witch was at the gate, sighing wearily, already tired of the ornery, ordinary man waving his finger in her face. It had startled Wren then how *old* her father was. She had always known her parents were closer to the ages of the grandparents of her playmates, that losing their first baby was a loss they'd never gotten over. That she had come along so many years later, when they had finally given up all hope. But it was stark to see the shock of his white hair next to the enchanted, glossy mane of the witch.

"My son was killed during the Year of Darkness," her father was insisting. "Get away from here before I make you."

Even Wren—who had been huddled in the chicken coop for hours at her father's insistence, her knees red with the imprint of the straw beneath them—knew the threat was empty. Her father was not a cruel man. He was merely afraid. Had been since the moment the farmer came banging on the door to let him know there was a witch in town.

"They won't take another child from me." Her father simmered and stormed, ranted and raved, anger turning his face ruddy and red. His fear was so thick that Wren nearly choked on it. But the pain behind his eyes, his frenzied fervor, was enough to keep her silent despite the way she watched the air crackle and shimmer around the witch. Her little heart ached, so desperate was she to be discovered. But the witch never looked toward the chicken coop. Instead she sighed dispassionately. Then Wren blinked, and the woman was gone.

As she relived the memory, the Witchwood grew darker, the colors swirling into shadows, the night endless and suffocating. It suddenly took a great amount of effort to force her legs forward. The dizzying roar of the trees echoed in her ears like the furious churning of water through a wheel. Everything was imprecise, like an off-pitch note or a too-bright flame. Wren wanted to crawl out of her own skin. Her heart was hammering. And through it all, a worry wormed its way into her head. *Wrong*, it seemed to say, but Wren couldn't tell if it was her surroundings or herself that was wrong.

The word tolled endlessly, like a bell, the darkness of its tone creeping across her body like the scurrying of beetles that sometimes crawled across the stale crusts of bread in the cupboard. *This is wrong.* Maybe she shouldn't have come here. Perhaps she'd make it through the trees and find that the witches didn't want her at all.

Would she be punished for having evaded them so long?

Something's wrong. Wren clapped her hands over her ears.

"What's wrong?" This voice was different from the one in

her head. Wren lifted her eyes from where they were fixed upon the grass and gasped as she took in the shining, shimmering outline of the woman before her. It was her mother, familiar in her broad hips and thick arms, her red hair piled atop her head. Her cheeks were plump and had the faintest hint of pink. She looked so alive. Which of course she couldn't be. Her father had burned the body. Wren had helped him scatter the ashes to the wind.

"What are you doing here?" her mother asked. Wren bit her lip so hard it bled. She focused on the pain, the bright, rusty tang on her tongue. She would not cry. She could not cry.

"I'm magic, Mama," she said, the words catching in her throat.

Her mother stared at her, shimmering. "Magic killed your brother, you know."

"I know."

"Are you wicked, Wren?"

"No, Mama." Wren took a step forward, but when she reached out a hand toward her mother, it moved right through. Wren had known it was just a trick of the light, a test of the trees, but disappointment still crashed over her like a wave.

"Then go," her mother said, her voice hoarse and sharp, her figure shimmering faster, as though the magic was fading. "Turn back and go home. Back to your father. Where you belong."

Wren choked back the lump rising in her throat. "I belong here, too."

"Save yourself," her mother said. But it wasn't her mother, not really. It was her image, perhaps, but not her heart.

"I'll show you," Wren said, careful and quiet. "I *am* good."

And though regret swirled in her chest, though she felt her heart splinter and crack, she walked away, past the image of her mother and deeper into the Witchwood.

She knew now it was the only way out.

Tamsin was screaming.

Wren hurried toward her, stumbling over sharp branches stuck in the muddy earth and leaping over logs as wide as she was tall. When she found the witch, Tamsin's eyes were wide with horror, her face pale, her gaze fixed on something Wren couldn't see.

"It isn't real," Wren said softly, her hand hovering over Tamsin's shoulder. "Whatever you're seeing, it isn't real." When Wren touched her lightly, Tamsin yelped with alarm, her face crumpling with hope and despair as she took in the girl before her.

"It's okay," Wren said, her shaking voice revealing how little she herself believed it. "You're okay."

"It isn't." Tamsin's mouth twisted wryly, her whole body still trembling. "I'm not."

Wren tugged on the tail of her braid to stop herself from reaching toward the witch. "What did it show you?" For it was clear that Tamsin had come face-to-face with something haunting, something as horrible as what Wren had faced.

"Nothing." Tamsin's eyes dimmed, her mind far away, wrapped up in another secret Wren was not privy to.

"I saw my mother." Wren could still see her shimmering outline, the hope in her eyes that Wren would listen and abandon her quest. "She told me not to give in to my magic. To go home to my father. And I walked away. Because I knew I had to keep going. I left her behind." She looked the witch in the eyes and made her hold on to the horror of what she had dealt with. "So don't act like you're the only one who has suffered."

Tamsin did not look away. Finally she sighed with resignation. "That girl who died? I'm the one who killed her."

Wren felt as though she'd been punched in the gut. "What?"

"I didn't mean to," Tamsin said, blinking furiously. "I was trying to save someone's life."

The fact that Tamsin, the most selfish and self-centered person Wren had ever met, had tried to do something that immense for another person was so unfathomable as to be impossible.

"Anyway, it didn't work. Two lives were lost, thanks to my spell. And I have to live with that. *I* did that." The witch busied herself with adjusting her cloak, her face pinched. "No one will let me forget it. Not even the Wood."

Wren started walking, brain buzzing. She had always suspected Tamsin's past to be fraught, but she now realized she had underestimated the depths of the witch's pain. The monumental weight of the guilt she was carrying.

"Where are you going?" Tamsin hurried after her.

"Getting us out of here. These trees will not defeat us." Wren stalked forward, chin up, shoulders back. She was magic, and she would not lose to the Witchwood. "Hurry up."

"I am hurrying," Tamsin said, her breath huffing as she worked to keep up.

"Your legs are longer than mine," Wren said, trying to keep

her voice light, although her stomach was still churning with the understanding of exactly how much power Tamsin held. It was one thing to watch her summon food or fire. It was another thing to imagine her with enough magic to end a life.

She shivered, hoping it passed as a reaction to the shadows around them, the breeze blowing straight into their faces. The whispers of the trees had faded to a dull ringing in her ears. In the distance were pinpricks of light, sparkling and twinkling like stars. The darkness that had crept up her throat, threatening to choke her, was starting to dispel. She was beginning to feel like herself again. Settled. Which could only mean that they were almost to the other side.

Wren reached for Tamsin's hand and pulled the witch forward, ignoring her startled cry. All that mattered was getting out of the Witchwood. Tamsin begged for her to slow down, but Wren could not, *would* not, until she saw a break in the trees, until she extracted herself from their tangled trunks and wanting branches.

Outside the Witchwood, the night was cool and calm. Wren dropped her sack and spun, giddy at the freedom of the wide open space. She had made it. She was in the Witchlands—she was in the world Within.

"What are you doing?" Tamsin pulled her hand free from Wren's grasp, still panting. Yet, despite her bemused tone, her eyes were wide with relief.

"Celebrating." They had done it. They'd made it through. Despite the horrors she had witnessed, she also finally had pure, indisputable proof that she belonged in the world of magic.

"You look ridiculous," Tamsin said, her eyes darting around the empty night.

"You're not a little bit excited?" Wren stopped spinning. "Didn't you grow up here? Won't people be pleased to see you?"

"Pleased?" Tamsin's face fell, her features pained. She looked like an entirely different person. Not the cold girl who had laughed when Wren demanded payment for her stolen eggs. This Tamsin looked sad. Vulnerable. Afraid.

"That's not the word I'd use," purred a voice. Wren and Tamsin whipped around to find a girl about their own age, her lips painted a vivid red, her hair dark and glossy. A long black cloak was draped over her broad shoulders, giving her the quality of a shadow. Her eyes, bright and frenetic, were fixed on Tamsin. Her lips quirked into a wicked grin. "Oh, Tamsin. I know the Coven put out the call to all witches, but surely you didn't think that meant you, too."

Wren turned to Tamsin, confused by the stranger's mocking tone. But Tamsin did not meet Wren's eye. She stared straight ahead, her face even paler than usual. She looked resigned, an emotion so wholly foreign on her usually smug face.

"Leya." Something dark and heavy lingered in the air between the witch and the stranger. Wren found herself desperate to catch Tamsin's eye, but she did not look her way. "What are you doing here?"

"*I* live here, remember?"

Tamsin shifted her weight awkwardly. "I meant at the border."

"Vera asked me to accompany her during her patrol. You

never know who might walk through the Wood." Leya twirled a dark curl around her finger. "I work for the Coven now."

Tamsin paled. "Vera's here?"

Before Leya could answer, a woman appeared where there had not been a woman before. She moved across the grass quickly in long, clipped strides. The woman was very beautiful, and absolutely terrifying. Her magic looped above her, less like a ribbon and more like a rope. Thick. Sturdy. Strong—perhaps *too* strong.

She was the witch in every ordinary folk's story, the one who charmed parents while stealing babies from their beds, who had a face of beauty but a cold, rotten heart. She looked as though she could take a bite through steel.

"Tamsin." The woman finally spoke with a voice as lush as poisoned wine. "You're looking . . . well." Her eyes lingered on Tamsin's muddy skirt and tangled hair. Wren recognized the set of Tamsin's jaw, the defiant fire in her eyes. Her defenses were high. This was not a woman she trusted.

"High Councillor." Tamsin gave the woman a deferential nod. Her voice was oddly strangled.

"Oh, come now," the woman said, her bloodred lips curving up in a predatory grin. "Is that any way to greet your mother?"

THIRTEEN

TAMSIN

It was dark in the tower, the black shadows of night seeping across the gray stone floor, yet Tamsin did not need a torch. She could have kept her eyes closed for how well she knew the twists and turns from the front door of the academy to the High Councillor's chambers.

Tamsin ran a hand against the cool, curved wall, her fingers dragging the way her feet wanted to as she followed her mother's clipped footsteps left, right, right, then another left before ascending a winding set of stairs.

She'd had to leave Wren down in the Grand Hall to face the Six alone. Those six ancient witches were all that remained of the old guard, the leaders before Vera and her friends had taken down the dark witch Evangeline and founded the Coven. The Six had always been performative—after all, their negligence was the reason Evangeline had managed to call forth dark magic in the first place. They were figureheads of power without follow-through. Magical law was neither dictated nor enforced, so witches roamed free, taking advantage of ordinary folk and one another alike. The Six had lived with magic so long that they'd forgotten it could corrupt. Could inspire chaos. Could destroy.

After Evangeline, the Six had ceded control of Within to the Coven. They were called in on the rarest of occasions to aid when the Coven could not. With Vera distracted by Tamsin, and the rest of the Coven out hunting the dark witch, it was up to the Six to interrogate Wren, a girl without a mark who had walked through the Wood. Tamsin wanted to be there with her. But what Tamsin wanted did not matter when faced with her mother.

Of course Vera had been waiting for her. Tamsin had been foolish to believe she could return Within and somehow evade all the people she so desperately wished to avoid. The High Councillor knew everything that happened Within. Naturally, she would know who was coming through the Wood.

Back in the hallowed halls of the academy, Tamsin was nearly suffocated by her memories. She could not escape her past, not even in her present as she followed her mother higher and higher up the spiral stairs. The Wood had reverberated with Amma's screams. Had shown her the shimmering outline of Marlena's body dropping to the floor.

Then she had been faced with Leya, her smug smile and the glittering eyes Tamsin had loved back when she'd had a heart.

She deserved Leya's venom. They had parted ways poorly. Tamsin had asked Leya to sacrifice everything but had offered her nothing in return.

She had been so consumed with Marlena that she had forgotten how to care about anyone else.

Vera touched the handle of a gray stone door and whispered a quiet word. A lock clicked, and the door swung open, revealing her private chambers. The antechamber housed two more doors, both made of wood. To the left was Vera's office, where she worked and disciplined. To the right was her bedroom, with its enormous four-poster bed and gold tub. Tamsin and Marlena had slept in her chamber as toddlers, but once their magic made an appearance, they were assigned beds in the dormitories with the other students.

Instead of settling into her personal chamber and offering up any of its numerous plush armchairs, Vera ushered Tamsin into her study, motioning for her to sit in the straight-backed chair reserved for those facing Vera's ire.

"I'll be with you shortly," she said, flashing her daughter a smile that was only teeth. And then she shut the door firmly behind her.

The room was smaller than Tamsin had remembered, the air stale. The tall shelves were still crammed with books; her mother's raven-feather quill still stood on the wide desk. Vera's favorite cloak, made of velvet black as midnight, hung from a peg near the door. But the chairs had been moved several inches to the left, the brick of the fireplace replaced with stone. The tapers Vera burned were now made from white wax rather than the black she had once preferred. Small things, hardly noticeable. But Tamsin noted them all.

Five years had changed the room, the way she, too, had changed.

She shifted in her chair, the sharp edge of Marlena's diary digging into her hip. She pulled out the little black book, turned it over in her hands. Tamsin had never imagined she'd be here again, suffocating in the tiny tower room, facing every terrible decision she had ever made. She ran a finger across the ragged edges of the diary, her heart sinking as it fell open.

Not again. Not now. Not here.

But she couldn't not look. The curve of her sister's handwriting was like a spell coaxing her closer, drawing her nearer.

You're not going to believe this (of course you won't; you're only a diary), but someone Within is using dark magic. The rains, the fires, the quaking, Amma's death. It's all the consequence of a spell. Someone's stupid, selfish decision, their need for power, is the reason my best friend is dead. I'm so furious I'm shaking.

Vera's falling to pieces. She's been locked in her study; she's stopped showing up to classes. It doesn't matter what we learn if the world's going to end. And even if the world doesn't end, Vera's world might. She thought that Evangeline was the worst of it. She and the Coven have been working so hard to build a new world, to gain the trust of the ordinary folk again. But it's already coming undone, and under her reign.

The only blessing is that the dark magic has not spread past the Wood. The world Beyond does not yet know what is happening Within. So naturally, Vera summoned Arwyn home to put an end to this once and for all. That's right, the most terrifying member of the Coven is back, with her emerald-bright eyes and her smile as sharp as knives.

I don't envy whoever is responsible for this mess. Whoever they are, Arwyn will track them down with her eerily attuned nose and her awful skeleton army. And then, once the dark witch is found, they'll have to face the wrath of my mother, a woman terrified of losing her position of power.

I wonder if they'll put her to death.

And I say "her" because I know who did it. Well, I think I do, anyway. We may not be very close these days, but I can still tell when Tamsin is hiding something. And she's a wreck. Sleeping all the time, her power fading in and out. She looks haggard, like she's suddenly aged a hundred years. She's guilty about something. This is the only explanation.

My sister is the reason my best friend is

dead, and to be honest, I'm having a difficult
time convincing myself that she doesn't
deserve what's coming to her. Amma is dead
because of something Tamsin did.

But what I don't understand is why. It doesn't
make any sense. Tamsin has more power in her
left hand than the rest of our class put together.
She doesn't need dark magic. She would never
use dark magic, because that would be breaking a
rule, and Tamsin's such a stickler for rules it makes
me want to scream. But this … this is something
different altogether.

What is my sister hiding? What did Tamsin
do?????

It was the same question her mother had asked her when
Arwyn brought her to the Grand Hall, flinging twelve-year-old
Tamsin onto the marble floor in front of the five other members
of the Coven.

"What did you do?" Vera's fingers had dug so deeply into
Tamsin's skin as she marched her daughter up the endless staircase
to her chambers that Tamsin had been black-and-blue for weeks.
Vera had thrown her daughter into a chair and glowered down at
her, the cracks already apparent in her usual pristine expression.

"She was going to die." Tamsin's voice was small.

"I told you no." Her mother's words were sharp enough to
slice through skin, but Tamsin didn't even flinch. "Do you think
this was easy for *me*, knowing my daughter was going to die? Do

you think you are the only one who cares for her?"

"But—but—" Tamsin stammered, her voice hoarse. "You didn't—"

"I *couldn't*," Vera snapped. "I wanted to. But I told you: We do not dabble in death." Her mother's face flashed with pain. "You've put me in a terrible position, do you know that? Do you have any idea what will happen when this gets out? My daughter, *my* child, the reason for all this destruction. They'll vote me out. They'll kill you. Did you stop to think? Do you *ever* think?" But her voice had lost its edge. "With one stupid, foolish decision, you have taken both my children from me."

"What are you talking about? Marlena's alive."

Vera pursed her lips. "When we break the bond between you—and we *will* break it," she said, stopping Tamsin's protests before she even opened her mouth, "Marlena will not survive it. Your magic is the only thing keeping her alive. When the bond is broken, we will lose her all over again. And you, well . . ." Vera busied herself with the papers atop her desk. "I do not think the Coven will allow you to live either."

Yet here she was, five years later, a flood of memories and guilt and wrongness. Tamsin had survived. Her sister had not. And she carried that with her every single day of her life.

The door opened, and the High Councillor swept back in. She leaned against the corner of her desk, and for a moment she said nothing, simply stared at her daughter.

"What—"

"I—"

They spoke at the same time, then paused, embarrassed.

Their words tumbled into each other's like bodies colliding. The room was off balance. They were not mother and daughter; they were two strangers. They did not know what to say.

"I'm glad you're here," Vera finally managed, her nails tapping against the desk.

Tamsin could hardly contain her shock. Her mother had been the one to cast her curse, the one to push her into the Wood, telling her in no uncertain terms to never return. Of course, that had been a kindness, in that she had pardoned her daughter from death. Still, Tamsin had never been able to shake the feeling that death might have been the kinder option. Five years of guilt was enough to drain the will to live from anyone, whether they could feel love or not.

But then she took in her mother's face, really and truly *looked*. She caught sight of wrinkles around Vera's mouth. Her mother had always looked pristine—her glossy black hair, her vivid red lips, long nails, rouged cheeks—due to the numerous spells that kept her effortlessly young and beautiful. But there was a crack in her composure, noticeable only up close. Something was wrong. Something was tearing her mother apart.

"I didn't do this, if that's what you're thinking. The dark magic. I wouldn't." Tamsin hated how small she sounded. Sitting there in front of her mother, she felt like a child.

Vera smiled sadly.

"What?" Her mother's expression was unsettling. Like there was more to the story than what had already come to pass.

"Look at you," Vera said, holding up a hand to caress Tamsin's cheek.

Tamsin stared at her blankly, Vera's hand like wind upon her skin. She felt no desire to greet her mother in a similar way. She could not even muster up a smile.

"I didn't do this," she said again, her voice stronger this time. Imploring. She needed Vera to understand. She was different. She was steady. She was careful. "I want to help. Who better to find the dark witch than me?"

Her mother gave her a searching look. "Who indeed?"

"I would be an asset. An aid. I've witnessed firsthand the horrors this spell has wrought. I see now. I understand. I know that what I did was wrong. Let me fix it. Let me help." Her knuckles were white, her fingernails pressed so deeply into the flesh of her palms that the creases would likely linger for hours.

All the while, Vera's face betrayed nothing.

"I'm glad you feel that way," she finally said, her eyes fixed on Tamsin's. "For I do require your help."

"You do?" Tamsin sat forward in her chair, apprehension forgotten. She had appealed to her mother, and rather than turning her away, as she had feared, her mother was welcoming her forward.

"I have knowledge," Vera said, "that threatens my position as High Councillor. Were it to be found out, I would lose everything I have spent my life building—the better world where our power is greater than currency, stronger than love, essential in a way that cannot be denied." She paused, letting her words hang heavy in the stale air. "I know who the dark witch is."

Tamsin let her breath out slowly as her mother's words sank in. "Then why haven't you stopped this?" The plague, the dark magic, all of it could end as soon as Vera said the word. The way she had when it had been Tamsin's spell. When it had been Evangeline.

Vera had instilled an understanding in her daughters that the fate of the world Within was worthy of ultimate sacrifice. Evangeline had been Vera's best friend, Tamsin her daughter. In the end, it hadn't mattered. The world Within was more important than the individual, greater than family. The choices Vera had made for Marlena's life, for Tamsin's future, were proof of that.

Hesitation stretched across Vera's face like a mask. Her uncertainty made her look small. "I cannot."

It was jarring to hear that phrase from the Coven's leader. Her mother was the most powerful witch in the world. She could do anything.

"Why not?" Tamsin's voice was so quiet she wasn't certain she had spoken aloud.

"Because this was my mistake. A miscalculation." Vera pushed herself away from her desk and moved toward her bookshelves. She kept her back to Tamsin, her fingers brushing the covers of books containing spells that were as old as the world. "When you are the Coven's High Councillor, your loyalty must lie with all witches," she said, tugging a slim book from the top shelf and flipping idly through the pages. "But when you are a mother . . ." She trailed off, looking uncomfortable. "Sometimes your priorities change."

Tamsin frowned. Vera had never seemed particularly interested in being a mother. Certainly, she'd been in her daughters' lives, as their teacher, an authority figure—a mentor, even. But not as a parent. Their relationship was not warm. Tamsin was a person, born from another person, valued and cherished for her power. Nothing more.

"But you didn't contact me. Not once in five years did I ever hear from you."

Vera closed the book and clutched it to her chest. "I knew you would find your way. You are strong. You were always going to survive. Your sister, however . . ." She trailed off again, her eyes far away.

"Didn't." Tamsin hated how bitter she sounded. It wasn't Vera's fault Marlena was dead. It was her own. Her rash decisions and desperate need to be loved had done this. And no matter what, she would always have to carry it, like a stone in her pocket, with every step she took on this earth.

"I'm sorry," Vera said, her eyes still focused on the stars shining outside the tower's tiny window. "It was the only way. The only way life Within could continue as usual."

Tamsin knew she was talking about her refusal to save Marlena. Tamsin saw her mother's reasoning despite the fact that she did not understand it. One could not come before the many. As Vera had said, her loyalty had to lie with all witches.

"It was my fault," Tamsin whispered, her breath hitching in her chest.

Vera set the book down on her desk. "No, Tamsin, it was mine. You couldn't stay here. You knew that. They would have killed you. I *should* have killed you, but you were so young. You had so much potential, and . . . you were my daughter. I couldn't bear to lose you. So I sent you away."

"I deserved it," Tamsin said, and the words felt right. Honest. "I killed her. Amma, too."

Vera sighed, running a hand through her river of curls. "I'm afraid it's not that simple." She swore darkly under her breath. "I had hoped this would be easier, but there isn't time to get it right." She exhaled sharply, moving back to stand before her daughter, her expression apologetic.

"Tamsin . . ." Her mother's voice shook. "The dark witch is Marlena. Your sister isn't dead."

FOURTEEN

WREN

Wren's wrists were bound, her knees pressed against an unforgiving marble floor. She blinked blearily in the dimly lit room, trying to get her eyes to adjust. It was massive, all vaulted ceilings, tall windows, and ornately carved columns. The high ceiling created an impossible chamber of sound—the music, the screeches, the lyricism of past spells, bouncing about the rafters in a cacophony so chaotic and grating that Wren wanted to slap her hands over her ears and run screaming from the room.

Instead she took a breath, trying to steady the nerves fluttering in her chest. The darkness was heavy and thick despite the hundreds of tapers lining the walls. Though each candle dripped wax, the fire hummed a tune that told Wren the flame would never reach the end of the wick. The light would never burn out.

Wren shifted, turning her attention to the nearly twenty witches filtering into the room. Some, with rainbow-colored magic, lined the stone walls, their eyes curious and expressions muted. Others were more stoic, their magic older, less colorful but more refined, gray like the sky or stone.

The six with ancient magic stood directly before her. Wren's nose was overwhelmed by the strong scents of their power (rain, lightning, figs, paper, sweat, and iron, respectively), and her eyes swam with the shimmering, protective enchantments they wore like cloaks. If she had to guess, she'd place their ages anywhere from one hundred to three hundred years old.

Wren squirmed within her bindings, her ears ringing. Leftover magic kept prodding her menacingly, like fire irons. She was in the Witchlands, yet it was nothing like what she had envisioned. She had pictured arriving with grace, exuding confidence, her power speaking for itself. Instead she was dirty, bound, and broken.

She wished Tamsin were with her. She also hoped she never saw Tamsin again. She took a breath, trying to steady the nerves fluttering in her chest. How could Tamsin have kept her mother a secret?

Even witches have mothers, Wren. She could practically hear Tamsin's flat expression, could perfectly picture the roll of her eyes. It wasn't as though Wren had assumed Tamsin would share *all* her secrets. What *was* surprising was the magnitude of those secrets, the truth of Tamsin's past. There was still so much about Tamsin she did not know.

Wren's many questions were silenced as she caught sight of the six ancient witches still staring suspiciously down at her.

"This meeting of the Six is in session." The witch who smelled of paper spoke. He was a wizened old man bent over nearly double, his eyes a milky white. He was perhaps the oldest person Wren had ever laid eyes on. Yet his voice was strong.

"I do not recognize you," the old man wheezed, "although of course my memory has been known to fail." Two of the six exchanged significant looks. "Who are you, and what are you doing with the banished witch Tamsin?"

Wren could do nothing but gape at him. *Banished?* She tried to reach for her braid, but her wrists were bound, the magic hot against her skin.

"Well?" the old man demanded.

Wren was having a difficult time finding her voice.

"She made it through the Wood, Barrow," a gray-haired woman said, her voice more patient than her expression suggested. "That means she's magic. The only question is, what kind?" She turned her attention to Wren. "What's your name?"

"Wren," she managed.

"Well, Wren," said the woman, "are you a witch?"

Wren darted her eyes around the room. She took a deep breath. "No," she finally said.

Whispers worked their way through the hall.

"Leya," a second gray-haired woman called. "Come here." Leya, the red-lipped girl who'd met them at the border, stepped forward, studying Wren with interest. An aura of magic—a full spectrum of colors, different from the single strands possessed by the witches—hung lazily about her head like a crown. There was no mistaking it: Leya was a source.

It wasn't until the girl's brown eyes slid up to the same space above Wren's head that Wren remembered that Leya, as a source, could see Wren's magic too.

The source stepped forward, circling Wren in a predatory way. She tapped a finger to her red lips theatrically. Nerves fluttered in Wren's stomach. Her whole life, she had hidden her true self from her father, from the world. Now she would be revealed before an entire roomful of witches.

Leya stopped moving. She could hardly be older than Tamsin. Her eyes were calculating, but not altogether unkind. As she reached out a hand to touch Wren, Leya's lips quirked downward, as if in apology.

She moved, faster than lightning, to wrap her hand around Wren's wrist. There was a jolt in Wren's blood. The source's fingers were like fire. Wren's magic slithered toward her like a snake, making her skin squirm. Leya made a small, thoughtful sound, then let go of Wren's arm, leaving behind the lingering scent of ocean spray and starlight.

"She is a source." Leya turned to face the Six. "Strong enough, but very undisciplined."

All six witches broke out in a flurry of heated whispers, their voices bouncing ominously off the black marble walls. But Wren only had eyes for Leya, her proud jaw, the restless energy in her hands. The two of them held the same power, but they'd led very different lives. Wren had kept herself and her magic hidden. Leya had been shaped by the Coven. It was like looking at a reflection in rippled water. A glimmer of what Wren might have been.

"Settle down." The gray-haired witch who had spoken first was on her feet, hands raised. The hall fell silent. The witch turned to Wren. "Now that we know *what* you are, why don't you tell us what you are doing here?"

Wren looked desperately around the room for a friendly face. Once again, she wished Tamsin were here, armed with a quick jab or dour remark. Instead she was alone, completely out of her depth. All she had was the truth. "Tamsin and I are here to hunt."

Leya let out a small splutter of incredulity.

The gray-haired woman held up a hand. "Are you?" She peered down at Wren with guarded interest. "And why should we allow you to hunt? A banished witch and an unregistered source?"

Wren swallowed. She didn't like the way the woman had said the word "unregistered." It made her sound like a criminal. Someone who had been intentionally negligent rather than torn in two, half her heart with the magic inside her, the other half with her fearful father.

"Because we are a team, twined together by a magically binding contract. We have no choice but to hunt. Unless you want to add our lives to your dark witch's body count." Her voice shook, her heart beating like the frantic fluttering of a moth's wings. She could hardly believe the brazenness of her words. More than that, she could hardly believe the truth of them.

Whispers built upon one another like rain during a summer storm.

"Very well." The first woman pressed the tips of her fingers together. "You will be allowed to hunt." Wren's heart swelled. "But we have reached another verdict: When the dark witch has been vanquished, you will return here to begin your training. From this day forward, you will be unable to pass through the trees back into the world of the ordinary folk. Your only place will be here, Within."

Wren froze, her palms sweaty and cold. "Sources cannot leave the world Within?"

She hated the way her voice shook, so weak it fell flat against the dark marble floor.

The witch raised a single white eyebrow. "*Sources* are permitted to leave, pending approval. You, however, are not."

Wren gaped at her. "Why?"

"Because you denied us your power. Sources are dangerous, Wren. Surely you know the stories. Even the ordinary folk tell them. Your power made the rise of the dark witch Evangeline possible. Sources allow witches to utilize magic consequence-free. Without feeling the effects of their spells, witches become greedy. They then turn toward dark magic for its ease, never mind the cost. We need to ensure that you are properly protected both from witches and from yourself. To do that, you must remain Within."

"But . . ." Wren scoured the room for a single ounce of sympathy. She was being blamed for the actions of one witch. But the eyes of the Six bored right through her. Leya's eyes would not meet her own.

"There is nothing more to be said." The witch coughed delicately. "Do you agree to serve the Coven?"

Now, when she did not want them, Wren could feel every single eye in the room.

Once she no longer loved her father, would she have the right to leave him too? It felt wrong to agree. To give up the possibility of seeing him again. But as she glanced at the stoic faces of the Coven, Wren knew that, once again, the choice she was facing had only one answer. If she wanted to live, if she wanted to find a cure for the plague, the only answer was yes.

"I agree to serve the Coven." Her voice dripped with resentment, but the Coven didn't seem to care. She was released from her bindings. Yet before she could rub the raw skin around her wrists, the woman reached out to grab her, squinting down at Wren's left arm. Wren squirmed beneath the witch's hot skin, but her grip was like iron.

"Leya, come."

The girl approached the platform. She still refused to meet Wren's eye, even as she offered the woman her hand.

The cloud above Leya's head swirled, extending a vein of violet. The source sent her magic forward, rushing toward the witch until the color had been drained from the cloud hanging above her head. It was an intricate dance, magic swirling through the echoing hall. Wren watched, openmouthed. It was the first time she had ever seen a source at work.

When the violet magic rested entirely in the witch's hands, she began to speak: guttural, twisting words. As she did, a blinding heat spread across Wren's inner arm like she was being stabbed by one thousand needles. Ink crept across her skin, arranging itself into a swooping arc topped by a line of four circles, each intersecting the next. The curved line took up nearly half her forearm, the ink black as night. As soon as the witch dropped her arm, Wren scuttled backward, pawing at the ink. It did not smudge.

"You are now a citizen of Within," the woman said. "There is no place for you in the world beyond the trees." She nodded curtly. "Here is your hunting license." She sent a scroll of parchment hurtling through the air. Wren caught it shakily and tucked it into her pocket. "Dismissed."

There was a flurry of movement, the creaking of bones as the Six removed themselves from the platform, filing out of the great hall with light footsteps. The crowd of witches who had gathered in the back of the hall dispersed slower, their eyes lingering on Wren and her new mark.

"Welcome to the fold." Leya's melodic voice sounded like a funeral dirge.

"Thanks. For everything," Wren said sarcastically, clapping a hand over her tattoo. The skin was still hot where the ink had been seared into her skin.

"The pain won't last." Leya pulled back her own sleeve to display the same symbol. The black of the ink had faded. It looked less severe, softer somehow, all curved lines and round shapes. "It will grow to be a part of you. Each circle is for an element: water, wind, fire, earth." She tapped each circle in time. "To remind us of the *source* of it all."

Wren snorted despite herself.

"Oh, good. You have a sense of humor." Leya glanced darkly toward the retreating backs of the Six.

Wren's legs had grown tired of supporting her. She sank to

the floor, the marble frigid against her skin even through her worn trousers. She couldn't be bothered to care.

Leya sighed impatiently, but she slipped to the floor as well, and settled her long skirt around her.

"I've never met another source." The words were out of Wren's mouth before she could pull them back. She was furious with Leya, but it didn't mean she wasn't curious about her too.

"We're very valuable."

"I'm certain that's what the Coven wants you to believe."

Leya frowned so quickly Wren wondered if she had imagined it. "The Coven wants you to believe a lot of things, but this is, in fact, true. There are hundreds of witches, but only a handful of sources. That's why they did all that intimidating whispering earlier. Your magic is worth a lot to them."

"They didn't seem to care very much about *me*." Wren fussed with the lace on her boot.

Leya raised her eyebrows so high they nearly disappeared into her hair. "That's because they're afraid of you. When witches cast a spell, it drains them physically and mentally. There's a limit to their power. But with a source, they can push those boundaries, take steps far beyond the scope of their limitations. Witches can do magic, but we *are* magic."

It was still strange to hear someone else refer to her as such. "There has never been a bit of magic in my family. Not even so much as an exceptionally talented gardener."

"No kidding," Leya purred, her vowels round and long. "There's . . . a lot going on up there." She waved her hand vaguely near Wren's ear. "It's really rather loud."

Wren frowned. She was always so preoccupied with the magic around her that she'd never stopped to consider what *her* magic was like.

"For years I tried to suppress it. Evangeline's sickness killed my brother, and so my father hates magic. I didn't want him to be afraid of me."

Leya made a soft clicking sound with her tongue. "I can tell. Your power moves in such a stilted way. It's like you're fighting too hard against what you are." Her eyes focused intently on the space above Wren's head. "You should give in to it. You'll be much more powerful than you already are." She gave Wren a significant look.

"Power is overrated."

"Power is everything." Leya's smile did not meet her eyes. "Especially to Tamsin."

"Power might be everything to Tamsin, but the truth certainly isn't. She didn't even tell me she was *banished*." Wren attacked the word the way she wished she could attack her travel companion.

Leya chuckled. "Not particularly forthcoming, is she? Some things never change."

Wren tugged on her braid, trying to fight the unease settling in her stomach. Leya and Tamsin had history. It made sense. The two of them were roughly the same age. They had both grown up in the Witchlands. They had probably studied together.

"You know her, then?" Wren tried to sound nonchalant, despite her sudden, desperate need to know every single thing about the witch.

"You could say that." Leya laughed darkly. "She was my best friend."

"'Was'?" Wren latched on to the past tense.

"I loved her." Leya shrugged. "I thought she felt the same, but all she cared about was power. When I wouldn't share mine with her, well . . . Can't trust a witch, am I right?" Something frenetic glinted behind Leya's eyes.

Wren tried and failed to fight the memory of their reunion. The vitriol in Leya's voice. The resignation in Tamsin's. There was something between them. Something even a five-year absence could not heal. "Anyway, it didn't matter." Leya's voice was flat. "In the end it all came down to Marlena."

Something caught in Wren's chest, a slow sinking of hope she hadn't realized she'd been carrying. The idea that there had been someone in Tamsin's life more enthralling than Leya, the beautiful girl sitting before her, was intimidating.

The idea that Wren was intimidated by a girl she had never even heard Tamsin mention was far more worrisome. She didn't understand why she cared, why she was sprawled on the floor, gossiping with Leya, when the entire trajectory of her life had changed. She could never go back to Ladaugh. She would never see her father's face again.

"Who's Marlena?" Wren tried to sound flippant, but the buzzing in her body made it clear exactly how badly she wanted to know. She wanted to know the type of girl who had stolen Tamsin's heart back when she'd had a heart to steal. She wanted to know the kind of girl Tamsin had loved. She wanted . . . Wren wanted the witch.

The feeling was startling yet certain. Unfathomable yet entirely true. Wren didn't know when it had happened, when she had begun to see Tamsin as someone to be desired. *Never learn to love someone untouchable,* the woman in Farn had said, but of course Wren had disobeyed. Had found herself in this impossible situation: falling for a girl who could not love.

She hated that Leya was there to witness it.

The other girl simply stared at Wren. Then understanding dawned across her face. "She didn't tell you." Leya began to laugh, an incredulous, hysterical sound that echoed around the empty room.

"Tell me what?" Wren's cheeks were growing warm. Her forearm, where the Coven's symbol lay, itched so fiercely it was painful.

"Oh. Oh no." Even as Leya continued to laugh, her eyes examined Wren with pity. "You don't even know what you don't know, do you?"

Wren's cheeks flushed with frustration. She hated being treated like a child. "I know things. We're a team."

"I'm sure that's what she told you." Leya pushed herself to her feet. "Careful there." She flashed Wren a small smile, the red of her lips garish against her white teeth. Then she turned and walked away, the swish of her skirt echoing like laughter, leaving Wren alone in the darkening hall.

FIFTEEN

TAMSIN

Your sister isn't dead.

Tamsin had spent five years yearning for those words, but now that she was finally faced with them, she didn't know how to react. She wanted to scream, wanted to retch, wanted to hurl her sister's diary across the room. It was more than she had expected to feel, considering that she had no store of love left in her heart. It was more, but it was still not enough.

Marlena was alive. She was out there, somewhere. For five years, Tamsin's twin had lived, and she had never known.

"But I saw her." A nagging disbelief pushed its way forward. Tamsin had been forced to stand on the black marble floor of the Grand Hall and watch her sister die. "When you severed the bond, she collapsed. I put flowers on her *grave*."

The betrayal was so enormous it felt as vast and impossible as the sea.

Vera pursed her lips, looking uncomfortable. "The bond was never fully severed. It was clever, tying your sister's life to your power. It made it nearly impossible for the source to extract the dark magic in its entirety. Like looking for a needle in a haystack. One small thread remained."

"When did you find out?" Tamsin's breathing was coming in ragged fits.

"Immediately after the bond was broken, I took your sister's body to the northern tower. I needed a moment alone to say good-bye. A mother should never outlive her child." Vera sniffed sharply. "As I clutched her frozen hand, I felt a pulse so faint I thought I was imagining it. But I wasn't. She still clung to the lifeline between the two of you. So I kept her hidden away in the tower. You and I buried an empty coffin.

"She stayed asleep all these years. It was a gift, really. If the Coven had ever discovered that she'd survived, if they'd guessed there was still a hint of dark magic left between you . . ." She trailed off, her long nails raking through her hair. "I made a decision to put my family first. I did what I had to do to save my daughter. And the world is paying for it now."

Tamsin laughed bitterly. She had spent so many years mourning her sister. Blaming herself. She let her breath out slowly, trying to control the rage bubbling beneath her skin. "All these years she was alive and you never told me."

Vera at least had the decency to look guilty. "When it came to Marlena, you had such a need to prove yourself, a need to be her champion, to secure her love. After what you'd done, I couldn't let you stay here. But I knew the only way to get you to go was to make you believe the worst."

"*I* did what I had to do. I saved her when you wouldn't." Tamsin still remembered Vera's pinched frown, the hard look in her eyes as she refused Tamsin's plea. "She might not have been powerful, but she was still worth saving."

Vera sighed. "You were always so focused on what was right in front of you that you could never see the bigger picture. You loved Marlena so much that you forgot about the rest of the world. But all *she* ever wanted *was* the world. And your actions nearly destroyed it."

It was all so impossible Tamsin could hardly wrap her head around it.

"I don't understand. If Marlena is asleep, how is she the dark witch?" She looked down at the diary, still clutched in her white-knuckled hands.

"She finally woke up." Vera glanced at the floor. "Your sister awoke and escaped from the north tower the morning of your seventeenth birthday."

Tamsin shook her head uncomprehendingly. "What do you mean, 'escaped'? How?"

"I don't know." Vera looked pained. "She shouldn't have been able to do it. I used blood wards to keep her locked inside. It would have taken an ordinary witch months to undo the number of enchantments. But she was just . . . gone."

Vera pushed herself away from the desk, her shoes clacking against the stone floor. "There was only a tiny thread of dark magic between the two of you, just enough to keep Marlena alive. I didn't expect her to wake up. I certainly didn't expect her to use it for her own purposes. To flee the academy. To cast her own spell." Vera settled herself carefully behind her desk, her hands folded atop several scattered pieces of parchment.

Her own spell. Surely that couldn't mean the plague had come from her sister. Evangeline's sickness had targeted those without power. Marlena knew what it was like to suffer at the hands of magic, had been outspoken about the dark witch's intolerance and cruelty toward ordinary folk. She would never have cast a spell that subjected others to the same terrible fate.

"She wouldn't." Tamsin shook her head. "She *couldn't*. She doesn't have the stamina. It doesn't make sense."

"And yet . . ." Vera sighed wearily. "I tried to suppress the plague, but the magic behind it is too furious. Too raw. I could not keep up."

Tamsin had never before heard her mother admit a limitation to her power. It revealed the sheer magnitude of their predicament. The urgency, the necessity of what they were facing. The reality of what one ill-fated decision had grown into.

"After Evangeline, we formed the Coven so that we would never have to witness such brutality again." Vera massaged her temples, her eyes squeezed shut. "We only recently were able to repair relations between witches and ordinary folk. This plague cannot continue. The spell must be broken."

Vera shifted slightly in her seat. "I fear it will soon be too late to return the world to the way it was. The Coven is exhausted. The queen wants a witch to burn for this. If anyone gets wind of the truth, I have no doubt that the rest of the Coven will strip me of my title and kill you in order to break the bond of dark magic that still exists between you and your sister. Without your power fueling her, Marlena will lose her life too."

Her mother was gazing at Tamsin with an emotion she could not name. "It is your bond that keeps your sister living. You must find a way to break it. You must stop her spell."

"Me?" Tamsin spluttered. "But if I break it, she'll die." It took everything she had to choke the words out.

Vera leaned across the desk. "Maybe. But maybe not. If you work together."

"How?" Tamsin despised the desperation in her voice. "Marlena hates me." The truth of it twisted in her gut like a knife.

Vera smiled sadly. "She doesn't hate you. You're just different people. And you were never willing to admit that." She straightened the stack of books beside her. "Find your sister, Tamsin. Make your peace. End this," Vera implored, "for all of us." And then she rose from her desk and swept toward the door, giving Tamsin a curt nod. She was High Councillor Vera again. Tamsin's mother was gone.

It was strange the way the light still fell at the same slant through the tall windows, the moon pooling on the floor beneath her feet. Tamsin stepped carefully, her skirt whispering against her ankles as she crept down the corridor the way she had so many times before. Only this time she was not sneaking out of bed to meet Leya, a flame concealed beneath her cloak. The two of them would not sprawl on the floor of the library, concealed by the dusty stacks, sharing secrets—and, occasionally, soft, searching kisses. There had been a delicious hope to the darkness then.

Now the west wing was empty, the dormitory doors flung open, revealing haphazardly made beds, lonely shoes, wrinkled robes. The inhabitants of those rooms had left in a hurry, likely sent back to their families in the wake of the new darkness. *Marlena's* darkness. It took some effort to even think her sister's name in such a context. It made no sense.

Tamsin paused, eyes catching on a room's four abandoned beds. She and Marlena, assigned to the same lower-form dormitory, had both claimed top bunks. Tamsin had wanted to see her sister at all times. Marlena had wanted to be closer to the sky.

She leaned against the door frame, slumping slightly against the smooth wood. Five years. She had gone five years believing her sister was dead. Five years and she had never suspected. Never doubted. And all the while, Marlena had slept, locked in a tower behind a shield of spells.

Would she have wanted Tamsin to rescue her? Or would she have been grateful to be left alone for the first time?

Either option made her feel ill. Either way, she had failed Marlena by being not enough or by being too much.

It was the reason Vera had insisted on her curse. When Tamsin loved, she loved too hard. It made her dangerous. Never before had that been so clear. Tamsin's love hurt people.

She scrubbed her eyes with the back of her hands, wishing desperately that she could cry. Anything to release the terrible,

terrible ache in her chest, the stiffness of her heart, the guilt pooling in her lungs. It was all her fault.

She had no idea what she was going to tell Wren.

Wren.

She had nearly forgotten about the source, left alone to face the Six. Tamsin hurried to the end of the corridor, faltering as the door opened before she reached it. She tensed, waiting for a reprimand or a gasp as the person on the other side registered her presence. Instead she was met with a familiar red-lipped frown.

It was odd knowing that once Leya had made her *feel*. For as she stared at her now, she saw nothing but a girl.

"Are you following me?"

Leya rolled her eyes. "Again," she said, her voice flat, "*I* live here, so in fact one could argue that *you* are following *me*."

Tamsin swayed slightly, exhaustion creeping through her bones like a morning frost. She used the wall to steady herself, rested her head against it.

Leya's eyes narrowed. "Don't do that."

"Do what?" Tamsin reluctantly lifted her cheek from the stone.

"Make me feel sorry for you. I can't handle that." Her words were harsher than her tone.

"I'm sorry," Tamsin said. "I haven't slept in two days."

Leya snickered. "No kidding. You look awful."

"I'm sorry," Tamsin said again.

Leya sniffed. "What's the matter with you?"

"What do you mean?"

"I mean that you were my best friend for ten years, and you've apologized to me more in five minutes than you ever did then."

Tamsin sighed, guilt flickering in her chest. Another casualty of her carelessness.

"I'm sorry," she repeated, then winced. Leya snorted.

"She really did a number on you, didn't she? I can see the earnestness written all over your face."

"Who?"

Leya blinked blankly at her. "My replacement."

"Wren?"

"No," Leya snapped, "the *other* source you brought along. Yes, Wren." She slumped against the wall next to Tamsin, pressing a foot up behind her. "How did you even find her? I thought we had every source in all four corners of the world."

So had Tamsin until Wren had appeared at her door. "She came to me."

"Of course she did," Leya muttered darkly.

"What does that mean?" Tamsin turned her head to face the girl who had once been her friend.

"That you were always going to be okay, no matter what happened." Leya turned away from Tamsin, her eyes fixed on the window across the corridor. "It means I did the right thing, telling you no."

Tamsin frowned. "That doesn't make any sense."

Leya's laugh echoed in the empty corridor. "Did you ever care for me? Even a little? Even just as a friend?" Her eyes flitted across Tamsin's face hopefully. "Before, I mean."

"Of course I did." The question was unfathomable. Even though she couldn't remember loving Leya, she knew she had.

She had been in awe of her, the way magic was so intrinsic to her person, the confidence she'd possessed. The way she made Tamsin feel important and full of potential.

"Then why did you ask me to help you?" Leya brushed her hair in front of her eyes the way she always did when she was close to tears. "They would have killed me, and you didn't care at all."

"That isn't true." But maybe in some small way it was.

Tamsin had thought that her return Within would be a chance for redemption. A way to set things right. But there was still so much to repent for.

"Just don't do the same thing to Wren," Leya sighed, sounding resigned. "She likes you, you know." Tamsin nearly hit her head on the wall in surprise.

"*Wren?*" Leya's words were unfathomable. "No, she doesn't. I'm awful."

Leya snickered. "Now, *that* we can both agree on." She pushed herself away from the wall. "Good luck," she said, "with whatever you came here to do."

"Thanks." Tamsin ran a finger absentmindedly against the black ribbon around her throat. "I'm going to need it."

"You probably won't," Leya said, smiling sadly before continuing down the corridor.

It was all Tamsin was going to get in the way of good-bye.

SIXTEEN

WREN

Wren was restless. Although the flames in the torches on the walls still burned bright, the outside sky had grown light. The fresh mark upon her skin had stopped its throbbing and become a sure, steady pain.

Still Tamsin had not appeared.

Wren shifted her position on the marble floor. She had lost feeling in one of her legs but was too exhausted to pull herself to her feet. She drummed an empty rhythm on the floor with her fingers, playing in time with the echoes of magic floating near the rafters.

Leya had left Wren alone with her thoughts, and rather than unpack the meaning behind the fluttering of her stomach and the twisting envy in her gut, Wren had given in to the sounds of magic: its broad, swooping notes, its grating scrapes, its lulling, unchanging pulse.

The hall was filled with it, the history of every bit of magic ever performed within the confines of its black walls. Some spells lilted with hope; others cried like crashing waves. Wren managed to find a melody: several bright, careful notes that kept repeating. She tried her hand at whistling, but her lips went dry with the effort.

Wren faltered, a note catching in her throat as the door at the back of the hall scraped open. She scrambled to her feet, wobbling slightly as she put weight on her dead leg.

Tamsin moved swiftly forward, the low blue flames cutting a sharp shadow across her face. Her jaw was set, her expression hard. She might have been carved from stone were it not for the wildness in her eyes.

It was an uncertainty, more contained than Leya's raw energy but less focused than the fire Wren had spotted within High Councillor Vera. Something was wrong, but even as Wren understood that an event of great magnitude had occurred, she watched Tamsin hide behind her steely expression, watched her build back up the walls that kept her safe.

"Hi," she said simply.

"*Hi?*" Wren blinked at her uncomprehendingly. "That's all you have to say to me? I guess I shouldn't be surprised, considering what else you couldn't be bothered to tell me. Not only were you banished, but your *mother* is the head of the Coven?" She threw up her hands helplessly. "Was this all just a joke to you? Am *I* a joke?"

"You're not a joke." Tamsin scrubbed a hand across her face.

"Well, you're making me feel like one." Wren was tempted to shout, thought that hearing her anger bounce off the vaulted ceiling might give her some release, but instead she crumpled, her left leg giving out and sending her back to the floor.

Tamsin stared down at her with trepidation. "Are you all right?"

Wren's laugh was a wicked, snarling thing that ripped through her throat and brought tears to her eyes.

"No." She fought to keep her voice level, but instead it came out as a growl.

Tamsin merely blinked. She didn't push, didn't ask her to explain. Wren wished she would. But when Tamsin offered up a frigid hand to help her back to her feet, Wren took it.

"You're always so cold," she said as Tamsin pulled her up. Nose to nose with the witch, Wren was suddenly quite aware of the stale taste in her mouth. She held her breath.

The witch stared at her with amusement. "Maybe you're just warm."

A blush crept across Wren's cheeks, the nearness of Tamsin disconcerting. She pulled her hand away and busied herself with her hair, unraveling it from its plait and brushing it out with her fingers.

"Your hair's red," Tamsin said, eyes narrowed, as though she'd only just noticed. Wren frowned, plucking at a strand, which was the same coppery bronze it had always been. She hadn't expected Tamsin to spend their journey waxing poetic about her appearance, but such a base observation made it clearer than ever how little she actually mattered to the witch. She made quick work of retying her braid. Leya was right. She was nothing more than a pawn in the witch's game. Easy to sacrifice.

"Are you ready to hunt, then?" Wren scowled at Tamsin. "In case you've forgotten, we have no choice." She tugged hopelessly on the ribbon around her neck. "At least the Six agreed with me there."

Tamsin blinked at her in surprise.

"Yes, they granted us a license," Wren said darkly, reaching for the slip of paper in her pocket and offering it to the witch. As she leaned forward, her sleeve slipped, revealing the circles of dark ink and the swollen pink skin beneath it.

Tamsin let out a low, full breath. The witch's gaze lingered on her like a hand hovering above a candle's flame.

"They *marked* you?" She did not reach for the parchment.

"Good job keeping yours hidden," Wren said, more tersely than she'd expected. "Caught me completely off guard. Hurt, too." She cradled her swollen arm carefully.

"I don't have one." Tamsin began to roll up her sleeve. "Well," she said dryly, "not anymore." Wren gasped as she took in the burned, mottled skin, twisted and stretched.

"What happened?"

"I was banished." The sleeve slipped back over her arm. Tamsin tried to smile. Failed. "So . . ."

"'So'?" Wren raised her eyebrows. "You can't possibly think that's the end of this conversation."

"Isn't it?" Tamsin turned on her heel and strode toward the door, her green cloak billowing behind her. Her footsteps clacked across the marble floor, the candles casting endless shadows across her determined expression. Wren sighed heavily as she hurried after her. She didn't know why she bothered. Leya was right: Tamsin was even more selfish and self-important than Wren had given her credit for.

She followed the witch through a dizzying maze of stone hallways and finally out into the morning light. Only it wasn't morning, not for more than a handful of moments at a time. The sun was having trouble staying put, streaks of dark magic pushing it across the sky so quickly that by the time Tamsin and Wren had made it down the front steps, the soft pinks of sunrise had faded into the sharp golds of mid-afternoon.

"Oh." Even though she knew it was a side effect of the plague, Wren couldn't help but stop to watch as the sun sailed behind a mountain range and the sky erupted into a dazzling sunset. The magic in the Witchlands was so strong it was as though Wren had been given a new set of senses. Colors were more vivid. The sunset smelled like the moment before falling asleep. "Isn't it beautiful?"

Beside her, Tamsin tensed. Wren tugged on her braid guiltily. She kept forgetting that the witch could find no enjoyment in even the simplest things. It was no wonder all her edges were so sharp. She had nothing soft to land on.

"The sky looks like it's on fire." Wren spoke carefully, keeping her eyes fixed on the rapidly changing colors. "Right above the mountains, the light is as bright as a daffodil, or freshly churned butter. Then there"—she gestured to the streaks of bright orange—"is the same color as a new flame. Or my hair." She bit down on her cheek to keep from laughing. "The orange is reflecting onto the clouds, turning them red like apples in autumn. Then it's blue, just the dregs of a new morning, but over there"—Wren pointed to the darkening sky—"that part's gone purple like the skin of an overripe plum. You know, the kind that dribbles juice down your chin when you bite into it?"

Wren glanced tentatively over at Tamsin, whose eyes were wide and glassy. "Are you all right?"

Tamsin flinched, her hand clenching into a fist. Wren realized too late that she had overstepped their tentative boundaries. Just because she found beauty in the vivid colors didn't mean Tamsin wanted to hear about something she couldn't appreciate. Her descriptions had angered the witch, had given Tamsin further proof that Wren was flighty and foolish. She closed her eyes, waiting for the blow.

"What are you doing?" Tamsin asked.

Wren opened her eyes. The sky was now as black as ink. Moonlight pooled on the witch's face, illuminating her wary expression. She hadn't moved an inch.

"I thought you were going to hit me." Wren's voice came out in a startled gasp; she was laughing despite herself.

"*Hit* you?" Tamsin's brow was wrinkled with genuine confusion.

Wren gestured awkwardly to Tamsin's clenched hand. The witch gave her a curious look before unfurling her fist, revealing tiny half-moon indentations on her palm.

"Old habit," she said, still staring at Wren strangely. "It's being back here. Remembering." She glanced over her shoulder nervously, as though she had revealed too much. "Come on. We have a witch to hunt." Tamsin snapped her fingers, and their things appeared. The witch threw her rucksack over her shoulder and started walking.

"Where are we going?" Tamsin didn't answer. Wren gathered her own bag and hurried to catch up. "You owe me about a hundred explanations, you know."

"Not here," Tamsin said firmly. Wren fell silent, not wanting to test her luck.

And so, while the sun rose and set with reckless abandon, they traveled across the Witchlands. They shuffled through blackened grass that nearly hit Wren's knees, ash and charcoal coating her tongue with every step. They passed through a valley of toadstools taller than two grown men—giant, spotted fungi that smelled of pepper. They avoided the footsteps of cottages that walked of their own accord—their great taloned toes digging into the dirt—and darted away from wells that cried for coins.

They struggled through swamps and marshes, past giant boulders shouting unhelpful advice, and ducked through craggy passageways that made Wren's skin crawl with the touch of a million insects.

Yet despite how far they traveled, despite the hills they climbed and the valleys they traversed, Wren could always see the gleaming black castle glowering intimidatingly behind her, its giant windows like eyes watching her every move. Waiting for her return.

Wren hoped the rest of the Witchlands was not as grand. Nothing so beautiful and cold could ever feel like home.

* * *

The inn was called the Wandering Woes, which Wren found to be a touch too fitting. She was certainly carrying more than her fair share of sadness. If the purplish bags beneath Tamsin's eyes were any indication, the witch was too. She was also holding all the answers.

"Now will you finally . . ." As Wren pushed open the front door, her words were forgotten. From the outside, the inn had appeared to be nothing more than a cottage, a small stone structure with a carefully thatched roof. She had expected to find a cozy kitchen, perhaps one or two rooms to rent. But inside was as grand as a palace.

The main room was the same size as the academy's marble hall, but it was much cozier. Tiny white lights floated near the ceiling, twinkling like stars. The back wall was covered in ivy, giving the room a fresh, just-after-rain smell. Long wooden tables sat in the center, fitted with colorful, mismatched chairs. There was a bar with hundreds of bottles of clear liquids infused with bright petals and dark spices. Flower-patterned china sat at every place setting, each cup filled with steaming tea that Wren could tell would never go cold. The inn was charming. It was welcoming. It absolutely sang with enchantments.

It was also filled with witches.

Witches whose heads turned toward them as soon as the bell above the front door jangled merrily. Wren tried to count them all, but their magic would not stay still. It darted and wove about the room, shooting sparks of every color she had ever seen (and some she hadn't), speaking in a hundred different tongues. The witches in that room were from all four corners of the world. They were of different ages, had different talents, different complexions, different memories, but they were all tied together by the same thing: magic.

"Well, this place used to be deserted," Tamsin said, her tone grim. "Come on"—she grabbed Wren's wrist—"let's find a seat. People are already starting to talk."

And they were. An energetic hum filled the room, the buzzing of gossip spreading like wildfire.

". . . got some nerve, showing her face here," a fair-haired witch whispered as they passed. There was a murmur of assent from the others at her table. "I'd rather die, if it were me. We all know what she did. How do we know she hasn't done it again? We should be hunting *her*."

There was a peal of laughter, hard and sharp as a stone corner. Tamsin set her shoulders; her jaw clenched. Wren scurried after her, several sets of eyes boring into the back of her neck. They made their way to the far end of the inn, where an old woman was wiping down a long table.

"Hazel." Tamsin's voice was soft. Tentative. The woman stopped wiping, but she did not turn around. Wren glanced at Tamsin, who looked nervous.

Finally the woman turned, revealing a waterfall of long silver hair and clouded eyes. "Do my ears deceive me?"

"They never have before, so I can't imagine why they'd start now." Tamsin glanced down at her shoes, chuckling humorlessly.

The woman's face broke into a wide smile. She held out a

wrinkled hand, waving for Tamsin to join her. She did, moving away from Wren, suddenly bashful as the old woman made a fuss over her.

"My eyes have given up on me, but I just know you're lovelier than ever. My girl, I thought you were gone for good."

Tamsin's face fell slightly. "I should be."

"Well, you're here now, and that's all that matters. Are you hungry? I think there's some stew left from dinner. Come."

The woman led Tamsin by the hand. Wren bit her lip to keep from laughing, settling herself in a chair of midnight-blue velvet. It was strange, watching Tamsin let down her guard. She looked younger, the sharp lines of her face relaxing slightly. Perhaps it was the warm orange flame flickering through the room or the way Tamsin's entire body had lost some of its rigidness as soon as the old woman had taken her hand.

Wren rolled out the crick in her neck, closing her eyes as she did. She could likely fall asleep on the spot. When she opened her eyes, a willow-patterned teacup and matching saucer had appeared in front of her. Wren curled her hands around the cup, which had filled itself with steaming tea.

Tamsin returned after several minutes, carrying two bowls of stew. Hazel followed after her, plopping down a plate of flaky pastries. The woman smelled of freshly churned butter, her ribbons of magic an herbal green.

"Oh, now," the old woman said, at last turning to Wren. "Who's this?"

"You already gave me two bowls, Hazel. You can't pretend to be ignorant now just so you'll get an introduction." Tamsin's words were harsh, but her tone was soft. Hazel gripped Tamsin's shoulder in a firm yet loving squeeze.

"I'm Wren." She hesitated, uncertain if she should extend her hand.

"I know." The old woman cackled, but it was a warm, inclusive laugh. "I'll leave you girls to your food and make up a room for you."

Tamsin settled herself into the plush pink armchair across from Wren. "Sorry about her. She means well, but she tends to meddle."

"She's nice." Wren blew softly on a spoonful of stew.

"We stayed here sometimes when we needed a break from the dormitories. When we wanted to feel as though someone actually cared for us, since Vera never seemed to have the time." Tamsin ran a pale finger around the rim of her teacup.

"We?" Was Wren sitting in the same seat Leya had once occupied?

Tamsin startled. "Sorry, I. I meant me." She took a sip of tea. "Hazel is kind. Perhaps too kind."

"No such thing," Wren said pointedly, trying to tamp down the squirm of suspicion in her stomach. "You should try it sometime."

"Ha. Ha." Tamsin's voice was flat.

Wren took a sip of tea just to have something to do with her hands. "So," she finally said, trying to keep her voice light, "we'll stay the night here?" She glanced out the window. The sun was already rising. "The day? The way the dark magic is pushing the sun through the sky, I've seen so many sunrises I no longer have any concept of time."

Tamsin almost laughed. "Suppose it doesn't matter now. The only thing that matters is finding her."

Her?

Surely Tamsin meant the dark witch, although her certainty that the dark witch was a woman was a new development.

"Tamsin." Wren glanced around, trying to keep her expression light. The buzz of gossip was still floating through the room, but the witches now seemed more focused on their conversations than on Wren and Tamsin themselves. "Will you please tell me what's going on?"

Tamsin ran a hand through her tangled hair. "I really need a bath."

Wren sighed deeply. "Will you stop avoiding my questions? If we're going to do this, I need to know what we're up against." She tapped her fingernails against her teacup, a soft tinkling filling the empty air between them as she stared the witch down. Tamsin looked away first.

Wren's mouth soured with the witch's silence. "I know how to keep a secret, you know. Not as well as you, obviously," she said pointedly. "Banished? I mean, you really didn't think to mention that before making me seal a contract?"

"Didn't your father ever teach you not to enter into contracts with witches?" Tamsin raised her eyebrows. "We're notoriously good at incredibly precise wording."

"He did, actually." Wren tried to suppress the pang she felt at the mention of her father. Tried to forget about the new reality of her life. "Anyway, I thought you were going to give me answers." She looked at the witch expectantly. "My patience is running thin."

Tamsin snorted. "No, it's not. You're never anything other than good and patient and kind." Her eyes flickered over Wren. "Which, frankly, is very annoying."

Wren rolled her eyes good-naturedly. "Says you. So?"

Before Tamsin could answer, Wren's stomach gave a ferocious growl. She smiled apologetically and lunged for the closest pastry. She couldn't recall the last time they'd stopped for food. She couldn't remember the last time they had properly slept, either.

"Don't choke," Tamsin said, watching Wren stuff half the pie in her mouth at once.

Wren let out a soft groan. The food was hot, the spices sharp, the pastry crisp. It was maybe the most wonderful thing she'd ever eaten.

Tamsin was watching her with horror. "You look like an animal."

"*You* look like an animal," Wren shot back giddily, her mouth full. A flake of pastry fell onto her shirt.

Tamsin wrinkled her nose. "Well done. That was devastating. Truly." She reached for her own pie. For the first time in days, she almost looked relaxed. But Wren was still on edge. *We. Her.* There was something the witch was still keeping secret.

Someone.

"Tamsin, who's Marlena?"

Tamsin nearly choked on her pastry. She coughed wildly, her face turning red. Wren fought the urge to get up and help her. She merely stared, waiting, until Tamsin had settled down and taken a giant gulp from the teacup in front of her. The witch's lips pressed into a firm line. Then, after another moment's hesitation, when Wren was sure the witch wouldn't answer, Tamsin said, "My sister."

Wren had thought she could no longer be surprised by Tamsin's reveals, but this one punched her in the gut. "You have a sister?"

Something complicated flashed across Tamsin's face. "A twin."

"So, earlier, when you said the only thing that matters is finding *her*, did you mean the dark witch, or did you mean your sister?"

The witch looked nervously over her shoulder. "I'll explain everything tomorrow."

Wren dropped the remaining bite of her pastry, eyes blazing. "No, you won't. You'll explain it now." She hoped she didn't sound as rattled as she felt. Tamsin's deflection was making her nervous.

"*Tomorrow,*" Tamsin whispered roughly. "When there aren't so many people around." Her eyes fluttered across the many colored cloaks of the witches in the room. "I promise."

She held Wren's gaze.

"My father taught me never to enter into contracts with witches," Wren said wryly.

Still, she didn't want to cause a scene amid so much magic. So, against her better judgment, Wren said nothing as the witch got to her feet, her stew untouched.

Wren watched as the tail of Tamsin's green cloak disappeared up the spiral staircase to the rooms above. An enchanted fiddle played a slow song, soft and familiar. It hit something in her heart, poked a place already bruised.

A twin sister. She'd have almost thought it a joke. And yet there was nothing funny about the hurt that had pooled in Tamsin's eyes.

Wren stuffed the final bite of pastry into her mouth. There were so many questions to ask when the morning finally came. Yet the one Wren found the most pressing was: Why, when Tamsin spoke of her sister, had she touched the book-shaped lump in the pocket of her cloak?

SEVENTEEN

TAMSIN

The world was dark.

Tamsin peered through the curtains, waiting for the light, but the sun had stopped its cycling. The sky was empty. Silent.

Tamsin exhaled, lighting a tiny flame, which she cradled in her palm. Wren was still asleep, her body splayed across the small bed opposite Tamsin's. The source had made quite a bit of noise when she'd finally come to bed, sighing and coughing falsely, flinging her boots across the room one heavy thump at a time. Yet Tamsin had not moved until she'd heard Wren's breathing slow.

She hadn't meant to slip, had meant to keep the truth about Marlena as close to her heart as possible in the hopes she might be able to feel it. But hearing her sister's name on Wren's tongue had been more than she could bear.

That tiny truth, that relief of confession, had cost her the upper hand.

She stepped into her boots and pulled on her cloak; then, careful not to disturb the flame, she slipped out the creaky door of the tiny attic room.

It was more than any other innkeeper would have given her. Not only did their beds have mattresses, but the room even had a proper washroom. It was no bigger than a shadowy closet, but still, Tamsin finally had the time to wash and detangle her hair, to change out of the clothes she'd been wearing for days. They had started to smell quite rank. Tamsin knew she could never thank Hazel enough for her kindness and her steadfast loyalty, even though Tamsin did not deserve it.

She extinguished her tiny fire as she entered the well-lit main room. Despite the darkness outside, quite a few witches were awake, scattered about, practicing their craft, trying to find a way to track the dark witch. To track *Marlena.*

Her sister was alive and out there, somewhere. She had been this entire time. Tamsin kept shifting from feeling foolish to feeling angry, from basking in relief to cowering with trepidation. Marlena wasn't dead. Her sister wasn't dead. Which meant Tamsin's spell hadn't killed her.

She didn't know what that meant for her guilt. She still had Amma's death on her conscience. Her dark magic had nearly destroyed the world Within. She was certainly not blameless. Tamsin still had plenty to atone for.

A gaggle of teenaged witches giggled from the corner where they were poring over an ancient grimoire. They took turns conjuring jars from the back wall, taking ginseng root and dried lavender, bay leaves and the bark of an ash tree, and pounding them all to a fine dust, which they scooped carefully into small leather pouches to be tucked in their pockets.

An older witch was bent over her table, a chunk of quartz in one hand, obsidian in the other. Her eyes were closed; her lips moved silently. She frowned and dropped the obsidian on the table, her hand searching for the next nearest stone. She grabbed a smooth black onyx. Opened her eyes. Frowned. Started searching through her stones again.

At the far end of the table, Rhys, a witch who had been a few years ahead of Tamsin in school, was shuffling their tarot deck, surrounded by several younger witches. They dealt a hand, their black-painted lips frowning as they took in the overeager faces. "Be quiet," they snapped, adjusting their cloak. "If you don't respect the deck, it won't respect you." Rhys's eyes flitted across the room to Tamsin, who quickly sat in the nearest chair, busying herself with the teacup before her.

Rhys had given Tamsin the same lecture years ago. Their reading had been right then—she *had* been acting brashly, and her impulsivity had come to haunt her in the end.

Tamsin drained her tea, squinted down at the dregs. The leaves were clumped at the bottom, but she could make no sense of them. Tamsin had no knack for divination. She was all about action. Which was, as she now knew, entirely the problem.

She cast the cup aside and pulled Marlena's diary from the

folds of her cloak. Now that her sister was alive, the words inside took on a new importance. A new burden. The door to the inn opened, and the pages of the diary went flying. Tamsin didn't know why the book bothered. She was already Within. She knew that her sister lived. Reading her words would only serve to remind her of the loss she'd thought she'd suffered and the pain she felt now. But Tamsin had never been one to protect herself from pain, and so she leaned forward to read.

I was right. Usually those are my three favorite words in existence, but writing them today brings me no joy. Arwyn came to the Grand Hall with that awful flute of hers and her horrible herd, crowing that she'd found the dark witch. You should have seen her face: Her eerily sharp teeth were practically falling out of her mouth, she was smiling so wide. And then who does she throw down onto the floor but Tamsin.

I was right. But in another sense, I was so terribly wrong.

Of course, Vera flew into a rage, hauling her up and out of the hall as fast as her heels could carry her. The rest of the room fell to whispers. What could Tamsin be doing with power like that? She was going to join the Coven someday, everyone was sure of it. She was an ideal candidate: talented, devoted, eager, selfless to a fault. She would have given her life to be charged with protecting the world Within. Instead it looks like she gave her life to protect me.

That's right. The dark magic she did? It's the reason why I'm alive. Without asking me, she pulled magic from the earth and bound my life to her power. So not only is Tamsin responsible for the rains, for the fires, for Amma, but I am too. Tamsin did this to save me, which means that I'm complicit. I'm a part of this whether I want to be or not.

And I hate her for it.

Vera brought me up to her office once she'd finished with Tamsin, and for a while she just stared. It was strange, like she was trying to memorize my face, which is absurd since it's the same as Tamsin's. But then she told me that she had to break the bond. It was her "duty" or something official-sounding. I wish I could say I was surprised. I know that Vera loves me—loves Tamsin, too, of course—but she loves Within more.

I don't even resent her for it. I truly don't. I wish I knew what it was like to love something so much you'd let your own daughter die. She didn't say so, of course, but I could see it in her eyes. When they remove Tamsin's power from me, I'm going to die.

Mortality is strange, in a way. Before, I was

always faced with long stretches in a white
infirmary, and since I knew there was always
the possibility of dying, I was always afraid. But
now that my life has an end date, I can't seem
to make myself feel … anything at all.

Tamsin stared down at the wrinkled page. She had taken the biggest risk of her young life, had pushed away her best friend, lost the respect of her mother and her teachers, all so she could save her sister. And now it was clearer than it had ever been that she'd made a mistake. Marlena wasn't grateful for what Tamsin had done. She *hated* her for it.

Tamsin rested her head in her hands. In no scenario could she have hung back and simply watched her sister slip away. The two of them were bound by a bond stronger than dark magic. If the roles had been reversed, wouldn't Marlena have done the same thing to save her?

The horrible truth came to her in the form of a chill, racking her whole body with a shiver so outsize that her elbow knocked her teacup onto the floor, where it promptly shattered into a hundred pieces. She swore and fell to her knees, carefully collecting the pieces in her palm.

"I thought you were a witch." Tamsin tensed at the sound of Wren's voice, but she did not look up. She continued to collect the shards of rose-patterned china.

"Tamsin." Wren nudged her softly with the toe of her boot. "Come on. It's time for you to tell me the truth."

Tamsin sighed and got to her feet, dumping the shards of

porcelain unceremoniously onto the tabletop. "I don't see what else there is to tell," she lied.

"You have a sister."

Tamsin fought the urge to correct Wren's tense. She was so used to thinking *had*.

"I was going to tell you," she said quickly. "But things are complicated."

Wren frowned. "Either you have a sister or you don't."

Tamsin very nearly laughed. "Exactly. That's why it's complicated." She exhaled, the mere fact of her breathing seeming to earn her several annoyed looks. She'd known that other witches resented her, some for the fact that she'd used dark magic, others for the fact that she was still living. Still, thus far the reaction to her return had been frigid at best.

She summoned their things, their bags appearing by their feet. "I'll say good-bye to Hazel, and then we're going to go."

"Go?" Wren's eyes darted around the room. "Why?"

"We've overstayed our welcome here." Tamsin heaved her pack over her shoulder, nodding toward the huddle of school-age witches, who were whispering hurriedly behind their hands, eyes fixed on the pair of them.

"Where are we going, then?" Wren fussed with her bag, her face pinched.

Tamsin ran a hand through her hair, dread souring her tongue. "Somewhere I can tell you the truth."

"Let me get this straight." Wren's voice was muffled from behind her sleeve, her expression impossible to decipher as they moved carefully through the darkness. "The dark witch is your twin sister, who you thought was dead but isn't thanks to the dark-magic bond between the two of you?"

The ground was soft and wet beneath their feet. The scent of sulfur permeated everything, had flooded their nostrils the moment they'd opened the door to leave the Wandering Woes. Wren had covered her nose, but Tamsin hadn't bothered. There was no escaping it. She wouldn't be surprised if the stink of rotting eggs clung to her skin for the rest of her days.

"Yes."

"Yes, what?"

"Yes, that's right." But telling Wren the truth hadn't made Tamsin feel better. In fact, it had made her feel worse. In the end, it all pointed back to Tamsin.

"All right," Wren said, squinting at the witch, lips pursed. "But I don't understand what this has to do with that little black book in your pocket."

"What?" Tamsin was so surprised her foot squelched dangerously close to a murky puddle. She had expected Wren to cry, to scream, to turn away from her once she had learned the truth. But she had underestimated the girl. Instead of fleeing, Wren stood her ground.

"Your sister is the dark witch," she repeated. "Which means *you* know who we're up against. I don't. That's why I need you to tell me everything." She looked as though she might crumble beneath the weight of all of Tamsin's evasions and lies. "So," she said pointedly. "The book."

"It's hers," Tamsin finally admitted, rummaging in the

pocket of her cloak and pulling out the diary. "It's Marlena's."

Wren let out a little hiccup of a giggle.

"What is it?" Tamsin snapped, feeling rather put out. "Why are you laughing at me?"

"I'm sorry," Wren said, one hand on her chest. "I just—I feel so silly. When Leya first mentioned Marlena, I thought—" She took a step forward, then shrieked as her foot sank into a muddy patch of grass. She scrambled to regain her balance, the ground slurping her leg into the squelching deep.

Tamsin lunged to grab Wren's elbow, but when her toes began to slip into the muck as well, she scurried back, letting Wren's arm go.

Wren's eyes widened with betrayal. "What are you doing?"

"Stop flailing," Tamsin commanded, charming her lantern to float next to her shoulder and fumbling with the tie on her cloak. "I can't save you if I'm stuck too."

Wren's face was twisted into a pinched, fretful expression as she struggled and writhed, sinking deeper into the muck with each motion. Tamsin shook out her cloak, clutched the hem tightly in her hands, and threw the hood to Wren.

"Grab hold. And quit moving. You'll sink yourself deeper if you keep squirming."

"It's cold," Wren moaned as she scrambled to grab hold of the cloak. "And it *stinks*."

Tamsin pulled at the cloak, the emerald-green fabric slippery beneath her sweating palms. Wren was submerged up to her waist. If she wasn't careful, she would slip under completely. "Right leg first. Slowly. *Slowly*." Tamsin's voice tensed.

"It's stuck," Wren said through gritted teeth as she sank a few more inches.

"Maybe it's a bog. Bogs are mostly water, after all. Can you swim?"

"No." Still Wren leaned back, her face plastered with a pained grimace. "It feels like I'm sinking further." She was, but Tamsin didn't want to tell her so.

"Move your right leg up. No, *up*." Tamsin's heart was pounding in her ears.

With a great grunt of effort, Wren freed a leg. Tamsin spotted the hint of a giant leather boot. Wren struggled, pulling hard on the cloak, but despite her shaking arms, Tamsin managed to hold her ground. After an immense amount of effort, and several more guttural sounds, Wren freed her second leg. Tamsin hurriedly pulled her upright.

Wren panted wildly, hair stuck to her sweaty forehead. Tamsin reached up to brush it away. She caught the faintest whiff of lavender before the smell was swallowed by the stink of the endless night. Tamsin mumbled a few quick words, and Wren's trousers dried instantly.

Wren, still struggling to catch her breath, stared at Tamsin with soft eyes. "Thanks."

Tamsin shrugged and busied herself with refastening her cloak. "You can't go dying on me now. We finally have a lead." But her attempt at humor fell flat, her shaking hands giving her away.

"I meant for the trousers." Wren offered up a soft smile. "But I *guess* thanks also for saving my life. Here." She stepped forward and tied Tamsin's cloak with a quick hand. "There you go."

As they stared awkwardly at each other, Tamsin caught another whiff of lavender. Something about Wren was different.

"Oh!" Tamsin finally managed. "Your eyes are green."

Strangely, Wren didn't seem as shocked. "And?"

"They were gray before."

"No." Wren frowned. "I'm fairly certain my eyes have always been green."

Tamsin shook her head wildly. She remembered Wren's eyes: the color of slate, the gray of rain-soaked stone. This new color was vivid and shocking. It made her want to stare. It made her want to look away.

"Why are you looking at my eyes, anyway?" Wren's tone was playful, but her smile was guarded.

"I'm not," Tamsin snapped, despite the fact that she obviously had been. She pulled away, leaving the lantern behind for Wren. Even as she walked away, she listened for Wren's footsteps to follow her.

It was the darkness, Tamsin told herself, that was throwing everything off. She had been awake for only a short time, but already she was exhausted, ready to throw herself back into sleep. The darkness meant that everything felt closer, more intimate, when all she had done was save Wren from a patch of mud. The darkness was even playing tricks on her eyes, changing colors, giving Tamsin glimpses of another life, one where she noticed the smell of a person's hair or the color of her eyes simply from staring into them.

But that wasn't who she was. That wasn't her lot in life. And so Tamsin swore she would not let the darkness play with her mind. She would not let the darkness win and break her already useless heart.

The innkeeper of the Fickle Fare recognized Tamsin too. But theirs was not a happy reunion. "All I have is a shack," the hawk-eyed woman said, her eyes beady and judgmental. "It used to hold my goats. But we fixed it up. Some."

Tamsin opened her mouth to protest, but the woman looked down her nose at Tamsin's left arm, as though she could see the mottled skin through the layers of clothing. It was enough to shut Tamsin up. This innkeeper knew exactly what she was responsible for. She knew she had been stripped of the Coven's sigil. Without it, Tamsin had no more status than a child stumbling Within for the very first time, their magic tumultuous and wild. She was not respected. She did not matter. Still, her mother was the High Councillor, and she had a hunting license issued by the Coven. The woman did not dare to turn her away completely.

"Fine." Tamsin turned on her heel and made her way around the small cottage to the shack behind. The door smacked the small bed as it opened. The room was practically a closet.

"Where's the other bed?" Tamsin detected a hint of panic in Wren's voice.

"Don't worry," Tamsin said, taking a tentative step into the small space. Her shins collided with the bed frame. "I'll just conjure another one. We could put it . . . here." She pointed to a space, barely large enough to fit the two of them standing up.

Tamsin closed her eyes and tried to focus.

"This is ridiculous—you're going to kill us." Wren put a hand on Tamsin's arm to stop her, but it seemed to have the opposite effect. Tiny sparks floated from her hand. She hurried to extinguish them before the bedspread caught fire. "Are you okay?"

"Fine," Tamsin snapped, embarrassed. She always had control of her magic. She really was behaving like a child. "We can just . . ."

They both stared at the small bed. Wren tugged on the end of her braid.

"What side of the bed do you sleep on?"

Tamsin stared at her uncomprehendingly. "I sleep on a bed. There are no sides."

Wren exhaled loudly. "Fine. I'll take the side by the wall; you can squeeze in here."

Tamsin blinked several times in quick succession. "We're going to *share* this bed?"

"Unless you want to sleep on the floor." Wren pointed at the stone surface covered in dirt and dust and mold.

"Why do *I* have to sleep on the floor?"

"Because you're full of secrets. If you bring them all onto this bed, there won't be any room left for me." Wren started to laugh—strange, hiccupping giggles that nearly caused Tamsin to laugh too. Instead she was sobered by logistics. How they would both fit. How she was supposed to lie so that she wouldn't disturb Wren, wouldn't touch her unnecessarily, wouldn't impose on her space, wouldn't make her uncomfortable.

When Wren finally stopped laughing, she scooted herself toward the wall, leaving Tamsin a sliver of space on the bed. The witch settled herself carefully onto the worn mattress and slid beneath a fraying quilt.

"Don't I get a pillow at least?" A chill had crept into her bones despite the fact that she was wrapped in the thin blanket. She was facing Wren's back, her whole body tense, trying not to touch her.

"Secrets," Wren reminded her, causing Tamsin to sigh in frustration.

"I'm sorry," Tamsin whispered into the darkness. "I just didn't want you to stop looking at me the way you do."

Wren shifted, turning toward Tamsin. "Like what?"

Their faces were so close. "Like maybe I'm not as terrible as I always thought."

"You're not so terrible," Wren murmured, her eyes drooping, her words thick with sleep.

Tamsin rolled over before Wren could change her mind.

Lying there in silence, listening to the wind whistle through the cracks in the walls, they worried their separate worries. They feared their separate fears. Tamsin felt something else, too. Just a flicker, like the sparks she had shot from her fingers. She hadn't been so near another person in years. Certainly not someone as good as Wren.

For Tamsin begrudgingly had to admit that Wren was not only a better person than she, but also someone who made her want to dissect her words, to think about her actions.

Wren made her want to be better.

"Tamsin?" Wren's voice was soft in the darkness. Tentative. She sounded breakable.

Tamsin tensed, certain that if she spoke, Wren would ask her to move to the floor. She couldn't. Wouldn't. Tamsin needed the warmth radiating from the source's skin. She needed to believe she was truly smelling lavender each time Wren shifted beside her.

Wren, forever describing sunsets and explaining smells, gave Tamsin a glimpse of the world the curse had taken from her. Wren's touch offered the warmth that had once been so elusive. Tamsin *needed* Wren, much as she didn't want to admit it. And so she lay still and did not reply. When Wren did not speak again, Tamsin exhaled softly, letting her mind run circles around itself, letting it wonder and letting it want, until the rise and fall of Wren's breathing became a lullaby that sent her off to sleep.

EIGHTEEN

WREN

Wren woke with her back against the wall, her cheek on Tamsin's shoulder, their legs tangled together. *Inevitable,* she told herself, *when two people share one small bed.*

Still, logic couldn't tame the fluttering in her chest.

Tamsin smelled of salt and sage, her skin surprisingly warm for one so cold. Wren reached up to brush Tamsin's hair from her face, and her fingers hit the ribbon around the witch's neck. The butterflies in her stomach stopped their fluttering. Wren was indebted to the witch, to every cruel, cold facet of her. Perhaps Wren didn't even care about Tamsin so much as envy her and her cavalier attitude, her absolutely infuriating propensity to keep secrets, her refusal to consider the feelings of anyone who wasn't herself.

Wren fingered Tamsin's silky curls as she pushed them out of her eyes. It was true that Tamsin was brash and complicated. Still, there was no denying there was something soft about her, something sweet that she took great pains to disguise. There were moments, glimpses of a grin, the sparkle of her dark eyes, when Wren saw again the person behind the curse—the girl Tamsin was but couldn't show. The girl Tamsin might have been if she could have loved.

When Tamsin spoke about her sister, it was clear how much she still cared, curse be damned. Last night, even, as they had maneuvered through the awkwardness of sharing a bed, it was almost as if . . . *No.* Wren wouldn't let her imagination run away like that. She had always been a dreamer. An idealist. Even now, Wren was fairly certain she could live forever on those tiny glimpses of Tamsin. That even the barest hint of the witch's true heart would be enough to sustain her.

Pathetic, she told herself as she extracted her other arm from beneath Tamsin's head. The witch sighed deeply and rolled from her back onto her side, so that she faced Wren. Her eyes were still closed, her face relaxed in sleep. Tamsin was undeniably beautiful, always, but without the ever-present tension and anger she held in consciousness, she looked different. Younger. They could hardly have a year's difference between them, but the load Tamsin carried aged her. Wren could help, if only Tamsin would trust her. But of course it wasn't that simple.

Wren wanted to cry at the irony of having fallen for a girl with a useless heart.

Carefully, so slowly she thought she might pull a muscle, Wren climbed over Tamsin's sleeping form. She didn't want the witch to wake, didn't want to have the necessary yet awkward conversation about sharing a sleeping space and how it meant nothing at all.

Nothing, Wren knew, could still mean so much.

She stepped across the shack and pulled on her father's boots. There was a pang in her chest as she thought of him, tossing and turning in their tiny cottage. She tried to picture his face but to her horror found that the image was fading. She had already lost the color of his eyes to Tamsin. When her father's face was meaningless to her heart, she would have no reason to hold on to the rest. He would slip soundlessly from the forefront of her memory, just another person she had passed in this great, wide world.

Perhaps that was for the best. Surely, it would be easier not to remember what she had lost.

Wasn't that the reason Tamsin seemed so defeated? Every day she had held the memory of her sister. Of the classmate who had died because of her. No wonder the witch was so closed off and cold. There was no room within her for anything but guilt and resentment and fear. Her entire life was a reminder of her failure. Of the rash mistake of a child.

That should not be enough to define her. She needed the chance to forgive herself. To make things right. But to do that, they had to find Marlena. Wren glanced at Tamsin, who was still snoring lightly. She pulled the witch's green cloak from the foot of the bed and pushed the door open slowly so it wouldn't creak. She made her way through the darkness to the inn, hoping to warm her cold hands with a cup of tea. Tea always had a way of helping Wren think.

This inn was not nearly as nice as the other, but the one thing both places had in common was that they were littered with witches. Keeping her head down, Wren slipped into a chair at the head of a mostly empty table. Tea poured itself into a metal tankard, hints of bergamot and cardamom tickling her nose. Wren took a long sip. The tea went down easily, hot enough to soothe her but not so hot that she burned her tongue.

She set to work sifting methodically through the pockets of Tamsin's cloak. She found string and buttons in one, in another a rind of cheese so hard it might have been stone. A third held a small brown pouch of dried herbs; another housed a round, pink crystal. None of the items glowed warm in her hand. None of them were magic. The pile of trinkets kept growing, new pockets appearing as soon as she thought she'd found them all. But none held Marlena's diary.

Wren paused, frustrated. Took a sip of tea. She had wanted to do something, to take action herself. Tamsin was so cagey when it came to Marlena's diary, as though it had secrets that might reveal themselves to Wren, secrets Tamsin didn't want shared. She never would have given it to Wren voluntarily. But if they were going to find Marlena, they needed a place to start.

Wren wanted to do that for them. She wanted to contribute, to do more than offer up magic when they needed to eat. She wanted to prove to Tamsin that they were a team, that the witch needed *her* as much as Wren needed Tamsin.

But to do that, she first had to find the diary within the depths of Tamsin's cloak. Not to read it, for that would be a violation of a perfect stranger, and if Marlena was anything like her sister, Wren knew better than to invite her wrath.

Rather, she hoped to get a sense of Marlena and her magic. If she knew the scent, the feel of Marlena's power, perhaps she could follow that trail to the real person.

Wren took another sip of tea. She was searching like an ordinary person. She wasn't searching like a source. She put the tankard down and spread the cloak out on the table. She closed her eyes, hands roving slowly over the thick fabric. She paid attention to the sensation, waiting for warmth, waiting for a hint that something enchanted was near. Her mind was so busy worrying about what to expect that she almost didn't notice the taste of honey on her tongue. She stopped, her hands hovering over a fold on the left side of the cloak. She lowered her fingers and felt the ghost of a pinprick. *There.*

Wren pulled the thin volume from its pocket, the leather cover soft and worn, the paper's edges stained and torn. At first she was unable to pry the cover open. Then, when the book finally fell open in her hand, she was met with blank page after blank page.

"All right," Wren muttered. "You don't want to reveal yourself to me. That's fine. You don't know me." She felt rather silly talking to a book.

A summoning spell whizzed past her right ear. Wren startled, glancing around the room at the witches immersed in their craft. One witch chanted softly over a book filled with scribbled runes; another stirred herbs into her teacup. A group of boys no older than twelve were summoning things from across the room, competing with one another to see whose spell could reach the item first.

None of them were shying away from their magic.

It's like you're fighting too hard against what you are, Leya had said. *Give in.*

Wren opened to a blank page at random. She slowly rubbed the paper between her thumb and pointer finger, freeing the traces of magic so that she could read them. She brought the parchment to her nose.

First came the overwhelming stink of sulfur. Wren gagged but forced herself to breathe through it. It was the same smell that had flooded her nostrils as they walked through the bog, the same smell that surrounded the victims of the plague. It was the stink of dark magic. She was on the right track.

After the scent of rotting eggs had dissipated, Wren caught a hint of salt. Her hair ruffled, as though catching a soft breeze. She squeezed her eyes shut, trying to block out the traces of magic in the room and listen to what the paper revealed.

A crunching, like the snapping of twigs. The crashing of thunder, a bright flash behind her closed eyelids like lightning. Her mouth tasted bitter, like charred wood. And through it all, Wren was lulled by a rhythmic roaring, though she knew not where it came from. Perhaps it was the earth itself.

"What are you doing?"

The magic died as quickly as it had come, the images fleeing so quickly that Wren began to wonder if they had ever been there at all. She opened her eyes to find Tamsin looking between Wren and the diary with apprehension.

"It wouldn't let me read it," Wren explained sheepishly, showing Tamsin the blank pages. "Not that I would have, even if I could," she added quickly. The witch's face relaxed. "But I can smell magic." She tried to hold on to the salt, the lightning, and the bitter ash. "I just thought—"

"That's right." Tamsin settled herself in the seat across from Wren and leaned forward on her elbows. "What does mine smell like, then?" She was staring right into Wren's eyes, her lips twisted in a mischievous grin.

Wren froze. It was oddly intimate, describing a scent to the person it emanated from. "Fresh herbs," she finally managed. "Rosemary and sage, mostly. Sometimes basil. Dill." Her face flushed. Wren resented her body for so mercilessly betraying her feelings.

"Huh." Tamsin was still staring at her intently. "Well, then, what did you find?"

Wren told the witch what she'd tasted, heard, and felt. Tamsin's expression softened with each detail, her eyes far away.

When Wren mentioned the rhythmic roaring and the smell of salt, Tamsin's focus snapped back to the present. "I know where Marlena is."

"You do?" It was Wren's turn to lean across the table. She had expected her clues to help, not to solve. "Wait, I actually did something right?"

Tamsin frowned again. "What do you mean?"

Wren squirmed, suddenly self-conscious. "I just . . . tend to not be very useful. I can sell an egg and make a broth, but other than that, my skills are rather limited." She shrugged, fiddling with the corner of Tamsin's cloak.

"Stop that," Tamsin scolded. Wren's hands stopped moving, but Tamsin shook her head. "Not the cloak. Your lack of self-appreciation. It's very irritating. You have power most people can't dream of. Start acting like it. You *matter*." Tamsin locked eyes with Wren, sending a jolt of energy through her blood. "Now come on." Tamsin pushed back from the table, gesturing for Wren to hand over her cloak. "We've got quite the walk ahead of us."

Wren had never been one to fear the dark, but the never-ending night had changed that. She clutched tightly to her lantern, the little blue flame dancing like the dread in her stomach with each step she took. The strange sounds of the endless night—shrieks and howls and scrapes—kept her close to Tamsin. So close that she kept stepping on the heels of the witch's boots, earning herself dark looks and weary sighs.

They followed a narrow path that took them far from the Fickle Fare, into a dense patch of woods. The air was thick with magic, making it difficult to breathe. A fine mist clung to the trees, dressing them with droplets as big and round as pearls in the lamplight. Between the tight-knit trees were endless patches of briars, the thorns so sharp that Wren and Tamsin had to pause and pick their way around for fear they would be caught forever.

It was quiet, save for the snapping of branches and the rustling of their clothing as they worked to extract themselves from the forest's clutches. Wren nearly cried with joy when the trees opened up to a glen, all rolling hills and rings of thick grass. The moss beneath her feet hummed softly, one solid, solitary note, which reverberated in her chest, taking the place of her heartbeat. She became the sound.

The glen was filled with rock formations: giant spirals, wild zigzags, tall towers, and careful clusters. Wren made to pass beneath a slab of rock balanced on two tall stones, but Tamsin pulled her back.

"Better not," she said, "unless you'd like to fall straight into the sky."

"At least then I'd have some idea where we're going," Wren muttered, but her heart wasn't in it.

"I can't believe I didn't think of this sooner. I should have known." Tamsin's mournful expression told Wren that she was talking not simply about their destination but about Marlena herself.

"How could you have?" Wren reached out a hand to touch Tamsin's shoulder, but Tamsin tensed. Wren pulled her hand away.

"She's my twin sister." Tamsin wrapped her cloak tightly around her. "I was supposed to know."

Wren tugged at her braid. She knew nothing about being a sister, but she knew something about what it felt like to fail family. "It's not your fault." Wren kicked at the grass. "I know you don't care what I have to say, but I hope you know it's true."

"I do, you know." Tamsin's voice was hesitant. Wren furrowed her brow. "Care," Tamsin clarified, staring determinedly at her boots.

Wren fought to keep a smile off her face even as she rubbed at the goose bumps lining the backs of her arms. She didn't want to scare Tamsin away with her emotions, especially since she knew Tamsin hadn't meant her words the way Wren wanted her to.

She *couldn't* mean them like that.

The witch led them up the side of a hill to level ground. They walked in silence together, Wren fighting the impulse to stop and collect bundles of wildflowers, their petals deep purple, bright blue, vivid pink. She didn't want Tamsin to think her frivolous. She didn't want to slow them down.

They did not speak again until they reached a roaring river, the water moving so swiftly and its magic so disjointed that it left Wren nauseated and shaky.

"Careful," Tamsin said. "The stones get slick." Then she was picking her way carefully across the flat stepping-stones that offered a path through the angry water. Wren exhaled sharply and followed, willing her feet to keep her upright.

On the other side was another forest, only this one was neither lush nor green. It was more the ghost of a forest, trunks and branches bare and blackened and burned. Ash settled on Wren's tongue, the taste familiar. She felt a swell of pride, despite the dismal scenery. Her magic had led them there.

Wren was so distracted that she forgot to watch her feet. She tripped over a giant branch and sprawled out on the hard dirt, the wind knocked from her lungs. She scrambled for her lantern, which had fallen beside her, and held it up to investigate.

She immediately wished she hadn't.

It wasn't a branch she had tripped over at all, but *bone*. What had appeared to be gnarled, petrified wood was actually a giant set of antlers still attached to a sharp snow-white skeleton. There was a terrible stench of spoiled venison. Wren nearly retched right there in the grass.

And then, before their eyes, the bones began to move.

Tamsin yanked Wren to her feet. She was too startled to protest the pain that shot up her arm. The skeleton groaned, clanking and clattering as it rose to all fours. A song composed of three high, sharp notes reverberated through the trees. It sent a chill down Wren's spine. It put her skin on edge.

"Okay, now listen to me," Tamsin said, her voice so quiet it was barely a whisper. "I'm going to need you to stay calm."

"I think we're past that." Wren had squeezed her eyes shut in hopes of staunching the tears that tickled at the edges. She had never seen anything so horrible. A deer without its skin—with nothing but the hard interior that gave it shape—wasn't an animal anymore. It was a monster. "Is it dark magic?"

"Worse," Tamsin said, her voice hard. "It's one of Arwyn's scouts."

The name meant nothing to Wren, but the look of terror on Tamsin's face said enough. She had no desire to come face-to-face with the sort of witch who would create such a gruesome creature. "Who's Arwyn?"

Tamsin's eyes flickered around the dark forest, the light from her flame casting strange, galloping shadows across the earth. "She's one of the Coven. She's, uh . . ." Tamsin trailed off, eyes lingering on the skeleton. "She's the one who turned me in."

Without thinking, Wren put a hand on Tamsin's shoulder. The witch flinched slightly, but she did not pull away.

The horrible song echoed through the clearing again, much closer this time. The skeleton before them lifted its head in the air, rapt. Leather and oil clung to the breeze. The air rattled with the creaking and clattering of bones. Arwyn was coming, bringing a herd of skeleton spies with her. A large foot stepped on a branch, the snap echoing through the empty air.

Tamsin had gone white as a sheet.

"Come on." Without thinking, Wren reached for Tamsin's hand. It was a testament to the witch's state that she did not protest; she merely allowed herself to be led. The trees were spindly and thin, hardly big enough to give them cover. But Wren wanted to keep hidden, wanted to protect Tamsin from the footsteps, the endless clacking that filled the air.

They crowded behind the largest trunk Wren could find, their shoulders pressed together, their hands still intertwined. Wren tried to steady her shaky breathing, but whether the root of it was fear or her proximity to the witch, she couldn't tell.

"It's all right," Wren whispered quietly, even as the clacking got louder. Even as she knew her reassurance was a lie. Tamsin was battling memories, was haunted by her past at every turn. Wren wanted to save her, but she didn't know how.

Then something nudged her other hand, something smooth and hard and cold. The white bone of a deer's antler.

Wren screamed as the skeleton scout shoved her, sending both Wren and the witch tumbling out into the open. They landed in a heap, their faces close, Tamsin's body pressed against hers. Wren hardly noticed the branch digging into her back. She was enchanted by the witch's lips. They were rounded in a small O of surprise, so close Wren could feel her hot breath on her cheek. For a moment Wren forgot about the woods around them, the skeletons, Arwyn, the plague. For a moment there was only Tamsin.

The witch's eyes searched hers, the air between them hushed and stilted. The magic between them thick enough to slice.

And then Arwyn cleared her throat, the bones of her skeleton lackeys clacking together as they settled.

"Well, well, well," she said, her voice sharp as a winter wind whistling through bare branches. Her skin was as translucent as morning frost, her hair shorn down to her skull. Her green eyes glittered in the weak light of her lantern, just as icy as the rest of her. "What do we have here?"

NINETEEN

TAMSIN

They were done for.

Tamsin felt it in the way Wren shifted beneath her. Knew it before she even looked into the tracker's eyes. There was no warmth there, nor had she expected there to be. Arwyn was precise. Exacting. Detached. She always had been. When Tamsin was a child, she'd been in awe of the woman, the way she carried herself, the authority she radiated. She was the only witch in the world who dared to enter Vera's chambers without an appointment.

That reverence was gone now. It wasn't that Tamsin resented Arwyn for turning her in—the Coven existed for the sole purpose of preventing the spread of dark magic, after all. Arwyn had only been doing her job. It was that Tamsin was embarrassed to have been caught by the witch she had respected most in the world. It was the way Arwyn's face had twisted in disgust as she took in the twelve-year-old's haggard appearance. As though Tamsin were not just a fool, but a stranger. The disappointment in her voice had hurt worse than any of her harsh words.

There was no trace of that disappointment now as the woman towered over the two of them lying in a crumpled heap on the forest floor. Now there was only anger, white hot like an iron in the fire. Tamsin scrambled to her feet, putting as much distance as possible between herself and Wren.

She focused on Arwyn's boots, trying to put aside the strange fluttering in her chest. Trying to forget the feeling of her body pressed against Wren's—a body that was soft and warm and had stirred something guttural and deep and desperate within her. She wanted to know what it meant, and, perhaps more important, how it was possible that she could feel anything at all.

"Hello," Tamsin finally said, meeting the older witch's eyes with as much dignity as she could muster.

Arwyn snorted. Apparently, Tamsin hadn't had much dignity to work with.

"What on earth are you doing here?"

Tamsin was startled to find that Arwyn was actually expecting an answer. Usually, the tracker's questions were rhetorical. She knew everything that happened Within and wanted everyone to know it. It was off-putting, watching the woman wrestle with her curiosity.

"We're here to hunt," Wren piped up, cheeks still burning red.

Tamsin shot her a sharp look. The girl did not know how to read a room.

Arwyn's mouth split into an empty smile. "Are you, now?" Her eyes silently appraised Wren, her patchwork clothes, her pink cheeks and freckled nose and eager eyes, bright and defiant. Tamsin felt suddenly protective of the source, resented how Arwyn's gaze lingered on Wren's too-big boots. As though her appearance somehow made her unworthy of respect.

"Yes," Wren squeaked, although she didn't sound particularly certain.

"Interesting." Arwyn moved her icy eyes back to Tamsin. "And who approved this?" Her fingers twitched as though ready to issue a binding spell, ready to clap iron around Tamsin's wrists and haul her back to the academy.

"The High Councillor." Tamsin hated the way her voice shook.

Arwyn's nearly invisible eyebrows shot up. "Vera knows you're here?"

Anyone who did not know the tracker could not have detected the hurt in her voice, but Tamsin knew her, had spent so many years studying her mannerisms and her tone. Arwyn felt betrayed. Vera had kept the truth a secret, had turned to her daughter in her time of need. It sparked something within Tamsin, something almost hopeful.

Perhaps she did still have a family after all.

"Yes." When Tamsin spoke again, her voice was stronger. She pulled the hunting license from her cloak pocket and offered it to the tracker as proof. Her hand did not waver.

Arwyn's expression soured. Behind her, her bone army clacked menacingly. Somewhere, far away, a bird called.

"I told your mother she was making a mistake when she banished you. I told her to kill you."

Tamsin had hoped her curse would make her impervious to that sort of hurt. But of course she felt it, every sinking inch of pain. It wasn't that she thought Arwyn was wrong. It was that she wondered if she was right.

If she had been killed, as precedent required, none of this would be happening. Marlena would not have summoned the plague. Dark magic would not be ravaging the earth. Arwyn would not be looking at her with renewed disdain.

"Well, she's alive," Wren piped up, her voice stronger this time, "and she's probably your best chance of finding this dark witch. So you should really let us get on with it." She glanced over at Tamsin appreciatively. Tamsin felt a flood of warmth. Wren knew everything, all her twisted, messy pieces, and believed in her anyway. Wren's voice silenced some of the doubt racing through Tamsin's head.

If Tamsin had died, Marlena would not have lived. Wren would not be standing here, eyes blazing with a fire Tamsin had never before seen. For better or for worse, Tamsin was here. Alive. She had made her mistakes.

Now she had the opportunity to fix some of them.

"Our best chance?" Arwyn's eyes pooled with pity. "Where did you find her?" she asked Tamsin with an empty smile. "She seems to be quite the yappy little guard dog."

"I'm simply stating the truth," Wren said, her bravado wavering slightly. "Just because you're too arrogant to see it doesn't mean it isn't fact."

Arwyn's hands balled into fists. Tamsin took a step toward Wren as though to shield her from the witch's wrath. But Arwyn merely chuckled.

"You think I'd waste my time on the likes of you two?" Her bone army rustled and settled. "If your mother had killed you when I told her to, we wouldn't be in this mess. But she betrayed me, betrayed all of us when she let you go. Our authority was tossed right out the window. And now there's someone else out there, testing our limits. Trying to see how much they can get away with."

Tamsin swallowed thickly, guilt roiling in her stomach. Arwyn was right, of course. She was always right.

"Rules are in place for a reason," she continued sharply. "After Evangeline, the Coven made a promise to hold witches to the highest standard. To never waver. But your mother did. And I can never forgive her for that." Arwyn exhaled, long and loud. "Do you think this is what I wanted? To monitor the activity of witches, making sure they don't take advantage of ordinary folk? Do you think I enjoy scouring the world for nonconsensual love spells?" She raised her eyebrows at Tamsin. "I could have become more. We all could have. But we made a promise, for the good of the world. For the good of all witches. And you broke that."

"I'm sorry," Tamsin said finally, her hand resting on the pocket that held her sister's diary. "I know it doesn't matter, that it doesn't change anything, but I am. I wish I hadn't done it, but

I did. That's the reason I came back: to help make things right."

The tracker rolled her eyes. "You have your mother's sentimentality. I told Vera that letting you live was a mistake, but she never listens to me when it really matters, does she?" Arwyn sniffed. "She must be rather desperate to have let you back Within. And this is how you repay her kindness." Her eyes flitted from Tamsin to Wren and back again. "Fooling around on the forest floor while the world falls to pieces. She always expected more of you than she should have. One daughter a disappointment, the other a disgrace." Arwyn pursed her lips thoughtfully as another breeze blew through the empty trees. "I'll let you two get back to it, then. Don't trip over my scouts again unless you've got something useful to share."

Arwyn pulled a small ivory flute from her belt and began an eerie song that made Tamsin's teeth ache. The skeleton herd jumped to attention, following as she turned away, bone clacking against bone. Her herd still gave Tamsin the heebie-jeebies. They had been with Arwyn for years, but Tamsin had never been able to figure out how the witch commanded bone with such ease. Despite all her prowess, Tamsin could not move so much as a mouse's skull.

"Well," Wren said finally, once the footsteps had grown silent, "now I know why you looked so frightened."

"And that was Arwyn in a good mood." Tamsin knew she was being flippant, but it was easier than letting the tracker's words hurt.

"She's terrifying, I can't imagine how you . . ." Wren trailed off and cocked her head. Listening. "What's wrong with the trees?"

Tamsin couldn't hear a thing. "I don't know what you mean."

"Look"—Wren rolled up her sleeves—"I have goose bumps."

Tamsin took in Wren's freckled skin, the tiny pinpricks of cold or fear or both that rose on its surface. For some indescribable reason, she started to wonder about all the skin she couldn't see.

"Tamsin." Wren's voice had gone sharp and high-pitched, the way it did when she was afraid. "Please. The trees are silent. It's worse than when they scream. It's like I'm trying to breathe underwater. Everything's muffled. I want to get out of here."

She grabbed Tamsin's arm right where the Coven's sigil had been stripped from her. It was the reason Tamsin kept her skin covered, a visible reminder of what her impulsivity had wrought. But beneath Wren's touch, Tamsin did not feel the scar's weight. Instead she felt a spark of possibility. Of redemption.

And so Tamsin nodded, wrapped an arm around Wren's waist, and guided her out of the wood.

She heard the sea before she saw it. The roaring in her ears drowned out her doubt, overpowered the churning nerves causing her hands to shake and her palms to sweat.

"I feel terrible." Wren's voice nearly floated away with the wind.

"Why?" Tamsin turned to her, surprised. "What did you do?"

Wren frowned. "I didn't *do* anything. I mean, my stomach hurts. I think I'm going to vomit."

Tamsin wrinkled her nose. "Please don't."

Wren shot her a sharp look. "Well, obviously I'm not going

to if I can help it. There's just this . . . clanging." She waved her hand around wildly. "This . . . roaring I can't seem to place, and the air is thick, and, oh!" She had turned toward the ocean, the little light from her lantern hardly bright enough to illuminate a single wave. "What is all that water?"

It took Tamsin a moment to realize that Wren had never seen the ocean before. "The . . . sea?"

Wren's eyes grew wide, her nausea apparently forgotten. She scampered forward like a child, bent to cup ocean water in her hand. "It's singing." Wren turned, beaming beatifically. "It's the nicest song. I'm sorry you can't hear it."

The airiness of her voice and the emptiness of her eyes were concerning. Tamsin yanked her away from the water. Wren had already wandered in ankle-deep.

"Your shoes are all wet now," Tamsin said to stifle Wren's protests. "If I hadn't come to save you, you would have walked straight into the sea."

"But the song. It was such a lovely song. The water only wanted me to add my voice to it." Wren sounded dreamy, soft as a whisper. Then her face went slack. She stopped walking and vomited loudly onto the sand. Tamsin recoiled, pinching her nose.

Wren wiped her mouth, her face pale and slick with sweat. "Something is really wrong here." Her eyes warily searched the coast, dotted with sloping sand dunes, littered with giant piles of gnarled driftwood stacked high as a wall. And, beyond that, something bigger. A light in the distance. "Do you think that's her?"

A mixture of panic and excitement welled up in Tamsin's chest as she moved toward the light. She scrambled and sank into the sand of the dune. Her legs screamed in frustration, her hands gripping the cold, silty grains in an attempt to steady herself. It was like trying to grab hold of a waterfall.

When Tamsin made it to the top, her excitement waned. There was a house . . . but perhaps calling it a house was too kind. It had the *structure* of a house—walls, doors, windows, roof—but the closer they came to it, the more apparent it was that it did not possess the sort of things that made a house livable. The front columns had crumbled away, the chimney was sunken, the doors had rusted hinges, and everything was coated with a thick layer of dust.

"Well, this looks promising." Beside her, Wren shuddered out a giant gasping breath. She pressed a hand to her mouth, her whole body tensing before she doubled over and vomited again into the sand. Tamsin hurried behind her and drew Wren's braid from over her shoulder, securing it far from harm's way.

Wren righted herself. "Thanks," she mumbled weakly. "It's the sulfur. Do you smell it?"

The wind shifted, and suddenly Tamsin did. It was a terrible stench, the smell permeating every inch of her. She nearly vomited too. Instead she nodded, trying to cover both her nose and her mouth while still allowing air into her lungs.

"There's so much dark magic here," Wren said as they approached the house, her skin a sickly green in the weak light pouring through the grimy front window. "Your sister has to be here somewhere." She looked as though she might faint.

Tamsin left footprints on the dusty front steps. She raised a fist to knock on the door, its wood weathered and worn. But before her knuckles had even grazed the door, it buckled, clattering from its useless hinges and falling to the ground with a crash louder than the waves.

A creeping sense of alarm slunk across the top of Tamsin's head, oozing down like the globby, sticky white of an egg. She didn't know what she would find when she finally came face-to-face with her sister. She didn't know who this new Marlena would be. Still, there was nothing to do now but forge ahead. She took a tentative step into the entryway of the dilapidated house. Wren, with one hand covering her mouth, followed.

The interior was just as dismal as the exterior. Wooden beams, rotted by age and the salt of the sea, sagged and crumbled, leaving the ceiling so low Tamsin often had to duck. The floorboards were loose, several missing entirely. One board buckled when Wren set down a foot. Tamsin had to yank her by the elbow to keep her from falling through.

There were ripped curtains, upturned chairs, and broken windowpanes, but though they searched through the destruction and rubble of every room—even braving a rickety staircase to the upper level—Marlena was nowhere to be found.

"I don't understand." Wren had curled up into a ball, her whole body shaking. "I can *feel* the dark magic. She should be right here."

Tamsin took in the bent nails, broken glass, and shards of mirror, but there was nothing to indicate that her sister had ever been there. Marlena was just as elusive as she'd always been.

Tamsin slumped to the floor, half with frustration, half with relief. "It doesn't make any sense."

She pulled the diary out of her pocket, but for once the black cover was sullen and still.

"What do you want from me?" she asked it, venom dripping from her every word.

Wren looked up from her knees, her eyes reflecting pools of pity. Tamsin's best hadn't been enough. *She* wasn't enough. She never had been.

"Please?" Tamsin hated how weak she sounded. How young and vulnerable and afraid.

A gust of wind, the breeze scented with salt, blew through the broken window, ruffling Tamsin's hair and rustling the pages of Marlena's diary. The book fell open on her lap. Tamsin gasped, the sound like a hiss in the dark, dingy room. It felt too simple. A trick. A trap. But there were the words in her sister's loopy hand, drawing her back in. Calling her name. Wren, her face still ghostly white, dragged herself closer to Tamsin, her hair tickling the witch's cheek as they both leaned forward to read.

I almost didn't bother to write. What can you say when you know you won't live to write again tomorrow? It's quite a bit of pressure, trying to make sure my final words are good enough. Not that I'd really know what good enough feels like. It's always been me scraping by, clinging by my fingernails to the bottom of the rope, hanging on for dear life. I suppose, if nothing else, I'll finally be able to relax. Stop trying too hard, even while I continue to end up exactly where I've always been.

I keep writing notes to Amma, folding them into the shapes her grandmother back in Kathos taught her. Tiny cranes, delicate swans, geometric frogs. She used to enchant them, send them hopping to my desk, floating through the air like they were flying. All I could ever do was slip my own notes into her pocket, but she pretended to be delighted all the same. I just keep writing and folding, writing and folding. I have a certifiable paper menagerie.

All the notes say the same thing: Come back.

I suppose that if tomorrow goes the way I expect it will, I'll get my wish. It won't be Amma coming back so much as me going there. But at least we'll be together.

And I'll never have to lay eyes on my sister again. It's funny, hating someone who shares your face. Every time I catch sight of myself in the mirror, I flinch. So I've shattered them all. My room no longer holds a single reflective surface, not even so much as a spoon. I don't want to remember what I wrought. I don't want to remember that I'm half of a terrible whole.

I haven't gone to see her. They're keeping her in a tower. I hope it has a window so she can see the way the Farthest Forest is ablaze with a terrible blue flame. Vera tried to put it out, taking no fewer than seven sources with her. It wasn't enough.

It's never enough, is it? We try and try our best, and it doesn't matter, in the end. I'm just one person, defined by my power—or lack thereof. Mine's just one heart.

I wonder what the world will be like without it. Without me.

I wonder who Tamsin will be without me too.

Beside her, Wren inhaled sharply. Tamsin stared down at the diary, trying to ignore the way Wren's eyes lingered on her face. She was hot and cold at the same time, a squirming, slithering wrongness settling in her bones. She hated that Wren had seen her sister's words.

Tamsin hated that *she* had seen them too.

She flung the diary down on the floor beside her, wrapped her arms around herself. She hadn't known the forest was on fire. There had been no window, just a tiny cot that she had hardly been able to pull herself from. She had been so tired. Dark magic didn't take a physical toll on the witch using it, but Tamsin had felt it emotionally. The reality of what she'd done—the consequences of her spell—had left her broken. Exhausted. A shell of the girl she had once been.

And then, the next day in the Grand Hall, when the Coven had gone to break the bond, Marlena would not meet Tamsin's eye. Soria, one of the Coven's sources, had asked them to stand face-to-face, their noses mere inches apart, and still Marlena would not acknowledge her. Tamsin had been desperate, had reached for Marlena's hand, but Councillor Mari had quickly restrained her.

So Tamsin could do nothing but watch as Soria dug deep in the space between them. She located the bond, and Vera cut it swiftly like a knife through flesh.

Tamsin had felt the life rush back into her at the same time it rushed out of her sister.

What she had done was undone in the blink of an eye.

She would never forget the sound of her sister's body hitting the floor. And now she knew that after that horrible day, Marlena had taken her place in the tower, sealed away from the world by stone without so much as a window.

"I don't know what to do." Tamsin's voice was rough. "I don't know how to find her. I never did. I never knew her at all." She kicked idly at a shard of broken mirror.

For a brief moment, she would have sworn she saw something flash in its depths.

She and Marlena had played a game when they were younger where they sat face-to-face, keeping their movements the same, their expressions exact. Back then, the imaginary glass between them had been clear and smooth. And then their magic had appeared, sending cracks running through them both. Cracks that still remained.

Tamsin picked up the shard of mirror and turned it over in her hands. She startled as the glass caught the reflection of a second pair of blinking brown eyes behind her. Eyes identical to her own.

She dropped the mirror and turned to face her sister.

"Hello, Tamsin." Marlena's voice was as dark as the night sky, and just as endless. "I see you found my diary."

TWENTY

WREN

Wren was seeing double. Of course she had known that Tamsin's sister would look like her. They were twins, after all. Still, it was disconcerting *how* identical they were—the long, dark hair, the round brown eyes. The way their foreheads wrinkled and pinched when they frowned. Their expressions were even the same: The scowl Wren had often seen plastered across Tamsin's face sat comfortably on Marlena's as she towered over them.

"How have you been, sister?"

Their voices were the same too. Lush and dark as night.

"You're alive," Tamsin said, getting shakily to her feet. They were even the same height. Wren pressed a hand to her eyes, but when she looked back, the sisters remained unchanged. Exactly the same.

"Well spotted." The scowl was still in place on Marlena's face.

"I didn't know." Wren's heart broke the same way Tamsin's voice did. Tamsin was staring at her sister as though she were a ghost.

"Yes, well, neither did I until recently." Marlena rolled her eyes. "Who's your friend?" She finally turned toward Wren, who felt self-conscious beneath Marlena's judgmental stare.

"I'm Wren." She pulled herself up, wavering slightly as another whiff of sulfur snaked into her lungs. She swallowed thickly, forcing down the bile that threatened to rise in her throat.

"Huh." Marlena did not seem particularly interested in her.

Wren couldn't blame her. The air between the sisters was ripe with tension and thick with words unspoken. Wren wondered if she ought to excuse herself, but then, where would she go?

"I'm glad you're here," Marlena said, her attention firmly fixed on Tamsin. "I wasn't certain they would let you back Within."

"I would have been here sooner, if I'd known." Tamsin's face was pained.

Marlena barked out a laugh. "Of course you would have been. Always the doting sister. I knew I could count on you. Although"—Marlena paused, her gaze far away—"the last few weeks have been rather eye-opening. Did you know that life is actually quite peaceful when you don't have to compare yourself to your sister? To the 'golden girl' of the world Within?" Marlena's lips had curled up into a sneer. "Did you know that once you were gone, I found my own power? I can do proper magic now. So maybe it wasn't that *I* was the weak one. Maybe it was that *you* were holding me back."

Marlena sent a stream of sparks from her hands. The room around them transformed before their eyes: A stone fireplace built itself quickly, housing a roaring orange fire. The walls lined themselves with bookshelves and giant potted plants. A carpet unrolled itself at their feet, slipping silently beneath their shoes. The shattered mirror put itself back together and hung itself on a wall above two green armchairs. A chandelier snaked its way around the newly repaired rafters, bathing them all in warm yellow light.

Marlena's magic made Wren woozy. She sank quietly onto the plush carpet, although neither sister seemed to notice. Marlena was smiling triumphantly. Tamsin was watching her sister with awe. Wren studied Marlena as well. She had expected the girl to show some sign of weariness, had expected the magic to take something from her. Instead she practically seemed to glow.

Which meant she was using dark magic.

"You never saw me as a person," Marlena said, circling Tamsin predatorily. "I was only ever a thing to be pitied. But I didn't ask for you to *save* me." Her voice was sharp as steel.

"I know," Tamsin said desperately. "I know, and I'm so sorry. It was my fault. All of it."

"You don't get to make my life about you," Marlena snapped. "Every time you looked at me, I could see the guilt swimming in your eyes. It was like you couldn't believe I could be happy if I wasn't as strong as you. But I was. Until you made me wonder if I shouldn't be." She laughed—a broken, screeching sound. "So are you happy now that I have unlimited power?" She swept her arms wildly to the side so that every book tumbled from its place on the shelf. "Is this who you wanted me to be?"

The room around them began to shake. There was a canyon between the sisters, all their unspoken resentment in the silence that hung heavy. Marlena glowered, her anger palpable. Tamsin retreated into herself, her shoulders slumping, her head bowed.

If Tamsin could not match her sister's anger, Wren would willingly step up and take her place. It couldn't have been a coincidence that on the same day Marlena escaped from the tower, ordinary folk began to fall ill.

"Why a plague?" She tried to keep her voice level, though the magic Marlena had used to shake the room had left a pressure pushing against Wren's chest. She struggled to breathe.

Marlena wheeled around to stare at Wren, looking at her as though she were a bug beneath a boot. "What are you talking about?"

Wren got shakily to her feet. Marlena was a passable actress. But Wren wasn't fooled. The plague was so destructive, so all-encompassing and inescapable, that it was impossible to ignore. "Your spell is ripping open the earth, draining the color and life from things. People are sick, their memories wiped clean, their hearts broken. Your magic is *hurting* people, Marlena."

Marlena merely blinked at her. "I have absolutely no idea what you are talking about."

"The plague that's erasing memories from the minds of

ordinary folk." Wren was having trouble imagining that Marlena, regardless of the anger she might feel toward her sister, could truly be so cruel, so uncaring.

Marlena shook her head uncomprehendingly. "I have no knowledge of any such spell. I wouldn't do something like that. I'm not Evangeline. I'm not *Tamsin*."

Tamsin, who had been standing quiet and still, flinched.

"That isn't fair." Wren's voice was low but full of warning. She tried to meet Tamsin's eye, but the witch was staring determinedly at the floor.

Marlena shot her a look of disgust. "And who are you to be lecturing me about what is or isn't fair?"

"My father is sick," Wren said, her heart clenching as she thought of him, his presence already hazy in her mind. "He has been taken down by your spell."

"I already told you," Marlena said, her voice rising, "I didn't cast any spell. I was asleep in a tower for five years, because *she* decided to tie my survival up with hers." She pointed a finger at Tamsin, her arm shaking with the same venom in her voice. "I didn't ask her to use dark magic—magic that killed my best friend and practically burned Within to the ground. But she did it anyway. And now that I'm alive, now that I have the possibility of a real life, you want to blame whatever's happening in the world on me? I don't think so."

Wren exhaled sharply. When Tamsin had used dark magic, strange things had happened in turn. The fires. The destruction. The death. None of it had come *from* Tamsin. The chaos had stemmed from her spell.

Once the bond had been broken, the world had quietly returned to normal. The thread between the sisters had been dormant while Marlena slept, the side effects nonexistent until Marlena had escaped from the tower, pulling strength from the bond that still connected the sisters. In doing so, she had woken the dark magic that had slept beside her for nearly five years.

And then Wren understood. The plague wasn't a spell Marlena had cast. It was a side effect of dark magic. Another consequence of Tamsin's five-year-old spell.

"No." The desperation in Tamsin's voice told Wren that the witch had pieced together the answer too. "This can't be because of me. Not again." She glanced helplessly around the room, her eyes finally meeting Wren's. "I didn't mean . . . I never wanted to hurt *anyone*."

Tamsin was haunted. Shattered. That much was clear just by looking at her. Something in Wren broke as she took in the pain behind Tamsin's eyes.

"I know," Wren said. And she did. Her father might be ill because of Tamsin's spell, but that didn't mean she would turn her back on the witch. Tamsin had started their journey harsh and arrogant, distrustful and mocking. But as they had traveled onward, the witch had unraveled, showing the soft, sweet, vulnerable sides of herself. Wren knew the plague was only a side effect. It was not magic borne from malice. It was a good intention gone horribly wrong.

She didn't need to punish Tamsin for her choices. Tamsin was doing enough of that herself.

"What a tender moment," Marlena snapped. "But I'm going

to need one of you to explain to me exactly what's going on."

Tamsin glanced nervously at Wren, who nodded encouragingly.

"The magic that you hold, the power that you feel . . ." Tamsin swallowed hard. "It's because of the bond of dark magic between us. It was never fully broken. That's how you survived. That's why you have this strength. Magic isn't affecting you the way it used to because you're using dark magic. You're not the one feeling the consequences. The earth is." Tamsin took a deep breath, twisting the hem of her cloak in her lithe hands. "And when you leaned on our bond to break through Vera's wards, the world rebelled. The plague Wren spoke of, it's because of us. A side effect of our spell."

"*Our* spell?" Marlena laughed bitterly. "Oh, no. *No.* You don't get to pin this on me. All I did was give myself the freedom I deserved. I didn't do anything else. I didn't ask for this."

"I know you didn't." Tamsin took a step toward her sister. "And I know I have no right to ask anything of you."

Marlena sniffed. "That's right," she said darkly. "You don't."

"But," Tamsin continued, her shoulders set determinedly, "we have to break the bond between us. It's the only way to restore the world to the way it was."

"Oh, break the bond *you* created? Give up the life *you* forced upon me?" Marlena stared at Tamsin pointedly. "Vera made it pretty clear all those years ago that if we break this bond, I'll die. So, thanks, but no thanks." Marlena rolled her eyes and turned her back on both of them, flopping into an armchair.

Tamsin's face paled. Wren was frozen with uncertainty. It

had been rather ridiculous of them to assume Marlena would happily sacrifice her second chance at life. Even if it was a second chance she hadn't asked for. Even with the world at stake. But if the bond wasn't broken, there was a chance the Coven would kill Tamsin, and then both sisters' lives would be lost in the process.

"What about Amma?" Wren's voice felt especially loud in the quiet room.

Marlena stiffened.

"You lost her to a side effect of dark magic. Now others are losing people they love to the very same thing. But you can do something about that. You can help us end this."

Marlena's face was hidden by a waterfall of hair, but her hands were white-knuckled and shaking as they gripped the armchair. A teacup, sitting delicately atop a saucer, shattered, sending shards of porcelain flying. From her corner, Wren caught a whiff of sulfur. The dark magic Marlena drew from was so close she could touch it. Nausea washed over her like a wave, bile creeping up her throat. Her skin was clammy and cold.

"How *dare* you." Each one of Marlena's words seemed to stab Wren in the heart. Ropes slithered around her legs and waist. She struggled to free herself from Marlena's bindings, but her hands grew tangled in the black ribbons of magic snaking their way around her, holding her in place.

"Marlena." Tamsin's tone was warning, but her sister made no indication she had heard.

"You might have read my diary"—Marlena got to her feet, shooting a dark look at Tamsin before returning her attention to Wren—"but don't presume to think that you know anything about me. Do you think I wanted this?" Marlena's voice tickled Wren's ear, and Wren shuddered. The heat of Marlena's anger lingered on her skin. "I lost *five years* of my life. My best friend is *dead*. My mother couldn't acknowledge my existence, lest she be put to death, and my own *sister* is the reason I'm in this situation in the first place. So don't," Marlena said, her voice dripping with poison, "pretend like we're the same. Not when you look at her the way you do. You're just another one of my sister's endless admirers."

Wren's stomach squirmed, her cheeks hot with embarrassment. She felt Tamsin's eyes on her but refused to meet them. Marlena had known Wren all of two minutes, and already she had seen right through her. Perhaps Marlena was right after all. Wren had no idea what she was doing. She was in so far over her head it was laughable.

"*Marlena.*" Tamsin's voice tripped over her sister's name.

"Oh, don't you start." Marlena rounded on her and ran a hand through her river of hair. It was still startling how alike the sisters looked. "I hate this. I hate who I am around you. Do you think I want to be this miserable? This resentful? All I wanted was to make it through the academy and get out of Within and as far away from you as I could muster. Do you know how incredible it would have been to live a life of anonymity? To have no one know Vera was my mother, no one know you were my sister?"

Marlena ran a hand over her face. "Amma was going to take me to Kathos. On a ship. I was going to see a whole new country." Her eyes were wide and far away, her voice soft, almost tender. "We were going to build me a brand-new life. And then *you* took her away." Tears clung to Marlena's eyelashes like flies to a spider's web. "You made her death my fault too. And I had no choice but to live with that." She let out a harsh bark of laughter. Perhaps it was a sob. Either way, the sound skittered across Wren's skin like a hundred beetles.

"Do you have any idea what it's like to lose someone you love?" Marlena took a step toward Tamsin, her movements swift and precise.

"Yes," Tamsin said, her voice so quiet Wren struggled to hear it. "I lost you."

A vase of white flowers tumbled from a table and shattered on the floor.

"Don't do that," Marlena said, hands shaking. "You didn't *lose* me; you made a decision without my consent. All this talk about how you *saved* me, but did you ever stop to think that maybe I didn't need to be saved? That I didn't see myself as someone to be pitied?"

Tamsin twitched, her hands in fists, pressing her fingernails into her palms the way she did when she was frustrated or afraid. Wren hoped it wasn't the latter. Dark magic hovered above them with its putrid stink and its icy grip. While Tamsin might have been the one to call the dark magic all those years ago, she no longer controlled it. Now it was fully in Marlena's hands. And the way the witch was smiling at Tamsin and Wren, she seemed prepared to use it.

"You don't have to fight us, Marlena," Wren said, her wrists screaming beneath her bindings.

"Oh, come now." Marlena let out a laugh, bitter and raw. "Why do you think I called Tamsin here? It certainly wasn't to talk."

Tamsin's hand grazed Wren's leg, loosening her bindings. Wren slipped quickly out of Marlena's ropes, letting them fall to the floor with a thud.

From across the room, Marlena toppled an armchair. Tamsin skittered out of the way. "Don't look so worried, sister. I'm just experimenting," Marlena said, her voice light and airy. "Oh, but you don't want that, do you?" She pursed her lips in an exaggerated pout. "You don't want me to be strong. You want me weak so you can care for me. So that you can remain superior. But I have to admit, having power is just as much fun as you always made it look."

"But it's dark magic." Tamsin spoke through gritted teeth. "You aren't feeling the consequences."

"Oh, and you are?" Marlena's face was pinched.

"I feel them every day," Tamsin said, her voice raw and honest. "I know what it's like to carry that weight. I don't want that for you."

"Of course you don't," Marlena snapped, a howling gust of wind blowing through the room. The plants shook in their pots; the pages of the books on the floor flapped and rustled. "You never wanted anything for me. That's entirely my point."

Tamsin's hand brushed Wren's own, so softly it might have been an accident. Wren frowned at her, but Tamsin's gaze did not leave Marlena. When Tamsin's fingers met Wren's again, she realized what was happening. Tamsin was asking for permission.

Tamsin was going to fight her sister, and to combat Marlena's dark magic, she needed a source. She needed *Wren*.

Thunder clapped. A flash of lightning bathed the room in white light. Still, Wren hesitated. When first they'd started their journey, Wren had been willing to do whatever she needed to take down the dark witch. She had been prepared to sacrifice one life for hundreds of others. But it was different now, seeing Marlena in the flesh. Watching Tamsin watch her. Tamsin would never forgive herself if something happened to Marlena. Wren would never forgive herself if something happened to Tamsin. But the fight would be lost either way if Wren did not offer up her magic.

She closed her eyes, trying to remember Leya's words, to focus her power and push it all to the forefront. She tried to imagine it running out of her like a stream. Slow and steady, a babbling brook rather than a roaring river.

Wren reached for Tamsin's hand, sparks flying as magic surged between them. Tamsin squeezed Wren's fingers. Wren squeezed back, sending the witch everything she had. Everything she was afraid to say. Wren's clammy hand held tight to the witch's icy fingers as Tamsin carefully siphoned Wren's magic and prepared to turn it all against her sister.

TWENTY-ONE

TAMSIN

The first time Tamsin and Marlena had fought, they were five years old. Tamsin had cried for an hour afterward. She had always been more sensitive, more emotional. Marlena had thrown her sister a wary glance before turning her attention back to the toy that had sparked their argument: enchanted blocks gifted to them by Councillor Mari.

In an attempt to distance herself from her tearful twin, Marlena used the blocks to build a castle around herself so that Tamsin could not come in. It was the first time there'd been a wall between them, and Tamsin hated it, pushed against Marlena's tower with her shoulder, with her hands, to no avail. Anger and hurt swirled within her, and, desperate, she tried to topple the tower with her mind. That did it, sent the blocks tumbling, revealing her sister again. Marlena blinked at her in surprise, asked Tamsin how she had brought her tower crumbling down.

Tamsin told her she didn't know. But there had been a warm glow within her, almost as though the power had gone straight from her mind to the building blocks. It was a glimmer of magic, and even then, young and curious, Tamsin had known not to say a word, not to give her sister any indication that there might be differences between them. Tamsin had held her magic close and waited for Marlena to catch up.

They were not so different now as Marlena stood before her, their past the wall between them, and the warmth from Wren's magic filling the hollowness in Tamsin's chest. Her skin danced with electricity, the same way it always did when Wren was near.

A saucer shattered, the shards skittering across the floor.

"Sorry." Marlena's face was split with a grim joy. Her eyes sparkled like cut crystal.

"You're not." Tamsin's shoulders tensed. The sheer magnitude of the moment weighed upon her so heavily it threatened to break her in half.

"I have to admit, this is quite exciting." There was a wickedness in the slant of Marlena's smile, curved just so that it might have been a sneer. "Knowing that I carry enough power to best you."

Now that she had read her sister's diary, Tamsin could pinpoint the moment Marlena had turned so hateful. As soon as Tamsin had cast the spell, Marlena had changed, her anger festering the longer the dark magic lived inside her. It was clear that as Marlena had slept, that darkness—her hatred of her sister—had only continued to grow.

For Tamsin, the time alone had done the opposite. For five years she had held the memory of Marlena close to her empty heart, and while she could never quite remember the way it felt to love her sister, Tamsin had always held tight to the knowledge that she *had*.

Now she was beginning to realize that love wasn't always enough.

Her love had brought her here, to this. Her love had caused her to do something unforgivable. She didn't blame Marlena for her hatred. In fact she understood it. Tamsin had spent so many years telling herself she had done what was best for Marlena. Instead it was clear that Tamsin had only done what was best for herself.

Now she was faced with making another decision—what was best for Marlena, or what was best for the world.

She was afraid of getting the answer wrong a second time.

In her hand was enough magic to stop her sister. But Tamsin had already almost killed Marlena once. She didn't know if she could do it again. Didn't know if her twisted, useless heart would allow it.

"Please don't make me do this."

"Do what?" Marlena's smile was mocking. It was still strange, seeing her face.

"You don't know what this connection between us has done to the world." Tamsin took a hesitant step forward, her hand slipping from Wren's. "Mountains are crumbling. People are forgetting who they are. If we keep this up, the earth won't be able to hold you, and what good will your power be then?"

"What would you have me do?" Marlena snarled, looking for all the world like a wild animal instead of a girl. Tamsin wondered at the beauty of her. She was so raw, so alive—perhaps even more so for having cheated death.

"*Help* me," Tamsin said, reaching out a hand to touch her sister's cheek. "I'm so sorry, Marlena. I never meant for things to turn out like this. I didn't mean to hurt you. I don't *want* to hurt you now."

Marlena recoiled from Tamsin's touch. "But what if *I* want to hurt *you*? You never think about what other people want, do you?"

"Are you telling me there's nothing I can do to repent? There's not a single, tiny part of you that is happy to see me?" Tamsin hated the way her voice shook. She was again a little girl locked out of her sister's tower, wanting nothing more than to be let in.

"Oh, Tamsin." Marlena's voice filled the room. "Surely it's clear by now this isn't going to be a teary-eyed reunion." She took a step forward, the candlelight catching on the glint in her brown eyes. "No, you're here to take my place as the sleeping sister."

Marlena moved about the room with a strange grace, shooting sparks forward that splintered the wooden floor beneath their feet. A sharp smack shuddered through the air, and the room shook with a violent quake. Dust floated down, streaking Wren's hair gray and coating Tamsin's lungs. She coughed, a deep hacking sound that left her throat sore.

"If you're asleep, our bond will not break." Marlena grinned cruelly, stepping lightly as the room continued to shake. "I'll leave you here to slumber, and escape this miserable place for good. Then I will finally, *finally* be free."

There was nothing left in her sister's eyes that Tamsin recognized. The Marlena she had known might have been sharp, but she wasn't cruel. She didn't hurt others for the fun of it. Tamsin gathered her hold on Wren's magic, its warmth swimming in her fingers and sparking in her toes.

She reveled in the raw power. This was who she was, who she was meant to be. She could stop everything now with the flick of her wrist. Command her enemy. Prove her prowess. She aimed a stream of light toward her sister. Yet at the last second, Marlena turned to face her. Tamsin wavered, changing her magic's course so that it hit the wall instead. Her sister was alive. She couldn't be the one to change that.

Marlena's eyes lingered on the ruined wall. "Come now. It isn't fun if it isn't a fair fight."

But nothing between the two of them had ever been fair. Tamsin sent a flash of light through the room toward her sister, bright enough to shock the eyes. She wanted to disorient Marlena, to get her to pause just long enough to catch her and restrain her. But Marlena merely let out an odd giggle, brighter than the light emanating throughout the room. She easily dodged the stunning spell Tamsin sent her way.

Tamsin felt the spell between her shoulder blades. She was out of practice, had overcompensated, let out too much of her reserve. If she wasn't careful, she was going to run through

Wren's magic too quickly. Marlena sent a jolt through Tamsin's arm that pushed her backward onto a broken chair. Tamsin swore, her shoulder and tailbone now aching in equal measure. She threw up a hand to defend herself, casting a wall of resistance around her as she extracted herself from the wreckage.

Marlena shot a rapid succession of sparks and charms her way, the magic burrowing into Tamsin's flimsy shield. It was growing weaker by the minute, the twinge in her back sharper the longer she held the spell.

Tamsin grimaced through her magic's toll, staring enviously at Marlena, who was issuing her spells almost lazily. Thoughtlessly.

The room gave another threatening quake. It was not until Marlena glanced nervously at the quivering beams above that Tamsin understood that the shaking was not of Marlena's design but a consequence of her power. Her sister was not used to the enormity of the magic she possessed. Were she more comfortable, Tamsin and Wren would not have stood a chance against her. But the magic was still unfamiliar to her.

Tamsin let down her shield and found only the slightest bit of warmth clinging to the tips of her fingers. She had too little of Wren's magic to draw from. The next spell was going to have to come from her alone. Tamsin whispered several soft words, and a wave of water crashed over Marlena, throwing her back and leaving her exposed.

It was the perfect moment to shoot off a disarming spell, but Tamsin, too, crumpled to the floor, her bones screaming with the effort. Wren, who had been huddled near the empty shelves, rushed to her, wrapping her clammy hands around Tamsin's shaking ones.

"What are you doing?" Wren kept darting looks at Marlena, who was spluttering on the floor.

"I can't hurt her." Tears mingled with the sweat dripping down her cheeks. Wren brushed Tamsin's face, her hands warm. The longer she held on, the duller the pain in Tamsin's body became. The shrieking of her bones turned to whispers, then to silence.

Tamsin's eyes searched for Marlena's shivering form, but her sister wasn't there. Tamsin swore. The room was small. There was nowhere for Marlena to hide. Yet she had all but vanished.

"Wren." Tamsin breathed her name so softly her lips barely moved. Wren frowned, leaning closer to Tamsin, but before Tamsin could whisper a warning, pale fingers were tangled in Wren's hair, pulling her up and away from Tamsin. Her absence set Tamsin to shivering again.

Marlena wrapped her hand around Wren's neck. Wren gasped for air, tears swimming in her eyes. Marlena flung Wren away with a force too terrible to be her own. Wren's body slammed into the far wall. She shuddered and went still.

Tamsin reacted before her mind caught up. She threw herself forward, scrambling for her sister, but Marlena vanished again. Tamsin stumbled, catching herself on a leg of the overturned side table.

Wren's head had lolled to one side, her eyes closed. A thin trickle of blood ran from her temple. Tamsin wanted to scream at Wren to wake up, that she couldn't die, not now. Wren couldn't leave Tamsin. Not before Tamsin understood her feelings. Not before she figured out *why* she felt anything at all.

"Marlena, you can't . . ." Tamsin didn't know how to put her pain into words.

"Yes, I can." Marlena was suddenly there, eyes sharp even as her voice wavered. "*You* did." She stared at Tamsin, accusation swimming in her eyes. "Were you so jealous? You hated that I had someone who cared for me *because*, not despite, so you took her from me."

Tamsin did not know what to say. Her spell had killed Amma inadvertently, and for that she was sorrier than she could ever express. But she did not want her sister to have to carry that same level of guilt. She couldn't bear for Marlena's heart to have another mar on its already bruised and battered surface.

"I'm sorry," she said, knowing the words were useless.

Sparks shot from Marlena's fingers, but they were nothing compared to the fire behind her eyes. "Why won't you fight?" She let out a shriek, unrestrained and wild, like the howl of a hungry wolf. "I can't win if you won't try." She pushed hair from her eyes with the back of her arm. "You're the one who made me like this." She flung her arms out wide. "Isn't this what you wanted?"

Tamsin shook her head sadly. "I never wanted this."

There was a groan behind her. Wren was starting to stir. Tamsin turned toward Wren's limp body, but even as she started forward, she was stopped in her tracks by an invisible barrier.

Wren's body jerked and jolted with tiny shocks. She writhed and flailed, her red hair falling from its plait and sticking to her sweaty forehead. Tamsin watched helplessly as Wren shuddered, pain written clearly on her face.

"Stop it." Tamsin clawed at the shield, her fingers finding nothing to hold. There was nothing to tear down, no wall to break through. All she could do was watch Wren scream as her sister laughed, low and sharp. *"Stop it."*

Marlena did not stop. Her spell did not waver. But the room did. A crack, deeper than before, forced its way through the floor, dividing the sisters so that they stood firmly on opposite sides.

"It seems that a line has been drawn." Marlena's tone was wry. It set Tamsin shaking with fury, the rage creeping through her, fueling her in a way that she had never felt before. Now that Marlena had hurt Wren once, she would do it again. Next time Marlena might even kill her.

Wren's life was in Tamsin's hands, had belonged to her since their lips had first met, sealing their pact. Tamsin had put Wren in danger by bringing her Within. She had not considered the consequences, much in the same way she had not considered the consequences of saving her sister all those years ago.

Tamsin sliced at the air, sending the shards of a broken teacup soaring toward Marlena, who darted easily away, shooting bursts of lightning back. Tamsin tried to keep Marlena's attention solely on her, to buy Wren some time.

She narrowed her eyes, focusing on Marlena's knees as she sent a stunning spell toward her sister. Marlena stumbled, swearing darkly as she nearly fell face-first. Tamsin's stomach twisted with guilt, watching her sister suffer at her hand. But on the other side of the room, Wren had gone still, covered with a sheen of sweat, her fair skin ghostly pale in the darkening room.

Marlena sent black ribbons flying through the air. Tamsin shot back a stream of spells, but Marlena's ribbons snaked their way past Tamsin's defenses. One slithered around her ankle, sending a jolt of exhaustion through her. Commanding her limbs became nearly impossible. Though Tamsin's brain screamed for her legs to move, for her lips to form the shape of her next spell, her body would not obey. A heaviness weighed her down, exhaustion rippling through her limbs. Tamsin wanted nothing more than to close her eyes and sleep amid the remains of Marlena's broken furniture.

Focusing her waning energy on the sharp shards of wood at her feet, Tamsin sent a chair leg hurtling across the room. Marlena brushed it away without a second thought. Tamsin fought against her drooping eyelids, but it was no use. The pounding in her head had returned. The magic was taking a toll on her body, while Marlena remained unscathed.

"Go to sleep, Tamsin." Marlena's voice was far, then very near. Tamsin forced her eyes open. Her sister's face swam before her. "Sleep now." Marlena's hand brushed against Tamsin's cheek almost tenderly. "Without you, I'll finally be free."

Tamsin's body screamed for her to get up, to fight back. She owed it to herself, to Wren, to the world falling to pieces. She was so close to saving them all, and yet even as she thought it, the light began to slip away. She was so, so tired. Tired of trying and tired of failing. Maybe it would be better if she just gave up. Gave in.

The room shook wildly. The roar of the ocean nearly drowned out Marlena's words. "Good night, sister." Marlena raised her arms, determination on her face.

It was fitting, in a way. Tamsin had always been willing to give her life for her sister. Now she finally would.

TWENTY-TWO

WREN

The day her mother died, the earth had shifted beneath Wren's feet—a great, rumbling quake that mirrored the breaking of her heart. As her father set to work methodically building the pyre on which to burn his wife's body, Wren fought to find her balance on a ground that would not stay still. Tried to reclaim her place in a world that no longer made sense.

No one else had ever mentioned the shaking. Not even her father, who had been working mere feet away from the ground where Wren stood. But she had always known it was the earth opening its arms to welcome her mother back to the dust from which she had come.

As the ground beneath Marlena's room began to shake, Wren wondered whom it would claim this time. She tried to open her eyes, but they felt sewn shut. Her bones were heavy and aching.

A high-pitched buzzing echoed in her ears, like a thousand baby bees. There was a flash of light so bright Wren could see it through her eyelids. A clatter. The scent of charred sage was overtaken by the stench of soured milk. Another clatter, louder this time. A soft swear. A sigh. And somewhere, far away, the crash of the sea.

Wren wrenched her eyes open. The room was ruined. Chairs were overturned, china shattered, tables broken, and a deep crack ran through the floor. A figure was kneeling next to a pile of pillows.

Marlena. Or was it Tamsin? Her vision was fuzzy. She couldn't tell the sisters apart.

Wren tried to focus. Her head pulsed with pain; her tongue was dry; her vision blurred. Strange that Marlena owned pillows the same color as Tamsin's cloak. Her brain buzzed droopily. She ought to tell Tamsin. Perhaps she'd find the coincidence funny. Maybe if she could make Tamsin laugh, a real laugh, just once, that would be enough to end all of this. Wren swept her eyes around the room, but the witch was nowhere to be found.

Movement. The kneeling figure brushed a hand over the pile of pillows, a dark curl catching on her finger. Wren's heart clenched as she realized it was *Tamsin* on the floor, *Marlena* above her. The ribbons of Tamsin's earthy red magic were no thicker than a sewing needle. Tamsin was helpless. Unable to fight back.

Wren braced her hands on the wall behind her, the structure grumbling like an empty stomach. She pushed herself up, as slowly as possible, not wanting to draw Marlena's attention. Her muscles screamed in protest. Her body ached as though she had taken a beating from a club fitted with a thousand tiny pins. Everything hurt.

"Without you, I'll finally be free." Marlena's tone was oddly grief-stricken, the way Wren's father's had been as he scattered his wife's ashes to the wind. "Good night, sister."

"Don't." The word escaped before Wren could think better of it. And really, she should have thought about it, for now she had the full attention of a witch armed with dark magic. Wren couldn't use her own power, couldn't fight back. All she could do was watch as darkness swirled around Marlena. Ribbons of dark magic clung to the girl like a shroud. But her attention was no longer fixed upon her sister. The tiny threads of Tamsin's clay-red magic still hung about her head. She was still alive.

"I thought I killed you." Marlena's eyes flashed with annoyance as she turned away from Tamsin's limp figure. "I might need Tamsin alive, but I don't need you, too." She shot a spark halfheartedly at Wren, but Wren, who was able to see the magic before it was thrown, dodged it.

Marlena's nose wrinkled with displeasure as the spark hit the wall beside Wren instead, and the quaking of the room turned to a full-blown roar. Marlena stared warily at a large crack that crept quickly toward the ceiling. Wren's stomach clenched. With Marlena casting spells at such a dizzying rate, there was no telling the effect the plague was having on the world beyond the trees.

Dark magic was forbidden because it was unbalanced. It was power pulled directly from the earth without anything offered in return. When Tamsin described the earth's reaction to dark magic, she made it sound as though it was the world that was behaving badly: *The world rebelled.* But how else could the earth exist if not for the power it held just beneath the surface? It was magic that made the rain fall, magic that made the trees grow, magic that guided the winds. It was magic that made flowers bloom and birthed animals and caused the sun to shine.

Now Marlena was stealing that magic, taking and taking and never returning. The sun had disappeared from the sky. People were losing their memories. Water howled and stone screamed. The earth wasn't rebelling.

The earth was *dying*.

"*Stop.*" Wren marveled at how authoritative she sounded despite the fear housed in every inch of her body. "That magic doesn't belong to you."

Marlena merely rolled her eyes, shooting another shower of sparks across the room. Wren dodged them again. The crack in the ceiling widened. A sliver of night sky peeked in, as black as the magic surrounding Tamsin's sister. It held not a single star.

The endless night was as hopeless as Wren felt. She couldn't evade Marlena's spells forever. Eventually, her body would give in to the pain, or the earth would open and swallow her whole. It was no use running away. Marlena needed to be stopped, but Wren could only sense magic, not fight it.

She was doing it again. Undermining her abilities before giving herself a chance to try. Wren was the one who had led them to Marlena. By using her senses. By taking her time. Trying not only to find the magic but to understand it. Perhaps if she thought of Marlena as just another sheet of paper in her journal, she could tease out the thread of magic still tying the sisters together. She could find a way to stop her—not like a witch, but like a source.

"Why are you looking at me like that?" Marlena had stopped shooting sparks and was staring at Wren with a wary expression. Dust fell from the cracks in the ceiling, streaking her dark hair with gray.

"Like what?" Wren wasn't certain what her face looked like, but she kept the expression in place.

"Like you aren't afraid of me." Marlena pressed her thin lips together until they all but disappeared. "I could kill you, you know." But this time she didn't sound so certain.

The earth beneath their feet gave another rumble. Marlena glanced around nervously.

"I know," Wren said slowly, softly, the coaxing way she sometimes spoke to her hens. "But killing me is not a good idea." She glanced up at the crack in the ceiling. She didn't want Marlena to use her power. The room was in shambles, its structure just as precarious as Wren's plan. At any moment it could collapse.

Marlena's eyes studied Wren suspiciously. They were so like Tamsin's it made Wren ache. "Why not?"

"Because I could help you." Wren fought to keep the fear from her face.

Marlena's lips quirked upward into the ghost of a smile. Her eyes glittered. Wren swallowed thickly. Magic scraped its way down her throat, leaving it as raw as if she had been screaming.

"And why would you do that?" Marlena eyed her in a way that made her feel exposed. The witch's gaze lingered on all of Wren's bruises and scars, all her tender places.

"Because I know what it feels like to be left behind." Wren's voice cracked, her breath hitching midsentence at the raw truth of her words. "I know what it's like when your best isn't enough."

Marlena's face darkened, but the magic swirling around her did not move to strike. "Is that so?"

"It is." Wren took a cautious step toward the girl. Her heart beat faster than the flitting of a hummingbird's wings. Her tongue was dry, the salty, sour taste of the air coating her teeth. Fear was an animal, uninvited and unbidden, leaving destruction in its wake. She would not give in.

The witch studied Wren for a moment before her fingers shot out and closed around Wren's wrist. Marlena's skin was as hot as a blazing fire. Her touch sent a wave of nausea through Wren, along with something darker. An emotion, desperate and heavy, settled itself in her chest. Wren forced her attention past the feeling, toward Marlena and her fiery skin, trying to find the girl's magic without giving away too much of her own.

It was exhausting. Wren was pushing back her own magic, funneling it so that it dripped out of her rather than poured. She was also pulling herself forward toward Marlena's power, keeping her senses alert, searching for the heart of the girl's dark magic.

Marlena's grip tightened, her fingers digging sharply into Wren's skin. Wren cried out, losing hold of her concentration. Marlena's eyes glittered wildly, her teeth bared in a feral smile. Then she sent Wren flying across the room.

Wren landed on her side, her elbow cracking against the floor, pain sparking through her body so quickly Wren could feel it in her teeth. She cried out, her body shaking as she curled into herself, trying not to cry.

"You must think me a fool," Marlena said, towering over Wren. "Just like everyone else, you underestimate me. You should really give me a bit more credit."

White-hot magic seeped into Wren until her organs, her skin, her heart, were all on fire. A scream echoed through the room. It took her a long time to recognize it as her own.

"Stop." Tamsin's voice cracked like the earth beneath them. She was on her knees, hair plastered to her sweaty forehead, her eyes dull and dark as she panted to catch her breath. Incredibly, Marlena obeyed her sister's command, staring with confusion as Tamsin tore at the broken floor with her bare hands, ripping away the splintered wood and sinking her fingers into the earth below.

Wren tried to get up, but she could barely see straight through the pain. She was going to be sick, the dark magic overpowering every one of her senses. Her vision was beginning to fade. She was useless. She was just as useless as she'd always feared.

Tamsin started whispering, so softly that Wren could not understand what she was saying, only that she was calling to the earth, asking for its power. It wasn't until the scent of sulfur caught in the back of her throat that Wren realized what Tamsin was doing.

She was summoning dark magic too.

It was so foolish Wren could hardly believe it true. Yet all the telltale signs were there: the stink of sulfur, the rumbling of the earth in protest, the inky black ribbons that clung to the witch like a shadow.

But louder than Tamsin's determination, than even Wren's fear, was the earth's desperate cry. It had no magic to spare, and if Tamsin used its power against her sister, the act would result in something so terrible Wren could not even imagine it. All she had was the world's fearful call, loud and insistent, inside her head.

If only there were something she could do. But she was housing too much sound: the scream of her own body, the clamoring of the earth, Marlena's shrieks of frustration. Tamsin continued to whisper, the air around her shimmering like a shield. Her sister's sparks ricocheted off the shining spell and smacked against the walls. Loud crashes split them into pieces. More and more of the night's endless darkness poured into the room.

With Marlena's attention focused elsewhere, Wren's vision started to return. She glanced desperately between the sisters. Each face was determined. Their decisions were made. Wren's arm ached, the bones shattered from her fall. She pushed herself shakily to her knees, her eyes on Tamsin. She had to get the witch's attention. She had to stop her before the world broke in a way that could not be repaired. Before Tamsin did something she would always regret.

As she clutched the threads of dark magic she had pulled from the earth, something raw flashed across Tamsin's face. Wren knew the expression well. She had worn it herself. It was grief, sudden as a summer storm and twice as destructive. This time, when Tamsin struck out, she would strike to kill.

But before Wren could call to her, Marlena darted forward, grabbed Tamsin's hair in a white-knuckled fist, and slammed her sister's head onto the ground. Tamsin let out a terrible scream, made worse by the fact that it lasted only seconds.

The room was silent, smoke drifting and shifting as ash scattered about their feet and wood crumbled above their heads. Wren could see nothing but the frantic waves of Marlena's dark magic. She couldn't see Tamsin, could not get a single whiff of herbs, saw no thread of magic, red nor black, emanating from her. She could see nothing but Marlena, standing alone in the middle of the room.

So Wren leaped at the girl, her ruined arm tucked tightly against her side, voice shrieking, hitting pitches even she herself could not hear. Her broken arm shouted with every minuscule jostle as Marlena writhed beneath her grip. The smoke caught in Wren's lungs. She struggled to breathe, coughing loud, scraping sounds. Her legs threatened to crumple beneath her weight.

Marlena swore, her hands in Wren's hair, tugging so hard Wren thought her scalp might rip from her head. Wren clawed at Marlena with her good arm, following her instincts, not her thoughts. Letting her senses lead, not her fear.

"Stop this," she choked out, her anger nearly as hot as Marlena's skin. "You're going to end *everything*." Fury hit her like a wave, like wind in a tunnel, as though she was sucking the life from her surroundings. The motion nearly bowled her over. For it wasn't anger but magic, unfamiliar and heavy, that pooled in

Wren. She reached out toward Marlena, not with her hands, but with that magic. And she *pulled*.

There was a snap.

Immediately, Marlena went limp and slumped to the ground. The world dulled, then suddenly became overwhelmingly bright, as though Wren had stared into the sun. A rush passed through her, like a howling summer wind. She was knocked to the ground yet landed softly, magic curling protectively around her.

Sound reverberated in her ears even as it echoed in a different pattern through the hazy room. The ache pulsed in her body, feverish and lingering. There was the unmistakable scent of sulfur, overwhelmed by the stench of rotting pears.

Dark magic clung to the room like cobwebs, casting thick shadows over everything. The air was heavy. Wren sucked in breaths, but it felt as though there were a pillow pressed against her face. The effort was so great as to be nearly impossible. There was another flash of lightning, and when the light faded, so had the darkness. It was still night, but the magic began to dissipate like a blown-out candle, the remaining threads of black floating lazily like smoke toward the sky. Stars appeared, their faint lights twinkling through the cracks in the ceiling.

The ground had stopped its shaking.

Marlena's body was splayed across the floor. Silent. Still. Wren tested the back of her hand against Marlena's forehead. The girl's skin was no longer hot, her cheeks no longer flushed with life. Her breathing had all but ceased.

"Wren?" Tamsin's voice was weak. "What's happened? Where are you?"

Wren skittered away from Marlena's limp form, her eyes wide and unbelieving. She had only meant to stop Marlena, not to destroy her. She pulled at her braid with shaking hands, but her scalp already ached from Marlena's attack. Her usual centering method did nothing to calm her.

"I'm . . . here," she called back, her voice catching in her throat, froglike and frightened. She surveyed the wreckage of the room, her eyes searching for a shadow. She cradled her broken arm like a baby against her. The pain had faded from a fiery burn to an endless dull throbbing. She wasn't sure she could feel anything anymore. She had broken something in Marlena, something irreparable, if the witch's limp body was any indication. She didn't know how she could face Tamsin.

A shadow pulled itself forward, its steps shaky and unsure. Tamsin stopped in the middle of the floor beside Marlena's body. Smoke curled about her sharp cheekbones. Her skin glittered like milk in the faint starlight. Wren caught a whiff of fresh sage.

But instead of shouting, as Wren had expected Tamsin to do, the witch pulled her to her feet and wrapped her arms around her so tightly she found it difficult to breathe. Together they stood among the wreckage, locked in an embrace as the world spun slowly on around them.

TWENTY-THREE

TAMSIN

Tamsin held on to Wren for dear life. And indeed it felt like the source was the only thing keeping her from falling to pieces, from shattering as easily as a teacup on the wooden floor. A tinny whistle buzzed incessantly in her left ear. There was a steady hammering at her temple where her head had met the floorboards. Her arms were scratched, bright red drops of blood wrapping her wrists like bindings. Yet the aching of her body was nothing compared to the splintering of her heart.

The fact that Tamsin could not love was irrelevant when faced with the sight of her sister lying lifeless on the floor. Marlena's mouth hung open, as though she'd had more to say.

Her eyes were empty. It was a punch to the gut, a stab in the side, seeing her sister splayed out in the exact same position she had been in five years ago, the first time Tamsin had watched Marlena die.

The one thing Tamsin had always promised herself was that she would never again hurt someone she loved, but then, in another moment of desperation, she had reached again for dark magic, this time to turn against her sister rather than to save her.

She was exactly the same stupid, impulsive girl she had always been. She hadn't grown at all. Her grief, her guilt, all her practice in self-restraint, had not actually made her better. In fact, here she stood, squeezing her eyes shut so she would not have to take in her sister's lifeless body. She was back exactly where she had started.

"I'm sorry." Wren's whisper was lighter than a feather. "Tamsin, I'm so, so sorry."

The source pulled away from her, her face streaked with tears. She cradled her arm like a baby, the bone splintered and awkward.

"Stop." Tamsin was grateful to focus on Wren's ruined arm. It was broken in at least two places. Wren sucked in a tight lungful of air at Tamsin's touch, her expression betraying exactly how much pain she felt. Focusing on the breaks one at a time, Tamsin pulled what little strength she had left to the forefront, sending it to the torn muscles and splintered bones. It was like scraping the bottom of an empty barrel. Wren, too, was devoid of magic, her stores depleted from the fight. So Tamsin worked slowly. Wren swayed back and forth, soft as the sea.

"Do you hate me?" Wren's voice was so small. Her eyes strayed to where Marlena lay, sprawled out on the wooden floor.

"How could I hate you?" And Tamsin meant it. How could she hate Wren for something that she herself had been prepared to do?

Her eyes skimmed the source still sniffling before her. Wren's eyes were glassy with tears, her hair streaked with dust and sweat. She had bright pink scratches across her cheek, and her skin was as white as a sheet, the freckles scattered across her nose more pronounced than ever. Tamsin wanted to count every single one, commit them all to memory so that even when she closed her eyes, she would see a constellation of Wren.

She reached up to wipe away the girl's tears, shuddering as her skin met Wren's. A rush, heavy and hot, thrummed through her like a wave of nausea. The feeling passed as quickly as it had begun, but in its absence, Tamsin became aware of a different kind of lightness. As though someone had lifted a particularly heavy item from a sack slung across her back, lightening her load.

Easing her way forward.

She kept her hand on Wren's cheek. This one strange girl had managed to throw off the balance of Tamsin's entire world. She had turned Tamsin away from emptiness and toward something . . . else. Something desperate and wanting and hopeful. Something pure. When she was with Wren, things were different. *She* was different, and Tamsin had no idea why.

"You're bleeding." Wren pointed to Tamsin's wrist, where a stream of bright red blood welled up and trickled down her arm like a waterfall.

Wren leaned forward to examine Tamsin's injury, her hair draping down like a curtain, sheltering the two of them from the dangers and the cruelties of the world. Tamsin wished they could stay hidden together forever.

Tamsin had always been afraid of *forever*. It was too broad, too all-encompassing. It left too much room for error and disappointment. But Tamsin had shown Wren all the messy, broken pieces of herself, and still Wren had not run. Instead she stood before Tamsin, biting her bottom lip in concentration as she tore a scrap of fabric from the bottom of her shirt. She wrapped it tenderly around the wound, despite the fact that Tamsin was a witch and could heal it herself.

Wren's eyes flitted up to meet Tamsin's. Their sharpness caused a jolt in Tamsin's stomach. Wren's cheeks flushed pink. "What?" She was still holding Tamsin's hand.

"I . . ." Tamsin was suddenly nervous. Words didn't seem like enough. They felt like too much. "Nothing." She was confused. Grief-stricken. She didn't know what to say. Her sister was dead. Again. She didn't know how her broken heart would survive it.

Wren's face fell somewhere between a smile and a frown. She studied Tamsin, her eyes boring into the center of her as though searching for the answer to an unspoken question. Tamsin hated this trepidation, this uncertainty.

She wished she could start all over again. Wished she could slam the door in Wren's face, ignore the way her freckles danced across her nose in the sunlight, tune out her stupid melodic voice and turn away her kindness. Tamsin wished she had never returned Within at all.

If she had stayed in Ladaugh, Marlena would still be alive. At the very least, she wouldn't be dead by Tamsin's hand. For Wren was an extension of Tamsin, by virtue of their pact. She had brought the source here. Which was why Tamsin hated herself for wanting to reach for Wren.

After all that had happened, despite Marlena's lifeless body on the floor, Tamsin wanted to comfort *Wren*.

It didn't make the slightest bit of sense.

Tamsin held on anyway. Sense was nothing amid the crashing waves of grief. She needed to touch someone, needed to remind herself that she was solid. That she wouldn't merely float away.

Her hand still cradled in Wren's, a flood of warmth creeping up her perennially cold skin, Tamsin tried not to think. Tried not to fear. Tried to simply listen to the heart lying dormant in her chest. She inhaled shakily, catching Wren's scent, sweet sweat mixed with something soft and floral. It was a pleasant smell, warm and safe. Made Tamsin feel certain rather than shaky and unsure.

But she wasn't supposed to smell nice things. Only awful things like sulfur and the stench of rotting food. This comforting scent had no place in her nose. The nervous churning of her stomach, that was more familiar.

Wren was still staring at her. Their faces were close enough that Tamsin could see the different shades of Wren's eyes. A forest green around the ring, fading into a yellow brown, the color of autumn leaves. Such vivid colors. Not only could Tamsin discern the shades, but she could describe them, the way Wren had described sunsets.

Something was happening.

Tamsin hesitated. Tamsin never hesitated; she simply took what she wanted and thought nothing of it. But she had seen the destruction that her love wrought. Who was to say it couldn't happen again?

She pulled away from Wren and stared determinedly at the floor. Her eyes caught a flicker of movement next to the hearth, so quick that Tamsin tried to tell herself it was only her grief. She hadn't actually seen Marlena's finger twitch.

But then—a low groan.

And her sister stirred.

Tamsin was by Marlena's side in seconds, scooping up Marlena's icy hand in her bandaged one. It was such a familiar scene. Tamsin fretting over her sister, hovering. Crowding her. She wondered if she should let go.

Marlena made the decision for her, scrambling up and out of Tamsin's grip. She bit her lip, eyes wary as she extended her arms, poised to attack. Tamsin waited for the blow. She deserved it after what she had almost done. But no spell burst forward, not even a shower of sparks.

Marlena looked flummoxed, her frustration turning quickly to anger. "Come on," she said, her voice breaking as she strained, trying to pull magic forward. But the air between them remained empty.

"I don't . . ." Marlena looked up at Tamsin, eyes wild. Desperate. "There's nothing to draw from. I can't reach the magic."

"What happened?" Tamsin turned to Wren. "When you thought you killed her?"

Wren looked uncertain. "I don't know. I thought she'd killed *you*, so I used my magic to reach into her. There was a snap, and then . . ." She trailed off, wringing her hands apologetically as she shrugged.

It was rumored that very strong sources could prevent witches from accessing magic, but Tamsin had never borne witness to it, had never heard of it happening anywhere other than in the writings of the ancients. It was a rumor. It couldn't be true. An untrained source couldn't possibly harness that kind of raw impulse.

Or perhaps it *was* the lack of training. Perhaps Wren had finally stopped thinking and started doing. Tamsin's breath caught in her throat. If Wren had truly cut off Marlena's access to magic, that meant magic could no longer hurt her. It meant that the thread between them was broken, yet her sister would continue to live.

Tamsin sank back to the ground, tears swimming in her eyes. She was exhausted. Overwhelmed with the impossibility of it all.

"What did she do to me?" But there was no venom in Marlena's voice. She sounded defeated. Utterly and completely wrecked.

"Your magic is gone, Marlena," Tamsin whispered quietly.

Marlena's face paled. "All of it?"

"I thought that was what you wanted," Tamsin said bitterly. "You're free now. Our bond is broken."

"That wasn't what I meant." Marlena shifted uncomfortably, slumping against the stones of the hearth. "Tamsin, I didn't mean to—"

"Let me know how much you hate me?" Tamsin laughed darkly. "You made that clear enough."

Marlena looked pained. "I don't hate you. I . . . resent you."

"Oh, because that's better," Tamsin snapped.

"It is, actually," Wren said. "Resentment can fade. Hate burns bright."

The sisters looked over at her in surprise. "I know a thing or two about what it feels like to resent you," Wren said, eyeing Tamsin sheepishly.

Astonishingly, Marlena laughed. A soft, bubbling laugh that held far less malice than Tamsin expected. It was not the wicked, twisted laugh of dark magic. It was the same laugh she'd had as a child. "You're ruthless," Marlena said, shaking her head. "Exactly her type."

Tamsin shot her sister a furious look. Marlena cackled again, the smile strange on her face. It had been so long since Tamsin had seen her sister's expression free of hatred that she almost didn't mind that her laughter was at Tamsin's expense.

But, far too quickly, Marlena sobered. "What happens now, then? Now that I've nothing, not even a spark of magic, to my name? What sort of reward will Vera grant you for disarming her rogue daughter?"

Tamsin frowned. "That isn't why she sent me. That isn't why I came."

"Ah, so there *is* a reward." Marlena pushed herself away from the hearth. "I wonder what she'll do to me. I escaped from her tower prison, after all. Threw the world into chaos using dark magic. And now I don't hold a single thread of power. What a disgrace. Maybe I should have died after all."

"Stop that." Tamsin's voice was harsh, her heart cracking as her sister spoke so flippantly about her existence.

"Why?" Marlena asked, her voice rising. "It isn't as though I have any other options. What am I supposed to do? I'm a witch without magic. What's the point?"

"You're alive," Tamsin snapped. "For better or for worse, that's what you are. Why can't that be enough?"

"Would it be enough for you?"

Tamsin hesitated.

Marlena smiled sadly. "I didn't think so."

Tamsin sighed heavily. This wasn't going the way she'd hoped. "I'm sorry," she said softly. "I'm sorry that I—"

"Don't." Marlena's voice broke. "Please don't. Apologizing might make you feel better, but it only makes me feel worse. So just stop."

"I . . ." Tamsin blinked at her sister helplessly. She had no idea what to say. She didn't know what Marlena wanted from her—or if she wanted anything at all.

"That's enough." Wren's voice was sharp. "Both of you. You're both alive. Together. You have the chance to start over. A *real* chance. And you're both fools if you don't take it."

She turned on her heel and slipped away, ducking through the shattered wall and out into the night. The truth of her words settled like a stone in Tamsin's stomach.

"Marlena, I—"

"Obviously, you're going after her." It wasn't a question so much as a command. "I know they cursed you, but even you

must be able to see what's happening between the two of you."
Marlena rolled her eyes, as though she didn't care either way.

"What?"

"Don't be an idiot. Go after her."

"But you and I . . ." Tamsin trailed off. She didn't know what they needed to do. Only that the space between them was still stagnant and stale.

"Not yet." Marlena looked pained. "I can't yet. Okay?"

Tamsin looked at her sister, really looked. Marlena's left eye was smaller than her right. She had a dimple in her left cheek, and her jaw was slightly square. Tamsin had spent so much time trying to fit them into the same box that she had never taken the time to see how they had grown on their own.

"Okay," she said, the enormity of her feelings too impossible to put into words.

She turned and followed Wren through the wrecked wall out onto the beach. She glanced up at the inky night sky. The moon was just a sliver, no thicker than a piece of thread. Stars shimmered above, offering the night a softness the never-ending dark had not held. She closed her eyes and breathed in the cool night air.

Wren was twenty paces ahead, staring out at the sea.

"The ocean looks different," Wren said, her eyes fixed on the water as Tamsin came to stand beside her.

The sea had settled, the waves no longer stormy but rhythmic, rising and receding gently, soft as a lullaby, leaving the sand dark where the waves had been.

"Do you think it's over? The plague?" Wren's voice was so hopeful that Tamsin could not bear to look at her face. She thought it might break her.

"I don't know. I hope so." Tamsin studied the piles of driftwood as though they were fortresses guarding a secret, keeping captive an answer. There was something she was supposed to say. Something she was supposed to understand about Wren and the way she made Tamsin feel. That she *made* Tamsin *feel*.

She turned to face Wren, her skin pale in the darkness, her hair wild and tangled above her head like a crown. Power looked good on Wren. Accentuated her rough and wild face. Tamsin opened her mouth to tell her so, but before she could speak, Wren held up a hand.

"I'm glad you didn't die," Wren said.

It was too dark to tell if she was blushing, but Tamsin imagined that she was, the familiar pink flush creeping from Wren's cheeks to her temples. Tamsin smiled. The silence was as heavy as the air before a storm.

Tamsin took a step toward Wren, the space between them practically nothing. She brought a hand to Wren's face, her thumb brushing dust from her freckled cheek, the rest of her fingers tangling themselves in Wren's hair.

"Wren, I . . ." It was as though she had forgotten how to speak. As though she had forgotten what words were for and why they mattered in the face of this girl with those blazing eyes and that ghost of a smile. For a moment, neither of them moved, the air crackling around them like a shower of sparks.

"It's okay," Wren said, misunderstanding her hesitation. She slipped carefully out of Tamsin's grip, one hand lingering on hers, until she pulled away completely, leaving Tamsin alone with the unfamiliar and infuriating feeling of wanting and the fear that she would never stop.

TWENTY-FOUR

WREN

The trees shuddered and sighed. When Wren and Tamsin had first passed through the empty forest, the branches had been thin and spindly. The trunks had stood like skeletons, their emptiness achingly clear. Now, although the branches were still bare, the bark was taking on new life. Color seeped upward from the gnarled roots as slowly as water dripping from a broken pump. Wren looked up. The trunks were taller, as though the trees were finally standing up straight. There was a buzzing in the wood, still whisper-soft, a thudding like a heart fighting its way back to life.

There was potential in those trees. A promise that the world might someday find its footing once again.

Above their heads, the sky was as dark as ever. Nearly one hundred paces ahead, Marlena carried a lantern, the light bobbing and weaving as she stalked through the trees.

Beside Wren, Tamsin was silent, her eyes fixed on the back of her sister's head. Wren nudged the witch lightly with her elbow. "You should go talk to her."

Perhaps it was because Wren knew she would never get the chance to see her father again—would never be able to tell him about her magic, her growth, the new world she'd found herself a part of—that she needed Tamsin and her sister to reconcile. Marlena was right there; that opportunity, that closeness, was a gift she wanted the witch to understand.

"She doesn't want to talk to me," Tamsin said without tearing her eyes from Marlena.

"You don't know until you try." Wren tried to sound encouraging.

"You can't fix everything, you know." Tamsin was finally looking at her. "I know you want to, but sometimes it isn't that easy."

That was something Wren knew well enough. Each shuffling step she took led her closer to the academy. She didn't want to return, but of course she had no choice. She was bound to this unfamiliar land. Her power bound to theirs.

Tamsin looked similarly haunted. Still, Wren was grateful for the company. She had expected Tamsin to join her in returning so that she could claim the boon but had assumed Marlena would put up more of a struggle. Yet, as they'd prepared to head back to the academy, the girl had followed them miserably to the door.

"I don't have magic anymore, and I'm not very good at fish-ing," Marlena had proclaimed darkly when faced with Wren's and Tamsin's questioning looks. "If I can't feed myself, there's no use staying here." Still, her eyes had lingered on the wrecked room before she turned determinedly on her heel and led the way across the beach.

Even the earth smelled different than it had upon their arrival. The putrid stink of dark magic had dissipated, over-powered by the sweet scent of a summer night. Wren breathed the warm air into her lungs, let it rush to her head. It tasted like freedom, something she knew was short-lived.

Still, neither she nor Tamsin walked with as much resigna-tion as Marlena. Before she could talk herself out of it, Wren quickened her step, hurrying to join Tamsin's sister.

"What does she want?" Marlena asked flatly, clearly fighting the instinct to glower over her shoulder at Tamsin.

"Nothing," Wren said honestly. "I wanted to see how you were doing."

Marlena laughed emptily. "As well as can be expected, which is to say, terribly."

"I never thought I'd meet someone surlier than Tamsin," Wren said without thinking.

Marlena appraised Wren for a second before allowing her face to split into a small smile. "Yes, well," she said finally. "Tamsin can't be the best at *everything*."

Wren laughed softly. "I suppose not."

Marlena exhaled slowly and ran a hand through her hair. "I'm sorry, by the way," she said. "For trying to, you know, kill you. I didn't mean it. The dark magic made me . . . I don't know what. I don't know who I am anymore."

Wren bit her lip, guilt flooding through her. She was the one who should be apologizing. She had sealed the girl's fate without even knowing it. "Well," she said carefully, "who do you want to be?"

Marlena blinked several times, almost uncomprehendingly. "I don't know."

"On the bright side," Wren said, offering Marlena a hopeful grin, "that means now you get to find out."

Marlena looked rather dazed. Wren slowed her pace to give the girl some privacy to consider her future anew.

"So?" Tamsin's voice was anxious, her eyes again fixed on her sister.

"Just give her time," Wren said gently.

Tamsin sighed heavily. "That's what I'm afraid of."

"I've got something that might cheer you up," Wren said, though the thought of what came next gave her no joy. Her whole body ached. Her mind was tired. Her heart battered. Better to hand over the last relic of her old life when she already hurt. What was one more bruise when she was already black-and-blue?

Tamsin looked at her curiously. "I don't need anything from you."

"Actually, you do." Resignation emboldening her, Wren pressed a finger to the ribbon around Tamsin's neck. "We hunted the dark witch. We ended the plague. Our time together is nearly up. Now I have to give you my love." She swallowed thickly.

"Your love?" Tamsin looked at her with surprise. "You told me you didn't want to love me."

Wren did not know whether to laugh or cry. The conversation in Tamsin's stiflingly hot cottage felt like it had taken place years ago. So much had changed. She hesitated, chewing on her already raw lip until the metallic tang of blood spread across her tongue. Tamsin had given her an opening. To discuss her feelings freely and fully.

For a moment Wren considered taking it. Tamsin's face was not twisted in confusion. Instead she looked almost hopeful. But of course that was nonsense. Only hours ago, Tamsin had been standing so near it would have taken no effort at all to close the space between them. But the witch had hesitated. She did not want Wren. She *could* not want her.

"My love for my father, I mean," Wren clarified, tamping down the flutter in her chest. It might have been her imagination, but Tamsin looked disappointed. "Unless . . ." She trailed off, her boldness abandoning her as suddenly as it had appeared.

"Unless what?" Tamsin prodded Wren.

"Unless nothing," Wren said quickly. It was too much. It was all too much. "Just take the love I promised you and be done with it."

"Oh." Tamsin looked wounded.

Wren sighed, a great melancholy sound. She hated herself for wasting their final hours together, for making Tamsin cringe. She hated herself for having spent so much time thinking about Tamsin when she should have been worrying about her father. She hated herself for always doing what she thought she ought to do instead of what she wanted. It got her nowhere, gained her nothing but sorrow.

"You're acting strange." Tamsin's voice was far away. "What's wrong?"

Love was a powerful and terrible creature. Wren refused to feed it. If she did not admit her feelings to herself, then she would not have to deny herself happiness.

Again.

Time after time Wren had kept herself from what she wanted based solely on what she thought others expected of her. She had sacrificed everything before anyone had asked, but even if that had helped them, it had destroyed *her*. Slowly but surely, Wren had become nothing but her sacrifices.

"Wren." Tamsin's hand was on her shoulder.

Wren stared at her desperately, wondering when she would finally allow herself to stop thinking and take what she wanted from the world.

"I . . ." Wren reached for Tamsin's hand, but the witch took a careful step back.

"I can't do this," Tamsin said, her eyes mournful.

Wren had been wrong before—she could still hurt. Her heart snapped audibly in half, sending shivers through her body. Her stomach curdled, her blood ran cold.

"Why not?" It was less a whisper than a plea.

"I couldn't do that to you." Tamsin stepped forward, her hand caressing Wren's cheek, her skin cool against Wren's own. Cool, but not cold. Something was different.

"Do what?" Wren whispered into Tamsin's palm, her heart

fluttering so fast she felt dizzy. She wanted to scream that Tamsin could do anything to her and she wouldn't mind one bit.

"I can't take your love for your father," Tamsin said, running her long fingers through Wren's tangled hair, "because that would hurt you. And I don't want to hurt you."

It wasn't what Wren had expected. She had been certain Tamsin had seen the way she stared at her, hungrily, as though she would consume the witch. She had been certain Tamsin was going to rebuff her feelings, deny her, and leave her defeated. She had not expected the air around them to still. She had not dared to dream that Tamsin would look at her with such tenderness, such trepidation. "Why?"

"Because I think I'm falling in love with you."

The absurdity hit her before the words were even out of the witch's mouth. Wren's tongue went sour and her stomach sloshed like the unsteady sea. "That isn't funny, Tamsin." The corners of her eyes burned, and she struggled to speak over the lump forming in her throat. "That isn't funny in the slightest." Tears soaked her cheeks, poured down her face, gliding down her chin and plummeting to the forest floor. Wren was an ugly crier, that she knew, but it didn't matter—not now that Tamsin had decided to make a joke of her, a mockery of her very real feelings.

Wren gasped through her fury. She had dared to hope, to think that she was different, that perhaps she could even break Tamsin's curse the way true love always did in stories. But she'd had no right to believe herself special. She clearly hadn't earned even a modicum of Tamsin's respect. She wasn't a heroine. She was a punch line. A fool.

The journey they had taken together meant nothing. Had changed nothing. Tamsin was just as cruel as she had always been, just as cold and unfeeling. Wren wiped her eyes on her sleeve and caught an inadvertent glance at Tamsin's face. The witch stood, stupefied.

"What's the matter?" Tamsin was watching with horror as Wren wept. "Did I do it . . . wrong?"

"If your intention was to make me feel foolish, then you've certainly succeeded," she snapped through a mouthful of salty tears.

"What are you talking about?" Tamsin moved forward, but Wren recoiled until her back met the stiff bark of a tree.

"You can't love anyone. It isn't kind to pretend you do, not when I . . ." She trailed off, tears still pouring down her face. She fished a handkerchief from her pocket and blew her nose indelicately.

Tamsin twisted her cloak between her hands. "Look, I know how it sounds." The witch took a step toward her. Wren pressed herself even more firmly into the bark of the tree trunk. "But I think I do, and I think . . ." Tamsin took a deep breath. "I think you love me, too."

Wren bit her already tender lip. "Do I?" She hated her cold, detached tone. This wasn't how the moment was supposed to go. Feelings *meant* something. They were supposed to be expressed slowly, carefully. Tenderly. Yet Tamsin had simply plopped hers out in the open without a second thought. Reckless, as usual.

Tamsin squinted at her. "I think you do."

Wren sniffed, finding it difficult to maintain eye contact. "What makes you say that?"

Tamsin glanced down at the forest floor. "Because when you're near me, I smell lavender on your hair. When you smile, I catch a taste of honey. Your skin is warm against mine, and when you touch me, I feel more than magic." She kicked at a pebble, her face flushing furiously. "None of that should be possible, not with my curse. I used to only be able to experience that kind of joy when I was drawing on stolen love. My reserves are empty, have been for ages, so I'm starting to wonder if, maybe, I'm drawing on yours"—Tamsin glanced up from the grass, her eyes boring hopefully into Wren's—"because *you* love *me*."

Something loosened in Wren's chest. "You feel?"

Tamsin took a step toward her. "When I'm with you, I do."

Wren studied Tamsin's eyes, the warmth that flickered in their depths. She was having difficulty breathing. Her heart hammered, louder even than the humming of the trees. But then she frowned.

"Does that mean you only love me because you feel love? That isn't . . . I mean, I don't want . . ." She trailed off, groaning with frustration at her inability to articulate. "I want you to love me because you do, not because you have to."

Tamsin's eyes went wide. "That isn't how it works. I can feel when I've taken the love of another, but that love has never forced me to return it. If that was how the curse worked, I'd be betrothed to half of Ladaugh by now. No." She shook her head firmly. "I feel when I'm with you, but I love you because I do."

Wren swallowed thickly, the black ribbon around her neck straining against her unvoiced protests. "But I still owe you." She pointed to her necklace. "If I don't pay you, I'll die."

Tamsin smiled hesitantly. "It's possible that this pact isn't very nuanced." She laughed softly to herself. "All it required from you was love. I think you might already be paying your debt. *If* you love me, that is." Her eyes suddenly went wide with horror. "Do you? Love me?" Tamsin tripped over her words, suddenly frazzled. It was the first time Wren had seen the witch anything less than composed. Her brittle shell had slipped, revealing someone hopeful and uncertain.

It was quite a bit of pressure, all things considered. Wren wanted her answer to be perfect. But she also wanted it to be true.

"I think so. But what if it doesn't last forever? What if some-day I stop? Will I owe you again then?" She didn't realize she was tugging on her braid until Tamsin patiently pulled her hands away and wrapped Wren's fingers in her own.

"I can't ask you for anything other than what you feel now. But that's enough. You, now, are enough."

Wren tried to look away, so intense was Tamsin's gaze. It made her nervous. There was so much she could not promise, so much she could not control. She might stop loving Tamsin some-day, or perhaps Tamsin would cease loving her. They could be torn apart by the Coven. They could be ridiculed by the world.

Or Wren could finally allow herself to be happy, however impossible that might sound. She could give in rather than give up before she'd even begun.

"Okay." Wren wasn't certain if she spoke or merely nodded, but it didn't matter. Tamsin's eyes were on hers; their fingers were intertwined, skin delighting in contact with skin. Every inch of Wren buzzed with anticipation as Tamsin moved closer still, until there was no more space between them. Perhaps there never had been.

It wasn't the first time the two of them had kissed, but it was the first time they were both aware of what it was. The act itself wasn't any different, still lips upon lips, chapped and wet and warm. But the intention was. This kiss was a question, an answer, fingers crossed, and a promise kept. It was hope. It was possibility. It was sparks across Wren's skin and a flutter in her stomach. It was roving hands and soft touches and lingering heat. It was bark pressed against her back. It was tiny gasps, Tamsin's mouth splitting into a smile that Wren matched with her own. Wren wanted to remember every second, wanted to be aware of every single sensation, but it was like trying to count the stars. Never before had she been so conscious of how many ways it was possible to feel. To want. To need.

The second kiss was much of the same.

The third was somehow even more.

After that, Wren stopped counting.

She focused instead on the way her skin shivered beneath the witch's touch, how she had never before considered the neck to be a place particularly suited for kissing (oh, how foolish she had been), how tender a tongue could be. Kissing the witch gave Wren the same sensation magic did. Kissing Tamsin made Wren feel like magic too.

"Called it." Blue light flashed behind Wren's closed eyelids.

"*What*, Marlena?" Tamsin sounded genuinely irritated as she pulled away from Wren.

"I thought you got lost." Marlena pouted. "It wasn't like I

was going to keep walking to the academy myself. Now I see you were just . . . otherwise engaged." She wrinkled her nose, a soft smile playing on her lips.

"Shut up." Tamsin sighed, running a hand through her hair. She glanced sheepishly at Wren, who was having trouble containing her gigantic grin. "Better get a move on."

Wren's stomach flipped, this time for an entirely different reason. She didn't want to reenter that echoing hall, didn't want to stand before the Coven. She didn't want to stay Within, especially when Tamsin couldn't.

Her fingers went limp. Tamsin shot Wren a curious look, but Wren plastered on a smile and forced herself to hold her hand tighter. She had given in to a want, and already she was facing the possibility it would be taken away.

Such was the way of the world.

"Wait." Tamsin slowed, pulling Wren back. "Let me just . . ." She flicked a finger, and the ribbon around Wren's neck floated softly to the ground. Wren bent to grab it, but it dissolved into nothingness before she could reach it. Wren glanced curiously up at Tamsin, who shrugged. "Now you don't have to wonder. You're free."

Wren opened her mouth, then clamped her lips shut, forcing them into a smile. "What about yours?"

Tamsin touched the necklace and shrugged. "I guess I've grown rather fond of it." She looked at Wren as she spoke. Wren shivered with a curious pleasure, twining her fingers through Tamsin's again.

The witch's skin was warm against Wren's own.

TWENTY-FIVE

TAMSIN

They made it to the Wandering Woes just as the sun rose for the first time in days. All three of them were beaten, battered, and bruised—both inside and out. Hazel's inn was the only place they felt safe enough to stop with Marlena in tow.

Wren and Marlena made for the inn's front door, ready to collapse, but Tamsin could not pull her eyes away from the sky. It was flooded with colors: soft blues, baby pinks, and bright glowing oranges nearly the same shade as Wren's hair. The sight brought Tamsin to tears. She told herself it was the exhaustion. Just because she was in love didn't mean she was soft enough to weep at colors cascading across the sky.

But she was. Tears rolled silently down her cheeks. Tamsin used her cloak, which she had taken off and slung over an arm when she'd grown too warm, to dry her face. Beside her, Wren said nothing, merely gave her hand an encouraging squeeze.

They slept through the day and most of the night, but Tamsin felt no relief. The threat of the Coven hung like a dark cloud overhead. She was haunted by the idea of facing Vera. Of having to own up to the bond—of admitting that *she* was the witch responsible for it all.

When they did depart, sent off with a package of honey, cheese, and bread from a wet-eyed Hazel, Tamsin grew teary too. Marlena, as usual, did not hold back—she cried frequently and frighteningly. But without the dark magic twisting her sister's emotions, each day Tamsin recognized Marlena a little bit more.

Once they reached the gilded doors of the academy, the sun planted firmly in the afternoon sky, Marlena hesitated. "I don't want to do this."

Neither did Tamsin. She had done as Vera had asked, had stopped the dark magic and saved her sister. But if the Coven learned that the plague was just another side effect of her five-year-old spell, Tamsin feared what they would do to her.

She was afraid of having to let go of Wren when whatever they had was only just beginning. Too much of her was tied to the world Within. Tamsin did not know how she was going to leave it behind again.

She turned to her sister, whose eyes were fretful, her mouth downturned. Their imaginary mirror still had cracks. Some shards had shattered completely, broken into so many pieces that the damage would never be fully repaired. But as Tamsin looked into her sister's eyes, she saw herself. She hoped that Marlena saw herself in Tamsin, too.

"Come on," Tamsin said, offering a hand to her sister. "We'll go together."

She pushed the front doors open with a soft whoosh, the sunlight straining to illuminate the dark marble floor. The air was thick and silent and stale. They made their way through the labyrinth of hallways without meeting a single soul.

Tamsin led the way up the familiar stairs to the High Councillor's tower, holding so tightly to Marlena's fingers that she feared her own would lose their feeling. Wren trailed behind, the worry on her face illuminated by the flickering blue flames of the torches lining the walls. Tamsin let them into the antechamber, pausing before the door to her mother's office. There was light coming from the crack beneath the door.

"Enter." Vera's voice was tense, calling them inside before they had even knocked. Tamsin pushed open the door, Marlena and Wren at her heels. Vera looked up from the paper she was examining. Her eyes widened as she took in the faces of her daughters, both very much alive.

In her haste to reach them, Vera's chair clattered to the floor. Then she was upon them, her arms pulling her daughters to her chest the way she had held them when they were little girls. Only now they were nearly as tall as their mother. Still, Vera's touch sent something warm flooding through Tamsin's chest. Her newly working heart felt the effects of her mother's relief.

"The bond?" Vera pulled away from them, her eyes darting

back and forth between Tamsin's and Marlena's identical faces.

"Is broken," Tamsin affirmed. She glanced at Wren, who was hovering awkwardly in the doorway. "Thanks to the Coven's newest source."

Wren gave Vera an awkward half wave. Stomach twisting anxiously, Tamsin watched her mother take Wren in. She hoped Vera's appraisal was positive.

"And what of the plague?" Vera's eyes had moved back to Marlena, distrust pushing its way to the forefront.

"Not Marlena," Tamsin interjected quickly, taking a step forward to shield her sister from her mother's scrutiny. "It was another side effect of my spell." She twisted the hem of her cloak nervously. "If you are to punish anyone, punish me."

Vera's eyes lingered on Tamsin for a moment, and then she sighed heavily. "You always were a bit of a martyr, dear," she said, tucking a lock of hair behind Tamsin's ear.

Behind her, Marlena snorted. "A *bit*?"

She and Vera shared a small smile. Tamsin cleared her throat. She did not particularly appreciate them sharing a joke at her expense.

"You were already punished," Vera continued. "I hardly think we need to add time to that sentence."

Tamsin frowned. She had been prepared to be banished twice over, if not executed. It was surely the least she deserved for causing harm to so many people. For putting the Coven in an impossible position. For forcing her mother to choose between her daughters and the world Within.

"There are, however, a few more pieces of business to

discuss," Vera said, stepping back to rest against her desk. "There is, of course, the matter of the boon."

Beside Tamsin, Marlena stiffened. Tamsin remembered her sister's flippancy, her belief that Tamsin had come after her only because she stood to gain something in return. And certainly, Tamsin could think of many ways to use the boon. But she didn't want her sister to think her an opportunist. She didn't want to ask for forgiveness for herself when she did not think she deserved it. But Wren deserved to live a life she had chosen for herself, not one that was forced upon her.

"I don't need a boon," Tamsin said quickly. "But," she added, turning to Wren, "Wren should take it. Ask for anything. Whatever you wish."

"What?" Wren spluttered. "I can't."

"You can." Tamsin took a step toward her. "I got you mixed up in all of this. Now I can get you out of it. Go home. Be with your father. Whatever it is you want, ask it."

"I . . ." Wren glanced shakily from Tamsin to Marlena to Vera. "Okay." She nodded resolutely. "I know what I want."

"Very well." Vera looked curiously from Wren to Tamsin.

"I ask that the Coven forgive Tamsin her transgressions and welcome her back Within."

"What?" Tamsin blinked stupidly. She had thought Wren would ask to be released from Within, and that they would return together to Ladaugh. She had not anticipated that Wren would give up her freedom for Tamsin's.

But Vera's face was pinched. "I don't know if that is something the Coven will allow."

"You're the most powerful witch in the world," Wren said. "Do you mean that you can't convince them?" She tugged briefly on her braid. "You don't truly believe the world is going to repair itself, do you? You *need* Tamsin." Her eyes skimmed Tamsin appreciatively.

"Wren, I don't think . . ." But Tamsin didn't know what she didn't think. The selflessness of Wren's action was more than she deserved.

"Hush," Wren said sharply. "I'm trying to do the Coven a favor."

Vera let out a low chuckle. "It seems as though my daughter has finally met her match." Her eyes lingered on Wren. "I will go to the Coven. I will present the situation and ask for their verdict." She pressed her hands together beneath her chin, her eyes on the three girls. "You all stay put. I'll be back soon with an answer."

Vera moved swiftly from her chambers, the door shutting firmly behind her. The room felt suddenly suffocatingly small. Tamsin slumped into one of the hard-backed chairs. Wren leaned against the door frame. Marlena wandered behind her mother's desk, pressing her fingers to the spines of the ancient books.

"Well, that's everything wrapped up neatly for the two of you, then." Marlena's voice was bitter. "Must be nice."

"We don't know what the Coven will say," Tamsin said quickly, defensively. So much of her life hung in the balance of the Coven's verdict. Arwyn, especially, was going to be a tough sell.

"They're going to let you back in," Marlena laughed softly.

"Wren's right. They need you. Me, however . . ." She trailed off, pulling a book idly from the shelf and flipping through the pages.

"You could stay here," Tamsin insisted. "There are plenty of things you could do. You could work in the library. You've always loved books. You could write. Research. You don't need magic."

Marlena shut the book with a loud snap. "You're doing it again."

"Doing what?" Tamsin gripped the chair tightly. Marlena had a way of making her feel foolish when she had only been trying to be kind.

"Deciding my life for me," she said, shoving the book roughly back onto the shelf. "I don't want to stay Within. There's a whole world out there filled with people who aren't magic. Now I'm one of them." She smiled sadly, eyes far away. "I always thought one day I might go to Kathos. Now I can." She brought a hand to her face and turned away. Tamsin knew her sister enough to recognize when she needed a moment.

She turned in her chair toward Wren, whose face was etched with worry. Her eyes drooped with exhaustion, her hair wild.

"You could have used the boon to free yourself," Tamsin said quietly. "I thought that was what you would do. We could have gone back to Ladaugh together. It would have been a decent life."

"It wouldn't have been enough." Tamsin was surprised to see fire in Wren's eyes. "You have power. I saw it back there, by the sea. You could be so much more than a village witch catering to the whims of ordinary folk."

Tamsin frowned. "I don't deserve that."

Being back Within, she had seen even more closely the

destruction her impulse had wrought. Watching her sister mourn a loss she would never fully recover from, Tamsin felt the consequences of her actions even more intimately. She was more certain than ever that she did not belong here among the people she had betrayed. The people she had hurt.

"What does that mean, 'deserve'?" Wren squinted at her, as though she truly wanted an answer. "Will you spend your entire life feeling guilty for what you did? Or will you try to redeem yourself with actions and deeds? Healing takes time." Wren glanced at Marlena, whose back was still to them, her shoulders shaking with silent sobs. "*Forgiveness* takes time. But none of it will happen until you allow it to."

Wren twisted a lock of fiery hair around her finger. "You told me to ask for what I wanted. And I *want* to stay. I hid from my magic for so long, fought against the pieces of me that weren't easy to explain. I want to know, now, who I am and what I can be. I don't want to hold myself back."

She laughed a little through shining eyes. "I wish I could tell my father. I wish I could show him who I truly am. All those years I gave myself up to be what I thought he wanted. But this is the truth. This is me."

She reached forward to brush Tamsin's cheek with her thumb. "And this is you. You were a child. Lost and desperate and afraid. You made a mistake. But if you don't forgive yourself, no one else will either."

Tamsin shivered at Wren's light touch. At the gravity in her eyes.

It felt too simple. To move forward, carrying the weight of

what she'd done without letting it hold her back. It was a delicate balance. Just like magic. Just like families and relationships and sisters who shared the same face but not the same heart.

Tamsin crossed the room to Marlena and wrapped her arms around her, resting her chin on her shoulder. At first her sister stiffened, tears still pouring down her cheeks. But then she let herself lean on Tamsin, collapsing into sobs. Tamsin held her close, the salt of her tears mixing with Marlena's, a hand in her sister's hair, as she did what she could to stop trying to fix and simply exist. Two girls—not halves, but two imperfect wholes.

Each of them enough.

The door opened with a soft click. Vera cleared her throat. Marlena shrugged herself out of Tamsin's grip, wiping her eyes with her sleeve. Their mother eyed her daughters with trepidation, her arms crossed tightly over her chest.

There was a small smudge of black kohl beneath Vera's left eye. A tiny thing, to be certain, but it reassured Tamsin slightly. All of them, regardless of power or past mistakes, were entirely and wholly human.

"The Coven has decided." Vera's tone betrayed nothing. "I explained that the plague occurred because our source did not fully sever the bond, which means this all occurred due to our negligence." Vera shifted slightly. "However, the Coven believes that we must uphold your banishment."

Tamsin went numb. Behind her, she heard a sharp intake of breath from Marlena and a gasp from Wren. Tamsin could not muster up the energy to be upset. All she was capable of was emptiness.

"Luckily for you, I have the final word." The ghost of a smile appeared on Vera's red-painted lips, but disappeared before Tamsin could determine if it was real. "You kept my secret. I owe you more than a boon. As High Councillor, I grant your curse and banishment lifted. You may return Within and live among us. You will aid in the revitalization, bringing Within back to its former glory. You will finish your studies. And you will *behave* as well as you are able." The smile returned to Vera's face. This time it stuck.

"If she's allowed to stay, does that mean I'm free to go?" Marlena's voice was ragged, her face blotchy, eyes red. "Now that the truth is out? My magic has left me. I've nothing to offer the world Within. So I'd like to leave."

Vera studied Marlena's face sadly. "Of course you can," she said quietly. "But you know the way the Wood works. If you have no magic, you may leave, but you can never come back."

"I know," Marlena said, so quickly it was clear she had considered every angle.

Tamsin admired her sister and her certainty. She was so sure she wanted to walk through the trees and leave Within behind. The same thing that had felt like punishment to Tamsin was freedom to Marlena.

"I'll just need a few supplies. Some food and clothing and coin to secure my passage on a ship."

Vera pursed her lips. "I don't like the idea of you venturing out there on your own, no magic to defend yourself."

"We'll go with her," Tamsin said quickly. "Just to the docks," she clarified, in hopes of softening Marlena's questioning glare.

"To see her off. There's one other thing we need to do out there in the world Beyond. Will you grant us a bit of time before Wren starts her training as a source?"

"I suppose the Coven may need some time to warm up to the idea of your return." Vera nodded hesitantly. "But do not dally. There's a lot to be done before life can continue on as planned. The earth needs us. And we need the ordinary folk to trust us again." Vera held out her hand. "Now give me your arm."

Tamsin pushed up her left sleeve. The pale skin was blotchy and scarred where Vera had burned off her mark. Tamsin had never fixed it. She had thought it her due punishment for letting her sister down. Marlena had died, and Tamsin was scarred. It had felt fitting. Yet even as Tamsin glanced at her sister, determined and full of life, she found she did not want to lose the memory of what had been. The forgiveness she still needed to earn. How grateful she was now.

"Perhaps the other one, then," Tamsin said, offering it up. Her mother nodded, tracing her finger across her daughter's skin.

Black ink followed her touch, arranging itself in a swooping arc that took up half her forearm, topped by four circles, each intersecting the next. The Coven's sigil settled into her skin.

A million tiny pinpricks welcomed Tamsin home.

Two days north of the Wood, they reached the docks and were able to secure Marlena passage on a ship to Kathos. She was going to find Amma's family, the grandmother she'd always spoken of so fondly. She was going to build the life she'd always hoped for.

Their walk through the Wood had been eerily quiet. It was almost as though the trees had been holding their breath, waiting for the sisters to speak. Tamsin took her cues from Marlena. She didn't want to tread on toes, to say something out of turn or make things even more complicated than they already were.

And they *were* complicated. Now that her curse was lifted, newly freed feelings buzzed about her like a swarm of bees. Each emotion was sharp and stinging, her attention pulled from hope to regret to adoration to embarrassment. She *felt* so much it was overwhelming. The leaves on the trees were so green they made her eyes ache. The breeze tickled her neck, distracting and delighting her. She had been born into the world anew.

But Tamsin's newfound feelings didn't negate her grief. She loved Marlena again, every piece of her sister, including the parts of her that were angry and hurt. Knowing that she was the reason for that hurt weighed on Tamsin. She wasn't used to being wrong. Wasn't used to consequences that lingered in her heart rather than her head. But she was living them now, reckoning with the fact that she had stolen so much from her sister. Given her a life she hadn't consented to live.

But Marlena—though her edges had softened since the bond had broken—had given no indication she had anything to say. And so all three of them had walked in silence through the hush of the trees, Wren darting nervous glances between the sisters.

As they walked, the trees offered them no horrors. There were no shrieks or shouts. The silence was punishment enough.

When they had exited the Wood, Marlena had not looked

back. And now, as they stood on the dock, Tamsin realized that she was the one who would be left behind.

"I suppose this is it, then." Marlena tried to smile, but her hands were in her hair, tying the strands into a hundred tiny knots. She was nervous, even if she didn't want to show it. "Good-bye." She bit her lip and turned away.

Tamsin stood, frozen to the ground. She couldn't watch her sister sail away with that as the final word between them. It couldn't be over. Not with so many things still unspoken.

Wren clearly felt similarly. She shoved Tamsin forward so hard she tripped, stubbing her toe on the worn, weathered wood of the dock.

"Marlena." Tamsin used her sister's shoulder to steady herself.

Marlena put a hand on Tamsin's elbow, almost absentmindedly, righting her. "I have to go," she said, gently untangling herself from her sister's grip.

Tamsin glanced pointedly down the dock, where the crew was still loading the ship, tossing sacks and rolling barrels into the storeroom. "It looks like you might have a minute. Please."

Marlena sighed softly but nodded. She stared at Tamsin expectantly.

"This belongs to you." Tamsin held out the diary, her fingers lingering on the worn leather cover. "I wish I had read it earlier. I wish I had known long ago what you truly thought of me. I never should have gotten us into this mess."

Tamsin cleared her throat, still surprised by the prickle in the corners of her eyes. "I know you told me not to apologize, but

I'm sorry, Marlena. I'm sorry for not seeing you for more than who I wanted you to be. I failed you. And you have every right to hate me for it."

Marlena flipped idly through the diary. "I never hated you, you know. Not truly." She looked up from the pages to her sister. "I just never wanted to *be* you. You wanted us to be the same, and I felt like I was always letting you down by being me."

"But I like you," Tamsin whispered, twisting her cloak between her hands.

"I like me too," Marlena laughed softly. "But I have to figure out who I am now. Without Amma. Without magic. Without Vera." She cleared her throat. "Without you." She looked out at the water.

"I just want you to be happy." Tamsin turned her gaze to the sea as well. "I hope you find what you're looking for out there. I hope that one day you write to me about your new life. And I hope that someday there's a place for me in it."

Marlena reached for Tamsin's hand. "I hope so too."

They stood there, hand in hand, as sailors shouted, waves crashed, birds called, and hope bloomed in the garden of Tamsin's heart.

She was not yet forgiven. She might never be. But it was a start.

Letting go was the first step.

Perhaps, one day, the two of them would meet again and take the next one together.

TWENTY-SIX

WREN

The world was waking up.

The earth's stores of magic were still depleted.

Wren continued to hear the screaming of stone, the muffled breathing of trees, the uncertainty of water. But she sensed hope, too. Every chance she got, she pressed a hand to a boulder, ran her fingers through the cool water of a reflecting pool. She offered drops of her own magic to the earth as a reminder of what had been. A promise of what was to come. And the world reached up to meet her.

There was much work to do. They were nearly four days on the road, most of their time spent picking paths through the broken branches, piles of rotting leaves, murky brown puddles.

The destruction they witnessed was endless. That the sun had returned to the sky only served to illuminate exactly how broken the world had become. Not a single structure in the city of Farn remained standing; the maze of alleyways was filled with the rubble of homes, the abandoned possessions of those fleeing the plague and their potential demise. The stench of death lingered an entire day in all directions.

Bands of frightened people huddled together on the outskirts of the city, setting up camps in fields of dead soil and withered crops, their wagons arranged in tight circles, studying Tamsin and Wren with suspicion even as they gave the groups a wide berth. People were hungry, dirty, defeated. The anger that had served them in the early days of the plague had dwindled to nothing, visible in their hunched shoulders and dull eyes.

Wren wanted to reassure them, to promise their safety, but no one was eager to speak to strangers, and certainly not ones so clean and finely clothed. There was no proof that they had suffered—although, of course, not all scars could be seen.

Now they were in the lowlands, only a day from Ladaugh and the countryside Wren had always called home. But the earth was devoid of color. It was all so stoic and sad.

"What are you thinking about?" Tamsin's hand brushed lightly against her arm, her eyes studying and serious. She no longer wore her green cloak. Instead her arms were bare, her ghostly pale skin finally exposed to the daylight.

"Nothing." Wren's footsteps crunched against the gravel on the road. Tamsin looked at her skeptically. "Everything." She shot the witch a small smile. "It's just overwhelming."

She gestured to their surroundings: the heavy white clouds hanging low in the sky; the detritus—soleless shoes, worn-down knives, broken ropes, torn clothing, empty sacks—littering the path; the field of tall summer grass to their left, dead, dried, and practically begging to catch fire.

"I don't know how we're going to fix this." She caught her bottom lip between her teeth. "*Are* we going to be able to fix this?"

Tamsin sighed, the sort of weary sigh Wren had come to associate with her. "I don't know. Vera certainly seems to think so."

"And what do you think?" She cozied up to the witch.

"That it's awfully early in our relationship for me to be meeting your father." Tamsin's tone was light, but her smile didn't meet her eyes.

Her father.

Unease blew through Wren like a strong wind. Each step suddenly felt like a struggle, trepidation spreading through her as she fretted over what she might find. There was no certainty that his memories could be replaced. That he would even still have his life. The cottage might have collapsed due to strong winds or the quaking earth. He might have starved.

Still, she was grateful to Tamsin for giving her the chance to find out. She would have been useless, stuck Within, not knowing her father's fate. It was a kindness she could hardly find the words for. If her father was dead, she would be able to put him to rest. If he still lived, she would have the chance to give him a proper good-bye and finally reveal the truth of who—and what—she was.

Her jaw clenched. Neither was an ideal outcome, but both were honorable. The duties of a daughter.

Tamsin flicked her cheek softly. "Stop that. You're going to ruin your teeth."

Wren shot her a sour look. Sleeping so close to another person had put all her bad habits on display. Tamsin was constantly chiding her for grinding her teeth. Wren had started teasing Tamsin for her snoring. Still, she wouldn't trade the nearness of the witch for anything. Not even for a more restful slumber.

With effort, she relaxed her jaw. She tapped her free hand against her leg, a jarring, jolting rhythm that mirrored the whistling in the wind. Tamsin stopped walking, catching her other hand so that she was facing Wren.

"It's going to be okay." She studied Wren carefully with those big brown eyes. There was a softness that made Wren's breath catch. There was *feeling* there.

"Is it?" She tried to squirm out of Tamsin's grip. It was too much, Tamsin was too much good in one place, and it made her feel guilty for having so much, for being *glad* that she had left her father behind for an adventure that had taken her far from home and given her a new one.

The witch put a hand under Wren's chin and forced her eyes back up. "It is. That's why we're doing this. So you don't have to wonder."

"I think I'm so nervous because I *want* to leave him. I wasn't supposed to, I always promised, but . . ." She trailed off, shaking her head. It was too impossible a thing to put into words. How much she wanted to study Within and embrace her power. How wrong she felt for that wanting.

"You're allowed to have your own life." Tamsin's expression

was conflicted. "You're allowed to want things. To leave people behind. To grow." She glanced behind at the road, although Marlena was long gone. "I see you. I've always seen what you could do. Who you could be if you'd only let yourself." Wren tried to pull away, but Tamsin's eyes were so fierce she found she couldn't move. "So what do *you* want, Wren?"

"You," she whispered, stepping closer and wrapping her arms around the witch's waist.

"That's cheating," Tamsin whispered, inches from Wren's lips.

"It's not," Wren insisted. For so long, she had tried to be exactly what other people wanted. She had given without a second thought. Ignored her own desires. Her own needs. But no longer. Being with Tamsin made her bold. "I want you. Can I have you?"

She brushed her lips against Tamsin's. The witch let out a tiny, contented sigh, and then she whispered: "Yes."

Ladaugh's town square was deserted. Abandoned stalls were littered with blackened, rotting vegetables and torn banners. The water pump dripped endlessly, tiny drops plummeting to the ground. Some of the cobblestones had cracked. Giant black birds, their feathers shining blue in the sunlight, soared over the wreckage. Wren shuddered, thinking of Farn, but Tamsin ushered her onward.

Most of the cottages had boarded-up windows. Some still had shadows of dark magic clinging to the rooftops. But all the stone huts remained standing. That eased Wren's fear some. But only a little.

"What if he's dead?"

"He isn't." Tamsin eyed the empty path warily, her tone uncertain.

"What if he doesn't remember me, then?"

Tamsin's hand tightened around Wren's own. "You're pretty hard to forget."

Wren smiled despite herself. Still, her stomach churned like the ocean during a storm.

She paused again at the front gate. The boots she'd left behind were gone. She swallowed the panic clawing its way up her throat. "I don't think I can do this." Her heart was hammering, her breathing quick and unsteady. She had the sensation of something crawling on her feet. She looked down. It wasn't her imagination. It was a cat—her stray. He was rather lean, his black fur matted and smeared with dirt, but otherwise he looked no worse for the wear. He rubbed against her ankles again, his large yellow eyes peering hopefully at her. Tears welled in the corners of her eyes, relief washing over her like a wave. He knew her. The cat knew her, which meant her father might remember her too. Wren gathered the cat up in her arms, smoothing his grimy fur and scratching him behind his ears.

Tamsin wrinkled her nose down at the creature, her hands remaining firmly at her sides.

"He's nice, I swear." Wren held him out like a baby toward the witch.

Tamsin offered one begrudging finger and tapped the cat three times on the top of his head. The creature hissed at her. Tamsin jumped away, scowling. "I don't care for it."

"You're being ridiculous." Wren gave the cat another squeeze. He struggled in her embrace, trying to gain his freedom. She eventually let him go. He licked his front paw, looking rather affronted.

"Well, the *cat* remembers me. That's a good sign, don't you think?" She stared, unmoving, at the front door of the cottage. She could waste all the time she liked before the gate, but it wouldn't change what was waiting for her inside. Better, then, to get it over with.

She stepped through the gate and was reaching for the door, the wood stripped and rough beneath her fingertips, when it swung open to reveal a man. Wren stumbled backward.

It wasn't her father.

"Tor?" Wren struggled to make sense of the scene. "What are you doing here?"

The tailor was staring at her with equal incredulity. "Just checking up on your da, like you asked."

Wren struggled to formulate a response. Instead she threw herself onto the tailor, sobbing into his shirt. "He's alive?"

The tailor patted her head awkwardly. "It was strange. There was a darkness, black as ink, that draped across the land. And then, six days ago, that darkness dispelled. It was like the storm broke. And everyone—all the afflicted—their memories came flooding back."

"Can I see him?" She hurriedly wiped her tears away with the backs of her hands.

"It's your house." Tor stepped past her into the afternoon light. His eyes fell on Tamsin, lingering awkwardly behind Wren. He frowned and turned away.

"Go on, then," she said, turning toward Wren, who had hesitated with her fingers on the front door. "I'll be right here if you need me." The witch offered up a soft smile. "Go."

Wren stepped inside. The cottage was stifling, a fire roaring despite the temperature outside. The stink of singed herbs—blackened rosemary, roasted thyme—lingered in the thick air. Wren coughed, holding a hand over her nose.

She stood in the middle of the room on the ragged carpet woven by her mother's hand. The bedroom door was open just a crack. Blankets rustled within. A man gave a throaty cough. "Papa?"

An intake of breath. Then her father's voice—timid, unbelieving: "Wren?"

"Papa." Wren flung the door open, tears starting up again as her stomach struggled to unknot itself, as the tightness in her chest loosened. Her father sat up, dressed and smiling. Not only was her father alive, but he *remembered* her.

"Little bird." His eyes shone as he took her in. "Are those my boots?"

Wren glanced down at her feet. She had almost forgotten the boots weren't hers. "I, uh, didn't think you'd miss them." She untied the laces, stepped out of the boots, and placed them against the wall where they belonged. Surely Tamsin could conjure her a new pair without much complaining. "There you go." She smiled guiltily. "You'd never even know they'd been gone."

Her father let out a laugh, loud and warm in the small space. "No, I suppose I wouldn't. Tor tells me I was a handful for a time there." He gave a soft chuckle, which turned quickly into a cough.

When he finally managed to breathe through the wheezing, he turned his full attention on her. "Now tell me," he said, patting the bed beside him. "Where have you been?"

Wren bit her lip. There was so much to tell him. So much he would not understand. She had grown up on their journey, but now, before her father, she felt like a fearful child again. She wanted to assure him she was still his daughter. That she was only a little different, and that it shouldn't change the way he looked at her. That what she was had nothing to do with the loss of her brother.

But even as she fretted, Wren knew that however her father reacted, it wouldn't change how right it felt to embrace who she was. And so she sat and told him the truth.

"I've been away, Papa," Wren said, tugging on her braid. "I went to the Witchlands and helped to end the plague."

Her father stared at her incredulously. "No, you didn't," he finally said, his frown deepening. "The only people who can make it through the Witchwood are witches. And you're not a witch."

"No, I'm not." Wren's nerves returned, stronger this time, so that she felt her fear in her toes. She wished that Tamsin had followed her inside. "But I am a source."

Her father shook his head uncomprehendingly.

She took a deep breath. "I'm magic."

He blinked at her, brow furrowed. "Are you sure?"

Wren's heart sank. "I've known for years. Kept it hidden because I didn't want you to . . ." She trailed off, her voice breaking.

Her father sat up straighter, his expression weighty with an emotion Wren could not place. "Didn't want me to what?"

"To be afraid of me," Wren finished, mouth trembling. "I didn't want you to stop loving me because of what magic did to my brother."

For too long, she had protected her father from heartbreak by tamping down her own desires. She had lived to serve him at the expense of herself. That was what he had wanted from her. That was her role as a daughter. And yet, instead of looking satisfied with her sacrifice, her father looked . . . devastated.

"You kept this hidden because you feared me?" He hung his head, shame radiating from him. "There's not a thing in the world that could make me stop loving you. That you didn't know . . ." He trailed off, staring down at his sheets. "That's my fault, not yours." He ran a hand across his face. "I'm sorry, little bird. I'm so sorry that I failed you." He looked up at her, a sad smile peeking through his scruffy beard. "Things will be different from now on."

Wren shifted on the thin pallet. "Actually, that's why I'm here." She folded her hands in her lap. She took a deep breath. "I'm here to say good-bye. The Coven wants me to train Within, and I want to go." Her father's brow wrinkled with confusion. "I'm going to live in the Witchlands," she clarified.

Her father studied her face, his eyes—the same green as hers, she could see now—boring into her. "And this is what you want?"

The question hung between them. Finally Wren nodded. "It's what I've always wanted."

Her father placed his clammy hand upon her own. "Then

go, little bird." His smile was small but true. "Go and do good." He cleared his throat. "It's high time I did the same. I cannot continue to let the past hold me back. I'm so sorry I let it hold *you* back."

They stared at each other, unspoken words filling the space. Wren didn't know how to say good-bye, and so she didn't. She kissed her father on the forehead, smoothed his sheets, and left the tiny room, trying not to let him see the way her hands were shaking.

Tamsin was standing in the middle of the carpet, staring at their meager home. Wren came up behind her and wrapped her arms around her waist.

Tamsin folded her arms around Wren's. "Are you ready?"

Wren extracted herself from the witch and looked around the tiny room. She had spent so many years here denying herself because she thought that was what was expected. What she was supposed to do. She tugged on the tail of her braid.

"Just one last thing." She pulled the knife from her belt, the delicate, ornate blade stolen from the Orathen hunter in Farn. Her hands were still shaking. She offered the blade to Tamsin, who stared at it blankly.

"What am I supposed to do with this?" Wren held out her braid. Tamsin's eyes widened in surprise. "Are you sure?"

She nodded. "Cut it off."

Tamsin stared warily at the knife in her hand. "Can't I just use magic? What if I slice your neck open?"

Wren raised her eyebrows. "Or you could just be careful and not slice my neck open."

Tamsin rolled her eyes. "Fine."

Wren held her breath as the witch hacked and sawed at her hair with the knife until the braid fell limp into her hands. It was heavy. Wren shook her head wildly, admiring Tamsin's work in the back of a ladle. The tips of her shoddily shorn hair barely brushed her jaw. She couldn't yank it, could hardly gather it into a tuft to tie at the back of her head. Her hair now looked nothing like her mother's. It was *exactly* as she had wanted.

Wren tossed the braid into the fire and watched the weight of the world's expectations go up in smoke. She opened a window to let out the stink. Her hair was the same color as the flames.

TWENTY-SEVEN

TAMSIN

Tamsin had never been one for sentimentality. Even before her curse had taken away the instinct to linger on fond memories, she had been more interested in what was to come than what had been. Perhaps that would have changed once she lost Marlena. But by then she could not feel, and so she could not linger. Could not dwell on moments past. Now, of course, everything was different, which was why she stood at her cottage's front door, her palm pressed to the warped, peeling wood.

"Are you . . . all right?" Wren stared up at her with the crease between her eyebrows that Tamsin always wanted to pinch.

"I'm fine," Tamsin snapped, old habits dying hard. She

grinned sheepishly. "I'm fine," she tried again, keeping her voice soft. "I just . . ." She looked down at her dusty boots. "I wanted to say good-bye."

Wren's mouth twitched. "Really?"

"Shut up," Tamsin said, but tenderly. "I know it's stupid, but . . ."

How could she put it into words? For years, the cottage was all she'd had. She had huddled by its fire to warm her uncooperative bones. She had stood in the middle of its floor, trading magic for strains of love strong enough to grant her the joy of a single sunset. Here she had done her best to make her life something worth surviving.

Now it was something worth living.

She reached for Wren's hand, soft, small, and warm in her own. A spark passed between them like a secret smile. The tension in her shoulders lessened. She caught a whiff of the summer air. Sweet like sunshine. Like Wren's laugh. Like the way the skin next to her eyes crinkled when she smiled.

It was still strange, the warmth that crept across her skin, the desire she had to tip her face toward the sky. She spread her arms wide, taking Wren's hand with her.

"What are you doing?"

Tamsin opened her eyes. Wren was staring at her with concern.

"The sun." Tamsin gestured upward. "Don't you feel it?" She caught sight of Wren's raised eyebrow. "Oh, don't you start. You've picked every wildflower we've passed. The ocean sings to you. You hear trees *breathe*."

Wren grinned guiltily. "I *may* have a tendency to get distracted sometimes. Okay, a lot of the time," she added quickly, swatting Tamsin's shoulder playfully.

"You're the worst," Tamsin muttered, dropping her arms but not Wren's hand.

"You love me." Wren's smile threatened to break her face, it was so wide.

"Someone's quite confident, aren't they?" Tamsin teased a strand of hair out from behind Wren's ear, still surprised by its new, shorter length. It suited her. Stopped her from hiding. Wren even stood up straighter now.

"But you do," Wren insisted, scrunching her freckled nose. It was clear she expected an answer.

"I do." Tamsin smiled, pushing open the door to her cottage.

Everything was exactly as she had left it. Nothing had rearranged itself in her absence. Her things were all tucked safely away in the cupboard. Flower petals lay forgotten in the hearth, their edges brown and curled. The room was stale with shadows and dust. Tamsin pried open the shutters, letting the light flood in.

"It's smaller than I remember." Wren paused in the doorframe, her eyes lingering on the ceiling, tracing ribbons of magic Tamsin couldn't see.

"Is it?" It was hard to look at the room objectively. She had lived so many of her worst years there, angry, cold, and alone. Fumbling with the idea of what it meant to be a witch without a home. A girl who could not love.

"Or maybe you're more. I don't know." Wren pulled out a

chair and plopped down into it. "I don't know what I'm trying to say."

"That's okay," Tamsin said, settling in across from her. "We've got all the time in the world."

"We don't." Wren drummed her fingers on the tabletop. "Vera is expecting us back soon."

Tamsin pursed her lips. "I didn't mean literally," she said, rather darkly. "I was *trying* to be sweet."

"Oh." Wren's eyes widened. "Oh no, I'm sorry. I ruined it. You said . . ." She paused, biting her thumb as she thought. "You said, 'We've got all the time in the world,' and the correct response should have been . . ." Wren narrowed her eyes, looking at Tamsin in that way she did, where she saw through her skin, deep down into the heart of her. Wren's lips quirked up into a soft smile, and she batted her eyelashes. "Do we?"

"Oh, hush." Tamsin rolled her eyes, but still she reached across the table and wrapped Wren's fingers in her own.

She was always reaching for Wren. Always entwining fingers, pressing palms, meeting lips. But it was all so new, so unbelievable, that if Tamsin went even a moment without contact, she started to fear that the next time they touched, she would no longer feel a spark. That one day she would wake to find it had all been a dream. Moments were so fleeting. So fragile. All Tamsin could do was hold on to the things that mattered and hope that was enough.

Tamsin reached for Wren, and, inexplicably, impossibly, wonderfully, Wren reached back.

They sat, tangled up together in the cottage that had housed her on so many of her worst days. Tamsin considered making tea just so she would have something to do. But it wasn't about *doing*; it was about lingering for one final moment in the place that had been home. About knowing she would never return.

Was it silly to mourn a place that had ultimately been temporary? Did that lack of permanence make it somehow less of a home? But then again, on that bed she had grieved for her sister, her life, the distance between before and after. At that table she had screamed her fury, explored her anger because it was an emotion she could revel in. On that rug she had paced, trying to tire herself out, trying to call sleep when being awake became unbearable.

Wren squeezed her hand. "Are you afraid?"

Across the table Tamsin startled. "Of what?"

Wren gestured vaguely with her free hand, glancing helplessly around the room. When she finally found the word, it came out breathless. "Everything."

Tamsin laughed, a helpless hiccup of mirth. "Yes." That one small word was hardly enough. There was still so much they did not know. So much that could still go wrong.

Wren exhaled slightly. "Me too."

Tamsin squeezed the source's fingers tighter before letting them go. She stared across the table, her brown eyes on Wren's green ones, hands already itching for Wren's red hair, her ears longing for the steady beat of Wren's heart. But she wanted a moment of wanting. A moment of appreciating what a person desired when she could, once again, desire.

Tamsin could want, and so she did.

Wren's face was painted with gold. The sun had begun to set, casting colors through the tiny room. Tamsin got to her feet, skirt sweeping behind her. It would never grow old, the colors saturating her eyes, filling the expanse in her chest—the heart she had never expected to come back to life. Tamsin clutched the windowsill, her knuckles white as the sun painted the sky.

The scrape of a chair, body heat behind her, a hand on her own.

There was a long road ahead. So many hurdles they had not yet encountered. Perhaps this love would last only a season. Maybe it would last forever. But of the many things Tamsin was afraid of, Wren was not one of them.

Love was not one of them.

And so she stood, her body pressed against another's, their hearts beating in time, and she *hoped*. Tamsin turned toward Wren, closed her eyes, and tasted joy.

ACKNOWLEDGMENTS

First and foremost, my unending gratitude to Sarah McCabe, without whom this book would not exist, and without whom I would be a lesser writer. Thank you for taking a chance on me.

To Jim McCarthy, my agent, whose work to prioritize and place queer stories in the world is one of the many reasons why I'm so grateful to have him on my team. Thank you for your guidance and encouragement, always.

To the entire team at S&S/Pulse/McElderry, Karen Sherman, Erica Stahler, to Virginia Allyn for turning my chicken-scratch map into something truly fantastical. To Tara Phillips for bringing Tamsin and Wren to life exactly as I pictured them, and to Laura Eckes, who turned Tara's art into the cover of my dreams—thank you both for making me cry next to that mailbox on Twenty-Third Street.

Kelly Quindlen, I promised you a paragraph, and you've done everything to deserve it. You started as an author I admired and are now a friend I admire even more. Thank you for your honesty, your wit, and your enthusiasm. To Jen Cox-Shah, for your eyes on my words, your heart, and your sincerity. I don't know what I'd do without the two of you. Thank you both for being ports in the storm of life.

To Kiana Nguyen, who makes me laugh harder than anyone, and who keeps me honest. Your input is invaluable, and your guidance is a gift. To Carey Blankenship, who pushes me forward and always keeps me in coffee. To Rey Noble, who fields late-night panicked texts and forces me to dream bigger. To Ashley Shuttleworth, who has been with me every step of the way on this journey—having a friend for the road has made all the difference. To Rachel Kellis for always letting me scream. This paragraph is proof that you *can* make friends on the internet.

To Katarina Havana, whose friendship cannot be reduced into words. Thank you for wine and laughter and late-night tears on the sofa, for cheering me on when this was still just a glimmer of a dream. To the og—ob's (Kat, Whitney, Claire, Tara, Rachel, Sophia, Dylon, Cedric, and Becky) for always letting me change the subject in meetings. To PK Weston, who told me I should have been an English major. To the "aunties" for . . . well, everything. To the Buchanans—especially Pat—for the unending enthusiasm and cheer. I'm so, so grateful to have you on my side.

To my family: my grandmother Charmaine, who believed in me before I did, and who has been a champion every step of the way. Thanks for always answering the phone when I call with good news. To Dylan and Rosa for always sharing in my excitement.

My parents instilled my love of words and books early on. Thanks to my dad, for telling bedtime stories that have survived all these years, for letting me practice my accents when reading aloud, and for always making me feel that writing a book was a matter of "when," rather than "if." Thanks to my mom, for taking me to coffee shops for reading time, for writing me stories for Christmas. Thank you for always being my first reader (and for reading this book upwards of ten times). Your input is invaluable, and I don't know who I'd be or what my writing would look like without you.

To my wife, Katie, without whom none of this would be possible. You know that, of course, but I still wanted you to see it in print. I once promised you all of my words, so take heart knowing that every single one is for *and because of* you.

And finally, thank you to my lonely, insecure fifteen-year-old self, for spending more time scribbling in journals than paying attention in class. If it takes ten thousand hours to become an expert, you're the reason I found my voice as a writer.